P9-CES-983

A LESSON IN SELF-DEFENSE?

Suddenly, Piper didn't care about horses or pistols or knives. She wanted to feel the possessive pressure of his lips, to inhale the masculine scent of this ruggedly handsome giant and lose herself in his encircling arms.

"Piper . . . the knife," Logan prompted, but his thoughts were as distracted as hers. The raw desire in Piper's eyes made it difficult to remember that he was attempting to teach her self-defense. What he needed at this moment was a lesson in self-control.

"I don't want to stab you," she whispered, her voice further betraying the turmoil of forbidden emotions that bubbled inside her.

"What *do* you want?" His rumbling tone resembled the purr of a tiger.

"I want to kiss you," she whispered shamelessly as she tilted her face to his.

His full lips rolled over hers, brushing against her mouth, courting her like a bee hovering upon a delicate flower. An involuntary gasp of pleasure ricocheted through her chest as his hand glided down her back to press her hips against the hard columns of his thighs. Piper could feel the ardent need she had aroused in him. She could taste him, touch him, inhale the heady aroma of him as if he were a part of her. And she knew she wanted to belong to him forever. . . .

EXHILARATING ROMANCE
From Zebra Books

GOLDEN PARADISE   (2007, $3.95)
by Constance O'Banyon
Desperate for money, the beautiful and innocent Valentina Barrett finds
work as a veiled dancer, "Jordanna," at San Francisco's notorious Crystal
Palace. There she falls in love with handsome, wealthy Marquis Vin-
cente—a man she knew she could never trust as Valentina — but who Jordanna can't resist making her lover and reveling in love's GOLDEN
PARADISE.

SAVAGE SPLENDOR   (1855, $3.95)
by Constance O'Banyon
By day Mara questioned her decision to remain in her husband's world.
But by night, when Tajarez crushed her in his strong, muscular arms, taking her to the peaks of rapture, she knew she could never live without
him.

TEXAS TRIUMPH   (2009, $3.95)
by Victoria Thompson
Nothing is more important to the determined Rachel McKinsey than the
Circle M — and if it meant marrying her foreman to scare off rustlers,
she would do it. Yet the gorgeous rancher feels a secret thrill that the towering Cole Elliot is to be her man — and despite her plan that they be
business partners, all she truly desires is a glorious consummation of their
vows.

KIMBERLY'S KISS   (2184, $3.95)
by Kathleen Drymon
As a girl, Kimberly Davonwoods had spent her days racing her horse, per-
fecting her fencing, and roaming London's byways disguised as a boy.
Then at nineteen the raven-haired beauty was forced to marry a complete
stranger. Though the hot-tempered adventuress vowed to escape her new
husband, she never dreamed that he would use the sweet chains of ecstasy
to keep her from ever wanting to leave his side!

FOREVER FANCY   (2185, $3.95)
by Jean Haught
After she killed a man in self-defense, alluring Fancy Broussard had no
choice but to flee Clarence, Missouri. She sneaked aboard a private rail-
car, plotting to distract its owner with her womanly charms. Then the
dashing Rafe Taggart strode into his compartment . . . and the frightened
girl was swept up in a whirlwind of passion that flared into an undeni-
able, unstoppable prelude to ecstasy!

*Available wherever paperbacks are sold, or order direct from the
Publisher. Send cover price plus 50¢ per copy for mailing and
handling to Zebra Books, Dept. 2809, 475 Park Avenue South,
New York, N.Y. 10016. Residents of New York, New Jersey and
Pennsylvania must include sales tax. DO NOT SEND CASH.*

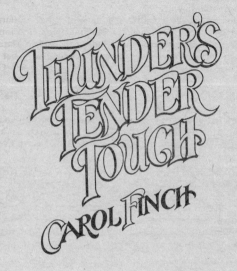

THUNDER'S TENDER TOUCH

CAROL FINCH

ZEBRA BOOKS
KENSINGTON PUBLISHING CORP.

ZEBRA BOOKS

are published by

Kensington Publishing Corp.
475 Park Avenue South
New York, NY 10016

Copyright © 1989 by Connie Feddersen

All rights reserved. No part of this book may be reproduced
in any form or by any means without the prior written
consent of the Publisher, excepting brief quotes used in
reviews.

First printing: November, 1989

Printed in the United States of America

Dedicated to:

My husband Ed
for his encouragement and support

And to my children
Christie Jill and Kurt.
Love you . . .

PART I

'Twas in the summer time so sweet,
When hearts and flowers are both in season,
That—who, of all the world, should meet,
One early dawn, but Love and Reason!
                                        —Moore

Chapter 1

June, 1859

The blistering Arizona sun beat down on the lone rider who trotted his paint stallion across the Gila River valley. Drawing the weary steed to a halt, Vince Logan peered across his sprawling ranch dotted with cattle. A hot wind dried the perspiration from Logan's bronzed face, a face that bore evidence of exhaustion and long hours of hard riding.

Home. The word had an empty ring to it and Logan silently substituted *headquarters* for *home*. He didn't exactly know what home was, having never had one that he could remember. But for the past five years the hacienda nestled beside the Gila River had been the place to which he returned between jobs. Arizona (the western lands that were clumped together to form New Mexico Territory) was as good as any place for his headquarters, he reckoned. It didn't matter all that much. As far as Logan was concerned, anywhere west of the Mississippi would have sufficed. He had trekked from the Mississippi to the Rockies for sixteen years, doing a little bit of everything if the price was right. And that calloused philosphy had earned him a reputation that usually preceded him wherever he went.

Logan was a loner, a slave to his own restlessness. Those who could afford to hire him for his legendary talents recognized that the name Logan provoked deep emotion among men who rode on both sides of the law. His name struck fear in those who carried rewards on their heads because Logan was relentless in pursuing his prey. For years now, he had hired himself out to cattlemen, businessmen, and marshals who found it necessary to fight back when the unorganized system of western justice fell short of the mark.

Nudging Sam, his paint stallion, Logan aimed himself toward the hacienda and a long-awaited bath. His backside ached from so many days in the saddle, and he wasn't sure whether he or Sam smelled more like a horse. Sam looked like one, Logan mused as he glanced down at his stallion's lathered neck. But he and his horse were sharing the same fragrance.

With careless ease, Logan stepped from the stirrup and slung his saddlebags over a broad shoulder. Moving with the panther-like grace that was an unconscious but striking characteristic of his, Logan strode across the sunbaked grasses and pushed through the front door of the hacienda.

Servants greeted him in fragments of Spanish and English, and Logan mustered the semblance of a smile before veering into the study to pour himself a drink, one he downed in one swallow.

"You look like hell," Harley Newcomb observed as he glanced up from the mound of mail that was piled on the desk.

"Good," Logan grunted, sloshing another drink in his glass and promptly swallowing it. "I wouldn't want to look better than I felt."

With droopy, silver-gray eyes he gazed at the wiry little man who had parked himself behind Logan's oversized desk. Harley looked like a dwarf behind it. But then, Harley looked like a midget compared to most large objects. Standing five feet eight inches tall in his boots and weighing a mere one hundred fifty-five pounds, Harley was thin-faced and thin-bodied. He was the nervous, restless type who ate like a horse and never gained an ounce, at least as far as Logan could tell.

Easing a lean hip on the edge of the desk, Logan stretched his brawny body sideways to retrieve a cigarillo from the top drawer. And then, performing the gesture that constantly got Harley's goat, Logan rolled a crisp two-dollar banknote, poked it in the lantern, and lit his cheroot with the flaming money.

Harley's pale blue eyes narrowed and his face puckered into a disapproving frown. "Why do you persist in doing that? Just to irritate me? You know it fouls up my bookkeeping."

The faintest hint of a smile slanted Logan's full lips upward as he inhaled the cigar and then blew lazy circles in the air. It was the first cigar he had enjoyed in three days.

"I earned every damned cent of my pay and I'll spend it as I wish," he told Harley flatly.

With his kerchief wrapped around his hand, Harley stamped out the fire before it spread to the stack of papers he had been rifling through for the past hour. "There's a helluva lot of difference between spending money and just plain burning it, Logan," he grumbled crankily.

Logan shrugged off the criticism and unfolded his tall, muscular frame from the desk.

To Harley's chagrin, Logan pivoted to swagger toward the door. Logan always did that—on purpose—and Harley said the same thing he always said the moment Logan returned from a tedious job. "Confound it, don't you want to know what's in the mail?"

Logan was interested in what job possibilities awaited him, but he pretended not to care. Harley knew that, but it still rankled him that Logan appeared so nonchalant. Harley supposed it was Logan's way of making his business associate feel he was carrying his load while Logan laid his life on the line.

"Mostly, I want a bath and a soft bed," Logan retorted over his shoulder, expecting Harley to clamber from his chair and scurry after him with his stack of letters. He always did. They repeated this ritual each time Logan arrived at headquarters.

"It's been a busy week," Harley declared as he shuffled the letters and quickened his pace to keep up with Logan's long, graceful strides. "You've gotten offers from here to California and all the way back to Arkansas. I've sifted out the jobs you wouldn't be interested in taking."

Logan's tanned face quirked in a grin. Harley was the world's worst at attempting to tell Logan what he should do. Nonetheless, Logan had allowed the wiry little man, who was three years his senior, to screen his mail for the past seven years they had been together.

A slight frown furrowed Logan's brow. He couldn't even

11

remember when or how he had acquired Harley during his vast travels. Harley had simply attached himself to Logan like a flea to a dog. He tolerated Logan's moods and became his friend, nursemaid, and whatever else Harley thought his companion needed at a given moment. He even found Logan women when he thought Logan was in the need of the company of the fairer sex.

While Logan was peeling off his dusty shirt and settling into his bath, Harley planted himself in a nearby chair. "I tossed out two requests for you to trail two wives whose husbands are sure the ladies in question have forgotten their vows to remain devoted until death do them part," Harley began. With a flair for the dramatic, Harley flung the two letters onto the end of the bed. His brows came together to form a line across his forehead. "So how do you feel about San Antonio this time of year? A group of cattlemen have had trouble with rustlers. They want to hire you as their detective and are willing to pay fifty dollars a day plus expenses and five hundred dollars for every outlaw you dispose of on purpose or in self-defense."

Logan made no comment. His features maintained a carefully blank stare as he lathered his hair-matted chest.

Harley set the letter in his stack of possible considerations. "If you aren't in the mood for Texas, maybe Tucson would be more to your liking," he announced as his blue eyes skimmed over the paper. "A group of miners who have returned to town to restock supplies and purchase livestock have found themselves approached by men bearing fake bills of sales intended to prove that their horses and mules are stolen property. The miners have been losing their newly purchased livestock and supplies as fast as they buy them."

His gaze swung to Logan, who had stretched out a long leg to scrub away the dust with the vigor of a washerwoman attending her weekly cleaning. "The miners are offering forty dollars a day plus expenses. One of the men is an old friend of mine," he added with a pointed glance.

Logan's silver eyes fastened on the third letter that Harley was tapping against his knee. He inclined his raven head toward the envelope. "And what's in that one?"

"This?" Harley looked so innocent Logan almost laughed.

Almost. There was very little in Logan's rugged, grueling life-style that provoked him to amusement. He lived hard and dangerously, and pleasure was seldom his shadow.

"I don't think you'll be all that interested in this one either. I don't even know why I brought it up here with me. You've been to Fort Smith, delivering prisoners for bounty, three times already this year. Besides, you could probably clear up the matter on this end without making the trip."

The evasive remark drew Logan's probing stare. "This end of what?" he wanted to know.

Harley heaved a sigh and his sunken chest fell. "Aw, you know, the business about the holdups and Apache attacks that have been plaguing Butterfield's stage line. Butterfield thinks there is a master plan to destroy his route between Missouri and California. But you wouldn't be interested," he insisted. "Hell, Butterfield would have you working for him full time. You'd be riding back and forth between here and Boggy Depot like a piece of unclaimed luggage."

"In case you've forgotten, Butterfield is the reason we have sold five hundred head of horses and the same number of cattle for use on his coaches and at the relay stations on the route," Logan snorted. "And may I also remind you that because of him we receive these excessive stacks of mail in half the amount of time we did before he won the postal contract last year."

"Well, he hasn't been asking us to supply him with livestock and beef lately," Harley argued resentfully. "He must have found someone to sell to him at a cheaper price. And then he had the gall to call in that no-account gunslinger, Royce Granger, because he was too tight to pay you what he knew you were worth. If you ask me, Royce is part of the problem. Butterfield wasted his money when he gave Royce this job. And you don't owe Butterfield anything special. He used to buy your stock, but he doesn't purchase much of it anymore. Business is business, but this isn't the job for you."

Unnerving gray eyes pierced Harley, causing him to squirm uneasily in his chair. Logan could stare through a man better than anyone Harley knew. Those probing silver eyes were Logan's most noticeable asset, and he employed that soul-

13

searching stare to rattle everyone who dared to cross him. It made a man think twice before he tangled with Logan.

"How much is John Butterfield willing to pay for my services as a stage detective and bounty hunter?" Logan questioned point-blank.

Harley let out his breath in a rush. "Five thousand dollars, plus expenses, plus the bounty on every head that's worth something on a wanted poster," Harley muttered begrudgingly. "But I'm tired of that grueling trip to Fort Smith. I don't want to be cooped up in that stage again. Fifteen days of riding over those rough roads wears calluses on my bony backside."

"You won't be going," he told Harley calmly. "If Butterfield's speculations are correct, I'll need you on this end of the stage line."

"Damn, you're going to take the job," Harley realized glumly. "I knew I should have let you light your cigar with this letter instead of that two dollar bill. Butterfield will have you tied up for months. The money he pays you will calculate out to a nickel an hour. You could make a lot more money during the time it will require to handle this job. You'll be crammed in a crowded stage with a bunch of tenderfeet who think they need to go back and forth to San Francisco just because Butterfield started a stage line that connects the East with the West."

Harley took a deep breath and rattled on before Logan could squeeze a word in edgewise. "Besides that, you always get surly after you've tromped around Indian territory, stirring up old memories. Your disposition is much better when you're wandering around through Texas and New Mexico Territory. Not only that, but you could get yourself killed just getting to Fort Smith with all the stage robberies and Apache trouble that's been reported. You might not live to collect your five thousand. . . ."

"And I'd foul up your bookkeeping for the very last time," Logan finished for him. "But then it would all be yours since I have no next of kin."

Harley bounded to his feet, his nostrils flaring, the veins in his face pulsating with irritation. It took little to provoke Harley's temper. He was a walking keg of blasting powder, and

14

Logan derived wicked pleasure in getting Harley's dander up.

"It isn't the money and you damned well know it!" he declared in that shrill voice that escaped from his vocal chords when he got steamed up. "I've been fussing over you for seven years. I don't want to see you get yourself killed protecting a bunch of dandies who have to resort to the stage because they don't have the savvy to trek cross-country. Nor do I want to see you sacrifice your life for a sack of cussed mail that is to be delivered to someone's Uncle George and Aunt Sally in San Francisco. You're a legend in your own time, the man who gets things done when the law doesn't have as long an arm as it should have in this part of the country."

"I don't consider myself a living legend," Logan remarked blandly, rinsing away the soap bubbles. "Most decent citizens find my presence in their towns intolerable. Half of them won't walk on the same side of the street with me. A legend?" Logan's tone hinted at incredulousness. "Like hell I am!"

"Well you are, even if you don't think so. And you've got scruples," Harley exclaimed with great conviction. "Most of the people you deal with aren't happy unless they've got something to complain about. They hire you to clean up their towns and save them from gun-toting bullies who flaunt their lightning-quick draws. And then as soon as you've done their dirty work for them, they want nothing more to do with you. They complain when they've got problems, and they have the gall to snub the very man who quells their troubles. They're all a passel of high and mighty hypocrites, if you ask me!" Harley wagged a thin finger in Logan's face. "They may turn a cold shoulder to you when the job is done, but you're still a legend to every damned one of them."

His shrill voice reverberated off the stucco walls, and Logan scoffed at his piercing tone. "Remind me to bring you along as a character reference if I find myself in need of one."

"I'm serious," Harley insisted hotly. "Rounding up ruffians and outlaws is a rotten job and I know somebody has to do it. But you deserve a helluva lot more respect from those so-called upstanding citizens you deal with. The West is a haven for desperadoes and thieves. I don't want to see you shot in the back while you're protecting a bunch of naive city slickers

15

from the East, ones who have no business crossing the badlands on Butterfield's stage. If they can't tote their own guns and fight to keep the money in their pockets they ought to stay home where they belong. It's not your civic duty to go rushing off to Fort Smith every time Butterfield sends out a plea for help."

Logan grabbed a towel and draped it around his hips. His gaze wandered over Harley's straight brown hair, his heaving chest, and his rigid stance. "And just what is it you think I should do, since you seem to have me and everyone else in the world all figured out?" he smirked.

Harley knew he was being baited. Logan had practiced the technique in his dealings and he had turned the skill into a fine art. But Harley was too quick-tempered not to rise to the taunt. That was the difference between the two men. Logan was always calm and controlled. Nothing rattled him. Nothing frightened him. Logan had done it all at one time or another. He had tested his abilities to their extremes. He was shrewd and methodic and calculating. Nothing moved that Logan didn't notice. He could appear totally unaware, and yet he was cognizant of all that transpired around him. No one was faster with a Colt .45. No one was more deadly with a knife or with his fists than Logan. His victories over worthy challengers had proved his expertise time and time again.

But in Harley's estimation, Logan had served enough time trailing murderers and thieves. The thanks he received came in the form of money, not in lasting friendships, not in the kind of respect the man richly deserved for his efforts. Harley was drawn to this man he counted as his friend. There was a helluva lot more to Logan than the rest of the world wanted to see. People used Logan to solve their problems. When he did, they expected him to ride off into the sunset and leave them to resume their lives.

"I think it's high time you found a nice woman and settled down to running this ranch," Harley announced. "You've gone looking for trouble and you've been well paid for resolving every crisis. Why, you have earned more than enough money to live out the rest of your life in the lap of luxury. And to hell with my bookkeeping and correspondences!" he added emphatically. "I'd be content to put down roots in one place instead of chasing all over the country after criminals. All you have to do is snap your fingers and Jenny Payton would marry you in a minute. Then the two of you could sit back and enjoy this pile of money you've made."

This was a recurrent conversation, one Logan found himself engaged in each time he returned to the Gila River valley. Sometimes Harley traveled with Logan, sometimes not. But this topic of discussion cropped up each time Harley sorted through the mail. Harley knew Logan would grow restless to roam so there was no sense hiding the letters and countless offers he received. But it didn't stop Harley from stating his opinion on what Logan should do with the rest of his life. Nothing stifled Harley. He spouted like Old Faithful.

"There is nothing to hold me here," Logan said with a nonchalant shrug. Leisurely, he stuffed a sinewy leg into a clean pair of breeches and then stretched out on his bed.

"That's why you need a woman like Jenny Payton," Harley contended.

A roguish grin twitched Logan's sensuous lips. "I don't recall ever being without Jenny or any other female when I wanted one."

Harley scowled. "I'm not talking about the kind of woman you bed to ease your needs."

"How many kinds are there, Professor Newcomb?" Logan questioned in mock innocence.

Clamping a tight rein on his temper, Harley counted to ten before responding. "There's two kinds, as if you didn't know. The kind you wed and the kind you bed."

"Even for a notorious freelance gunman like me?" Logan taunted his exasperated friend. "I thought you just said the respectable citizens ostracized me and that they should all be throttled for their self-righteousness."

Harley was becoming more frustrated by the second. One would have thought, after having this same debate so many times, that he would be prepared for Logan's rebuttals. But Logan never made the mistake of employing the same arguments twice, and Harley wasn't quick-witted enough to counter Logan. He could always think of what he should have

17

said *after* Logan was long gone.

"I still think you should consider Jenny Payton," he declared. "She worships the ground you walk on, as near as I can tell. She would fit in nicely around the ranch and she would make you a fine wife. Hell, she probably understands you as well as you allow any female to know you." Harley breathed a heavy sigh and stuffed his hands in his pockets. "It's time you started living your own life instead of straightening out everyone else's for them."

Logan rolled to his side. Lord, he was tired. Logan had chased down a crafty outlaw who knew this wild country as well as he did. It had taken a week of relentless riding to track the scoundrel down. And then, when he finally fell into Logan's trap, the man refused to give himself up. The renegade had chosen to battle his way to freedom or die trying to escape. The townspeople had sent out a posse to assist Logan, but the men only arrived in time to cart their public nuisance back to the coroner. It was the end of a long killing spree and Logan didn't regret that the *hombre* hadn't lived to stand trial. But he did regret the extra time spent tracking the ruthless murderer and rapist. It had cost him several days and countless hours without sleep.

"I'm going to see Butterfield," Logan murmured as his black lashes fluttered down to block out the late afternoon sunlight that spilled through the window.

Harley knew Logan would and it infuriated him to no end. He had wasted his breath spouting his opinions. "Well, Butterfield could have come to you," he grumbled sourly. "After all, the man owns the blessed stage line. He ought to be the one riding it out here to confer with you."

"Send off a letter telling Butterfield I'll be in Fort Smith after I've had a few days' rest. And then jot a note to Carter, Danhill, and Rader," Logan requested as he massaged his aching temples.

Harley stared frog-eyed at the brawny form that made the double bed appear half its normal size. "What the blazes do you want with them?"

From beneath a thick fringe of lashes, silver eyes opened to twinkle with mischief. "It isn't what *I* want with them, Harley.

18

It's what *you* want with them. You are going to help Butterfield restore order and safety to his stage route."

Harley slammed his sagging jaw shut. He didn't have the foggiest notion what Logan was planning, but he would find out later, whether or not he wanted to know what part he would play in Logan's scheme. Grumbling, he stalked back downstairs. His notes to the three men Logan had named did not contain more than three words: "Logan needs you." Carter, Danhill, and Rader would come without question. Harley knew that as surely as he knew his own name.

Sitting behind the oversized desk, Harley drummed his blunt fingertips and grumbled to himself. Wasn't it just like Logan not to explain what he was planning until the last minute? Harley could speculate all he wanted, but he doubted he could puzzle out Logan's intentions. But Logan knew exactly what he wanted to do. It was his nature to keep the rest of the world in the dark until the matter was mentally organized to his satisfaction.

Blast it, sometimes Logan's secretiveness aggravated Harley to the point that he contemplated strangling the brawny giant. And the only thing that prevented Harley from appeasing his frustration was the fact that Logan was six feet three inches and two hundred thirty-five pounds of cougar-quick reaction and rippling muscle. A man didn't mess with Logan unless he was a daredevil or a self-destructive fool, Harley reminded himself. Logan didn't like to be touched, and he took it unkindly when a man thought to put a bullet through him.

Yes, Logan was the shining example of the kind of man most people were afraid to tangle with. But deep down inside, beneath that armor of deadly calm and ironclad control, was a lonely man who needed a friend. Harley Newcomb was that friend. Harley knew there was a lot of good in Logan, even if most folks were afraid to look inside him and take the time to learn what really made him tick. Considering his hard shell, Logan had a soft core. But he allowed very few people to know that. Harley knew and he wished other folks could see the man who hid behind that protective wall.

Harley might grumble and complain about Logan, but he was steadfast in his friendship for the legendary shootist. He and

Logan were good for each other. But what would be even better would be for a woman to come along to draw out the raw warmth and hidden goodness from the deep well of unrefined emotions that very few people even knew existed in this giant of a man. Jenny Payton could probably come closer to exposing Logan's emotions than any woman he had known. But getting that human tumbleweed to put down roots would be the difficult part, Harley mused pensively. If Jenny couldn't persuade Logan to make her his wife, Harley doubted that any woman could.

Well, I'll just keep harping on the subject, Harley decided. Maybe in another year or two he could wear Logan down and get him to at least consider marriage. Logan was going to grow old before his time if he didn't slow his reckless pace. But there was something in Logan's constitutional makeup that made him restless. Maybe it was his unfortunate childhood or the hazards of the profession Logan pursued. Harley didn't know for certain, but he wasn't giving up on Logan.

The man needed a wife and family so he would come to consider this ranch in Gila Valley as his home instead of his headquarters. Logan needed a reason not to leave home. The right woman could make all the difference. The problem was, Logan never took the time to really get to know a woman. He didn't have relationships with women, only fleeting affairs. Even Jenny Payton was more of a convenience than she should have been after the three years they had known each other. But it was no matter. Harley resolved to nag Logan until he changed his ways. Sooner or later Logan would realize his longtime friend knew what was best. Logan was just stubborn to the core, Harley reminded himself. In fact, Logan was probably the most headstrong man to walk the face of the earth.

A spiteful chuckle bubbled from Harley's lips. What Logan needed was to run headlong into a woman who was as bullheaded as he was. Then the two of them could return to the ranch and butt heads for the rest of their days. At least that would keep Logan home!

Wearing an ornery smile, Harley sent a prayer heavenward, requesting that just such a female cross Logan's path. If the good Lord believed in justice he would answer this particular prayer. What Logan needed was a taste of his own medicine to straighten him out. Something had to give, after all. Logan couldn't pursue this rough and tumble pace forever. It would kill him if some cowardly bastard didn't shoot him in the back first!

Chapter 2

Fort Smith, Arkansas
July, 1859

Piper Malone straightened her stylish pale blue silk dress adorned with royal blue trim. Primly she adjusted the matching plume bonnet as she moved gracefully down the street. Her fair, delicately structured features wore a determined frown. Her soft lips were compressed in irritation —the same turbulent emotion that had sustained her for the past two weeks.

Like an arrogant fool, Piper thought she could second-guess her greedy stepfather and that wily weasel Grant Fredricks. Her miscalculation had led her on a frantic chase from Chicago's elite districts to the mud-caked streets of Fort Smith—a city of three thousand citizens, many of whom possessed faces Piper was sure she had seen on various wanted posters between Illinois and Arkansas. From what she had noticed thus far, Piper was sure law and order were the exception rather than the rule in this rowdy town.

Piper was certain she had wasted her time in the exclusive boarding schools her stepfather had insisted she attend in the East. Since she had left Chicago she hadn't employed a smidgen of the education she had received. Trekking west was like touring a foreign country. Her stylish garments were two years ahead of fashion in Arkansas, and the English dialect spoken in this part of the country, compounded with a

Southern drawl, was nothing like Piper was accustomed to hearing.

Shaking off her meandering thoughts, Piper squared her shoulders and flounced toward the sheriff's office. Otis Potter's handlebar mustache uplifted at the corners and his heavy brows arched in an expression of surprise and curiosity when Piper breezed in, looking breathtaking and yet sorely out of place in her fashionable garments, garments that put the women of Fort Smith to shame.

"May I help you, Miss?" Sheriff Potter inquired as he stumbled to his feet, awed by this delicate vision of poise, refinement, and beauty. He couldn't remember seeing a woman who intrigued him so quickly and effectively as this stunning blonde. She possessed the greenest eyes he had ever seen, and her lips looked as soft and inviting as wild pink roses. Otis could have stood there drooling for the next few minutes if her soft, seductive voice hadn't brought him back to reality.

"I hope so, sir," Piper declared with a cordial smile. "I am looking for a man."

A wry grin pursed Sheriff Potter's lips as he smoothed his unruly mustache back into place. With a face and body like hers, she wouldn't have far to look for a man, he mused. She could have any man she wanted, and he would like to be first in her waiting line. Lordy, he felt like a lovesick schoolboy, knocking knees and all!

"Is there a warrant out for the man's arrest?" he managed to question over his half-paralyzed tongue.

Piper shook her silver blond head, causing the renegade strands that clung to her temples to spring back into loose, alluring curls. "You misunderstand, Sheriff. I am searching for a man who is proficient in locating fugitives who do not wish to be found."

"You're looking for a bounty hunter?" Otis choked out in disbelief.

Her eyes turned a darker shade of green. "Not just an ordinary bounty hunter, but rather the best private detective between here and California, someone who is worth the price I intend to pay him."

Sheriff Potter wilted back in his chair, one that creaked

beneath his heavy weight. "There is a man named Royce Granger who might take you on as a client now that his last job has been terminated. He is reasonably competent with a pistol. . . ." Otis suddenly recalled the rumors that were buzzing around town. "But there is another man, name of Logan, who is the best detective and shootist between here and the Pacific," he informed her. "He is due in town any time now. Logan is to meet with the president of the stage line." A slight frown knitted his brow. "But, come to think of it, I'm not sure either one of them is the kind of man a proper lady like you would want to associate with."

"Is this Logan experienced and competent?" Piper questioned somberly.

The sheriff would have laughed out loud at the understatement, but the young lady had no way of knowing there weren't enough words to aptly describe Logan's legendary talents. Giving his head a nod, Otis leaned his hands on the desk. "Logan has combed this part of the country, rounding up fugitives, for as long as I've been here. He's been shot at, shot up, and shot down, but he always manages to survive. Oftentimes he's been judge, jury, and executioner. If there is anything the man hasn't done, I'd hate to venture a guess as to what it might be. He's served as a cattle detective and battled in range wars. He's handled a few matrimonial investigations, served as a U.S. marshal, a hired gunslinger, and sometimes he can be the meanest son of a b . . ." His face colored profusely. "'Scuse me, ma'am. I forgot myself."

Otis cleared his throat and reminded himself he was talking to a sophisticated young woman whose delicate ears were probably unaccustomed to profanity. "As I was saying, Logan can track a bird in flight and locate men who can disappear into thin air. He's got eyes like an eagle, ears like a fox, and a nose like a bloodhound." Otis eased back in his chair to stare pensively at the dazzling blonde. "But, like I said, I'm not sure he's the kind of man a proper lady usually does business with or would even wish to speak to on the street." Potter gave his head a firm shake. "No, I don't think it would be such a good idea to seek Logan out. He wouldn't suit you."

"What is wrong with Logan?" Piper demanded to know.

"Well . . . he's . . ." The sheriff stammered to formulate his words. "You might say he's a bit rough around the edges. He's sort of a cross between a rattlesnake and a grizzly bear. Most people shy away from him unless they're desperate for help. Logan minces no words and he doesn't care much for Easterners."

Piper raised a proud chin. "He doesn't have to like me. He only has to work for me. I am desperate for a bloodhound, Sheriff, and I want the best one to be found. It is vitally important that . . ."

Piper flinched when the office door clanked against the wall, sending a trickle of dust dribbling from the woodwork. Half-turning, she glanced at the massive specimen of a man who filled the portal, then peered wide-eyed at the smaller man whose hands were bound with rope. The prisoner's face was bruised and swollen and a bandana encircled the wound on his shoulder. But it wasn't the haggard appearance of the captive that held her spellbound. It was the shaggy, raven-haired mountain of a man who filled the doorway. Piper felt her gaze and her thoughts drawn immediately back to him. The mere sight of this brawny giant caused her heart to tumble pell-mell in her chest.

Logan tilted his head back ever so slightly, scrutinizing Piper from beneath the wide brim of his brown felt hat. Shock waves rippled through her when Logan fixed his piercing silver eyes on her and raked her gown with a stare that revealed neither pleasure nor disgust. He simply stared straight through her in that unnerving way of his. Piper felt as if she had been thoroughly examined and picked apart. It was the most unsettling sensation she ever remembered experiencing in all her twenty-one years.

Her breath stuck in her throat, and it was several seconds before she could drag in much-needed air. By that time Logan's penetrating gaze had trekked across the heaving swells of her breasts to the trim indentation of her waist, settling finally on the feminine curve of her hips. Piper felt the most peculiar need to cover herself, as if she were standing there stark naked. Reflexively, her trembling hand moved upward, shielding herself from his scorching stare. She was sure the side effects would linger long after he released her from the incredibly potent spell cast by those piercing silver eyes. And they most certainly did! Piper was still quaking, even after Logan cooly dismissed her to focus on his prisoner.

Clad in buckskin, moccasins, and leggings that extended up to his knees, Logan stood like a portrait of formidable masculinity. His lithe body rippled with muscle, and the sensual rhythm of his movements caught and held Piper's wide-eyed gaze. Ominous power and potential strength emanated from his steel-honed body. Each breath he took caused the deerhide clothes to strain across the massive expanse of his chest. His shoulders were broad and they swelled with whipcord muscles. The hard columns of his long legs were exposed by the skin-tight breeches he wore. A wide leather belt fitted with a sheath, bowie knife, and two revolvers was draped around his lean hips. He looked for all the world like a swarthy renegade who called no man master.

His facial features drew Piper's eyes upward like a magnet. His skin was bronzed from the excessive hours he had spent in the sun. A decade of hard, reckless living was stamped on his craggy but undeniably handsome face. The thick strands of hair that protruded from the band of his hat were every bit as black as his eyebrows. His full, sensuous mouth carried a cynical slant that left Piper wondering what ironic twist of fate carved this man into the forceful creature he was. There was a definite arrogance about the way he held himself, the way he moved with masculine grace. Each step was calculated and precise. No motion wasted even a single iota of excessive energy.

Piper felt certain that constant danger and wary disdain were his ever-present companions. She could almost feel their presence in the room. She doubted this brawny giant trusted anyone but himself, and the eerie aura that surrounded him shouted things about his personality. He looked as cold and unapproachable as a rattlesnake. His very presence caused Piper to shiver with excitement tempered with apprehension.

Piper was stung by the sensation that she had trekked into a territory where angels would fear to tread. She doubted this dynamic man was a stranger on the devil's playground. His somber facade indicated he had been to hell and back on several occasions. But even his clash with demons had failed to find him a worthy challenger. And yet there was something wildly fascinating about the man. He possessed a certain mystique, a subtle charisma that intrigued even the most cautious of souls. Common sense warned Piper to keep her distance, but some unexplainable need compelled her to him. She felt like a kite being tugged against the wind, steadily towed along the invisible line between him and her.

As she stood there feeling intimidated and awestruck all in the same moment, she felt her lips go bone-dry. Instinctively, her tongue flicked out to moisten them. Honestly, she mused as she attempted to compose herself, I feel like a victim trapped between a rock mountain and a towering grizzly bear. And those eyes! Lord, they were like liquid silver—hot and bubbly and soul shattering. When Logan cast another glance in her direction, Piper wanted to look away, needed to look away, but she couldn't drag her gaze from this swarthy creature that appeared to be half-man, half-savage, and one hundred per cent male.

Although Piper was the first to admit she was naive about men, having spent half her life stashed in a boarding school that was teeming with other females, she couldn't recollect ever meeting a man who had such devastating effect on her. Logan demanded her respect without requesting it. His very presence in the office diminished its size to a cubicle no larger than the space this towering giant occupied. He was like an immortal god who was to be revered and idolized . . . but from a safe and cautious distance.

The man frightened her in the strangest way. It wasn't the feeling that he could crush her in his large, powerful hands or squash her flat if he felt inclined to sit down on top of her. Piper was sure he could make mincemeat of her if he had a mind to. But the apprehension she experienced stemmed from the peculiar sensation that her will and determination would be nonexistent compared to this powerfully built man. It was as if her own identity had been swallowed up by a stronger, more dominate force. And what truly unnerved Piper was the feeling that it would be pointless to resist a man such as this.

He would ultimately win, no matter what the challenge.

Logan's face and voice were trained to express very little emotion. He rarely permitted himself to display what he was feeling, whether it was pain, pleasure, or grief. Shutting himself off from the world had become habit with him, one necessitated by his dangerous profession and inspired by instinct. But the presence of this dazzlingly attractive young woman struck him like a physical blow. Jeezus, she was so damned pretty she took his breath away! It was like having the sun confined to the office in which he was standing. He could feel the intense heat of her radiant beauty.

From beneath a fan of long, curly lashes a pair of sparkling green eyes peered up at him with angelic innocence. Along the encircling brim of her dainty bonnet, silver blond curls teased the soft, creamy texture of her face—a face God had labored over with loving care. Two delicately carved brows arched over extremely large eyes set above her pert nose. Her skin was like satin—the color of peaches and cream, and those lips! lips as exquisite as pink velvet, naturally curved up at the corners, even when she wasn't smiling.

Logan's astute gaze made another deliberate sweep of her assets. He gazed at one hundred pounds of the most well-sculptured beauty he had ever seen. The thought of how this enchanting goddess would look if she were lying naked beside him in bed left a warm throb of desire pulsating through him. She was a veritable vision of loveliness, one that could instantly arouse a man and leave him gnawing with forbidden hunger.

Logan was assaulted by the most ridiculous impulse imaginable. He found himself yearning to bridge the space between them, snatch this shapely bundle of femininity off the floor, and cart her off like some lusty caveman. But accompanying that compulsive need came the strong, bitter realization that he and this gorgeous nymph had absolutely nothing in common.

This young woman was the epitome of refinement and gentle breeding. She possessed polished manners and sophisticated charm that had been perfected into an art. She had it all—the delicate bone structure, the eye-catching poise, the arresting

29

figure, and the best clothes money could buy. She represented everything Logan wasn't and had never wanted to be. She was expensive silk and lace; he was raw leather. She was the personification of what Harley Newcomb had ranted about in his most recent tirade—the symbol of respectability, and yet she was a hopelessly naive individual who fit into the West like a square peg in a round hole.

Fort Smith was the last outpost of civilization that lay beside lawless Indian Territory and the other wide open spaces to the west. In an instant Logan knew this breathtaking beauty had no business in this rugged, raucous town, or in any community west of the Mississippi for that matter. She would be sorely out of place anywhere except in the elite society of aristocrats who inhabited the East.

After what seemed forever, Logan managed to drag in the reins to his wandering thoughts. Determinedly, he turned his attention to Sheriff Potter, who was also having trouble keeping his eyes off the comely blonde in seductive blue satin.

"This is Cactus Jack," Logan declared, giving his prisoner a rough shove toward the door that led to the row of cells. "He's worth two hundred dollars dead or alive. But Butterfield and I will be glad to forgo the bounty if you'll turn your back while I persuade Jack to reveal who is responsible for the plague of stage holdups near Apache Pass."

Piper blinked like an awakened owl when she heard the deep resonance of Logan's voice. Her gaze swung to Cactus Jack. He looked as if he had already been given the third degree with a pair of meaty fists. She didn't have to be a genius to determine to whom those fists belonged. The bruises on Jack's face were the identical size of Logan's knuckles.

"I ain't sayin' no more than you already beat out'a me," Jack mumbled out the side of his mouth that wasn't cut and swollen.

Without waiting for Sheriff Potter to take charge, Logan herded his captive into his cell and slammed the door shut with a decisive clank. "You'll talk," Logan assured him confidently. A deadly smile dangled from the corner of his lips as he raked his battered prisoner. "I'd bet your life on it, Jack."

With the silence of a stalking tiger, Logan propelled himself toward the front door. "I'll be back later to interrogate Jack and discuss who owes whom for his trouble." His penetrating gray eyes slid from Potter to the curvaceous blonde who hadn't dragged her gaze from him for more than a second since he appeared at the door. Logan stared at her with cool disapproval before refocusing his attention on Potter. "Let me know when you've turned your office back into a county jail instead of a parlor for Eastern debutantes. I certainly wouldn't want to offend the lady with my uncivilized methods of interrogation." He glanced at Piper as if she were a pesky insect, and his tone implied he couldn't have cared less whether he offended her or not. That was the exact impression Logan intended to leave with Piper before he made his hasty exit.

His snide remark caused Piper's back to stiffen. Of all the nerve! She had said or done nothing to warrant the man's cynical sarcasm. He had walked in and taken over Potter's office like a king returning to court, rapping out biting criticism without provocation.

The sheriff opened his mouth to inform Piper of the man's name and occupation, but he was cut off before he could utter a second syllable.

"I know who he is," Piper assured him as she lifted the front of her full skirts and marched toward the door. "But you forgot to mention Logan's monumental arrogance. Obviously he has allowed his unseemly reputation to go to his head."

Sheriff Potter couldn't contain the titter of amusement that trickled from his lips. "He's a cocky rascal, ain't he?"

Piper yanked open the door before glancing over her shoulder at the grinning sheriff. "That, sir, is the understatement of the decade!"

Once outside, Piper resolutely drew herself up and followed in the direction Logan had taken. She wasn't surprised to note the glances Logan was receiving. Passersby took a wide berth around him, their quiet murmurs rippling down the boardwalk like waves on an ocean. She seemed to be the only one who had little to say about the new arrival in Fort Smith.

For a few minutes Piper continued to trail behind him at a safe distance. Silently she composed what she intended to say once she mustered enough nerve to approach the notorious gunslinger.

Logan paused to lean his shoulder against the supporting beam of the mercantile store. Reaching into his pocket, he extracted a cigarillo and clamped it between his teeth. He sensed rather than saw the woman who followed in his wake. He caught the alluring scent of jasmine that had fogged his senses while he was in Potter's office. Again Logan was stung by the same ludicrous urge to scoop her up and taste those inviting lips before some other reckless devil beat him to it.

Darkness was beginning to settle over the streets, bathing the world in shades of hazy pastels. The other women who dared to venture out at dusk had armed themselves with a male escort. All except this sultry blonde, Logan thought in irritation. The naive little fool. Didn't she know better than to go prancing around unchaperoned in these streets? She could be mauled before she knew what happened to her. The lovely nymph's assailant would be a lusty man in pursuit of a wench who could ease his basic needs. Logan ought to know. He was craving the same thing at this very moment!

Without turning to glance at Piper, Logan stared down the street lined with thirty saloons. "Are you following me, lady, or are you lost?" he snorted derisively.

Logan had seen Piper's kind before. *Gapers* he called them. They stared at him as if he were a side show from a circus. Butterfield had let it be known that Logan would be arriving to rid the stage of its robbers and thieves. All the stage agents he had confronted en route to Fort Smith had mentioned the fact they knew he was coming. And everyone he had encountered in town had glanced at him with grim recognition. Hell, he didn't need a sign posted on his chest. They all knew who he was. But the respectable citizens of Fort Smith simply steered clear of him without offering a smile or nod of greeting. All except this naive bit of sophisticated fluff who belonged in some elaborately furnished parlor in Boston or Philadelphia, he thought cynically.

Shock registered on Piper's flawless features. How had Logan known she was following him? He had never once glanced behind him and she had been as inconspicuous as a church mouse. All the previously rehearsed phrases abandoned her as Logan pivoted to stare at her from beneath that veil of coal black lashes.

"I have a proposition for you, Logan," she squeaked, finally, her voice two octaves higher than normal.

A rakish grin tugged at his sensuous lips. Logan made no attempt to disguise his frank appraisal of her statuesque figure. Recklessly, he reached up to grasp the unlit cigar and tucked it back in his pocket. "You surprise me, lady," he drawled in taunt. "I didn't think you looked the type to be tossing around propositions." He regarded her with a mocking stare, one that rudely and purposely focused on her full breasts. "Am I expected to pay handsomely for your virginity?"

How did he know, at a glance, that she was innocent of men? She certainly didn't have that information embroidered on her sleeve! Honestly, the man was a wizard, along with whatever other incredible talents he might possess.

In deliberate intimidation, his laughing silver eyes mapped her shapely terrain, silently assuring her that he knew exactly what lay beneath her blue gown. "Whatever your price, sweetheart, I wouldn't mind sampling your charms. Besides, you look like you could use a little experience."

His remark was so ridiculing and his perusal so thorough that Piper swore he had reached out to fondle her with those tanned hands even as he mocked her innocence. The arrogance in his grin caused her back to stiffen like a ramrod. In Piper's estimation, his hauteur was only exceeded by his incredible audacity. The combination of those two annoying characteristics set spark to her temper.

Piper reacted without thinking (and afterward, when she had time to contemplate her retaliation, she was startled by her own bravura). The palm of her hand cracked against his grinning face like a thunderclap. But Logan never flinched or changed expression. Damnation, one would have thought her blow to his cheek was as insignificant as the brush of a breeze against his chiseled face.

Logan thought his ribald remark would have sent this prim sophisticate dashing off, crying a river of tears and gasping in indignation. The fact that she dared to strike him nearly shocked him out of his moccasins. He was purposely trying to get rid of her. He didn't like what he was feeling deep down in the previously untouched recesses of his soul. This chit disturbed him, frustrated him, aroused him. He knew she was off limits, and yet as he stared into those flashing green eyes he felt another pang of forbidden desire gnawing at him.

Determined of purpose, Logan again tried to put this lovely dove to flight before the lusty beast within him decided he really didn't want her to go. "Do you want me to bathe and shave before I bed you, honey?" he goaded her sardonically. "Or have your wildest fantasies compelled you to spread yourself beneath the likes of me, just the way I am—an uncivilized character out of your dime novels, just like the ones who supposedly haunt the wild West?"

Whoopp! Piper emblazed her handprint on his cheek—the same cheek she had smacked the previous minute. Even though the side of his face pulsated with stinging pain, Logan didn't grimace or move a muscle. He stood there in mute amazement. This chit was either an utter fool or an idiotic daredevil. He would have thought his last crude remark would have sent her off in hysterics. But she stood her ground as if she had been planted in it.

City slickers and Eastern bluestockings were supposed to go scurrying off, revealing their true colors the moment they were challenged. So why wasn't she hotfooting it back to Sheriff Potter's office, demanding that he arrest Logan for his shameful behavior?

Piper punished him with a scathing glower. Their eyes locked and clashed. Her face flushed with outraged fury. Her kissable mouth quivered with irritation, and her gorgeous body trembled with indignation. Her clenched fists were white against the folds of her blue gown. She looked as if she wanted to mutilate him, and she might have tried if he wasn't looming over her.

And oh, how he could loom! He must have practiced that technique as often as he practiced his lightning-quick draw. But Piper had endured as much of his intimidation as she could tolerate. Every glance he flung in her direction silently criticized her. Every comment was meant to expose her secret weaknesses. Well, Logan wasn't perfect either, not by a long shot, and Piper proceeded to tell him so.

34

"I have endured your acidulousness as long as I can."

"My what?" Logan did a double take. "What the devil does that mean?" he wanted to know that very moment.

"Your sour sarcasm," she translated into simpler terms. "And I will have you know that whatever it is that lies below your belt buckle that you're so proud of doesn't interest me in the slightest, Logan," she hissed like a disturbed cat. "In fact, I've heard more appealing offers from drunks lying facedown in the streets. All that interests me is your reputation as a freelance shootist and private investigator."

She fired another round of insults like bullets, and Logan instantly decided this minx was as quick with her tongue as she was with her hand.

Piper hadn't realized she possessed the nerve to stand up against this powerful package of masculinity. But Logan's wisecracks had unearthed the kind of courage Piper had never been forced to call upon in all her twenty-one years. Quite simply, he brought out the worst in her, and she reacted as she never had in all her life.

"Do you think just because I'm a civilized female that your savage lusts and ruttish ways appeal to me? You have nothing I couldn't get from any other man if I wanted it. You may charge a fee for that swift draw you supposedly possess, but I'm willing to bet you have to pay for sex, just like the other low-minded, good-for-nothing scoundrels that swarm these streets." Inhaling a deep breath, she plunged on before she lost her new-found courage. "All that you have to your credit is that you are obviously a sincere person, no matter how terribly misdirected your intentions. No one would purposely pretend to be such a boorish ass!"

Murmurs rippled through the crowd like the first winds of an approaching thunderstorm. Never in his life had Logan permitted anyone, except Harley, to speak so disrespectfully to him. It shocked him that he had stood silent while this saucy sophisticate had her say, especially since curious bystanders had paused to listen to her spout degrading insults at him.

It would have been simple to shut her up. Why the devil he didn't do just that was a question he couldn't quite puzzle out. Perhaps it was astonishment that paralyzed his tongue and his reflexes, but whatever the reason, he had allowed Piper to scorch him with her blistering remarks.

If Logan thought he was shocked by her outburst, Piper was doubly surprised at her audacity. To make matters worse, it had suddenly occurred to her that she had stooped to Logan's disgusting level. She had snapped back at him as if she could support her insults with the same fearless methods with which a man of Logan's profession backed his. Lord, had she completely lost her mind? No one purposely insulted an infamous gunslinger unless she wanted to attend her own funeral. Haunted by that unsettling thought, Piper closed her mouth and glanced away from her antagonist.

Odd, Logan couldn't remember the last time he was provoked to irrepressible laughter. But this gorgeous she-cat caused him to chuckle in pure, unadulterated amusement. She had spunk. She probably couldn't handle herself in the face of true adversity. She would probably get herself into serious trouble trying to protect her virtues, but she did have spirit. He'd give her that!

Still snickering, Logan clutched Piper's arm. "Come on, honey. You can escort me to my hotel room and tell me about this mysterious proposition of yours," he offered.

Piper yanked her arm from his grasp as if she had touched live coals. The sizzling sensation rattled her. She detested Logan and his attempt at male domination. And yet his touch stirred her the way no other man's had. He provoked contradictory emotions within her, and Piper had difficulty coping with the riptide of feelings that he alone evoked from her.

"I can walk on my own accord, thank you very much," she bit off testily. "And I am not, nor will I ever be your honey!" Tilting a defiant chin, Piper stamped along beside him, pausing occasionally to glower at the bystanders who struck up another round of fast and furious gossip. They were probably wondering why she would permit herself to be seen in the company of this ornery varmint. Well, Piper was wondering the same thing!

Logan was an expert at reading faces. He knew exactly what the passersby were thinking. The fact that he allowed the company of this stunning blonde disturbed him. He thought she would have flown off in the opposite direction by now. He had purposely mentioned the hotel, certain she would be offended by the kind of intimate privacy he suggested. Damn, the lady beat anything he had ever seen! He had her pegged as a babe in the woods, but she appeared to have more intelligence and gumption than her breed of women usually possessed.

Sometimes a man had to be cruel to be kind, Logan reminded himself, as he peered at the indignant beauty. He had actually tried to do her a favor by trying to get rid of her. But this sassy chit had ignored her chance to scamper to safety.

As Piper strode along beside Logan she realized she had learned things about herself the past thirty minutes that she hadn't known before. She possessed far more courage and self-confidence than she suspected. The fact that she had stood her ground against this mountain of male invincibility, without allowing him to browbeat her, was a point in her favor. She had also acquired more daring than she believed possible. It felt good to vent her frustrations. She hadn't done that since her mother married that weasel Hiram. Piper had bitten her tongue, refusing to cause dissension, even if she did detest Hiram. Those five years of pent-up emotion had suddenly erupted, and Logan just happened to be in her line of fire. Now that her mother was gone, Piper didn't have to keep the peace with that money-hungry leech or with any other man. Once she caught up with that sniveling lout Grant Fredricks she would also give him a good piece of her mind! Damn him for deceiving her. . . .

The erotic brush of Logan's arm against her shoulder jolted Piper back to the present. Once she had calmed down she realized Logan was purposely antagonizing her just to get a rise out of her. He had taken one look at her and decided not to like her because she was a naive Easterner. Well, it didn't matter what Logan thought. She needed his assistance. She wanted Logan to locate Grant Fredricks and retrieve her inheritance. Then she would stake Grant out to bake in the sun and let him burn to a crisp. She would even stoop to doing business with this impossible man if it meant she could eventually satisfy her vengeance toward Grant. Tolerating Logan would be worth the trouble he caused her.

Chomping on that vindictive thought, Piper hurried to catch up with Logan's long, lithe strides. She didn't give a hoot if the townspeople thought she was crazy as a loon for consorting with this notorious shootist. She needed him and that was the beginning and end of it!

Chapter 3

Recognition dawned on the innkeeper's face when Logan swaggered into the hotel lobby. He glanced momentarily at the lovely blonde, unable to suppress the shock of seeing Logan with such a respectable young lady. Without voicing a word about the obvious mismatch, the proprietor retrieved a key and turned the ledger to his guest.

A wicked smile pursed Logan's lips as he scribbled his name on the ledger. "Shall we share a room and save on expenses?" Logan questioned Piper.

The suggestive tone of his voice sent an unwanted tingle down Piper's spine. Land sakes, Logan hadn't even asked her name, and he had suggested several intimate propositions that had already earned him two well-deserved slaps in the face. The man was positively impossible!

"No thank you," she cooed with sticky sweetness. "I have already reserved a room."

Shrugging nonchalantly, Logan pulled a two-dollar bill from his pocket to light his cheroot in his customary manner. Aghast, Piper snatched the bill from his fingertips and stamped out the flame on the hotel desk. When she had tucked the singed cash in her purse, she glared at Logan with such icy disdain that it took him a moment to recover from frostbite.

"No matter what our creed, background, or ancestry there are certain tenets we should all observe." When Logan looked puzzled by her comment, Piper hastily defined the word that provoked his muddled frown. "Tenets are rules and regulations, Logan. We do not burn money!" she chastised, before flinging him a withering glance. "Honestly, the way you squander money one would think it grew on trees."

Logan stared at the purse in which she had stuffed his two-dollar bill and then focused on her snapping green eyes. He opened his mouth to counter her comment, but Piper pirouetted and marched toward the steps. Damn, but she was a saucy little snip, he mused as he watched the graceful sway of her hips. And if they were going to spend much time together he was going to have to find himself a dictionary. Piper's command of the English language left him floundering to determine whether or not she had insulted him.

After requesting a bath, Logan hurried to catch up with the curvaceous blonde. When she started into her own room, directly across the hall from his, Logan grasped her by the arm and shepherded her into his suite. While hot water was being carted into the room by a stream of attendants, Piper shifted uneasily from one foot to the other. Again she was unnerved by two conflicting emotions. When she was with this awesomely built man she felt safe and protected. And yet she had never felt quite so uneasy in the presence of a man. She doubted her ability to successfully handle this swarthy rake. Logan was nothing like the properly mannered aristocrats who had courted her the past three years.

Piper lingered too long in thought. A startled gasp tripped from her lips when she realized they were alone in his room and that Logan was looming over her. He loomed all too well, Piper thought resentfully. Logan's ominous stature left her with the uneasy feeling that to protest or struggle against him would be a waste of time and energy.

Awkwardly, she tilted her face to peer into his bronzed features. The lines that bracketed his mouth weren't as harsh as she remembered them. He was studying her as if she were the first female he had ever seen, even when she knew that was laughable.

Logan stared down into her exquisite face. He knew he could do whatever he wanted to this alluring minx and no one would stop him, certainly not her. She didn't have the strength to counter his assault. That realization brought his hand upward.

His thumb drifted over her silky cheek. It was every bit as soft and smooth as he imagined. She was the most exquisite creature he had ever touched. If she had been any other woman Logan would have tugged her into his arms and devoured her with his usual brand of impatience. But it would have seemed sacrilege to be rough with this delicate angel. And yet, Logan wasn't sure he knew how to be gentle. He had never bothered to try.

To Piper's surprise, Logan abruptly retreated a step, pivoted, and doffed his buckskin shirt. Effortlessly, he positioned the dressing screen between Piper and his waiting bath. Although he was vividly aware of her presence in his room, he didn't glance back to see her reaction when he partially disrobed in front of her.

Piper's wide green eyes assessed the bronzed expanse of his back, taking note of the scars from bullets that had penetrated his rib and shoulder. If he knew to what extent his half-nude body affected her he would have enjoyed some small consolation. But he was too busy struggling with his own emotion to notice her look of feminine appreciation.

"What's your name, honey?" Logan questioned as he peeled off his breeches.

Piper gritted her teeth, annoyed that he had flagrantly disregarded her request not to call her honey. "Piper," she informed him stiffly. "Piper Malone."

Piper . . . Her name reminded him of the story of the Pied Piper, who lured children along behind him. It was one of the few fairy tales he recalled. Considering his childhood, it was a wonder he knew any bedtime stories. But in this alluring siren's case it wasn't children who helplessly trailed along behind her. It was an endless rabble of men who were hopelessly infatuated by Piper's unrivaled beauty and hypnotic poise. Odd, Logan mused as he sank into his bath. This green-eyed blonde stirred strange, unfamiliar feelings that he was at a loss to explain. If he truly believed in witches he would have accused her of being one!

"What sort of proposition did you have in mind, Piper?" Logan questioned as he plucked up the sponge and saturated it with water.

41

The sound of her name tumbling from his lips, and their close contact from moments before, had her heart cartwheeling around her chest like an acrobat. Willfully, Piper collected her wits. Her purpose? The proposition? Why the devil was she here? She was so rattled she couldn't remember.

After another uneasy moment, her malfunctioning brain began to operate properly. "I would like to hire you to locate a man for me." Her voice became steadier as she progressed. But it took incredible self-control not to dwell on the fact that there was a naked man behind the dressing screen—possibly the most virile, muscular specimen she would ever encounter in all her life. "After questioning the supervisor at the stage station, I learned that Grant Fredricks left Fort Smith on Monday, bound for San Francisco. I want him taken into custody and charged with theft."

An annoyed frown furrowed Logan's brow as he hastily bathed and dried himself. "What does this man mean to you?" he inquired. "And why do you want me to fetch him back to you?"

Piper's hand knotted and uncurled in the folds of her gown. Her lovely features puckered in a frown. She didn't want to inform Logan of all the details. "I don't want him back," she told him frankly. "I didn't want him in the first place. Grant conspired with my stepfather to swindle me out of the trust fund that I was to receive today—my twenty-first birthday. Some birthday this turned out to be." Her voice was laced with bitterness.

A frustrated sigh escaped her lips as she wrestled with the unpleasant memories of her past. Her stepfather had been as shocked as she was when he discovered his conniving plan had gone awry. Grant had outfoxed both of them. He had made off with the fortune Hiram had schemed to control.

"How much money are we discussing here?" Logan demanded.

Piper chewed indecisively on her bottom lip. She wasn't sure she should confide in this professional gunslinger. Why was he interrogating her anyway? Didn't his kind usually accept a job, no questions asked?

"The amount is not as important as the principle of righting an injustice," Piper insisted. "I am prepared to pay you one hundred dollars to return the satchel of cash to me and to scare the living daylights out of Grant Fredricks."

"One hundred?" A peal of incredulous laughter rang in his chest. This naive minx didn't have a clue what the going rate for a private detective was. One hundred dollars? Hell, that was pocket change to him!

After he had changed into his clean black breeches and stockings, Logan emerged from behind the screen. Piper caught her breath when her eyes fell to his wide, muscled chest and the dark furring of hair that tapered down to his waist. Never had she been so compelled to reach out and touch a man. She simply couldn't imagine how his dark flesh would feel beneath her inquiring fingertips. There wasn't an inch of flab on his rugged body. He looked like a perfectly sculptured bronze statue—the very image of masculinity and vitality. Honestly, he was so appealing it left her lightheaded.

Logan swore under his breath when Piper's eyes roved over his exposed flesh with unguarded fascination. It wasn't that he didn't enjoy the rapt attention he was receiving, but it made it damned difficult to concentrate on conversation. He should have donned his shirt. Her appreciative stare made him want things he knew he shouldn't take from this innocent nymph. Damn, he was going to suffer a heart seizure while he was trying to be noble!

"Feminine curiosity, Piper?" Logan mocked. Jeezus, if she didn't quit staring at him like that he was going to lose what little control he had left! "I thought you said you only wanted me to hunt down Grant Fredricks for you."

Her face flushed from the base of her throat to the roots of her silver blond hair. How dare he suggest that she was fantasizing about him! She was, but a gentleman would have been considerate enough not to tease her! "I haven't the slightest inclination to . . ." She lied to save face, but Logan's explosive laughter interrupted her denial.

"Haven't you?" he drawled in that intimidating tone that Piper had already come to detest. "I've made a living reading people's faces, honey. And thank you." A cocky smile dangled in the corner of his mouth. "It's nice to be noticed, even by a fluffy little sopisticate."

"Dammit, will you please put on your shirt!" Piper flared in helpless exasperation.

His brow jackknifed. "I didn't know refined ladies were allowed to swear. I thought their delicate ears burned when they were forced to endure profanity. It must be twice as painful when the lady herself is the one who utters such curses," he taunted mercilesssly.

When Piper wheeled toward the door, his hand snaked out to entrap her. Wearing a mischievous grin that annoyed her to no end, Logan spread her fingers and pressed them against the muscular wall of his chest. He didn't think her animated features could turn a deeper shade of red, but they did.

"The proposition . . ." she chirped in reminder. "One hundred dollars . . ." Lord, her heart was pounding so loudly she couldn't hear herself think.

Logan employed her slender arm as a rope, pulling her ever closer, swamping her with the fresh, clean scent of him, making her far more aware of him than she wanted to be. "The payment I would demand from you might call for something other than money, Piper," he informed her, his voice ragged with a desire he was tired of fighting.

He was going to kiss her, right here in his room, right smack dab on her lips! He was going to clutch her against that extremely masculine chest. And Piper, despite her valiant attempt to control herself and salvage her pride, was going to melt all over him. She could feel the sensation spilling over her. Damn him! Was this another of his cruel attempts to humiliate her? Did he derive wicked amusement from preying on her illogical attraction to him?

Logan felt her betraying body sway helplessly toward him. Her thick lashes fluttered down and her features froze in a frown. It looked as if this stunning vixen had buckled beneath his overpowering persuasiveness, but it was evident that she resented the sensations he had stirred in her.

"Look at me, little dove," he murmured hoarsely. "You're going to kiss me with your eyes open, seeing me, not some other man you've conjured up in your mind."

Piper was too rattled to understand what had prompted his

remark. Timidly, her lashes swept up to survey those glistening pools of silver. That was a mistake. She already knew how potent his gaze could be. At close range, the spell cast by those hypnotic eyes was absolutely devastating. Her heart was paralyzed. It refused to beat. Piper stared breathlessly at the sensuous curve of his lips. Her senses were fogged with his manly scent. She could feel the searing imprint of his body against hers and her knees threatened to fold up like an accordion.

When his sinewy arm stole around her waist, it reactivated her stalled heart, sending it galloping in triple time. And finally the sweet agony was over. Almost hesitantly, as if he also resented the compelling attraction between them, Logan lifted her delicious body against him and bent to taste her lips, savoring her innocent response. A shudder rocked him when he felt her sweet mouth melt beneath his skillful kiss.

Jeezus! Had he somehow become separated from his common sense? Only minutes before he had warned himself not to get this close. But the moment she turned away he had reflexively pulled her to him. What the sweet loving hell did he hope to accomplish? Piper Malone was an innocent angel who had strayed from paradise, and he was only a few miles this side of hell. They were worlds apart. They were totally different and shouldn't be sharing this soul-shattering embrace!

The swiftness with which Piper found herself set to her feet, without the possessive pressure of Logan's hands and lips to sustain her, left her staggering. Piper stood there clutching the back of a nearby chair, blinking like a startled owl. Sweet mercy! Kisses weren't supposed to do such incredible things to one's brain and body, were they? She felt like a tree that had been uprooted by a cyclone. She couldn't stop quaking.

"I've thought it over and I don't want the job," Logan growled in a hateful tone that knocked Piper completely off balance.

"Why?" was all she could get out before her vocal cords collapsed in her throat.

Logan spun around to glare at the wall, employing the time to recompose himself. Jeezus, he felt hot and cold and shaky. After a moment he pivoted to study the myriad of emotions reflected in Piper's bewitching green eyes. "Lady, you don't belong here," he told her candidly. "You're like a duck out of water. I suggest you catch the next stage back to wherever the hell you came from and post a warrant for your boyfriend's arrest. I've got better things to do than tromp across the country trying to retrieve your dowry. Hell, I'll give you the money myself and you can forget about this ridiculous search! How much did you lose, three or four hundred?"

Piper felt the rise of fury pulsating in her cheeks. Logan had pulled her into his room, kissed her blind, and then turned her down flat! Men. They were all so certain of their superiority. They used a woman for their own lusty purposes and then tried to make her decisions for her. Confound the man. He delighted in making her feel cheap and incompetent and unimportant.

Three or four hundred dollars, Piper thought with a disgusted sniff. A lot he knew about it. Just because Logan had money to burn he assumed that she would leap at his offer and go slinking off like a whipped pup. Well, she wasn't going to accept his cash and return to Chicago! She had come this far and she would go all the way to San Francisco if need be.

"If you won't consent to help me, I'll follow Grant myself!" she muttered resentfully.

A bubble of incredulous laughter rattled in his broad chest. "You? You don't know beans about life in the West. It's damned wild, especially if you're a defenseless female who probably never handled a gun or knife and couldn't straddle a horse to flee to safety if the situation demanded it." His gray eyes raked her with scornful mockery. "You're out of your element, honey. To make matters worse, the stage company has been harassed by road agents, all of whom would take one look at your luscious body and whisk you off to satisfy their lusts."

To prove his point, his hand clenched in her silky hair, wrapping it around his fist like a rope, dragging her face to his. Logan roughly devoured her lips while his straying hand fastened on her buttocks, crushing her against his rock hard thighs.

Piper felt as if she were riding an emotional pendulum that

swung from giddy pleasure to revulsion. Moments before he had held her gently against him. Now he was purposely hurting her, antagonizing her. But along with his rough abuse came a stark awareness of the man himself—something Piper hadn't expected to feel once the repulsion of being manhandled wore off. And it evaporated much sooner than it should have!

Although she told herself she despised Logan, her body paid no attention to her brain. His touch branded her with fire and she melted, unable to control the flood of sensations that splashed over her. It baffled Piper that she could despise Logan and still feel this illogical compulsion for his touch. But rhyme and reason flew out the window the moment he encompassed her in those powerful arms.

Logan had defeated himself at his own game. What had begun as an attempt to overpower Piper had become tormenting pleasure. When he felt his hands wandering over her in a caress rather than a disrespectful grope, he jerked away as if he had been stung. Growling under his breath, Logan wheeled around to retrieve his money belt. After extracting several bills, he bridged the space between them in swift, impatient strides. Although Piper gasped at the feel of his fingertips against her breasts, Logan promptly stashed the cash in her bodice.

"Consider the money a birthday gift. Happy twenty-first, honey." There was very little sincerity in his tone, only a gruffness that infuriated Piper all the more. "Now get the hell out of here," he muttered crossly. "I've got things to do and none of them include playing nursemaid to a defenseless bluestocking. If you know what's good for you, you'll stay away from me and go back where you belong."

Piper found herself removed from her position in front of the door and quickly deposited in the hall. For several moments she stared unblinkingly at the door. Mercy, her emotions were in a tailspin. She had been kissed senseless, fondled, insulted, and thrown out of Logan's room so swiftly that her head was whirling like a carousel.

Piper wobbled across the hall on legs that functioned as inefficiently as stilts. Entering, she glared at the huge tomcat that lounged on her bed.

"The man is absolutely impossible," she declared to Abraham.

Abraham pricked his ears, stared leisurely in her direction, and then flexed his claws. Annoyed that Abraham showed so little concern, Piper stamped across the room to stare down at the coal black cat whose neck was encircled by a natural collar of white hair. His four white stocking feet were sprawled in front of him while he lay negligently on his side. Abraham reminded her of a king lounging on his throne. His golden eyes displayed no compassion for the emotions Piper had been forced to endure.

"I offered to pay him good money to find Grant, but would Logan accept it?" Piper answered her own question since Abraham hadn't been blessed with the gift of speech. "No, he rudely rejected the proposition and told me to go home! The nerve of that man. He . . ." Piper expelled her breath when she realized she was ranting at Abraham as if he were personally responsible for her troubles with Logan.

A muffled curse tripped from Piper's lips when she cooled down enough to remember her luggage was still at the stage depot. It had been impossible to tote Abraham's reed carrying case and her belongings to the hotel all at once, so she had left her luggage behind. She knew Abraham was thankful to be rid of the cramped basket in which Piper had forced him to ride during their trek to Fort Smith, but there was still the matter of retrieving her luggage.

Grumbling to herself, Piper pivoted back toward the door. Remembering the money Logan had stashed in her bodice, Piper reached into her chemise. Her eyes widened in surprise when she counted the five hundred dollars Logan had thrust at her. He had handed her a small fortune just to get her out of his way. Why? He barely knew her. Gunslingers weren't supposed to be generous and protective, were they? He owed her nothing. It seemed out of character for a man with Logan's notorious reputation to attempt to pacify her, especially after the raffish way he treated her. She hadn't expected him to have a heart or the least bit of concern about what might happen to her. To hear him talk she was a public nuisance. So why had he offered her money? She knew he had no use for her kind.

Piper threw up her hands in exasperation. She couldn't decide if she admired or despised Logan. He infuriated her when he tried to tell her what to do, when he took outrageous privileges with her. Yet she was baffled by his attempt to protect her from trouble.

She supposed she truly should appreciate his concern, even if he had chosen to insult and intimidate her in hope of getting rid of her. That was simply Logan's way, she realized. He did not employ diplomacy and tact as she had been taught to do. But Piper was still determined to salvage her trust fund if at all possible. If she couldn't locate someone to assist her she would hunt down Grant all by herself! Logan wasn't going to change her mind with his tactics.

Chomping on that thought, Piper exited from her room to retrieve her luggage and to find nourishment for herself and Abraham, who was in the habit of enjoying a snack before he settled down for another of his evening naps. She wasn't going to spare that exasperating Logan another thought. If he refused to help her she would manage without him, somehow or another!

Puffing on his cheroot, Logan studied John Butterfield, who sat behind the desk in the back room of the stage office. Butterfield was a man of imposing size and stature. Even at age fifty, John had worked tirelessly to win the mail contract and to ensure that his stage route didn't suffer any unnecessary delays. But the past few months he had endured Apache raids on his relay stations and the unnerving appearance of road agents who ransacked the mail and relieved passengers of their coins and jewelry.

Hiring Royce Granger to act as his stage detective proved futile, John mused sourly. Royce hadn't rounded up even one desperado. The stages were still being waylaid in New Mexico Territory, and the money Butterfield had spent for a hired gun had been a wasted investment.

John Butterfield surveyed the powerfully built man who lounged negligently in his chair. Although Logan's controlled facade suggested nonchalance, Butterfield was well aware of the man's competence in the face of adversity. Why he hadn't hired Logan in the first place was beyond him. He had attempted to cut a few corners, but he would have been money ahead had he paid Logan's exorbitant fee. Besides that, Logan had proven dependable since the first time they met. John had purchased prize stock from Logan and had no complaints with their business arrangements. He would still have been doing business with Logan if he hadn't located a man who sold his stock cheaper than this rancher and detective. But if Logan could rid John of his one major headache—stage holdups—he would resume their business arrangement, even if livestock could be purchased at a lower price elsewhere.

"I have the feeling my problems are complicated," John began bitterly. "There seems to be method to these delays and holdups." His breath came out in a rush. "I'm beginning to wonder if some of my employees are mixed up in this. There are too many details taken into account when one of the coaches is robbed. It's as if the road agents know which stage carries passengers that can provide the most loot."

Logan had arrived at the same conclusion after forcing information from Cactus Jack, who had been riding with the band of highwaymen who attacked the stage Logan had traveled in on his journey east. Cactus Jack had grudgingly admitted that some of the stage agents were working as spies for the outlaws. Logan might have gained more information from the bandito if Sheriff Potter hadn't insisted that the prisoner remain in one piece. Potter's presence had handicapped Logan from utilizing some of his more drastic methods of persuasion.

"I want to handle this my own way, John," he declared in a no-nonsense tone. "If I take the job, I want no questions asked and I will feel no obligation to any demand you might make. It will be my way or no way at all."

A faint smile crossed John's lips. When did Logan handle anything except in his way? He never buckled beneath outside influences or suggestions.

Without posing any argument, John twisted in his seat to retrieve five thousand dollars from the safe. With a mute nod,

Logan carelessly stashed the roll of cash in his pocket. As if anyone would dare attempt to take money from this skillful private detective, John thought to himself. A man didn't cross Logan unless he was bent on self-destruction.

"I want results and I'm not about to tell you how to manage your affairs," he assured Logan. "And if all goes well, I will also be expecting a shipment of your livestock to supply my coaches and furnish meat to my passengers. You can name your price."

Returning the smile, Logan leaned forward to brace his elbows on the edge of the desk. His expression sobered as he stared Butterfield squarely in the face. "Now that we understand each other, I'll tell you what I have in mind. But the information is to go no further than this office. If it does, you may find you have wasted good money. Every damned stage agent between here and Tucson knew why I was coming east. I don't like having everyone know what I'm about, especially those I'm tracking."

As Logan unfolded his plan John grew even more confident he wasn't spending a frivolous cent on this professional shootist. What Logan proposed was as inventive and resourceful as the man himself. When Logan swaggered out of the office a few minutes later, John felt sure it was only a matter of time before the Butterfield stage was running on schedule and without unfortunate robberies or delays. John was certain he would sleep much better this night. Logan had taken the worry off his hands. Firing Royce Granger and hiring Logan was the smartest thing John had ever done.

Logan ambled down the street toward the hotel, serenaded by the music that wafted from the numerous saloons. He paused momentarily to glance at the lights that sprayed across the dirt streets of Fort Smith. Lord, he could use a drink and a soft, willing woman. . . .

The screech of a female voice brought his head around to locate the source of the sound. His blood ran cold as the distraught voice reminded him of the comely blonde who had preyed on his mind for the past two hours. Reversing direction,

51

Logan dashed toward the frantic squawks. His stormy gray eyes pierced each concealing shadow like a cat stalking his prey in the darkness.

The sight of two silhouettes struggling for dominance as they bumped against the wall of the bakery shop brought all of Logan's senses to life instantaneously. Like a cougar crouched on a rocky ledge, Logan pounced off the boardwalk and into the alley.

Piper scratched and clawed at the whiskey-saturated lecher who had attacked her while she was overburdened with her luggage. She had attempted to strike him with her satchels, but his groping hands had invaded unclaimed territory no other man had ever touched. Revulsion speared through Piper as she fought to prevent him from lifting her gown higher than he already had and placing his filthy hands on her thigh. Her stylish gown had been ripped from her neck as if it were tissue paper, exposing the generous swells of her breasts to his leering gaze. And now the despicable ogre was trying to tear the lower portion of her dress into shreds so he could have his way with her.

The warning Logan had issued earlier that evening came back to haunt Piper. He had predicted that she would get herself into trouble. Now she was going to be raped and she had no weapon at her disposal. Her fists and sharp nails hadn't fazed the groping galoot. . . .

A growl, one that sounded almost inhuman, echoed in the darkness. Suddenly the foul-smelling hooligan who had attacked her was launched through the air. In disbelief, Piper watched the scalawag crash against the side of the building. With bare breasts heaving, Piper stared at the muscular giant who had come to her rescue. Mercilessly, Logan pounded her assailant flat enough to fit into one of Butterfield's mail pouches.

Piper had never seen another human pulverize another as swiftly and effectively as Logan was doing. The crack of his fists against her assailant's whiskered face sounded like a carpenter driving nails. Painful grunts erupted from the man's lips as he attempted to protect himself from one blow after another. But the varmint would have needed a shield if he hoped to deflect Logan's fierce attack. Logan was all fists, feet, and flying fur. His legs were as lethal as his arms and the swarthy giant was making short shrift of the scalawag.

Another blow, one delivered by moccasined foot to the groin stole the last of the man's breath. As his knees buckled beneath him, Logan's meaty fist connected with his jaw. With a thud, the scoundrel pitched forward onto the ground to taste the dirt beneath Logan's feet.

Like a homing pigeon returning to roost, Piper flew instinctively at Logan. Her hand locked behind his broad back and she clung to him as if she never meant to let go. She had been riddled with fear the previous moment and now she felt safe and protected once again. That contented emotion caused her to linger, to bury her head against his laboring chest. She savored the feel of his sinewy body and inhaled the masculine aroma that replaced the offensive smell of perspiration and whiskey.

Stunned, Logan stared down at the shapely bundle of femininity who was plastered full length against him. He could feel Piper's breasts boring into his shirt and he was instantly aroused by her nearness. Jeezus, he had been three weeks without a woman and he didn't need to be reminded of that fact, not when temptation was practically squeezing the stuffing out of him! Didn't this naive little imp know better than to hug a man unless she expected to be hugged back?

Involuntarily, his brawny arms began to fold around her, to reassure her, to caress her. . . . Logan caught himself the split-second before he cradled Piper against him and sought out her delicious mouth. He wouldn't be giving the kind of aid and comfort she expected and needed if he allowed their embrace to continue, not when desire throbbed in his loins. Already he was left wanting something she couldn't give.

Muttering at this minx's uncanny knack of arousing him without even trying, Logan braced the heel of his hands against her quaking shoulders and shoved her an arm's length away. That too was a mistake. The pale golden light of distant lanterns bathed the luscious swells of her breasts left exposed by her gaping gown and chemise. His eyes fell to the creamy mounds that seemed to beg his touch. The desire he had attempted to control the previous moment raced through him again. Logan was assaulted by a gnawing ache that did nothing to sweeten his disposition.

Still grumbling at the incident that had thrown them together and from the hunger that raged within him, Logan gave Piper a firm shake. Her blond head snapped backwards, spilling the glorious strands from beneath her lopsided bonnet. Like a toppling waterfall, sprays of sunbeams and moonbeams cascaded over her bare shoulders to lie enticingly against her breasts. Logan swore he would never forget the alluring sight of her, even if he lived to be one hundred. She stole the breath from his lungs and left his paralyzed heart dangling inside his rib cage. Struggling for control, Logan raised his wandering gaze to glower into her misty green eyes.

"Jeezus, woman, there's a nine o'clock curfew in this town," he snapped. "Anyone who wanders out to these streets after that hour is openly inviting trouble. You got exactly what you deserved for your idiocy!"

His rough shake and his whiplash tone brought Piper to her senses. Anger mastered the sentimental emotions that had poured out of her when Logan came to her defense. His eyes burned into her like molten silver, scorching her, ridiculing her. Honestly, the man was so dispassionate and cold he probably bled ice water. She would like to shoot him and find out for certain!

Proudly, her chin tilted as she fought to compose herself and blink away the mist of tears that clouded her eyes. Her trembling hands moved upward to cover her bare flesh. Determinedly, Piper struggled to salvage what was left of her dignity.

"Well, no one informed me of any curfew," she muttered resentfully. "How was I supposed to know vampires emerged from the darkness to scare the wits out of unsuspecting women?"

"Dammit, I told you this wasn't a civilized city where a lady can go parading about. There are no policemen to patrol these streets," he growled into her flushed face. "You foolish Easterners don't have the sense God gave a mule!"

He couldn't have hurt her worse if he had struck her with a

54

deadly fist. Nursing her bruised pride, Piper spun around to collect her purse and her scattered belongings. She didn't have to stand here and endure another round of Logan's scathing insults. Damn him, he was so rude and intimidating that she swore she would rather die than thank him for saving her from disaster.

Growling like a disturbed lion, Logan snatched the heavy satchels from her fingertips and clamped onto her arm. "I'm taking you back to the hotel and locking you in your room," he informed her crossly. "And in the morning, go buy yourself a pistol. You're going to need one if you plan to court catastrophe every couple of hours."

Piper wormed free of his grasp. She had suffered enough stinging insults from this big ape for one day. Her temper, sorely put upon already, snapped. Her irritation caused her to forget to employ the tact and diplomacy that had been drilled into her head at boarding school.

"I don't need you to accompany me to the hotel," she said scathingly. "I can manage just fine all by myself!"

A deep skirl of laughter reverberated in his massive chest. "The same way you took care of your overzealous friend?" he taunted sarcastically. His eyes raked her exposed flesh like sharp silver talons. "Or were you anticipating rape? Maybe you encouraged the poor man to take what he wanted from you."

Piper had never been so furious and outraged in all her life. The very idea of suggesting she had invited that scalawag to maul her! In a burst of fury Piper struck out, itching to wipe that ridiculing grin from Logan's craggy features, aching to satisfy her vengeance. If her schoolmaster could have seen her, he wouldn't have believed her to be the prim and proper young woman who had graduated *magna cum laude*.

Logan caught her dainty hand before it collided with his cheek for the third time that day. His piercing silver eyes held her hostage, as did his clenched fist.

"I've been lenient with you twice, sweetheart," he bit off tersely. Logan wondered who irritated him more—Piper for daring to come at him with claws bared or himself for permitting this tempting beauty to stir unfamiliar feelings

55

within him. "If you try to slap me again, I'm going to slap you back." A wicked smile pursed his lips as he increased the pressure on her fingers. "You might find yourself as black and blue as that hooligan who attacked you."

"You derive great satisfaction from your despotic ascendancy, don't you?" Piper shot back, grimacing when he applied even more pressure to her hand.

Logan muttered in frustration. How could he defend himself when he didn't know what the hell she was even talking about? "Can't you talk plain English?" he snorted grouchily.

Her flashing green eyes swept over his overpowering physique, hating him, hating herself for being so aroused by his nearness. Piper resented the paradoxical emotions that tugged at her when she stared into his ruggedly handsome face. She was constantly lashing out at Logan in an attempt to compensate for her frustration. "You think you can browbeat everyone you meet. . . ." Her gaze fell to the noticeable bulge in his breeches and she realized she had affected him in ways she hadn't expected. Even during their tussle, Logan was as physically aware of her as she was of him. It was hollow consolation that she moved him to any sort of emotion—even if it was simple lust.

Logan was vividly aware of where her eyes had strayed. Hell, he even knew what she was thinking—that he may have been a brawny, intimidating beast but he still succumbed to her powers of femininity. It rankled him that she was enjoying even a smidgen of satisfaction at his expense.

"Well, what did you expect?" he snorted defensively as he thrust her hand away. "You're standing there with your breasts pouring out of your gown. I'd have to be blind not to notice you. I've been without a woman for more days than I care to count." Another intimidating smile, the kind that stoked the fires of Piper's temper, curved the corners of his mouth upward. "Unless you want to remedy my situation, you damned well better find something with which to cover yourself. I find myself wanting a woman and you are all too convenient."

His candid remark left her no time to relish the satisfaction of knowing she had aroused this mountain of a man in ways even he couldn't control. Blushing profusely, Piper rifled through her satchel to retrieve a shawl. With her back stiff as a flagpole, she grabbed her luggage and stomped into the street without awaiting her escort.

Twice she was confronted by men who paused to leer suggestively at her. When they opened their mouths to fling a lurid comment, she glared daggers at them and they immediately backed away. Since she had successfully countered the threat of trouble, Piper grew more confident with each step she took. Wearing a proud smile, Piper struggled up the steps with her armload of luggage.

Inhaling a deep breath, she set the satchels aside to retrieve her key. A startled yelp erupted from her lips when she caught sight of Logan propped against the wall behind her.

"You needn't think your haughty looks saved you from trouble," he drawled as he pushed away from the wall. An ornery grin rippled across his sensuous lips. "It was my presence a few steps behind you that spared you from catastrophe, honey."

Logan reached out a tanned hand to close her pretty mouth as her bright green eyes widened and her jaw gaped in surprise. "If you don't believe I had any influence while you were carelessly flirting with trouble, why don't you prance back down the street without my trailing behind you and see just how far you get," he challenged her.

Leaving her to chew on that thought, Logan let himself into his room. Piper seethed with frustration as she struggled to carry her luggage through the door. Stamping a dainty foot, she glared at Abraham, who hadn't moved a muscle since she left him earlier that evening.

"You could have offered to help," she muttered and then rolled her eyes. Lord, she was so furious she had forgotten Abraham was a spoiled, helpless pet. After inhaling a deep breath, Piper slowly expelled it, fighting for composure. Why had she allowed that impossible man to upset her so? He derived satisfaction in ruffling her feathers. Well, from now on, she wouldn't let him know how much he rattled her. It would probably kill her, but she was gong to make an attempt to be civil to Logan. Her ultimate satisfaction would come in having him think he didn't upset her. Determined in purpose, Piper left her room to rap on Logan's door.

Logan hadn't expected to find the comely blonde at his door, gracing him with a smile. Indeed, he had anticipated a whack on the cheek, a barrage of highfalutin' words he couldn't define, or a pride-slashing insult. The fact that Piper appeared calm and composed knocked him sideways. Logan didn't know how to handle this gorgeous chit when she was being nice to him.

"Thank you, Logan," she said sincerely. "I suppose I'm not as capable as I should be in this raucous town. In the future, I will be more cautious and less trusting. Your criticism was justified and I shall try to profit from what you told me."

When she had turned and closed the door to her room, Logan expelled a harsh breath. Jeezus, he was letting that female get to him! He was too aware of her, of her moods, of her needs. But what disturbed him most was the monstrous craving she aroused in him. Sleeping with this gnawing hunger that had mushroomed into a gigantic craving was going to make for a long, fitful night, Logan knew.

Sure enough, Logan's sleep was haunted by enormous green eyes and a flowing cape of silver blond hair. Lips as soft as rose petals played softly against his. Twice he awoke in a cold sweat. Damn, he was left wanting that minx in the worst way, and she didn't know the first thing about appeasing a man. Hell, she knew even less about passion than she did about defending herself!

Expelling another colorful curse, Logan punched his pillow and closed his eyes. He wasn't going to spare that nymph another thought. She was out of his life forever and he was glad of it!

Chapter 4

After making her toilette, Piper peered down at Abraham, who hadn't bothered to stir from his resting place at the foot of the bed. Even though she loved the oversized tomcat dearly, she was the first to admit she had pampered and spoiled him to excess. Piper shouldn't have brought Abraham with her, but she couldn't very well leave him in Chicago with Hiram. Why, the scoundrel would have sold Abraham along with all the other family possessions.

"Climb in your basket," Piper instructed the tomcat. "I'll sneak you a few morsels at breakfast."

Abraham looked as though he would prefer to have his breakfast served in bed. But at Piper's insistence he rose on all fours, stretched leisurely, and then crawled beneath the lid of the basket Piper had purchased as his improvised carrying case.

Clutching her purse in one hand and the reed basket in the other, Piper proceeded downstairs. Since Logan had refused her proposition, Piper decided to seek out Royce Granger. Even if he couldn't match Logan's legendary skills. Granger couldn't be more difficult to deal with than Logan, Piper consoled herself. Surely he would accept the job and the generous fee she offered.

After inquiring at the registration desk, Piper learned that Royce Granger wasn't staying at the hotel. When she checked at the second hotel, she was told Granger had rented a room but that he had left a few minutes earlier. The innkeeper suggested she try the restaurant that Granger usually frequented when he wasn't shuffling cards and conversing over a bottle of whiskey at his favorite stomping ground—the Buckhorn Saloon.

With impatient strides, Piper marched down the street, ignoring the leering glances from men who monitored her progress. Using the description the innkeeper had given her, Piper scanned the establishment to locate Royce Granger. To say she was disappointed in the man's appearance was an understatement.

Royce was muscularly built, but he wasn't nearly as tall and formidable a figure as Logan. He possessed a mop of carrot red hair and a generous smattering of freckles. His ruddy complexion clashed with the unruly cap of hair that jutted from the sides of his face. And his ears! They reminded her of the size and shape of those found on an elephant. It was obvious the good Lord had been in a hurry when he scooped up the features He had plastered on Royce Granger's face.

Well, at least she didn't find herself physically attracted to Royce the way she had been to Logan. It would be easier to deal with a man who didn't evoke a riptide of emotions within her.

Squaring her shoulders, Piper marched purposefully toward Royce. Her foremost concern was locating someone to assist her in her search, even if the man wasn't quite as capable as Logan was reported to be.

Royce had noticed the bewitching beauty the moment she entered the restaurant. His keen brown eyes raked Piper, instantly liking everything he saw and eager to see more. He couldn't believe his good fortune when the stunning blonde smiled and walked straight toward him.

"Sit down, honey," Royce invited with a roguish grin. "I've been waiting for you all my life."

Honestly, every man in Fort Smith must have considered every woman to be his "honey," Piper mused disgustedly. If she heard that endearment uttered so loosely again she was going to scream in frustration! And if Royce Granger had indeed been waiting for her all his life he still had a long wait ahead of him.

As Piper eased into the chair and set the basket on the floor, she whimsically wished Abraham were a bulldog instead of a lazy tomcat. She might need him to chew on Royce's leg if the varmint dared to do what he looked as if he were contemplating doing to her. His lusty intentions were printed on his winged brows in bold letters, and Piper didn't like what she was reading in his expression.

"I have a proposition for you, Mr. Granger," she announced in a businesslike tone.

His carrot-colored brows lifted suggestively. "I'm game for anything you suggest, honey," he purred.

Piper ignored the lurid innuendo. She hadn't thought it possible, but she actually preferred Logan's insults and his candor to Royce's fumbling attempt to seduce her. His roguish grin did more to repulse her than arouse her. If Royce was the last man on earth and she was the last woman, Piper would have rejected his advances, even if it meant the termination of the species.

Piper raised a determined chin. "I wish to hire you to find someone for me."

Royce's eyes flooded over her bodice. "Since I'm between jobs, I'd be glad to accommodate you. And my payment won't even involve the exchange of money. . . ."

If Piper hadn't been desperate she would have slapped Royce silly. But Royce was her last resort. "I am only offering cash," she told him firmly. "I do not intend to become part of our bargain."

Leaning his elbows on the table, Royce smiled wryly. "Maybe we can work something out. . . ." His voice trailed off when a long shadow fell over him. An annoyed frown instantly plowed his brow.

"You're not taking the case." Logan's low growl caused Piper to flinch as if she had been stabbed in the back.

Piper hadn't heard Logan approach and she wasn't the least bit thrilled to have him interrupt their conversation. Twisting around in her chair, Piper reacquainted Logan with her look of disdain (as if he could have forgotten). "This is none of your concern," she bit off. The nerve of this man! How dare he meddle in her life after he had flatly refused her proposition.

From beneath the wide brim of his Stetson, silver gray eyes

riveted over her. "I'm making this my business." The rumbling purr in his voice hinted at barely suppressed irritation. "You don't need Granger. You're going back where you belong, lady."

"Now hold on a minute," Royce snapped gruffly. "I'll decide whether I want to take this job."

When Royce's right hand, minus the top portion of his middle finger, eased toward his holster, a scuffle of chairs and retreating footsteps resounded around the restaurant. Customers poured out the door without finishing their meals.

Logan's hand was already resting on the butt of his Colt .45. "Don't be so damned defensive, Granger," he said quietly. His stormy gray eyes locked with Royce's smoldering brown ones. "You're just sore because Butterfield fired you and gave me your job."

"Back off, Logan," Royce growled.

Piper vaulted from her chair to glower first at one man and then the other. Honestly, there were times when Logan made Satan look like a saint. This was one of those times. Why was he brewing trouble? Why couldn't he just go away and leave her alone?

"I have yet to meet two bigger or more arrogant fools," she declared with great conviction. "We are *not* having a gunfight over this matter!"

For what seemed forever both men stared each other down. Granger knew he was no match for Logan's lightning-quick draw. He had hoped to bluff Logan since there was a woman present. But for some reason Logan wouldn't budge. It made him wonder what connection Logan had to the shapely blonde. Logan seemed intent on making her business his business.

"We'll talk about this after you get rid of your fire-breathing dragon," Royce told Piper with a derisive snort. "I'll be at the Buckhorn Saloon if you want me."

As Royce lumbered around the table he stubbed his toe on Abraham's basket. The tomcat, startled from his nap, scrambled out before his basket overturned with him in it. Caterwauling, Abraham sank his claws into the table cloth to pull himself onto higher ground. Cursing in surprise, Royce automatically reached for his pistol. His Colt misfired, blowing a hole in the floor. The sound was followed by the clatter of dishes and a flying tablecloth. The avalanche of cups and plates, compounded by the barking pistol, frightened Abraham. With a feline growl, he darted across the room with the hair on his back standing on end.

"What the hell . . . ?" was all Logan could get out before Abraham leaped at the window in attempt to escape.

"Abraham!" Piper shouted at the hysterical cat. But her voice was drowned beneath the crash of another set of dishes.

Logan watched in mute amazement as the oversized tomcat bounced off the window, shattering the dishes on the table on which he had landed. Yowling in panic, Abraham shot across the restaurant toward the door that one of the braver customers was kind enough to hold open for him. Snatching up the basket, Piper dashed outside to retrieve her runaway cat. When she was out of earshot, Logan focused his full attention on Royce.

"Turn the lady down and keep your distance from her," he advised with a meaningful glance.

Royce drew himself up to proud stature. "I don't want any trouble with you, Logan. But you're sorely mistaken if you think I'm going to let you tell me which clients to refuse."

With that, Royce stamped out the door and aimed himself toward Buckhorn Saloon. Logan had just finished paying for the damages caused by Piper's crazed cat when she reentered the restaurant.

"Sit down," Logan ordered brusquely. He never asked when he could command. And usually when he demanded that someone sit, they sat. There weren't many people who dared defy him. Logan wasn't sure if the shapely blonde was a fool or just plain stubborn, for she glared rebelliously at him and refused to park herself in the chair.

"I paid for the disaster wrought by that cussed cat and I'm offering to buy your breakfast," he snapped impatiently. Still Piper refused to stir a step. Roughly, Logan clamped his hands on her stiffened shoulders and physically stuffed her in her chair.

Damn that man, Piper silently fumed. How dare he order her about as if she were his chattel. "You might have said please," she muttered resentfully.

Logan folded his tall frame into his seat and flung her a mocking smile. "With you, I doubt it would have made a damned bit of difference." His eyes fell to the basket from which two golden eyes were staring warily at him. "And what the sweet loving hell are you doing toting around that crazy cat?"

"Abraham is a pet," she defended tartly. "And he has more sense than some of us!" Her accusing glare pinpointed the "some of us" to which she referred.

"I hate cats," Logan snorted in a disparaging tone. "They are such sneaky looking creatures."

"I'm sure Abraham will be crushed by that news," Piper commented flippantly, her tone assuring Logan that Abraham would be nothing of the kind.

Logan ordered their breakfast without consulting Piper as to her preference. When the waitress walked away, Logan stared straight into those mutinous green eyes.

"You don't want a man like Granger working for you," he told her bluntly. "Royce is unscrupulous. He'll take your money and probably a helluva lot more than you planned to give. In his case, there is a fine line between a vigilante and a desperado. He has no qualms about playing the law to his advantage."

"Since you refused to help me, I don't see what concern it is of yours who I consult," Piper sniffed in annoyance. When the waitress set her meal before her, Piper stabbed her eggs until they weeped on her plate. "I am not giving up this crusade, Logan. I want my inheritance back and I'm willing to go to any length to recover it." Swiftly, she stuffed the money he had given her the previous night into his hand. "I don't want your charity. I only want what is rightfully mine. Grant took my trust fund and I am going to retrieve it."

She wasn't just foolish, she was damned stubborn, Logan decided. This naive Easterner didn't have a clue as to what kind of trouble she could get herself into. "Your precious inheritance won't do you any good if you're dead," he growled.

He wasn't sure why he was so exasperated with Piper. Everything she did annoyed him. Even her impeccable table manners aggravated him. They served as a reminder that there were many obvious differences between them. She was dainty, refined, and naive and he was rough-edged, educated by firsthand experience, and seasoned in the ways of the world.

"With your stunning good looks you can return home and entice some wealthy bachelor into marrying you. That should be compensation enough for your losses."

Indignation registered on her exquisite features. "I don't want to marry to resupply my missing funds. I want what is lawfully mine," she reiterated in an emphatic tone that was punctuation in itself. "I will recover my inheritance, no matter what obstacles are flung in my path. No one is going to tell me I can't do what I want to do, especially not you!" Still glaring at him, Piper leaned down to feed a slice of bacon to Abraham, who gobbled his meal in three ravenous bites.

Logan scoffed at her foolhardiness. "You and that fat tomcat are going to strike out on this dangerous crusade? What a fearsome twosome that will be!"

Piper compressed her lips, refusing to rise to the taunt. Logan made it difficult to be civil. Indeed, he thrived on baiting her. But she wasn't going to lose her temper with him again today. It served no useful purpose. It was far more effective to be pleasant to him. That tactic left him with the impression that he hadn't succeeded in irritating her. The less satisfaction he received the better Piper liked it.

When Piper finished her meal, she dug into her purse to pay for her breakfast. But Logan raised his hand to forestall her.

"I said I was buying," he reminded her, pushing her money away. "As fanatic as you are about coins, you'll want to pinch every penny."

There it was again, that cocky grin and that ornery sparkle in his eyes that challenged her to pick up the gauntlet. The man was always spoiling for a fight. Since he disliked her, he delighted in badgering her. But Piper had resolved not to indulge in his annoying games and she would be damned if she took his bait.

"Thank you for the breakfast," she cooed pretentiously. "Good day, Logan." Her smile, though brittle as an eggshell, remained intact until she scooped up Abraham's basket. "I sincerely hope you choke on your toast."

Logan chuckled at her softly uttered curse. Piper was trying very hard to cling to her prim and proper manners, but he had riled her. He had detected the flicker of anger in her eyes before she masked her irritation behind that forced smile.

Yes, Logan had aggravated her. And he would go on harassing her until she lost what was left of her temper. Before long she would throw up her hands in defeat. When she finally packed up and left, Logan would bid her good riddance. He liked Eastern sophisticates as well as he liked cats. The fact that he found himself far too attracted to that dainty bit of fluff was more than enough reason to want her out of his life. They had absolutely nothing in common. The sooner she was gone the better!

When Logan stepped into the street a quarter of an hour later, he glanced toward the bawdy houses on Chippy Hill. There were women enough there to help him forget his unreasonable fascination for that troublesome minx. And if he didn't get some satisfaction—and quickly—he might find himself turning to the one woman who had already complicated his well-organized life with her very presence—Piper Malone.

But the fickle hand of fate was conspiring against Logan. One glance toward Buckhorn Saloon had him growling under his breath. There, poised outside the unseemly establishment, was Piper. She had apparently transported her pudgy tomcat back to her hotel room so he wouldn't hinder her while she was window peeking. From the look of things, Piper was trying to gain Royce's attention without barging into the saloon.

An amused smile replaced Logan's sour frown as Piper performed her ridiculous antics. She resembled an oversized bird flapping its wings in preparation for flight.

When Piper realized someone was watching her she turned, displaying a sheepish grin. But her smile became an instant glower when she realized it was Logan who was amusing himself at her expense.

One thick brow arched to a mocking angle. "Are you testing

your wings, little dove?" he tittered. Her very name and the nickname he had bestowed on her seemed very appropriate. This little bird was testing her wings in a world where she didn't belong. After touching his forefinger to his tongue, Logan determined the wind direction. "It seems conditions are right for your flight *east.*"

Forgetting her vow to defeat Logan with kindness, Piper glared poison arrows at his infuriating grin. "I'm not leaving here, no matter how much you intimidate me," she told him in no uncertain terms.

His broad shoulders lifted in a nonchalant shrug. "Have it your way, lady. Fools are always the last ones to realize their mistakes. You'll never recognize trouble until it marches up and sits down on you."

From beneath the hooded veil of long black lashes, Logan stared down into her fuming frown. The laughter had evaporated from his silver eyes. They became as cold and hard as steel. "Go home, Piper," he ordered firmly. "I don't want to see you hurt. And you will be if you continue to pursue this daring quest."

The fact that he cared in the least startled her. Logan could read the surprise in those green eyes that dominated her enchanting face. It took a great deal of willpower for Logan not to reach out and caress her satiny cheek with a bronzed finger. He wanted to touch her but he managed to contain the impulsive urge. It would only intensify his forbidden desire for her. *That,* he didn't need.

Although Piper was momentarily stunned by his comment, Logan doubted it would have much effect on her. He predicted this stubborn minx wouldn't budge from Fort Smith until he had stripped her of every alternative. Mulling over that thought, Logan pivoted on his heels and ambled into the saloon. He had bypassed another chance to appease his male needs, but he felt compelled to foil Piper's plans (for her own good, of course).

With determined strides, Logan aimed himself toward the gaming table where Royce Granger was pondering his hand of cards. It was his intention to keep Royce occupied so Piper would have no opportunity to speak with him. By the time they parted company Logan would make certain Royce had consumed so much whiskey that he would be in no condition to converse with anyone.

A wary frown knitted Royce's brow when Logan invited himself into the poker game. Without ado, Logan folded his brawny frame into the vacant chair beside Royce.

"I came to apologize," Logan announced. "I've always made it a policy never to get into a gunfight over a woman. You and I have had our disagreements, but I'm willing to let bygones be bygones."

Royce stared dubiously at Logan's outthrust arm. It was difficult to shake hands with the man who had shot the end off his middle finger. But Royce decided it was healthier to be Logan's friend than his enemy. Clasping Logan's hand, Royce gave it a firm shake.

"Apology accepted." A lopsided grin dangled from the corner of Royce's mouth. "I can't say I've never fought over a female. And the one in question this time was a pretty piece of fluff. But she ain't worth gettin' killed over."

Logan's low laughter rumbled in his chest. "None of them are, Royce," he contended, "not when females populate half the world. For every one a man lets go, there are at least two females who are willing to accommodate him."

"I'll drink to that!" Royce said enthusiastically.

Logan kept Royce drinking toasts to every tidbit of philosophical mumbo jumbo he could conjure up. And every hour on the hour, Logan noticed Piper peeking through the window to determine if Royce was still seated at the table. Logan made sure Royce was, and that infuriated Piper to no end. But when Royce challenged Logan to a drinking contest he wondered if either of them would be able to rise from their chairs and stumble to their respective rooms.

Jeezus! The sacrifices I've made for that green-eyed witch, Logan mused as he tipped another glass of whiskey to his lips. By early afternoon the walls of the saloon had turned a hazy shade of gray. By late afternoon, Logan swore he had drunk himself blind. He could barely see the walls at all.

When Royce determined it was time to declare the winner of their drinking contest, it was all Logan could do to drag his feet beneath him and weave toward the door. Royce announced that whoever could stagger the farthest without collapsing in an unconscious heap would be crowned the victor of hand-to-glass combat.

"I feel fit as a fiddle," Royce boasted over his paralyzed tongue.

"The whiskey didn't faze me either," Logan slurred out, struggling to grasp the swinging saloon door before it slapped him in the chest.

"All I need is a breath of fresh air," Royce insisted. "It always revives me, as if I never guzzled a single drink." To add credence to his boast, Royce sucked in an enormous breath of air.

Propping himself against the outer wall of the saloon for additional support, Logan watched, blurry-eyed, as Royce's chest swelled to phenomenal proportions. But Royce didn't look as if the deep breath had cured him. His eyes rolled back in his head and he weaved unsteadily on tree-stump legs. To Logan's relief, the breath Royce had inhaled caused him to become top-heavy. Like a huge redwood toppling beneath a lumberjack's axe, Royce swayed backwards and landed with a crash.

Logan had accomplished his purpose of rendering Royce incapable of listening to Piper's pleas for assistance. The poor man might not rouse unless someone stepped in the middle of him on the way into the saloon—if even then. But Logan had no time to gloat over his victory. He had gone to such great lengths to keep Piper away from Royce that he couldn't help but wonder if he would survive the hellacious hangover he would be sporting the following morning.

Jeezus, he was drunk! He couldn't remember feeling quite so dazed and disoriented. After waiting for his eyes to catch up with his rotating head, Logan struggled to get his bearings. It took concentrated effort to inch along the boardwalk. Pushing away from the supporting post, Logan wobbled across the alleyway and stumbled onto the next boardwalk. With the speed of a turtle, Logan propelled himself toward the hotel. Although he longed to inhale a steadying breath, he didn't dare, not after watching Royce collapse in a drunken stupor. If he could just tackle the mountain of steps that led to his upstairs room, he felt sure he could locate his door.

Staring grimly through bloodshot eyes, Logan peered up the Pike's Peak of steps that towered above him. One foot in front of the other, Logan mumbled to himself as he began his tedious climb. One foot in . . .

An agonized groan erupted from his lips as one of the steps flew up and hit him in the face. Clutching the banister, Logan pulled himself hand over hand. Wobbling on rubbery legs, Logan navigated his way down the hall like a blind man feeling his way down an unfamiliar corridor.

Fumbling into his pocket, Logan fished out his key. But he realized the worst was yet to come. Stuffing the key in the lock proved as difficult as threading a needle blindfolded. The contrary key kept leaping out of his hands to clank on the floor. And to make the situation practically impossible, Logan couldn't even see the cussed lock! After making several futile stabs with the key, Logan slurred out a string of colorful expletives that orbited through his skull and vibrated in his ears. He was running out of time. The world was spinning furiously around him. If he didn't reach his bed he feared he would collapse in front of his door. Frantically, Logan made another attempt to stuff the key in the lock. If he didn't get results this time he vowed to break down the door. He had no intention of being found sprawled in front of his room when that saucy minx exited the hotel. Piper would mock him mercilessly. That thought inspired Logan to find a way to gain entrance to his room, and quickly!

Chapter 5

Piper had heard the commotion on the steps and her ears were burning from the salty curses that were chasing each other down the hall. The rattle of the lock on the door across from her room piqued her curiosity. If Logan had returned from his drinking spree, Piper fully intended to seek out Royce.

It was Piper's misfortune to ease open her door at the moment Logan lost what was left of his temper. After pounding viciously on the portal, Logan shoved his shoulder against it. Since the door didn't give way, he wobbled back a few steps, lowered his head, and charged like a rhinoceros. After he bounced off the unyielding door he stumbled over his own feet. His momentum sent him staggering across the hall to collide with the door from behind which Piper was spying on him.

A startled squawk erupted from her lips when Logan's drunken body thudded against hers. The horror of knowing this muscular giant was about to fall on top of her provoked instant panic. Piper tried to remove herself from his path, but Logan was clawing air in search of support. Piper found herself the recipient of a hug that squeezed the breath out of her. What little air that was left in her lungs erupted in a pained grunt when she hit the floor—squashed flat by Logan's heavy weight.

"Get up, you big ape!" Piper hissed, when she managed to inhale a vital breath of air.

"I'd be glad to," Logan mumbled groggily as he braced

himself on his elbows. "Just as soon as I figure out which way is up."

The room was spinning like a top. A haze of black fringed the perimeters of Logan's vision. Through the echoing tunnel of his ears he thought he heard the caterwaul of a cat. His eyes swept up to see Abraham spitting at him from his perch on the bed. Growling, Logan swung an arm at the offensive feline, who yelped like the coward he was and sprang to safety.

"Damned useless cat," he snorted, as he struggled up on all fours. From his vantage point, Logan stared down at the petite female pinned beneath him. "Not now, honey, I'm too drunk to make love to you."

Piper sputtered in outrage. The very idea! How could Logan even think she would want to have him sprawled on top of her—drunk or sober! "Get off me!" she railed indignantly.

Logan simply couldn't resist. Her pouting lips lured him closer, his inhibitions drowned in the bottle of whiskey he had guzzled. His big body settled exactly over hers, acquainting her with one of the more popular positions of passion. His mouth slanted across hers, devouring her, stripping her of what little breath she had inhaled before Logan's muscular body engulfed hers.

Piper was too stunned by his ravishing kiss to struggle. Before she knew it her body responded to the unfamiliar sensations that channeled through her. To her astonishment, she found herself kissing him back. For crying out loud, didn't she have one iota of willpower? She should have been pounding her fists against him, cursing him. But instead, she was enjoying the feel of his masculine body meshed intimately to hers, delighting in the hungry kiss that put her senses to flight.

"Mmmm," Logan slurred as he raised his ruffled, raven head. "A taste of heaven."

Like a lumbering elephant, Logan lifted one heavy leg and then an arm so Piper could roll to her feet. While she stammered in embarrassment Logan peered at her bed as if it were his salvation. Shamelessly he crawled toward it. As he hoisted himself onto the mattress Piper hopped up and down in offended dignity. But Logan paid her no mind. Now that he was in a prone position, he wasn't going to rise until the room ceased its furious revolutions around him. Piper could scream at him until she was blue in the face, but it would take an act of God to rout him from her bed.

"You can't stay here," Piper snapped furiously. "Where am I supposed to sleep?"

Logan mumbled something undecipherable in response and flung out a limp arm. A victim of his own curiosity, the cat had taken a perch on the headboard to watch the goings-on. Logan's hand accidentally slammed against the side of Abraham's face. The unintended blow caused Abraham to yowl in pain. Using Logan as a springboard, Abraham launched himself toward safety once again. As luck would have it, his path landed him directly on Logan's groin.

It was difficult to ascertain who screeched the loudest. Logan yelped in surprise and discomfort as Abraham's daggerlike claws dug into the private part of his anatomy. Abraham hissed furiously when Logan instinctively backhanded him. As the tomcat flew off the bed, Logan groaned and swung blindly. This time his hand connected with the night stand, sending the lantern crashing to the floor.

God, he felt sick. He wanted to die. That damned cat was howling up a storm and Piper was reading him the riot act. But Logan was too far into his cups to utter a word in his own defense. He simply slipped into the swirling abyss. With a thankful sigh and a prayer that, if he did indeed survive to view another sunrise, he would feel considerably better. Without a fight, Logan surrendered to the pitch black darkness that circled over him like a looming vulture.

With her fists clenched on her hips, Piper tapped a dainty foot in impatient rhythm. Logan had turned her room into shambles. He had scared off eight of Abraham's nine lives. Now Logan was sleeping off his drunken stupor on her bed, of all places! One would have thought this oversized demon had been sent up from the fiery pits of hell to torment her.

Well, Logan isn't going to deter me from my purpose, Piper promised herself. Snatching up her purse, she stomped out of the room to seek out Royce Granger. And while she was gone she hoped Abraham would claw that sleeping giant to shreds. It was what Logan deserved, damn him.

Employing a few of the inventive curses Piper had heard erupting from Logan, she stared down into Royce's freckled face. He was still lying in front of the saloon like a misplaced doormat. Bracing her heel against his arm, Piper attempted to shake him awake. Each time she jarred him, his head rolled against one shoulder and then the other and his tongue fell out of his gaping mouth. In his inebriated condition, absolutely nothing fazed Royce.

Grumbling, Piper marched back to the hotel with the morsels of food she had retrieved for Abraham. But she spitefully hoped the tomcat had feasted on the unconscious ogre who had made himself at home on her bed.

Logan, like his drunken cohort, hadn't moved a muscle since Piper exited a half hour earlier. He still lay spread-eagled, his broad chest rising and falling in methodic rhythm. After her frustration ebbed, Piper surveyed Logan's arresting assets. The man was incredibly well built. His mere size was intimidating, and his muscular physique complemented his tall stature. His dark skin and coal black hair set him apart from a crowd. He was a man among men, and Piper could not help but admire him.

"We are so very different," Piper mused aloud. When Abraham realized his mistress was only talking to herself, he curled up beside Logan, who made a warm pillow when he wasn't swinging wildly at anything that moved. "How can I be so fascinated with him, knowing we are worlds apart?"

The opportunity of touching Logan without facing the repercussions overwhelmed Piper. Like a child admiring a statue, Piper traced her index finger over the distinct lines of his face, memorizing the feel of his clean-shaven skin beneath her inquiring hand. Tentatively, her fingertips drifted across his sensuous mouth. She remembered, with vivid clarity, how his lips felt when they took firm possession.

Continuing her explorations, Piper ran her hand over his muscular shoulder to measure the wide expanse of his chest. The potential strength and energy that lay beneath her hand

74

caused her to sigh in feminine admiration. Touching Logan was like examining a jungle cat in repose. There was simply something intriguing about him, and Piper couldn't force herself to withdraw.

Her eyes fell to his strong and sometimes gentle hands. They were brown and calloused and decidedly masculine. She wondered if they could ever be tender and loving hands. She knew he could be rough, but there had been times the past two days when she had detected a hint of gentleness in him. But Piper doubted if this unruly renegade had spent much time mastering the art of tenderness. In his profession, warmth and gentleness were not necessary traits.

Curiously, Piper also wondered if Logan would be a considerate lover or if he . . . Banish the thought! Piper gave herself a mental slap for allowing her musings to detour down such sordid avenues. She didn't give a fig if Logan was rough or tender with a woman. If she hadn't found herself pinned so suggestively beneath him the previous hour that lurid speculation would never have entered her mind.

And yet, after a woman found herself in such an intimate position, staring up at a man who had probably forgotten more about lovemaking than she would learn in a lifetime, it was perfectly natural to wonder.

Of course, I will never find myself in that vulnerable position again, Piper assured herself confidently. If Logan hadn't been rip-roaring drunk he wouldn't have kissed her and he wouldn't have pressed his virile body to hers. Most of the time he behaved as if he resented this strange physical attraction between them. Logan responded to her because she was a woman, because it was second nature to him. But he didn't like her as a person. It was only her feminine body that aroused him, not the personality attached to it.

Despite her attempt to discard her wayward thoughts, Piper could still picture herself looking up into Logan's whiskey-drugged features. She could still remember the feel of his powerful thighs lying provocatively between hers, feel his muscular chest molded to her breasts. And when he had glanced down at her from all fours, Piper had been stung by the most peculiar sensation. She had the premonition that being possessed by a man like Logan would resemble being swallowed alive. Logan would overwhelm her, envelop her. She would lose her identity to become an integral part of that awesome strength.

A startled gasp tripped from Piper's lips when Logan groaned in his sleep and rolled to his side. She had lingered too long in thought to escape the heavy arm that curled around her shoulders. Before Piper knew what had happened, Logan had cuddled her to him. From very close range she was forced to stare at his broad chest and the muscular arm that prevented her from moving.

But that wasn't the worst of it! Logan squirmed again and she found herself mashed beneath him. His dead weight kept her flat on her back. His chin was nestled against her cheek as if she were his pillow. Piper flushed six shades of red when her naive body reacted to the feel of a man's leg lying across her thighs. Piper could barely draw a breath. Arching to throw the big oaf sideways would be a waste of energy, she predicted. She may as well have tried to hurl aside a boulder.

Piper was assaulted by another round of odd sensations that had no business attacking her innocent body. She didn't like what she was thinking and feeling. It was most unladylike, but she was forced to endure these tingles since she was pinned to the bed.

After what seemed forever, Logan stirred enough to roll away. Propped upon both elbows, Piper peered pensively at the raven-haired rake. Something had to be done. There was no telling when he would flop on top of her and squash her flat again. And yet, there was no way to remove him from her bed. In his condition, he couldn't be held responsible for his actions. Piper doubted if he would even remember falling into her room. The man's brain had been pickled with whiskey. And honestly, one would have thought hers had been too the way she was drooling over him like a lovesick schoolgirl!

Heaving an exasperated sigh, Piper prepared for bed. She refused to miss a night's sleep just because Logan had accidentally wound up in her room. It would not be a particularly pleasant night's sleep, she reckoned. But it was all to be had unless she wanted to camp out on the rug. Obviously, that wouldn't make a comfortable pallet, since Abraham had turned up his nose at the prospect of sleeping on the floor.

Cautiously, Piper eased beneath the sheet on the edge of her bed. Abraham stirred slightly and then resumed his place between Piper and Logan. He didn't approve of sharing his side of the bed with the oversized brute, but there was no way to rout him. Put quite simply, both Piper and Abraham were stuck with Logan for the night.

As if he were clawing his way up the walls of a bottomless well, Logan fought to return to consciousness. When he opened his eyes he was greeted by a lighter shade of darkness. Moonlight splattered through the partially drawn curtains, casting a faint light in the room. Logan winced when a pair of golden eyes peered back at him. Disliking the creatures as much as he did, he wasn't pleased to find a cat in his bed. But what shocked him out of his moccasins was the feminine form that lay on the other side of the cat!

Jeezus! What was this curvaceous blonde doing in his bed? Had he . . . ? Logan couldn't think past the fog that clouded his brain. The last thing he remembered was watching Royce Granger keel over in a drunken heap. What had he done to Piper during his brief lapse of sanity? Logan needed to know, but he was almost afraid to ask.

The creaking of the bed brought Piper awake with a start. Pulling the quilt beneath her chin, she peered at Logan's silhouette in the shadows. Piper realized now that she should have formulated what she intended to say when this inevitable moment arrived. Now that the instant was upon her, she couldn't think of a single solitary thing!

"What are you and this damned cat doing in my room?" Logan muttered as he massaged his aching head.

The drunken galoot was obviously suffering from amnesia, Piper diagnosed. He didn't even know where he was!

"This is my room, Goldilocks," she sniffed sarcastically. "You're the one who has been napping in someone else's bed."

"Goldilocks?" Logan repeated bemusedly. His upbringing hadn't included a large repertoire of children's fairy tales.

"What the hell is that supposed to mean?"

"You're just like the little girl who wandered into the home of the three bears. . . ." Piper clamped down on her tongue and rolled her eyes heavenward. Why was she trying to tell a bedtime story to a grown man? "Oh, never mind," she grumbled crankily.

It was obvious that analogies were wasted on Logan. Knowing he had never heard of Goldilocks made her wonder about his childhood. She wouldn't have been surprised to learn he had been raised by a pack of wolves.

Logan studied Piper's face among the shadows and frowned puzzledly. If he was in Piper's room, sharing the same bed, he must have seduced her. Had he enjoyed it? Surely he had. He couldn't imagine why he wouldn't. He had been speculating about how it would feel to have her naked body in his arms since the moment he laid eyes on her. Perhaps he had succumbed to his fantasies while his common sense was saturated with whiskey.

"Did we make love?" he asked with his usual amount of candor.

Piper was grateful for the darkness that disguised the sudden flood of color in her cheeks. "Certainly not!" she sputtered indignantly. "I wouldn't have permitted it and you were too far into your cups to do anything except stumble over your own feet!"

"Are you sure you wouldn't like to?" Logan teased, knowing what her answer would be.

Piper sat up so quickly that it startled Abraham who sank his claws in Logan's chest before bounding to the floor.

"Argh!" Logan howled when he felt Abraham's spiked paws pricking his flesh. "I swear I'm going to kill that pesky cat. I'm not his private pin cushion!"

"You're the one who is sleeping in his place," Piper reminded him tartly. "And now that you have regained your senses, kindly take your leave."

Logan leaned over her, bracing his arms on either side of her. She was so temptingly close that he could almost taste her sweet lips. Logan blamed his impulsiveness on his bout with whiskey. It had him saying and doing the strangest things.

Without ado, he helped himself to her tempting lips. Sizzling sensations shot through his body, leaving him wanting more than just a kiss. Instinctively, his arms encircled her as he half covered her soft, supple flesh. Lord, it would be so easy to forget his vow to keep his distance from this luscious nymph. He could lose himself in the magic of passion. Piper was the stuff dreams were made of, and he had been weeks without a woman.

Although Piper swore she would never allow herself to be tempted ever again, she felt the swirling sensations swamp and buffet her. Logan's mouth was playing tenderly against hers, cherishing the taste of her. She should never have permitted herself to speculate about him as a lover. Her betraying thoughts had joined forces with her wayward body, leaving her adrift in a sea of tingling anticipation.

When Logan's straying hands migrated across her breasts to tease each taut peak Piper felt the flame of desire begin to burn within her. She knew she was flirting with trouble, but she was helpless to stop herself from enjoying his caresses, reveling in the forbidden pleasure his touch evoked. She knew she wasn't woman enough to tame a man like Logan, but something within her accepted the challenge of leaving her mark on this mountain of a man.

The spark of passion leaped between them, igniting fires that Logan feared would burn out of control. He wanted this lovely nymph—madly, passionately. And yet he didn't want the complications that could come from seducing this innocent goddess. Even when he knew they were wrong for each other, he was sure lovemaking would feel right with Piper. It was that unsolvable conflict that had frustrated him from the beginning.

Calling upon his crumbling willpower, Logan broke his embrace. If he didn't put a respectable distance between them now, he wouldn't be able to leave her without appeasing the hungry craving she so easily aroused in him.

"I charge a fee for initiating virgins," he announced, knowing the remark would infuriate her. It did. But again Logan reminded himself that he had to be cruel in order to be kind. The magnetic attraction between them was too explosive, too tempting. He had to put a stop to their encounter before they lost their heads and did something they might later regret.

Piper's body became as stiff as a rail as she was subjected to Logan's pride-slashing jibe. To further annoy her, Logan climbed over her instead of rolling off his side of the bed. She was so furious she was sputtering inarticulate phrases that made not an ounce of sense. It annoyed her to no end that Logan could take something pure and sweet and spoil it with his insulting remarks. How she could respond so helplessly to a man who behaved like the very devil was beyond her. It was apparent that she was a poor judge of character. She was trying to see things in this infuriating scoundrel that weren't really there.

"I hate you," Piper spat when she recovered her powers of speech.

Logan scoffed at her curse, purposely stoking the fires of her temper. He and Piper needed to be at odds once again. It was all that saved them from this illogical attraction for each other, one that had no future.

"Consider yourself lucky, honey," Logan drawled non-chalantly as he swaggered toward the door. "If I had been Royce Granger I wouldn't be wandering back to my own room right now. You would have lost your virginity, just to recover your missing inheritance." He paused to glance at Piper, who was lying rigidly on her back with the hem of the sheet resting beneath her chin, clenched tightly in her fists. "All I stole was a kiss. There was no harm done. Things could have been more intimate if I had wanted them to be, but I didn't. I like my women skilled and experienced in the ways of passion. Some men aren't so discriminating. And if you're smart, you'll steer clear of Royce and every other man in this town. Go home before you lose more than you can possibly gain."

Piper watched in frustrated silence as Logan wandered out the door. She was sure he was still battling his bout with liquor when she heard a thud in the room across the hall. It sounded suspiciously as if Logan had missed his bed on the first try.

Aggravated with him though she was, she could not suppress the smile that pursed her lips. She could picture him falling flat on his face. It was a pity she couldn't have been there to see him. Turning her attention to Abraham, she patted the empty space beside her. Abraham hopped onto the bed to resume his place, purring contentedly now that Logan had made himself scarce.

Logan was right, Piper mused as she settled down to sleep. She was virtually helpless in this man's world. If Logan had really wanted her he could have taken her and she wouldn't have known how to stop him. . . . With each new milestone they passed in this rocky relationship, Piper found it more and more difficult not to surrender to the awakened passion that silver-eyed devil aroused in her. Piper hated to admit it to herself, but her feminine curiosity was leading her deeper into the web of forbidden desire. If ever there was a man who could tempt her past the point of no return, it would be Logan. It was fortunate he had found the will to walk away, because Piper doubted she could deny the unfamiliar craving Logan evoked from her. . . .

Piper stopped herself before she dwelt too long on those wanton thoughts. They had the power to reactivate the sensations provoked by Logan's experienced kisses and caresses. Willfully Piper concentrated on other matters.

There was only one thing left to do, she decided as she stroked Abraham's broad head. If Logan wouldn't accept the job of searching out Grant, and if he wouldn't permit her to contact Royce, she would have to assume the task herself. But she wasn't giving up just because Logan discouraged her. She would let him think he had won, but he was going to help her with her crusade whether he realized it or not.

A muffled giggle bubbled from Piper's lips as she snuggled beneath the sheet. The next time she felt intimidated by that overpowering rogue, she would conjure up the vision of the besotted man who had stumbled into her room. Logan hadn't seemed so threatening a few hours earlier. Indeed, he had been quite comical, especially when Abraham sank his sharp claws into his chest and the crotch of his breeches.

Piper couldn't think of one good reason why she liked that domineering, outspoken, overbearing rake. But incredible though it was, she was hopelessly drawn to him, even when he made her so furious she couldn't see straight. He had been cut from a rough scrap of wood. His mysterious background aroused her darkest suspicions. He had tried to dictate to her since the first instant they met. And yet, despite his many annoying faults, there was something about Logan that lured her to him, even when better judgment advised her to back away.

She found herself wanting to understand what motivated a man like Logan, to test her reaction to him. Yes, it was dangerous and foolish to attempt to befriend him, especially since he seemed hellbent upon driving wedges between them. But his magnetic appeal defied logic. That devilish charm of his would tempt a saint. And since she wasn't within shouting distance of sainthood it was little wonder she was infatuated with him.

Somehow or another, she was going to maneuver Logan into teaching her things that would aid her in her trek west. She may as well put her eagerness to spend time with him to practical use. Of course, she would let him think she had decided to give up her search and return home. But he was going to become her instructor just the same. For once she was going to win against that stubborn giant.

Pondering that thought, Piper drifted off to sleep. But her dreams picked up where reality left off. It wasn't the anticipation of learning to survive in the West that motivated her. It was the tantalizing memory of the man who had inspired her wildest fantasies that left her wanting to discover the meaning of passion. Her subconscious flirted with those titillating speculations, ones that her conscious mind hadn't permitted her to contemplate.

In her dreams, Piper imagined how it would feel to lie in Logan's powerful arms, to eagerly return those passionate kisses that so easily aroused her. Of course, Piper knew she could never allow their relationship to progress into intimacy. She reminded herself of that very fact when she awoke in the middle of a lifelike dream. She knew she was suffering from a silly romantic notion that plagued women who had virtually no experience with men. Her overactive imagination was running away with itself, that was all. Making love to a man like Logan could never be as splendid as she allowed herself to believe. He probably didn't have a tender bone in that brawny body of his.

He would probably be more interested in taking pleasure than in giving any in return.

After chastising herself for dwelling on those sordid thoughts, Piper closed her eyes and begged for sleep. The following day would be long and trying, she predicted. She had to find a way to convince Logan to teach her to survive in his rough and tumble world.

And there wasn't going to be any more kissing and caressing, she promised herself faithfully. Logan didn't really like her. Each time he touched her she knew, deep down in her heart, that he would be satisfied with any woman. Anything she felt for him would be wasted emotion.

The best she could hope for was a friendship between them, and that was asking a lot for a man who was definitely a loner. He preferred it that way. Logan had made it clear that he wanted nothing to do with a naive city slicker like her. And if she had any sense, she would remember that any romantic inclinations she might have toward Logan would only end in heartache. He wasn't particularly fond of her or her cat. He had made that clear enough. Now if only she could convince her foolish heart that she was growing a mite too attached to a lost cause!

Chapter 6

With the lunch basket she had borrowed from the restaurant in one hand and Abraham's carrying case in the other, Piper approached Logan's door. Setting the picnic basket aside, Piper knocked repeatedly. After waiting several minutes her shoulders slumped in defeat. She had purposely delayed until this late hour, permitting Logan time to recover from his hangover. But apparently he had bounced back from his bout with whiskey much quicker than she expected and had already left for the day. Just when she had given up on him, Logan inched open the door to peer at her through eyes that were streaked and swollen.

Piper would have laughed out loud if she hadn't wanted to avoid antagonizing him. The opportunity to get even for all the rotten things he had said to her was staring her in the face, but Piper deliberately bypassed the chance to intimidate him, even if he did deserve it.

A hellish headache plowed through Logan's skull and an agonizing throb beat in rhythm with his heart. The monotonous hours he had spent on the stage without sleep, compounded by his drinking spree, had caught up with him. If Piper hadn't disturbed him, Logan felt certain he could have slept the entire day away.

A muddled frown creased his brow as his blurry gaze drifted over her trim-fitting breeches and revealing shirt. His bloodshot eyes nearly popped from their sockets. She filled out her outrageous garments so effectively that a wave of unwanted desire splashed over him, hellacious hangover and all.

What Piper did to a pair of men's breeches and shirt could be labeled a crime. No one looked as good in trousers as she did. Jeezus! She was alluring in a gown, but her new attire called even more attention to her arresting curves and swells. She hadn't been safe in the streets when she was dressed like a sophisticated young lady, but the empress's new clothes would make matters worse! Men would stampede over each other to get their hands on this curvaceous minx.

"What the blazes are you up to?" Logan growled. "Are you auditioning for a career in the circus?"

Piper had grown accustomed to his rudeness. She had come to expect the good morning insults he always instituted for greetings.

"I have another proposition for you to consider," she announced, undaunted. Pushing the door open, she breezed into his room without invitation. While Logan gaped frog-eyed, Piper retrieved a roll of bills from her purse. "As I told you before, I do not accept charity. This is for Abraham's damages to the restaurant and for my meal. I don't expect you to pay my way. Considering the hazards of your occupation, you should be more frugal with your money. After all, you risk your life to earn it. I should think . . ."

"Get to the point," Logan grumbled grouchily.

When Piper started to protest the fact that he had stashed the money back in her lunch basket, along with the five hundred dollars he had tried to give her earlier, he flung her a burning glare. For argument's sake, Piper accepted the gift. This was not the time to rile him. She needed his help, and by damn he was going to give it, even if she had to bow to him like a slave to a king.

"What the hell are you planning?" Logan demanded impatiently.

"I thought I would portray Little Red Riding Hood, who . . ." Piper clamped her mouth shut as Logan's face puckered in a muddled frown. Blast it, why couldn't she remember that Logan knew nothing about fairy tales? With his limited experience from childhood, Piper began to think the man had actually been born at the age of thirty.

Clearing her throat, Piper restated her intentions without alluding to Red Riding Hood and her confrontation with the big bad wolf, even when it was a suitable comparison to her encounters with Logan. "I learned several valuable lessons from you the past few days," she declared, as she impulsively reached up to arrange the tousled raven hair that lay across his forehead. When she realized what she had done she jerked her hand back as if she had been bitten by a snake. "You made me realize there might be times when I need to know how to defend myself and that I might also need to learn to straddle a horse. I will be glad to pay you if you will teach me to fire this pistol. . . ." Piper opened her lunch basket to produce the Colt .45 she had purchased at Logan's suggestion. "And I would appreciate it if you would show me the proper techniques of riding. Although I have been educated in the finest schools, my experiences are limited. . . ."

"I'll say," Logan snorted caustically, still staring at her newly purchased pistol.

Piper overlooked his usual sarcasm and continued. "If you refuse to teach me to ride and shoot, I will simply attempt to teach myself by trial and error. And if that fails, I will see if Royce Granger has recovered enough to offer instruction."

Logan's silver eyes toured her tantalizing curves. There were things he could teach her, but none of them had to do with self-defense. The arousing thought stalled in his mind. He didn't want to remember how much he'd wanted her when he roused from his stupor. Well, he wasn't going to think about that anymore. It was mental suicide, and he always got carried away in those lusty fantasies.

This bewitching beauty was a threat, Logan mused as his gaze betrayed him. She made him feel vulnerable and out of control. In the past Logan had known women (and there had been plenty of them, believe you him!) in one-dimensional relationships that involved hopping in and out of bed. He didn't want to spend any more time with this tempting pixie. Hell, he needed to get her out of his life before she took up permanent residence in his brain.

"I promise to go away and never come back if you will instruct me in these underdeveloped facets of my education," she tempted him, without admitting that she had every intention of going away . . . to the *west*, not the *east* as he anticipated.

Logan studied the alluring sprite for a long, pensive moment. Oh hell, what would one more day hurt? he asked himself. Tomorrow he would be on the westbound stage and he would forget he had found himself intrigued by this naive beauty. Besides, he rationalized, she needed to learn a few techniques of self-defense, even if she were spinning in the social circles in the East. One never knew when one might need to ward off an overzealous aristocrat.

"All right, little dove," he heard himself say.

The pleased smile that blossomed on her lips threatened to melt him into sentimental mush, but Logan caught himself the split second before that happened. The grin that radiated from her exquisite features reminded Logan of staring at a spectacular sunrise. Rarely had he given her a reason to smile. Mostly he provoked her to glare murderously at him.

When Piper impulsively reached up on tiptoe to press a grateful kiss to his bronzed cheek, Logan groaned inwardly. Jeezus he hated what she did to him. He should never have agreed to this. She was too distracting, and he was flirting with frustration by spending another day with her. He would regret getting to know even more about this attractive chit, of that he was certain. Every moment he dallied with Piper brought him a step closer to forgetting his resolution to keep his distance. No doubt he would spend the hours trying to keep the lusting beast within him imprisoned in chains. Damn, some fun this was going to be, he mused sourly. One look at her revealing attire and he ached. This picnic of hers would prove to be a test of self-denial. . . .

His thoughts dispersed and a disdainful frown clouded his brow when he recognized the other basket Piper had brought along with her. "That cussed cat isn't going," Logan declared sharply.

Piper lifted her chin a notch higher. "Abraham needs some fresh air. I'll ensure that he doesn't come near you," she promised him.

"He's a menace," Logan snorted, and then wished he hadn't

employed such an explosive tone. It aggravated his throbbing headache.

"Abraham feels the same way about you," she countered. "Not that I share his low opinion," Piper added hastily, trying to keep the peace. Logan was in no mood to be harassed, and she couldn't risk having him back out now.

Grumbling under his breath, Logan reluctantly nodded his consent. He pulled on his moccasins, picked up the lunch basket and escorted Piper onto the street. The stares they received enroute to the blacksmith's barn left Logan frowning in bemusement. Piper hadn't batted an eye at being seen in her outrageous attire. But it wasn't the appreciative stares and wolfish whistles from other men that concerned him. Men naturally gawked at this tempting beauty, no matter what she was wearing. He had expected it. It was the glances *he* was receiving after passersby finished ogling Piper that really miffed him.

As near as Logan could tell, his mere association with this dazzling nymph had somehow earned him a smidgen of their respect. Why? Damned if Logan knew, but all of a sudden, the citizens of Fort Smith weren't taking a wide berth around him. Some of them even nodded a greeting to him when they passed on the street. For some reason, they had come to the conclusion that he wasn't as dangerous as they suspected if this lovely lass allowed his company. It was as if his association with Piper had enhanced his reputation.

"Is something amiss?" Curious green eyes lifted to survey the contemplative frown that clung to Logan's craggy features.

Logan managed the semblance of a smile and nodded mutely when another passerby touched the brim of his hat in silent greeting. Damn, this beat anything he had ever seen!

"I don't know whose reputation has been altered the most since we dared to parade down the street together," he smirked. Actually he did know, but it had become a habit of his to needle Piper every chance he got.

Her shoulder lifted in a careless shrug that surprised Logan. He had expected her to take offense. "It's unimportant what others think," she insisted. "Besides, it's no one's business."

In full view of anyone who cared to look, Logan abruptly

pulled Piper's luscious body against his hard, unyielding contours, forcing her to prove her bold declaration. His mouth came down on hers, savoring and devouring her all in the same moment. A taunting smile pursed his lips as he raised his raven head to gauge her reaction to his public display of affection. He waited, expecting her to turn all the colors of the rainbow when she glanced sheepishly about her. But those enormous green eyes never wavered from his dark face. She didn't seem to care who had been watching them. And to Logan's utter astonishment, her small hand lifted to cup the side of his face.

"I'm aware that you can be rough and abusive," she told him softly, completely disarming him, "but I much prefer the tender touch . . . like this. . . ."

Never in his wildest dreams did he expect Piper to kiss him back. But she did—in front of God and everybody! Her gentle embrace boiled his brain into the consistency of jelly, and the rock hard muscles of his legs melted like butter left unattended on a hot stove. Her countertactic was far more devastating than a blow to the midsection. Indeed, he would have preferred it.

When Piper gracefully withdrew to proceed toward the stables, Logan was the one who glanced sideways to see who was staring in his direction. A mischievous smile tugged at Piper's lips as she strolled toward the barn. Logan had been testing her, purposely trying to embarrass her. But after their volatile encounters the past few days she had decided to counter his insults by turning the other cheek. It wasn't always practical to fight fire with fire, but rather with a bucket of water.

Logan might not ever learn to like me, she mused, but he is going to learn to respect me. And he wasn't going to bully her anymore, either. Force didn't always imply brute strength. There were other ways to deal with a man who was as overpowering as Logan. Even though she wasn't his match physically, she was intelligent and inventive. If she couldn't get *through* that hardheaded varmint she would simply go *around* him. But one way or another he was going to honor her request to teach her to be competent with horses and weapons. And Logan was never going to know until it was too late that he had been skillfully manipulated.

For a tenth of a second Piper chastised herself for her underhanded tactics. But then she rationalized by reminding herself that she had never before dealt with a man like Logan. The situation demanded that she devise subtle ways to control him. He was going to do exactly what she wanted and all the while he was going to think it was his idea. Yes, she was scheming, but she was desperate for assistance. She needed Logan.

If only I weren't so irresistibly drawn to him, she thought with a heavy sigh. He was so different from the other men she had known. He fascinated her, challenged her. And every time she peered into those spellbinding silver eyes her heart ran away with itself. Every time she stared at his powerful physique, strange, uncontrollable tingles assaulted her. Logan was probably more man than she could handle, but she wanted instruction from no other man. Odd as that sounded, even to her, it was the—

"Why did you do that?" came the gruff voice behind her.

"Do what?" Without glancing in his direction, Piper surveyed the horses in the stalls.

Logan growled under his breath. "Why did you kiss me back?"

With sylphlike grace, she pirouetted to confront his black scowl. "I like you, despite the fact that you are always trying to erect walls between us." One delicate brow arched over her sparkling green eyes. "Are you afraid of me, Logan? Afraid you might fall hopelessly in love with me? Or are you worried that I might be falling in love with you? Are you trying to prevent it? Do you think I want to change you, to tame you to suit my tastes?"

Piper shook her head negatively in answer to her own questions. "Indeed not! I am only trying to broaden my horizons. You have constantly brought it to my attention that I need to learn to adapt to the ways of the West, just for my own protection. You were absolutely right, and I am only conceding that fact to you."

Two thick brows flattened over his narrowed gray eyes. "Don't feed me that diplomatic prattle. That doesn't explain why you kissed me back," he growled like a disturbed lion. "I like horses but I don't go around kissing them. Just spare me the tact and answer me."

Again Piper did the unpredictable. Her fingers curled into the lacings of his buckskin shirt, bringing his face and (more particularly) his sensuous lips to hers. With the slightest breath of a touch, she kissed him, slowly and thoroughly.

Logan's legs buckled at the knees. Jeezus! Was this the same straightlaced female who had slapped him silly for making suggestive innuendos? Mercy, nowadays he never knew what to expect from Piper. He felt like a duck that woke up in a new world every day. How could he deal with a woman who was so unlike the rest of her gender? She was changing day by day, evolving into a female who belonged in a class all by herself, and Logan was at a loss as to how to handle her. Once he had been able to incite her fury with his insults, but now even intimidation didn't faze her. She was calm and confident, and he was the one who was floundering.

"I'm kissing you first for the same reason I kissed you back," she informed him in a throaty whisper.

His nearness had an arousing effect on her. Each time she dared to step inside the magnetic field that surrounded this dynamic man she was stung by the same fiery sensations. He stirred her, and there was no sense trying to hide it. Logan was astute enough to sense her reaction to him. She may as well use it to her advantage.

"I find you attractive, despite your numerous faults," she confessed. "Honestly, sometimes I think I like you more than you like yourself. You strive to prove yourself to the rest of the world, as if you felt a need to be more than equal. Is there something wrong with simply being a normal man?" Her expressive eyes searched his craggy features. "Must you always hide behind that hard, impenetrable shell of yours?"

"I can't be a normal man," Logan blurted out. "I'm a half-breed."

The remark was meant to set her back on her heels. Most Easterners were terrified of Indians because of the horror stories they had heard. Half-breeds were always looked upon as second-class citizens. Logan had fought that stigma all his life.

He was a half-breed gunslinger with two strikes against him. That was why people went out of their way to avoid him. He waited for disapproval to register in those lovely green eyes. But it didn't, much to his surprise.

Piper broke into a smile as her gaze drifted down his well-structured torso. Then she stared him straight in the eye. His abrupt confession answered many of the questions that had been buzzing through her mind. He had tripped back and forth between two civilizations and had never truly been at home in either of them, she guessed. That was why he had a chip the size of the Rock of Gibraltar on his shoulder. But Piper intended to chisel away at it, bit by bit.

"Your Indian ancestry has added character to your face." Her fingertips limned the dark skin that wrapped around his high cheekbones and angular jaw. "You are very attractive, Logan. But I'm sure women have told you that hundreds of times before."

Damn, she didn't seem to care that he was an outcast of both Indian and white society. While Logan stood there wondering at what exact moment he had lost control, Piper pivoted to study the horses and grapple with the conflicting emotions that gnawed at her.

Why was she being so bold with him? She had never dished out compliments to men. Most of them, men like Grant and Hiram, didn't deserve flattery. They were all conniving bastards, and women had to tolerate them since they populated half of the world. Men were also scoundrels, she contended. She ought to know. She had been courted by men from every occupation, and not one of them had proved to be worth his salt until she crossed paths with Logan. This giant of a man had walked up and looked down his nose at her as if she had contracted leprosy. Perhaps the fact that he had never catered to her was what fascinated her most. She had never been challenged by a man and she liked that. It was better than enduring empty phrases of flattery that were uttered to soften her defenses. At least with Logan she knew exactly where she stood. He didn't have much use for her, but at least he was honest about it.

Casting aside her meandering thoughts, Piper focused her

complete attention on the row of horses. One dainty finger indicated the roan gelding that was stamping around in his stall. "I should like to ride that one," she announced. "He looks sound."

Logan's mind shifted gears as rapidly as Piper's did. The subject of conversation frustrated him. He didn't want her to like him. It was safer that way. Although he was convinced he would be a happier man once Piper was out of his life, he had the uneasy feeling he was going to miss this troublesome little imp.

He flung aside his musings and concentrated on Piper's comment. The lady didn't know beans about horses. The experienced eye could note several flaws in the steed, none of which Piper could detect. "The roan would throw you in a matter of minutes."

Her inquisitive gaze swung back to Logan. "How can you tell?" she questioned earnestly.

"By the way he's staring at us, the way he's tossing his head," Logan pointed out. "He's got too much spunk and he's too young for an inexperienced rider." His sinewy arm stretched out to indicate the bay mare that was calmly standing in her stall. "She looks to be a seasoned mount and she knows her place."

Piper stiffened defensively. "Why? Because she's a *she?* How like a man to make that ridiculous re . . ." She bit her tongue a moment too late. Piper had resolved not to instigate arguments with Logan. He was too proficient when she met him on his own battleground. She was going to keep the peace, even if it killed her.

A wry grin dangled on Logan's lips as he opened the gate and grabbed the mare's halter. "Most females do recognize their proper place," he snickered. "There are, however, a few exceptions."

"Thank you for the compliment," she replied.

"It wasn't meant as one," he said candidly.

Before Piper rose to the taunt, the smith warily approached the mismatched couple. Piper's eyes widened in disbelief as Logan peeled off several bills to rent the steed. Lord, he could have bought the whole horse for the amount he paid to borrow her for the day!

"Why are you such a spendthrift?" she snapped without thinking.

"What difference does it make to you?" Logan shot back as he tossed the saddle over the bay mare. "I earned it and I'll spend it as I see fit."

"I only hope you can make it as fast as you squander it," she muttered.

"John Butterfield paid me handsomely to stop the disturbances along his stage line," Logan informed her blandly. "If I die, I can't take the money with me."

"Exactly what kind of disturbances?" Piper gulped apprehensively. If road agents were attacking the stage, the trust fund Grant had stolen from her could be stolen from him!

Logan misread her startled expression as concern for personal safety. "It isn't going to matter, honey," he assured her. "The only holdups reported are in West Texas and points beyond. No trouble has arisen to the east of Fort Smith. Since you are going back home where you belong, you have no need for worry."

Like hell she was going east! But Piper promptly swallowed that particular comment before it found its way to tongue. She wasn't telling Logan of her plans and risk having him attempt to stop her. She was going to do what she had to do, and the training Logan gave her would help her do it!

Piper was jolted to her senses when Logan, who had already mounted, leaned down to pluck her off the ground. His strong hand folded her elbow, positioning her behind him on the mare. The feel of his masculine body pressed familiarly against hers provoked a jolt of a different nature. Piper could feel his hips against her inner thighs, feel the bunched muscles of his back brushing against her breasts.

"Hold onto me or you'll wind up in a broken heap," he warned as he nudged the horse into the street and maneuvered the two baskets on his lap. Logan spitefully hoped Abraham would decide to peek from his case and fall flat on his face. Jeezus, he never thought he would be carting a cat around with him. If Harley could see him now he would be rolling in laughter.

95

Reluctantly, Piper placed her hands on his waist. The mare trotted down the street, jostling Piper from side to side. A bubble of amusement rattled in Logan's chest as Piper bounced along behind him. She was going to be bruised and sore the following day, he predicted. He was also prepared to bet his right arm that she hadn't been on the back of a horse in all her life. If she had, she had gained nothing from the experience.

"Clamp your legs around the mare," he instructed. "Move in rhythm with her motion. Feel her beneath you and become a part of her."

Piper speculated on the suggestive contents of his sentence and the sultry tone of his voice. It didn't sound as if she were receiving a riding lesson, more like a symposium on mating customs. Her face flushed scarlet red.

"You have to let her know you are always the one in command," Logan went on to say with a mischievous grin. "Make her move to suit your needs." Expertly, he touched the reins to the mare's neck and then veered right and left as he followed the dirt path that led away from town. Once they reached the meadow Logan quickened the mare's pace. "If she thinks she controls you, she'll run away with you. And never trust her," he added meaningfully. "When she lulls you into complacency she might take the opportunity to throw you. She'll wait until you have your guard down and then she'll leave you in a tangled heap."

"You don't trust me, do you?" Piper blurted out.

Logan swiveled his head around to peer at Piper's agitated frown. "I was talking about the horse," he managed to say with a poker face.

"You were not and I damned well know it," she accused.

"Tsk, tsk," he taunted mercilessly. "Ladies of quality shouldn't curse."

"And men like you shouldn't be so mistrusting and they certainly shouldn't try to tell women what to do!" Dammit, it was practically impossible not to become annoyed with Logan. He was a master at baiting her into an argument. Even when she tried to meet this impossible man halfway it still wasn't enough! Sometimes he made her so frustrated she wanted to throw him down and round up a herd of horses to trample over him!

"Do you want to learn to ride or do you want to argue?" he mocked.

It was easier to antagonize Piper than to get along with her. When they were enjoying each other's company it made him uneasy. He felt he had somehow lost command of the situation, and he wasn't accustomed to being at a loss. This green-eyed blonde kept his emotions in turmoil and Logan didn't appreciate fighting the mental wrestling match that her presence always instigated. Quite frankly, he didn't want to care about her. Knowing he did, even a little, frustrated him.

Piper clamped her mouth shut so quickly she nearly bit off her tongue. Silently she listened to Logan's instructions, even when she swore he was using the lesson to stab her with innuendos and subtle jibes that had nothing to do with riding a horse.

Halting the steed, Logan hooked his arm around her waist and set Piper on her feet. With graceful ease he stepped from the stirrup, juggling both baskets in his hands. But he happened to snag Abraham's carrying case against the pommel of the saddle (on purpose, not accidentally, mind you). As the basket tumbled pell-mell to the ground Abraham let out a yowl that would have roused the dead. With wicked glee, Logan watched the pesky tomcat scratch and claw his way from the upturned basket. He was delighted to see that Abraham had landed on his back instead of on his feet.

As Abraham bounded off across the meadow Piper opened her mouth to protest Logan's spiteful prank, but he quickly drew her attention to the mare. "Now it's your turn," he announced. "Let's see if you've been listening to my instructions."

When Piper took up the reins, the mare pranced in a tight circle and then dropped her head to nibble on the grass. While the mare was preoccupied, Piper stuffed a booted foot in the stirrup and struggled into the saddle.

"What the hell are you doing?" Logan croaked.

She stared at him as if he had ivy growing out his ears. "I'm mounting the horse." Wasn't that obvious? Why was he asking stupid questions?

97

"Not from that side," he grumbled. "Always mount on the left unless your horse is accustomed to being crawled all over like an Indian's pony."

"Well, honestly, I don't see what difference it makes," Piper mumbled defensively as she stamped around the steed. "Both sides look the same to me."

Logan bit back a grin as Piper clambered atop the mare without his assistance. He was too busy studying her shapely derriere to remember the courtesy of helping a lady onto her horse.

After tugging at the reins to lift the mare's head, Logan showed Piper how to hold the leather straps in her hands. "Remember to let her know who's boss," he instructed. "And don't forget what I told you about keeping a firm and constant pressure on the reins when you want to change directions. If the mare resists the command, be persistent."

Piper mentally listed all the instructions Logan had given her. Concentrating, she pressed her knees to the steed's flanks, urging her forward. Gaining confidence, Piper reined the mare in a figure eight. When she felt comfortable with the walk she nudged the mare into a trot. After several minutes Piper kicked the steed into a gallop. Recalling what Logan had said about becoming a part of the horse's natural movement, Piper strived for accurate precision.

As the mare gobbled up the ground beneath her hooves, Piper felt the breeze rush past her face. There was something exhilarating about straddling this powerful animal. The thrill of controlling a thousand pounds of finely honed horseflesh stimulated her, and Piper thirsted for more. Nudging the bay mare again, Piper thundered across the meadow, racing against the wind. She was stung by the wild sensation that she could fly, that the mare had sprouted wings to soar. . . .

And then suddenly, panic gripped Piper. Directly ahead of her, just beyond the high rise of ground, was a winding creek. She was upon it before she could react. When she gathered her wits it was too late. The mare launched herself over the creek, causing Piper to jerk backward in the saddle. When the mare's four hooves hit the ground simultaneously Piper experienced both flying and crashing.

Expelling a bloodcurdling screech, Piper watched in terror as the ground leaped up at her. A thorn bush reached out to snare her, diverting her from landing on solid ground. She crashed with a decisive thud that knocked the wind out of her. Pricking pain stabbed at her hip as she shook her head to halt the revolving stars that twinkled before her eyes.

Piper groaned miserably. She couldn't get up, didn't want to get up. Every bone and muscle in her body was still reverberating. She felt like a tuning fork that had been clanked against metal. She could feel herself vibrating in rhythm with the throbbing pain that ricocheted through her. Piper assured herself she might eventually rise from her unceremonious heap. But she would never, *ever* mount that vicious mare again!

Chapter 7

Before Piper could check for broken bones or gather her legs beneath her, strong hands clamped around her waist to set her upright on the ground. Her knees buckled beneath her and she clutched at Logan's strong shoulders for support. Piper could feel his big body shaking in silent amusement, and she glared shadows on his beaming smile.

"Don't you dare laugh," she ordered brusquely.

Logan tried not to, he truly did. But he simply couldn't contain himself. He kept seeing Piper soaring in flight, crashing into the briar patch. A snicker tripped from his lips, even when he attempted to camouflage it behind an artificial cough. His laughter caused humiliation to stain her cheeks. When she tried to draw herself up another pain gouged her in the hip.

"I hate that horse," Piper growled, eyeing the mare with contempt.

"It wasn't her fault," Logan countered between chortles. "You tried to gallop before you mastered trotting. You can't learn to ride in one easy lesson. . . ."

His voice trailed off when he noticed Piper had contorted her body to peer down at her backside. He knew exactly what had happened without posing any questions. And without delay, he pushed her to the ground. Despite her furious protests, Logan quickly loosened her breeches and tugged the garment from her hip.

"Hold still," he demanded as he retrieved his bowie knife.

Piper had never been so mortified in all her life! Logan was digging thorns from her derriere, one neither he nor anyone had ever laid eyes on. The palm of his left hand lay against her bare flesh while he used his knife to remove the embedded thorns—all five of them. Piper wanted to dig a hole and crawl into it, never to be seen or heard from again.

While Logan performed minor surgery, his all-consuming gaze flooded over the creamy smooth flesh of her buttocks. He wasn't sure who was hurting the most—Piper with her thorns and her humiliation or him with his frustrated desire. She couldn't have ached worse than he did. His entire body was beating in a steady throb.

"How dare you!" Piper spewed, writhing in vain for freedom.

"You're welcome," Logan mumbled absently, too distracted by his arousing thoughts to care how embarrassed she was.

Finally, Logan completed his ministrations and pulled her breeches back in place, though with great reluctance. "Next time, keep the mare at a slow canter or you could wind up with a broken neck instead of thorns in your . . ."

"I know where they were," she bit off.

His silver eyes raked her in slow deliberation. "So do I . . . on one of the prettiest derrieres I've ever seen."

He couldn't know how much that reckless remark hurt and Piper wasn't about to tell him. Even Piper couldn't understand why she was so aggravated to hear him mention that he was a connoisseur of a woman's anatomy. Why, he had probably slept with more females than she had met at boarding school, damn him!

Leaving her standing there, silently seething, Logan swaggered over to retrieve the mare. When he offered her the reins, Piper gave her tangled blond hair a negative shake.

"I've enjoyed my first and last riding lesson," she told him. "When the mare and I parted company it was forever."

"When you take a fall, the best thing to do is climb back on," he insisted.

"No." Her smudged chin tilted to a rebellious angle.

"Yes." Logan hooked a muscular arm around her waist and promptly deposited her in the saddle, whether she wanted to be there or not. She didn't.

Piper grimaced uncomfortably when she felt the hard leather beneath her tender backside. "I'll never forgive you for this," she grumbled at Logan.

Heartlessly, he patted the mare on the rump, sending her off in a trot. "I can live with that."

As the steed and her reluctant rider trotted off, Logan leaned back against a tree, crossing his arms and legs in front of him. He really couldn't pinpoint why he was smiling. He just was. His eyes never wavered from the shapely beauty who breezed across the meadow. Her silver blond hair undulated behind her like a flag as the mare stretched out into an easy canter. Although Piper hadn't wanted to remount, she had finally accepted the challenge. She had taken his instructions to heart, practicing the techniques he had taught her. She possessed a natural grace and poise that her inexperience in the saddle couldn't overshadow. In admiration, Logan studied the lady and her steed as they loped across the prairie in one rhythmic motion.

For a whimsical moment, Logan pictured this bewitching sprite thundering across the grass-carpeted Gila River valley. She would be the rose of the desert. . . .

Shaking away the ridiculous thought, Logan propelled himself toward the lunch basket. That fantasy would never collide with reality. He was catching the westbound stage at 3:30 the next morning, and Piper would be riding on the eastbound stage that was due to leave Fort Smith in two days.

They would never see each other again, and that was exactly the way Logan wanted it. This bewitching nymph amused him and frustrated him all in the same moment. He hadn't liked the way his heart skipped several vital beats when she flew headlong from her steed. He wasn't accustomed to being frightened for a woman, fretting over her. He didn't appreciate this helpless hunger of desire that constantly gnawed at him. He detested wanting something he couldn't have and certainly didn't need.

Dammit, he and Piper were as different as night and day. Her knowledge came from textbooks. Piper had been taught proper lessons of etiquette, poise, and manners. It showed in

103

everything she did. Logan's vast and varied knowledge was based on experiences in a wild and lawless land. The education he had received at the schools established in the Cherokee nation had prepared him to communicate with whites, but very little else. Trial and error were his instructors, and they taught him most of what he needed to know to survive in the West. He had grown up like a tumbleweed, bearing a grudge, feeling alone, unaccepted and unwanted.

Logan squeezed back the unpleasant thoughts of his formative years. Piper was right about him. He had carried a gigantic chip on his shoulder. Resentment and revenge had motivated him. He wanted to prove himself competent to live in the world of the red man and the white man alike. He had learned to handle a gun with experienced ease. He had learned to fight like a panther, who employed all four appendages as weapons against its competitors. The money he had made selling his gun hand had been his way of keeping track, of getting even, of assuring himself that he wasn't just a half-breed but a man to be reckoned with.

In the beginning, Logan had imagined each man that he faced in a shootout to be the bastard who had raped his mother—his own father (whoever and wherever the hell the scoundrel was). But over the years of constant wandering the bitter resentment faded. Now Logan only took a man's life when he was left with no alternative. But he never let himself forget that those he was forced to kill were murderers, thieves, and rapists like his own father.

"Am I improving?" Piper questioned as she slid to the ground.

His eyes surveyed the lively bundle of beauty. He realized, quite suddenly, that the mere pleasure of female companionship had been nonexistent in his life before Piper came along. Yet ironically, this sophisticated blueblood did not belong in his life. They were, as the saying went (at least Logan thought he had heard the adage somewhere along the way), like two ships passing in the night. And something about two twains never meeting. Or was that another adage entirely? Logan couldn't remember. The literature he had picked up over his thirty-one years was a mite sketchy. Hell, when Piper started referring to Goldilocks and Red Riding Hood he didn't have the foggiest notion what she was talking about. For all he knew they could have been the ones who rattled off philosophical phrases about passing ships and twains. . . .

"You're doing very well with your riding," he complimented, casting his pensive thoughts aside. Absently, Logan dug into the picnic basket, pulled out a chicken leg, and munched upon it. "When you return home, buy yourself a gentle mare and keep practicing until you can rein her to a halt without flying over her head."

Piper's eyes dropped to the lunch basket. She wasn't about to return home while Grant Fredricks was running around loose with her inheritance, but she couldn't tell Logan that. He would forcefully stuff her on the eastbound coach and send her packing.

"I'll keep practicing until I'm as accomplished in the saddle as you are." She could promise him that much without revealing her intentions. Hesitantly, she glanced at the brawny giant who was sprawled on the ground beside her. "Will you tell me about yourself, Logan?"

The question surprised him and he frowned disconcertedly. "What do you want to know?" If she asked him how many men he had dropped in their tracks, the way most inconsiderate, unthinking folks did, he would strangle her!

"You mentioned your Indian ancestry," she commented as she eased onto her uninjured hip to savor their midday meal.

The aroma of food brought Abraham from hiding. Logan glared disdainfully at the tomcat who accepted the chicken wing Piper handed him and then crunched loudly upon his feast.

"I'm half Cherokee," he said bitterly. "My mother was raped by a drunken trapper. When I was ten years old the tribe was herded into a camp and then prodded down the Trail of Tears to their allocated lands in Indian territory. My mother died, along with the other four thousand souls who perished along the way. They were underfed, underclothed, and infected by white men's diseases."

"It must have been . . ." Piper began sympathetically.

"It was living hell," Logan interjected with a resentful

105

snort. He didn't know why he was telling Piper about his childhood. He had never revealed the story to anyone but Harley, and only after he had badgered Logan about it for two years. He had only known Piper for a few days and he was spilling the confession at her request. Jeezus, she had him saying and doing things he would never have expected of himself.

The grim picture Logan painted caused Piper to shiver. If Logan carried a grudge it was certainly well-founded. Her life had been a bed of roses compared to his. At least it had been until her mother married her stepfather. Piper had considered Monica's second wedding date as her entrance into hell. Hiram had insisted that Piper be carted off to boarding school while he squandered her mother's fortune. When Monica passed away, Piper was told she had died of an incurable disease. But Piper knew better. Her mother had died from depression and constant harassment. Monica had realized that she had married Hiram because of loneliness, to fill the emptiness in her life. But her second marriage of five years had been a disastrous mistake. Monica had not been the kind of woman who knew how to stand up to a man, to fight back. She had given up and withdrawn into herself, and she had chosen to die rather than to live in misery.

Piper had resolved never to buckle to a man the way her mother had done. Never would Piper allow a man to destroy her life. And when she finally caught up with that scheming varmint Grant Fredricks, he would rue the day he had tried to swindle her out of her livelihood! And if Hiram thought she would allow him to take control of her money he had another thing coming. Piper was nothing like Monica.

The vengeful thought regenerated Piper's determination. Clutching her new pistol and bullets, she rose from the ground and sought out a target. As she fumbled to load her weapon, Logan's steady hands folded over hers, offering instruction. She paid very close attention, hanging on his every word, trying to ignore the tingles and goose bumps that cropped up when he dared to venture so near her.

Standing directly behind her, peering over her shoulder, Logan showed Piper how to handle the weapon and take accurate aim. "Never try to bluff if you are forced to defend yourself," he told her earnestly. "Aim at your intended victim's belt buckle if you want to ensure that he won't be around to harass you again."

When Piper raised her arm to look down her sleeve, Logan pushed it back where it belonged. "When you point at your target you don't raise your trigger finger to eye level and try to sight it." His hands settled on her waist, forcing her to rest her forearm against her hipbone for steadiness and extra support.

"Grip the Colt between the last joint of your thumb and forefinger so there is a straight line between the muzzle and your elbow." He placed her hand just so on the pistol. "Aim as if you were merely pointing your index finger. Instinct will determine how grave your situation and how accurate you must be if you are to survive a duel."

When Piper squeezed the trigger, Logan snorted in disgust. "Jeezus, woman, you aren't supposed to close your eyes. How the hell do you expect to see where you're aimed? You don't close your eyes, you don't even bat them!"

"I didn't mean to—"

Piper's defensive protest was cut short by Logan's irritated grunt. "If you want me to teach you the proper techniques, you are going to do it right after I tell you how. Now keep your eyes open. You can blink when the smoke clears." Logan grumbled under his breath and retrieved his own pistol. Spitefully, he selected Abraham's carrying case as his target. "Firing a pistol should look like this. . . ." The first shot sent the basket flipping into the air. Abraham, who was lounging beside it, screeched in terror and darted up a nearby tree. The second shot put the upended basket right side up again.

"You tried to kill my cat!" Piper snapped furiously.

With smooth precision, Logan glided his pistol into its holster and displayed an ornery smile. "No," he contradicted. "I was only blowing air holes in his basket. If I had aimed at him I would have shot him right in the—"

"You don't particularly like me either," Piper sputtered as she stared at Abraham, who looked as if he had suffered the shock of his life. "Do you intend to blow my feet out from under me as part of my shooting lesson?"

107

Logan redirected her toward her target. "I was only making a point," he insisted. "A novice with a gun in hand is more dangerous than a ruthless gunslinger. I hit what I was shooting at because I employed the proper and most effective techniques. If you had taken aim at the basket you would have killed your cat."

"You would have loved that, wouldn't you?" she harshly accused. "Nothing would make you happier than to see me murder my own pet."

"Forget that damned cat and pay attention," Logan growled impatiently. "You have to cock your pistol after each shot, so don't fumble around and let it discharge accidentally or you'll blow off a toe." Logan repositioned her arm in the proper place against her side and squared her shoulders. "What you need now is a great deal of practice. You must refine your skills, just as a cardsharp practices with his deck of cards. Learn to draw, cock, and fire in one fluid motion. Once you have mastered all that you can concentrate on accuracy and speed."

The tree at which Piper aimed was safe the first three times she squeezed the trigger. But with Logan's constant instruction she began to hit her target. And then suddenly, the pistol was snatched from her hand and a steel blade lay against her throat. Her body stiffened as Logan's muscular body mashed against her back, evoking wanton sensations that had no business arousing her at such an untimely moment.

"This is the weapon a woman should learn to handle," he murmured so close to her ear that another herd of goose bumps stampeded down her spine. "If you had a knife the night your assailant came at you, he wouldn't have been able to lay a hand on this lovely body of yours without paying the price."

His close contact was having a staggering effect on Piper. She tried to concentrate on what he was saying but her body was paying no attention.

Logan was having the same difficulty. He had meant to catch her off guard but he hadn't meant to tempt himself with her nearness. But now that he had, he had difficulty controlling the hunger that gnawed at him. Roughly, he spun Piper around and folded the stiletto into her fist. Logan told himself to ignore the tantalizing scent and the feel of her feminine contours. This was to be her lesson in self-defense, even if his betraying thoughts had something more stimulating in mind.

"If I attack you, insert the blade between my ribs. No man is going to argue with a woman who holds a knife to his side. . . ."

But Piper didn't lay the blade against his ribs or his neck or anywhere else. Her body was immobilized by the churning emotions that had been nagging at her each time Logan touched her. Suddenly she didn't care about horses or pistols or knives. She wanted to feel the possessive pressure of his lips moving seductively over hers. She wanted to inhale the masculine scent of this ruggedly handsome giant and lose herself in his encircling arms.

Her curly lashes fluttered up to peer into those entrancing silver eyes. Piper felt her heart melt when she focused on the sensuous curve of his lips. She marveled at the rugged lines of experience that were chiseled on his bronzed face. She looked at him and wanted things she knew she couldn't and shouldn't have. But it felt so right when she was in his arms, as if she belonged there.

"Piper . . . the knife," Logan prompted her, but his thoughts were as distracted as hers were.

Piper was too inexperienced to hide her longings, and the raw desire in her eyes made it even more difficult to remember he intended to teach her self-defense. What he needed at the moment was a lesson in self-control. His was suddenly nonexistent. His body had gone up in flames, and the tender torment of holding her close was slowly killing him—mentally, physically and emotionally.

"I don't want to stab you," she murmured, her voice further betraying the turmoil of forbidden emotions that bubbled inside her.

"What do you want?" His rumbling tone resembled the purr of a tiger. The steady beat of his heart had accelerated and his pulse leapfrogged through his blood. Jeezus, feeling her body molded intimately to his was nine kinds of hell. He should have kept his distance!

"I want to kiss you," she whispered shamelessly as she tilted her face to his.

The word *no* formed on his lips, but Piper kissed it away the instant her sweet mouth rose to meet his. Logan felt a soul-shattering shudder ripple through him. The wall of ice around his heart melted beneath the warmth of her gentle touch, and his body answered *yes* as he returned her kiss.

Piper had prepared herself for the rough domination of this swarthy giant. It wouldn't have mattered though, she reminded herself dazedly. She wanted him so badly she wouldn't have cared if he ravished her, so long as he satisfied this burning need that blazed in the core of her being. But Logan was the epitome of gentleness as he cradled her to him and took possession of her lips. Logan had become a gentle giant, and Piper's eyes misted with the rare rapture of his loving touch.

His full lips rolled over hers, brushing against her mouth, courting her like a bee hovering upon a delicate flower. His tongue traced the curve of her lips and then guided them apart to explore the soft recesses within. An involuntary gasp of pleasure ricocheted through her chest when his hand glided down her back to press her hips against the hard columns of his thighs. Piper could feel the ardent need she had aroused in him. She could taste him, touch him, inhale the heady aroma of him as if he were a part of her.

Piper knew she was flirting with danger, but, fool that she was, she couldn't stop herself. It was insane and reckless and yet she wanted him to caress her. She wanted him to satisfy this compelling ache that she had never experienced until Logan had awakened her slumbering passions.

Maybe he wasn't the man for her. And perhaps she would live to regret surrendering to the needs he instilled in her. But he had taught her so many skills already that it naturally seemed to follow that he should be the one to unveil the mysteries of passion.

Another quiet moan tripped from her lips when his roaming hands tunneled beneath her shirt to make contact with her quivering flesh. Unleashed desire swelled inside her. Sweet fires of longing burst into flame when his fingertips teased the rigid peaks of her breasts. And then she felt his practiced hands traverse her ribs to glide along the band of her breeches. Over and over again, his exploring caresses scaled her stomach

110

to encircle each throbbing bud before they drifted provocatively to her waist.

There was something magical about the way he touched her. His hands were strong and commanding and yet amazingly gentle. It was as if he were weaving a spell over her with his skillful caresses. And while he was discovering the sensitive points on her flesh, he took her lips under his, savoring her, sharing each ragged breath.

Piper was too delirious with forbidden pleasure to recall the exact moment when Logan had laid her in the grass and bent over her. But he was there, staring down at her with those entrancing eyes that shone like polished silver. He always looked faintly dangerous, but now it was worse. He was looking at her in a way that made her go hot all over. Her will was suddenly his own and, oddly enough, Piper wanted it that way.

Logan held her gaze as his fingers tripped across the buttons of her shirt, ones that gave way to his gentle insistence. As the fabric fell away, his eyes burned across her bare flesh, memorizing each arresting curve and swell, cherishing the sight of her as if he had unwrapped a precious gift.

Piper watched his eyes drift over her exposed flesh, but she couldn't meet his sizzling gaze when his hands weaved intricate patterns on her skin. Even though she relished the pleasure of his touch, there was a certain shyness that accompanied the intimacy of baring herself to a man.

"Piper . . ." The sound of her name and the husky resonance of his voice drew her reluctant gaze back to his face. "I want you to watch me touch you," he murmured raggedly. "I want you to see the pleasure your beauty gives me. Never have I looked upon or touched anything so exquisite. . . ."

Was this the same man who insulted and teased her, who tried to push her away when she attempted to reach over that rock wall of self-reserve that he usually hid behind?

"But I've never . . ." Piper protested shakily.

"I know, little dove," he whispered as he bent to graze his lips over the dusky peak of her breasts. "And that's what makes touching you so priceless. . . . You're pure and soft and no other man has seen the glorious sight of you. . . ."

Piper swore her entire body had caught fire and burned

111

when his hands and lips took possession. His prowling fingertips and warm lips were everywhere at once, sensitizing and arousing. She couldn't control the convulsive quaking, the streams of sweet agony, the shocked gasps of excitement and anticipation. Piper had been towed into the whirlpool of reckless pleasure, and she didn't care if she drowned in these wondrous feelings. Logan could have done whatever he wanted to her and she would have begged for more. He had made her a slave to obsessive desires that blossomed out of nowhere to consume her. Modesty bowed to the satisfaction of being loved by this sometimes frustrating and yet wonderfully intriguing man.

As his moist lips scaled her shoulder to reclaim her mouth, Piper's inquisitive hands dived beneath his shirt to explore his hair-roughened belly. She wanted to return the pleasure he had given, to learn his magnificent body by taste and touch.

A shuddering groan erupted from Logan's lips as her untutored hands located the sensitive points of his flesh and transformed muscle to mush. Instinctively, his body moved above hers, half covering her petite form. His knee insinuated itself between her thighs, wanting more than this innocent elf knew how to give. Logan yearned to see every exquisite inch of her, to feel her soft, supple body imprinted against him. He wanted her to lose her innocence to him. He ached to teach her the ecstasy of lovemaking and brand his memory on her soul. . . .

That tantalizing thought speared across his mind as he shifted to pull her full length beneath him. Logan resented the garments that separated them. Impatiently he rolled to his side and tugged at her breeches, allowing his hand free access to the rest of her silky flesh. His fingertips probed and teased until Piper breathlessly arched against him. Her own impatience to satisfy the need he had instilled in her left Logan trembling with a monstrous craving.

He lay down upon her, letting her feel what she did to him, letting her know how much he wanted her. Before he came to her, appeasing their obsessive hunger for each other, he wanted her to understand what awaited her. Her innocence made him take special pains to prepare her, to fully arouse her before he taught her the meaning of passion's fulfillment.

Logan had never been so caring and cautious with the woman in his arms. But he didn't want to frighten or hurt this inexperienced nymph. They had dared too much, but it was too late to turn back. His male needs had taken command of his mind and body. He wanted their lovemaking to be the essence of dreams, a sweet lingering fantasy she would cherish when she returned to her world and left him alone in his.

The feel of his bold manhood pressing against her thighs sent Piper into wild abandon. She was shocked by the changes that overcame him and yet she shamelessly wished him to end this sweet, tormenting agony. Logan had led her deeper and deeper into the sensual world of passion, making her a prisoner of desire. She wanted to feel him inside her, to experience the ultimate bliss of lovemaking, to satisfy this maddening hunger that stripped her of her senses and left her a creature of burning need.

"I want you . . ." Logan growled in disturbed desire.

The jingle of harnesses and the rumble of an approaching wagon shattered Logan's fantasies and sent him plunging into the depths of frustration. Muttering at his momentary lapse of common sense and the abrupt interruption, Logan pushed himself away to help fasten Piper back into her clothes.

Paralyzed by the lingering sensations, Piper watched his nimble fingers fly over the gaping garments. "Logan, I . . ."

His thunderous scowl caused the words to die in her throat. Abruptly, he yanked her to her feet and scooped up the lunch basket. Even Abraham knew better than to display his contrariness when Logan barked the order for him to climb into his carrying case.

With swift, efficient ease, Logan swung Piper into his arms, baskets and all, and placed her in the saddle. In one lithe motion he eased behind her on the mare and took up the reins.

"Next time you better stab me," he grumbled in her ear. "I think it would be a helluva a lot safer for both of us. We're playing with fire, honey, and you are the one who would have been badly burned."

113

Oblivious to the ride back to town, Piper sat rigidly against Logan—ashamed, embarrassed, and totally appalled with herself. What strange spell did this man hold over her? She had practically begged him to seduce her. She had never made such suggestive overtures to any other man. And suddenly she found herself surrendering to a man who had no desire to entangle himself in a lasting relationship with any woman, least of all her—the naive Eastern bluestocking, as he so disrespectfully referred to her.

Sweet mercy, what a fool she had been. Logan had probably lost what small amount of respect he might have held for her. He called her a city slicker, a tenderfoot. He mocked her lack of experience in passion and in life. And she had let him touch her intimately, wanting him the way she had wanted no other man. He knew of her vulnerability for him, and now she had handed him another weapon to use against her. As if he didn't have enough already! she thought dispiritedly.

To make matters worse, Logan hadn't bothered to let her down gently after they had been interrupted. He was a worldly man, wasn't he? He should have known what to say to smooth over a situation that had gotten out of hand. But he didn't really care about her mortification. The moment the spell had been broken he crept back into that hard shell of his like a turtle! He had never once said he liked her, only that he wanted her, that it aroused him to know he was taking what no one else had taken from her.

But it wasn't I who made the difference, Piper told herself bitterly. She could have been any one of a number of women and it wouldn't have mattered to Logan. She was just another of his many women, and he enjoyed seducing all of them.

Oh, what a fool she had been! Piper hated herself for buckling beneath her womanly curiosity. Facing Logan after what they had shared was worse than standing before a firing squad. God, she wanted to die instead of living with her humiliation. He would probably scratch another notch on his pistol, and she would become just another casualty of love and war.

Piper's silence had Logan growling under his breath. He knew what she was feeling. She was thoroughly ashamed of herself for permitting him to touch her so intimately because she knew he wasn't good enough for her. Being an innocent, she had merely been experimenting with passion to appease her curiosity and she had driven him crazy with wanting. But when she came to her senses she had realized she should have searched elsewhere. He was just a notch above a savage and she was just a step below royalty. She knew they could be good together but not good for each other—not when they were worlds apart. Piper refused to look at him because she didn't want to see the man she had allowed to caress her, the man who had very nearly stolen her virginity. Even if they had made love it would be the same as it was now—stilted silence. When the loving was over Piper would have opened those enormous green eyes and she would have seen him as he was—the rugged, uncultured renegade who was a far cry from the man of her dreams.

Jeezus! He should never have let her talk him into teaching her anything! He was the one who was learning things that he would have been better off not knowing. She had almost discovered how human he really was, how vulnerable he was with her.

But in a few hours he would step into the stage and he was going to forget this entire week. He didn't want to remember the frustration, the forbidden desire of wanting a woman with whom he had nothing in common except an attraction that burned hot enough to melt the stars and leave them dripping on the night sky. Dammit, as glorious as it would have been to embark on the most intimate of journeys, it wouldn't have been enough when reality returned.

The moment he set Piper to her feet in Fort Smith Logan vowed to erase her memory from his mind and never spare her another thought. What was the matter with him? He knew he couldn't love away the differences between them. He was what he was. And what he was *not* was this naive little bluestocking's experiment with passion! She had wanted him for all the wrong reasons, and he had wanted her because he had been without a woman too long. They had been caught up in a fire that had very nearly blazed out of control. It was a disastrous mistake and Logan was going to forget this tête-à-tête ever happened.

115

He had been better off when he was antagonizing Piper. He should have left well enough alone.

Tomorrow I will be long gone, he reminded himself. He couldn't shake the dust of Fort Smith off his moccasins quick enough. Damn, he must have been out of his mind to let this attraction between them get so far out of hand!

Chapter 8

Piper paced her room like a caged cat while a bored Abraham glanced at her and closed his eyes. For more than two hours she steamed and stewed. She and Logan had parted company with a stiff nod and without a word. She had heard him leave his room the previous hour and she wondered if he had gone to the bordellos on Chippy Hill. She hadn't satisfied his craving for a woman. She was a novelty to him, but she was too innocent and inexperienced at . . . at everything!

Stop this! Piper shouted at herself. Logan meant nothing to her, nothing at all. She had come west for one purpose—to track down her missing inheritance. That was the beginning and end of it. Logan refused to help her so she was going to solve the problem by herself. He wouldn't assist her and he didn't like her, so that was that. There was no reason for her to feel rejected. From the outset, she knew Logan was the kind of man a woman should avoid like the plague. Sheriff Potter had warned her. But she had been overly tempted and she had taken it on the chin. Whatever was between them was over as quickly as it had begun, so that was that too. And it *was* over, Piper told herself firmly. But why didn't she feel a bit better after having this conversation with herself? Piper's shoulders slumped. God, if she could rewind the hands of time she wouldn't have thrown herself at Logan like an eager naive fool. . . .

To Piper's bemusement, an envelope slid beneath her door, and then the door across the hall quietly closed. She didn't know where Logan had gone, but obviously he was back. Curious, Piper retrieved the envelope and gasped in disbelief when she examined its contents. A gold ring, inset with diamonds and emeralds, sparkled up at her. Her eyes immediately fell to the note that had nothing more than Logan's name scrawled on it.

Scarlet red rage blinded her as she left her room to pound on Logan's door. How dare he try to buy her expensive trinkets! Did he think he could compensate for the embarrassment he had caused her? Did he presume to pay for favors with gifts purchased with money that meant nothing to him? Did he buy extravagant trinkets for all the women he had toyed with during his wanderings? Well, maybe his other women appreciated tokens of his affection, but not Piper, and she fully intended to tell him so!

When the door swung open, Piper shoved the ring into Logan's belly, along with her doubled fist. "I don't want this!" she snapped furiously.

Her hateful tone spurred his irritation. Although he had vowed never to spare Piper another thought, her memory had tormented him the entire day. He had offered her an expensive gift to match her tastes, but he didn't even know why he had yielded to the impulse of buying her the ring. It just reminded him of her and he thought she should have it. The gift had been his way of apologizing for what had happened. But obviously he wasn't good enough for her and neither was the ring. He should have known nothing in Fort Smith suited her. Uppity, fickle little snip that she was!

"Well, it sure as hell won't fit me," Logan growled into her flaming red face.

"Then give it to another of your conquests," she hissed, her green eyes swimming with anger and unshed tears. "I don't need to be reminded of what almost happened between us." Her watery gaze fell to the butts of the two pistols that were strapped on his hips. "Shall I initial the notch on your gun, Logan, or can you remember each one of your victims without being prompted?"

She had just confirmed his darkest suspicions with her snide remark. Piper, regal queen, had teased and tempted him to

118

amuse herself and now she resented the intimacy between them. He was to have been her reckless fling before she stepped back into her own world. Now she was feeling guilty and she wanted to ensure he didn't happen into her town and embarrass her further in front of her sophisticated friends. Well, she needn't have bothered with this melodramatic scene of hers. Logan had no intention of looking her up . . . ever!

"I don't want to remember what happened either, sweetheart." His endearment sounded like a curse and that was exactly how he meant it. "But since our little fling wasn't all that spectacular, I doubt I'll even recall your name by the end of the week."

Oh, how she would love to kick him into splinters! Well, she would forget him twice as fast as he forgot her. Just see if she didn't! "I don't accept frivolous gifts from men, especially from a spendthrift who goes through money as if it were water. If it means nothing to you, then it means even less to me!"

Dammit, wasn't that just like a woman, Logan thought sourly. A man offered a female an expensive token and she hit his head off for spending the money. Women! Who could get along with such illogical, temperamental creatures?

Dammit, wasn't that just like a man, Piper mused resentfully. A man thought he could put a price tag on a woman's affection for him and buy her off with trinkets. Passion meant nothing to Logan because he seduced her with his body but never his heart. Well, if jewels were all he had to offer, she didn't want them. Men! They were absolutely impossible.

Logan's attention swung from Piper's lovely, animated features to the ring that lay in the palm of his hand. Confound it, he had intended for them to part company on tolerable, if not friendly terms. It was sentimental and not at all like him to care one way or another, but he did. After his spitefulness had worn off that afternoon he realized he didn't want to leave Piper on a sour note. He wanted to savor the vision of this lovely nymph. The memories of their time together were twenty-four karat gold, and Logan had tried to purchase a gift of equal value. Although he and Piper had their differences of opinion, she was as close as he could ever hope to come to

119

perfection. It was the only time he had gotten to know a woman other than just in a physical sense. Piper was trying to spoil the sweet memory of their afternoon together. It was wondrous and unique, even if she was ashamed of it.

Quickly, Logan skimmed his fingertips over the lacy neckline of her gown and dropped the ring into a private place that would force Piper to undress if she wanted to retrieve it (which of course she wouldn't). Her outraged gasp died beneath his unexpected kiss which stole her breath from her lungs.

With no warning, Logan pulled her to him, melding his muscled flesh to her soft curves. Piper forgot what she had been so furious about. The feel of his powerful arms and thighs molded familiarly to her set off a chain reaction, one exactly like the helpless sensations that had consumed her that afternoon. She had been on a slow burn most of the evening, not so much from anger but from frustrated desire.

Logan's kiss, one that had begun as a forceful embrace, became a tender possession. The last sediments of her anger were swept away, leaving the raw emotions she had fought so hard to control. The feelings came back, intensifying, creating gigantic new cravings.

Piper instinctively strained against his hard contours, as if she couldn't get close enough to the compelling flame his kiss ignited. Her arms seemed to possess a mind of their own. They glided over his broad shoulders to caress the taut tendons in his neck. She held him to her, absorbing his strength, even when she knew she should be flinging herself away. But it was so difficult to deny herself when she knew this would be their last private moment together.

Logan was long past thinking. He had done so much of it that afternoon he had worked up another throbbing headache. Now his body was responding to innate feelings, wanting Piper again in the wildest ways. His hands mapped her soft flesh, memorizing her luscious shape, fantasizing about how it would feel to love her, really love her in all the rapturous ways that he ached to teach her.

It would be so easy to make love to her. She had again succumbed to the spark of passion that leaped between them, just as she had that afternoon. They started wildfires in each other, despite their differences, despite their similarities. But none of those things seemed to matter when she was in his arms. They were like long lost souls who had rediscovered each other in paradise. Their afternoon together had become a stepping stone that led into the world of forbidden pleasure.

When Piper returned his kisses and caresses with the same ardent impatience, streams of liquid fire bubbled through Logan's veins. Lord, he ached up to his eyebrows with the want of her. But he couldn't send her back to her world, stripped of her innocence, and that was exactly what was going to happen if he didn't regain control of his raging passions. No matter how he tried to make it right in his mind, he knew it was wrong to take advantage of Piper. If he did, she would wind up hating him more than she did now.

It took incredible willpower to step away when his body was instinctively drawn to her. But Logan clamped an iron hand on his primal desires and set Piper to her feet.

Piper wobbled unsteadily before she could maintain her balance without his support. Her lips still tingled and her body sizzled with awakened passion. He was teasing her with his masculinity, giving her pleasure and then quickly snatching it away, leaving her to burn. It humiliated her that she possessed not one iota of self-reserve when it came to this brawny giant. He enfolded her in his arms and her brain malfunctioned. All her self-inspiring sermons were forgotten the moment his sensuous lips slanted across hers. Her body had betrayed her again. She had been instantly and totally aware of him since the moment she walked into his room. She swore she would carry his disturbing image around with her for the rest of her days. She could close her eyes and he would be there taunting her, teasing her, making her want him in ways that no other man could satisfy.

Like a blinking owl, Piper cast enormous green eyes on Logan. The sensuality in her features and the color of her kiss-swollen lips had Logan growling under his breath. Did she have any idea how beautiful and desirable she was? Did she know how difficult it was for a man to keep his hands off her? Jeezus, she was the maddening combination of heaven and hell.

Touching her was heaven and restraining himself from taking what he wanted was worse than suffering the eternal tortures of hell.

Fishing into his pocket, Logan handed Piper a roll of uncounted bills. He didn't care how much money he had given her, only that she had been fully compensated for her missing trust fund. When she tried to protest, he employed the same tactic as before.

After the money was stashed in her bodice, Logan glared stormily at her. "If you want to retreat with the same virtues that you possessed when you entered my room, you'll take the ring and the money and leave," he growled into her enchanting face. "My stage leaves tomorrow at 3:30 in the morning, going west. Yours departs Wednesday afternoon, going east. I won't deny that I want you. I'm a man with a man's needs and you are too damned desirable for your own good. A tumble in bed may appease your curiosity about men and satisfy my hunger for a woman, but it won't change what tomorrow holds."

His breath came out in a frustrated rush. "I don't want to hurt you and that's the God's truth. I don't want you to despise me. For some reason that matters; I don't want to spoil your propriety or your reputation. It's already been damaged enough by cavorting with a man like me. I could easily take from you what you really aren't prepared to give. I think you know that as well as I do, but our passions keep cluttering our thinking." His hands clenched on her forearms. His silver eyes probed into hers with such intensity that she flinched. "I'm not going to leave you the way that bastard father of mine left my mother. Do you understand what I'm saying?"

After Piper had nodded mutely, he released her. Sighing heavily, Logan reached up to push the renegade strands of silver-blond hair from her face. "We came from two entirely different worlds, you and I. I won't tamper with fate. Now get the hell out of here before I start asking myself when I turned into such a damned noble gentleman and decide to take you to bed, no matter what the consequences you might face when I'm gone."

The low growl in his voice caused her feet to retreat toward the door. He looked angry and frustrated and, as always, dangerous. Piper wasn't sure exactly what provoked her fear. It was a combination of things, she supposed. And when Logan spoke in that low, threatening tone, she heard and she believed.

Logan was the kind of man a person didn't cross, especially when he resorted to that rough, rumbling tone. He reminded her of a snarling cougar, poised to pounce. For a long moment, she continued to stare at his ruggedly handsome face, one that looked as if it had been carved from granite. She wanted to debate the issue, to declare that she had no intention of returning home, to confess she was willing to take the risk. But the smoldering fire in his eyes and the unyielding look that was stamped on his commanding features quelled all argument.

Piper was fully aware now that he wanted her as much as she wanted him. Of course, it wasn't the same for him, being a man, but the fierce attraction was there. That was her only consolaiton as she wobbled to her room and sat down before she fell down.

Flouncing down on the bed, Piper absently stroked Abraham's head. What peculiar emotion was eating at her? Why was she so helplessly drawn to Logan that she wanted to sacrifice her innocence, even when she knew he would tire of her as quickly as his passions cooled? What, precisely, was there about him that continued to intrigue her so? Why did she want what she knew she could never have? She had always prided herself in being logical and sensible. But there was nothing logical and sensible about what she felt for that silver-eyed devil. Why, she didn't even know his first name! In fact, she knew very little about his past, his preferences, nothing but sketchy details! So why did she feel compelled to him? It made no sense at all.

Forcing away these thoughts, Piper hugged her pillow. Well, perhaps nothing could ever come of this ill-founded infatuation, but she was not going east. Not even the forceful, overpowering Logan was going to stop her from journeying west. Logan would be on the same stage, or at least riding along beside it. Fleetingly, she wondered if she was determined to travel west because she knew that was the direction Grant had taken or because of that raven-haired demon who had somehow taken possession of her soul.

Well, whatever her reason, she was westbound, even if it was over between her and Logan. He wanted it to be over. He had always resented his desire for her. A stage full of passengers would prevent them from forgetting their vows to put an end to their illogical attraction. It was over, Piper convinced herself. It had to be over. That was the way Logan wanted it and nobody argued with the legendary shootist and won!

PART II

Misses! the tale that I relate
This lesson seems to carry—
Choose not alone the proper mate,
But the proper time to marry.
                    —Cawper

Chapter 9

More than an hour before the stage was to depart, Piper was standing in line behind three men and one other woman. Impatiently she waited her turn at the ticket counter. When the stage agent smiled sympathetically at the woman in front of her, Piper tensed with apprehension.

"Are you traveling alone or with a male companion?" the conductor inquired of the middle-aged woman.

"Alone," the woman responded airily. "My husband is the commander of Fort Lowell in New Mexico Territory."

"Then I'm afraid, I can't sell you a ticket," he told her apologetically. "Mr. Butterfield is concerned about the holdups and Indian raids that have been taking place on the western end of the route to California. Until the disturbances have been quelled he instructed us not to permit female passengers to travel without the consent of their male escorts."

"My husband will be furious when he learns you wouldn't sell me a ticket!" the woman spumed.

The stage agent tried to be civil, but it was difficult when the old hen, dressed in her fine feathers, was squawking at him. "Then perhaps you should write and tell your husband you will need a military escort," he suggested. "Mr. Butterfield made the rules for your safety and I'm obliged to comply with them."

When the woman flounced away, muttering in irritation, Piper gulped. The stage agent peered inquisitively at her, and

Piper forced a faint smile. But when he repeated the same information to her, the smile slid off the corner of her mouth. She found herself staring into the unyielding face of a man who refused to bend the rules for anyone. Piper was faced with a critical decision and she quickly made up her mind what to do. Raising a determined chin, she rattled off her comment, only to see shock register on the stage agent's face.

Slipping quietly into the hall, Logan stared at the door across from his room. Impulsively, he reached up to rap upon it and then had a change of heart. He wasn't sure he wanted to be haunted by sleep-drugged green eyes and a tangled mane of silver blond hair—the tantalizing picture of how Piper would have looked if she had awakened from a night of splendid passion in his arms.

Remembering her appearance the previous evening—her lips swollen from his devouring kiss, her eyes darkening with aroused desire—was enough to torment Logan. No, he wouldn't put himself through that agony again. He had a stage to catch, and the last image he carried from Fort Smith should not and would not be that of Piper Malone. He didn't need to tell her goodbye. He needed to make a hasty exit and forget that saucy minx even existed.

Doing an about-face, Logan moved silently down the hall, trying to put the bewitching blonde from his mind. He had business to attend, an armload of it. If the information he had dragged out of Cactus Jack was accurate, he did indeed have his work cut out for him. Jack hadn't wanted to talk when Logan went to visit him in jail, but he had. Logan had been ruthlessly persistent with his prisoner. The outlaw wouldn't name names, but he had revealed valuable information that would aid Logan in his search for the ringleader of the desperados who were harassing Butterfield's stage line.

It was a damned good thing he had something else to occupy his attention. If not, Logan would have been more frustrated than he already was. Piper Malone had made a strong, lasting impression on him, and even now, he could almost feel the imprint of her soft body on his hard flesh, taste kisses that were as addicting as cherry wine. . . .

Forget her, Logan scolded himself harshly, in thirty minutes he would be seated on the coach, rumbling westward. And in two days Piper would be headed east. Logan purposely hadn't inquired as to which eastern city she called home. He didn't want to know where to find her in case he was assaulted by some ridiculous whim to seek her out after he had concluded his business for Butterfield.

Logan sighed, remembering the long hours he had spent in the coach, dreading the long hours ahead of him. The coach was constructed to hold from six to nine passengers, and the boot in the rear was built to carry the pouches of mail and luggage. It was supported by heavy iron wheels set far enough apart to keep the vehicle from toppling over. The body of the coach was reinforced with iron and swayed on six layers of sturdy leather straps called thoroughbraces, which acted as shock absorbers. But in Logan's estimation, the thorough-braces only took half the discomfort out of the jolts and bumps they rumbled over. Plainly speaking, the ride was still unbelievably rough, and those with weak stomachs were constantly queasy. The cab rocked back and forth like a cradle while it simultaneously bounced up and down over the rough roads.

Logan inwardly groaned at the thought of folding his oversized body into that cramped space for the next two weeks of traveling day and night. Only inclement weather and slick roads were cause for lengthy stops. And there had been times Logan had prayed for a downpour, anything to give him an excuse to climb down from the confining coach.

Four muscular horses, two of which were from his stock, pawed and snorted in anticipation of thundering off down the familiar route. Heavy leather curtains covered the windows to ward off the dust, rain, and cold. Russet leather lined the interior, which was illuminated by candle lamps. The seats were arranged so the backs could be let down to form a makeshift bed that allowed passengers to sleep like sardines in a can when they were finally overcome by exhaustion.

On top of the cab was a seat on which the driver and conductor strapped themselves to prevent being ejected on rough roads. The drivers and conductors worked sixty mile stretches without rest, then climbed down to catch up on lost sleep while a replacement took over the next leg of the journey. To Logan's way of thinking, the drivers and conductors earned every penny of the $150 they were paid monthly. They constantly subjected themselves to bad weather, rough roads, and the threat of road agents.

Still grumbling at the thought of confining himself to the narrow cubicle, Logan entered the office to consult with the stage agents. Most of them usually offered him a fleeting glance and then promptly looked the other way. But that was not the case this time. For some reason, the men smiled cordially and nodded a greeting to him. Logan wasn't accustomed to receiving this kind of attention from anyone and it made him wary.

Logan became even more suspicious when the conductor, who had never offered him anything remotely close to a smile, actually smiled. He strongly disapproved of Logan's profession and reputation and made it a habit of ignoring Logan if at all possible.

"There is no need to bother, Logan," the conductor declared with another smile. "Your wife already purchased her own ticket."

Logan was thunderstruck. "My wife?" he croaked like a sick bullfrog.

"Yes, sir, and may I say she's the prettiest thing I've seen in a long time," he added confidentially. "I didn't know you had gotten married." The conductor outstretched a hand. "I extend my congratulations."

Stormy silver eyes scanned the chairs that lined the walls. Logan glared at the shapely bundle of femininity who sat in an inconspicuous corner. A silk bonnet hid the woman's face. When Piper slowly raised her head to bat her big green eyes at him, Logan swore under his breath. That little liar. All this time she had him thinking she had accepted his advice and had planned to return home. But she had intended to do nothing of the kind. That virago was determined to plant herself on the wrong stage, heading the wrong direction!

Logan gnashed his teeth as Piper lifted her left hand to draw his attention to the emerald and diamonds that encircled her ring finger.

"She is charming, isn't she?" Logan managed to say to the conductor in a pleasant tone. But there was nothing pleasant about the glare he leveled at Piper. If looks could kill, she would have been pushing up daisies.

"To be sure!" the conductor agreed enthusiastically.

Damn that little minx. When he got her alone he was going to shake the stuffing out of her!

"I never would have thought a man like you could have ensnared such a sophisticated . . ." The conductor's face colored noticeably when he realized he had put his private thoughts to tongue. "Er . . . , you've done yourself mighty proud, Mr. Logan."

Mr. Logan? Logan blinked in disbelief. My, he had suddenly acquired an air of respectability—all because the stage agents thought he had married this lovely Eastern bluestocking. Jeezus, didn't that beat all!

When Logan glared at Piper, looking as if he were about to blurt out the truth about her charade, she gracefully rose to her feet. Bridging the space between them, Piper curled her hand around Logan's elbow. "Did you see to your last-minute arrangements, my love?" she purred sweetly. "I feared Abraham and I were going to have to board the stage without you. . . ."

Before Logan could squeeze a word in edgewise, the conductor took the passenger list from the agent and announced their immediate departure. Like a breeze, Piper sailed toward the door and into the coach with Abraham in tow. Logan was left growling like a disturbed lion.

Damn her stubborn hide! She had no business traveling west. She could get herself killed . . . or worse. That defiant sprite had latched onto him for protection since the stage refused to assume the responsibility of unescorted females. No wonder the conductor had allowed her a seat. Who could better protect his supposed bride than the freelance shootist who had been hired to guard the stage?

Hell, everyone in Fort Smith knew why he had come to confer with Butterfield. And that was the very reason Logan

131

demanded that Butterfield disclose nothing about his plans. Gossip was bad enough, but exposing his intentions would spoil his chances of rounding up the thieves who had preyed on the stage line. And what he didn't need was a supposed wife while he went about his duties. On top of all else, the gossips would have a field day with this pretended marriage to that sassy little city slicker. Jeezus!

As Logan pulled himself into the coach, the other passengers sidled sideways to permit him room to sit beside his "wife." Why Logan didn't eject her from her seat, shove her to the ground, and expose her scheme was a question he continued to ponder while they jostled down the street and onto the open road.

Damnation, this wasn't at all what he had intended. He glowered furiously at Piper's sunny smile. She, in turn, reached up to smooth his irascible frown.

"I know you detested rising at such an outrageous hour, my darling, but do try to look more sociable," she cooed up at him. "I don't want the other passengers to think my new husband possesses a surly disposition. Honestly, they will be wondering what redeeming qualities I saw in you that made me want to speak the vows."

Logan's fingers clenched into his knees, which were tangled around each other in the cramped space he occupied. His fuming gaze fell to the tomcat who had crawled from his basket to perch upon his mistress. "Keep that cussed cat on your lap and off of mine," he muttered bitterly.

Piper bit back a snicker. Logan looked comical, all wadded up in a tight ball, glowering mutinously at her and Abraham. Although she wasn't particularly comfortable either, Logan resembled a towel that had been haphazardly thrown in a corner.

"Abraham knows where he is welcome and where he isn't," Piper assured him so sweetly that Logan nearly became nauseated from listening to her sugary tone. "But I will clamp a tight grip on Abraham in case he strays."

"And I will try to display my charming nature," Logan purred back at her. But Piper wasn't fooled for a second. She knew that rumbling resonance in his voice indicated suppressed anger. Leaning close, Logan grazed her cheek and then bit rather than nibbled on her earlobe. "When I get you to myself, you're going to wish you hadn't connived to win yourself a seat on this stage."

"That is no way for a man to speak to his loving wife," she admonished. "One would think you have something against marriage." Piper leaned away before Logan chewed off her ear.

"I have nothing against wedlock," he defended tartly, "as long as it doesn't involve me. Now that it does I—"

The gigantic rut in the washboarded roads caused the coach to bobble like a bouncing ball. Unprepared, Piper went flying. Her head slammed into the top of the coach before she ricocheted against Jedediah Smith's shoulder. The rotund gentleman, who sat directly across from her, expelled a grunt as Piper bounced off him. All that prevented her from landing in his lap was the steely arm that abruptly clamped around her waist. More roughly than necessary, Logan stuffed Piper back into her narrow niche beside him.

While Logan was restraining Piper, Willis Worthington was screeching in pain. Abraham had bared his claws the moment he went flying and they had stuck in Willis's chest. The passenger was still shrieking when Logan leaned out to pluck Abraham up by the back of the neck. With one fluid movement, Logan opened the lid of the basket and shoved Abraham inside while the cat was still yowling at the top of his lungs.

"The next two hundred miles are the worst roads you'll ever have the misfortune of enduring," Logan told Piper with wicked glee. "I hope you suffered no ill effects from yesterday's riding lesson. This jaunt by coach will undoubtedly add to whatever discomfort you have been experiencing." His mocking gaze fell to the basket on her lap. "And keep that crazed cat caged. If he goes flying again he'll have all of us ripped to shreds."

Piper was plenty uncomfortable after her riding lesson and her fall into the briar patch. But she would have died before she confessed that to Logan. Each bump and rut that fell beneath the coach's wheels provided a new test of endurance. Piper did, however, manage to bear the pain without complaining. She would tolerate most anything if it provided the opportunity to pursue Grant Fredricks and her missing inheritance. No cost was too great, Piper assured herself as she squirmed restlessly on the seat.

The scheme that had hatched in her mind the instant before the ticket agent sent her away from the stage depot had sounded ingenious at the time. She had been desperate, and pretending to be Logan's wife seemed to be her only salvation. But Piper didn't have the foggiest notion what was in store for her. The coach ride she had taken to Fort Smith hadn't seemed so grueling as this jaunt through Indian Territory. The paths weaved over and around the valleys and foothills of the timber country near the Winding Stair and San Bois mountains like a snake slithering across rugged terrain. There were scores of creeks, congested with cedars, redbuds, and scrub oaks, to ford and steep slopes with which to contend.

And Logan's assessment of the road conditions was accurate. If the driver had missed a single bump, Piper wouldn't have believed it. Her backside felt like a pin cushion and the bruises she sustained after riding the mare had been bruised again! Although she wiggled and wormed to locate a more comfortable position there was none. But what aggravated her the most was the ornery grin that hovered on Logan's lips when he tipped his Stetson forward to block out the rising sun while he caught a catnap. He had sprawled out, wedging her between him and Samuel Kirby, who sat on her right. Piper was forced to remain as erect as a flagpole, her elbows jammed against her ribs, ones that were already tender from her flying leap into the thorn bush.

The first streaks of sunshine warmed the sky, but the timber was still heavy with dew and swaying shadows. The coach bumped along its winding path, jostling passengers to and fro. Piper still sat like a statue, pressed between two oversized men. Her bones and muscles screamed each time the coach hit a rut, each time she dared to squirm on her seat. Her head ached from the blow she received when she collided with the top of the cab. After that brain-scrambling experience she was beginning to understand why the term *sorehead* had been coined. Any passenger who rode the stage was likely to become one by the time he reached his destination. One would have thought the stage company could have done something to smooth out the craters in these roads!

When Piper bounced up and down like a yo-yo for the umpteenth time, Logan reached over to wedge her shoulder behind his, preventing her from being launched into orbit around the inside of the coach. Bracing himself, he waited until the stage had plowed through the deep rut before grinning over at Piper.

"Enjoying yourself, honey?" he murmured sarcastically. "You had your heart set on coming west." His mischievous smile broadened to display pearly white teeth. "I do hope you are having the time of your life, because this is as good as it gets."

"Surely you exaggerate," Piper grumbled as she readjusted her lopsided bonnet and righted Abraham's tilted basket.

Logan shook his head. "I never exaggerate."

And sure enough he hadn't. The road got worse long before it got better!

Piper had just nodded off when the conductor's bugle sounded to alert the agents at Skullyville of their arrival. The passengers were allowed a ten-minute stop while the fresh relay of horses was hitched to the coach. Logan shuffled Piper out of her seat to stretch her legs, but her appendages had fallen asleep the previous hour and walking was difficult. Clinging to Logan for support, Piper wobbled about like a newborn foal. Her gaze swept the small log cabin station, which was manned by two stubble-faced agents whose cheerfulness was wasted on her. She felt miserable, and she had only regained the circulation in her legs when Logan propelled her back to the coach and folded his brawny body beside her.

Until they arrived at the next station, spaced twelve to fifteen miles apart, like all the others, Piper's head nodded first in one direction and then the other, bringing her awake with a start. Each time her eyes popped open from a moment's sleep, she found Logan smiling at her with that infuriating I-told-you-so grin that he wore so well. But Piper refused to complain. She knew Logan was waiting for her to grumble about her discomfort and the deplorable conditions. She refused to give him the satisfaction of being able to mock her.

After pausing at Brazil Station, the passengers spent another three hours being bounced and flung helter-skelter over the washboarded roads and mud holes. The conductor's bugle sounded again and Piper roused slowly from her short nap, instinctively trying to stretch. Catching herself, she folded her arms primly in front of her and muffled a yawn.

Holloway's, the next station along the route, was referred to as a home station, or so Piper was told. It was a farmhouse that provided a homecooked breakfast for passengers. After clambering from the coach and setting Abraham free to stretch his legs, Piper wobbled inside and sank down at the table. Willis Worthington, one of the fussy passengers, turned up his nose at the prospect of paying a dollar for coffee, eggs, and biscuits. But Piper gobbled her meal without complaint and kindly thanked the man who had prepared it. When she reached into her purse to retrieve her money, Logan frowned disapprovingly.

"My dear wife, now that we are married I will assume your expenses." Just to annoy her, he paid twice the requested amount and then lit his cigar with a two-dollar bill.

"One would think you have a limitless supply of wealth," she muttered as they strolled onto the stoop to gaze at the rolling hills choked with pines, dogwoods, and scrub oaks.

"You don't wish me to spend my money on you or on a decent meal?" he questioned flippantly. "Just what would you have me do with it? If you detest my frivolousness, why did you marry me?"

Piper rolled her eyes and reminded herself that she wasn't going to permit Logan to drag her into an argument. He was enjoying her misery, delighting in taunting her. "You know perfectly well why I had to charade as your wife," she replied airily. "I wanted to be on this stage to track down Grant."

"Ah, but at what costs," he chuckled, grinning devilishly. "I may decide to name a price for the use of my name, *Mrs.*

Logan." His callused hand cupped her chin, raising her exquisite face to his naughty grin. "What if I threaten to tell the conductor you aren't really my wife unless you submit to all your wifely duties . . . each time lust overcomes me."

Logan let the comment hang in the muggy morning air, allowing Piper to draw her own conclusions as to what he expected. Her eyes flashed hot sparks.

"You assured me that I am not woman enough to satisfy the lusting beast within you," she countered.

"I may become less particular now that you are the only available female within three hundred miles."

His remark stung like a wasp. "You can go to hell, Logan," she hissed poisonously.

A goading grin stretched across his sensuous lips as his fingertips sketched her lively features. "If you refuse any of my demands, you could find yourself stranded at one of the two hundred stage stations between here and San Francisco, waiting for me to rid the route of marauding Indians and ruthless road agents. Knowing you were left to bide your time in some out-of-the-way post might cause me to take my own sweet time about solving the problems that face the stage line."

The feel of his hand on her cheek and the intensity of his silver eyes caused Piper to flinch uncomfortably. She had been fighting these unsettling sensations the entire time her body was mashed against his muscular frame in the stage. That, compounded with the uncomfortable ride on bumpy roads, had already worn her nerves to a frazzle. Logan's insinuation didn't help matters.

As much as Piper hated to admit it, she could easily visualize how it would feel to lie beside this swarthy giant, to feel his arms encircling her, to feel his hair-roughened body pressed intimately . . .

The blush that climbed from the base of her throat to the roots of her silver blond hair provoked Logan to chuckle. "I can see by the look on that lovely face that you know exactly what it would be like between us. There was a time when I tried to be noble and keep my distance from you. But you have made yourself fair game by masquerading as my loving wife." His arm stole around her, bringing her full length against him, unchaining the forbidden memories. "I may decide this charade of yours can work to my advantage as well, maybe even better than it will work to yours. . . . My conscience is no longer bothering me, little dove," he whispered against her flushed cheek. From now on, what I want I take. . . ."

"I hear congratulations are in order," the stage agent declared as he strolled onto the porch to interrupt what looked to be an intimate conversation. "I didn't know you had traveled to Fort Smith to get married." His ringing laughter filled the morning air as his roving eyes toured Piper's arresting figure. "And all this time rumors have been flying that your only reason for coming east was to help Butterfield dispose of pestering road agents."

Logan never unfastened his probing gaze from Piper's pulsating face. Nor did he remove the lingering hand that traced her delicate features. Piper trembled beneath his unexpected gentleness and his unblinking gaze, one that still held intimate promises of things to come.

Lord, what had she gotten herself into? Logan was demanding that she compensate him for embroiling him in her scheme. Heavens, he had practically come right out and said he would expect her to become his private whore! This is to be my punishment, she mused dejectedly. He was offering passion without affection. It was to be *his* revenge and *her* torment.

"Even a man with my reputation can succumb to Cupid's arrows," Logan murmured, smiling wryly at Piper.

Touching this lovely pixie set off a series of tingling sensations that Logan no longer had to control, especially since the rest of the world assumed them to be man and wife. And Piper deserved what she was getting, he assured himself. She had permitted herself to become his pawn, and his conscience no longer bade him to keep his distance from her.

Using the situation to his advantage, Logan bent to taste her soft lips, feeling Piper tremble in unwilling response. "It seems this match of beauty and the beast agrees with me."

The agent grinned broadly. "Well, you have certainly done well for yourself, Mr. Logan," he complimented. "Mrs. Logan is a most attractive woman." His all-consuming gaze testified to his approval of this shapely lass in pink silk.

As the agent walked off to check the harnesses for the new team of horses, Logan dropped his hand and turned away. That was the third time that day he had been complimented on his false marriage. It was also the third time that men who rarely acknowledged his presence walked right up to offer congratulations.

Odd, he thought pensively. His "marriage" to this green-eyed goddess had earned him instant respectability—something he had struggled to attain all his life. And if the agents at every stop continued to congratulate him on his recent marriage they would have him believing it. . . .

The sound of a screaming pistol interrupted Logan's thoughts. Instinctively, he reached for his Colt and slammed himself against the outer wall of the cabin. But the shots were not coming at him. Curiously, he craned his neck around the side of the building to locate Piper, who had sailed away the moment the stage agent took his leave.

A stampede of humanity came pouring out of the cabin to determine what had happened. All eyes turned to Logan, who had located the source of the racket and was smiling in quiet amusement. "My wife," he chortled, pointing to the bundle of pink silk who was blowing holes in a tree limb. "After I taught her to shoot she decided to perfect her marksmanship."

"With her looks, I think it's important that she learns to protect herself," the conductor commented, totally absorbed in watching Piper. When he realized his blunder, he colored slightly. "Of course, with a husband of your reputation she probably will have all the protection she needs," he hastily added.

Nodding mutely, Logan strode off the stoop. After having purposely taunted Piper with the possibility of sharing his bed when the opportunity presented itself, Logan speculated that she was envisioning her "husband" as her target. She wouldn't dare antagonize him since she needed his help in her scheme. But she wasn't beneath taking her irritation out on the tree and pretending she had blown her "husband" to smithereens.

Logan had read her thoughts correctly. Piper was indeed filling Logan's image full of bullet holes. She was frustrated and her scapegoat had become a defenseless tree rather than the sap of a husband she had selected for herself.

When the conductor announced their departure, Piper tucked her pistol in her purse and ordered Abraham to climb into his basket. Tossing a pretentious smile to Logan, Piper reseated herself in the coach. It was unnerving to know that her scheme (one that had seemed so ingenious at the time) could so easily backfire in her face. If she didn't play along with Logan he would expose her lie. And if she did submit to him, she suspected she would become another of his conquests. Damn, what a mess she had made of things.

It was different between them now. There was an underlying tension between them, one provoked by her charade. Logan no longer wanted her because he was attracted to her. He wanted her because he knew he could have her. She had placed herself in a vulnerable position and Logan liked that. The situation was a familiar one to him—the lion toying with his prey, playing the waiting game. He was taunting her, biding his time. If and when he seduced her, it would be to prove his point, to end the challenge. Piper would become a slave to his lusts, nothing more.

That depressing thought did nothing to improve Piper's mood. The coach ride was barely tolerable as it was, but the apprehension of wondering what was in store for her wrought havoc on her nerves. She found herself involved in an intimidating cat-and-mouse game, and sooner or later, she knew she was going to be gobbled alive! Logan wouldn't be gentle with her. He would seek to prove his dominance over her. When he deflowered her, it would be all her fault. She should have known Logan would turn the situation to his advantage. He always did.

It was no wonder his talents as a private detective and shootist were known far and wide, she mused disconcertedly. Logan was calculating, methodical, and relentless. No one eluded Logan. Piper should have realized she was dealing with a man she couldn't possibly handle. Now she had become one of his challenges! What could she have been thinking when she planned this charade? She must have taken leave of her senses.

Chapter 10

By the time the coach stopped at Buffalo Station, where they were served their evening meal, Logan had been congratulated more times than he cared to count. Each time a new conductor took charge of the passenger list, Logan was assaulted by another "I didn't know you had gotten married." The barrage of repetitive comments was beginning to annoy him, but it didn't frustrate him half as much as the peculiar feeling of possessiveness that overwhelmed him when Piper nestled into her niche beside him in the coach. Logan found himself yearning to curl his arm around her shoulders and cradle her supple body against him each time she dozed. It aggravated him that the other male passengers ogled her with obvious interest. Piper was supposedly married, and still the three men stared at her, silently picturing themselves in Logan's position.

Damned lechers, Logan thought disgustedly. They gaped at the sultry blonde when they thought he wasn't looking. But he noted their speculative glances and he knew exactly what they were thinking. He saw them thinking the same thoughts that had buzzed through his head since he barreled into Sheriff Potter's office. They have their nerve, Logan mused sourly. Piper was his wife and they were . . .

The thought caused Logan to wince as if he had been stung by a hornet. Jeezus! What was he thinking? Her cunning charade actually had him behaving like a jealous husband. We aren't married and we never will be, Logan told himself stormily. He was merely giving a performance for the other

141

passengers' benefit. If he knew what was good for him, he would remember that it was just an act. He couldn't afford to become emotionally involved with this stubborn beauty. When the opportunity presented itself he was going to send her packing.

"I'm sick to death of these long hours of sitting in confinement and choking down those tasteless meals," Willis Worthington grumbled as he squirmed on the leather seat.

Logan frowned irritably at Willis. The way the man was carrying on one would have thought he had been force-fed boiled rats for supper. Willis's body had been dormant for hours on end, but he had certainly exercised his lips with constant complaints.

Willis's deep-set eyes swung to the oversized young man who sat beside Piper. "Samuel needs proper nourishment. I'm taking him to San Francisco to challenge California's string of professional boxers." A derisive snort burst from his thin lips. "By the time we arrive, Samuel will be ten pounds lighter than he was when we left St. Louis!"

Piper surveyed the muscle-bound young man who looked to be thirty pounds heavier than Logan and a good two inches taller. Curly reddish blond hair capped his wide head and accented his boyish face. His brown eyes held a rather blank look, even though he seemed to be a personable fellow. Although Samuel was long on brawn he was a mite short on brains. He seemed harmless enough and he smiled at her constantly. Piper wasn't certain what she expected of a boxer, but in her estimation, Samuel didn't possess the killer instinct, not like Logan. Samuel reminded her more of a St. Bernard puppy than a professional boxer.

A speculative frown knitted her brow as her gaze turned to Willis. She had noticed the smaller, older man had been fluttering around Samuel like a mother hen. Samuel had permitted Willis to order him around since the moment they departed Fort Smith. Willis had indicated where Samuel was to sit in the coach and where to position himself during meals. She pitied Samuel Kirby. For all his obvious physical strength, he allowed the fast-talking Willis Worthington to do his thinking for him.

Piper had speculated on the association between the two men. Now finally, after two days of close contact in the coach, Willis had revealed that he was Samuel's boxing promoter.

Logan's expression revealed nothing, even though he had his fill of Willis's arrogance and his sour disposition. Willis had the vanity of a peacock and nothing seemed to be good enough for him or his young protégé.

In critical inspection, Logan looked Willis up and down. Willis was pushing forty-five and stood barely five feet four inches tall. His wire-rimmed glasses set on the bridge of his short nose and he was constantly shoving them back in place. A scant smattering of freckles were splattered across his chalky cheeks, and his brown hair jutted from beneath his derby hat like dried up corn shocks. His stylish clothes hung off his thin frame, suggesting he hadn't physically exerted himself to make a living. Willis was a leech who preyed on the talents of others. He was presently promoting Samuel Kirby, but Logan doubted Willis would be loyal enough to stand by the young man if another opportunity arose.

Because the situation demanded it, Logan had tolerated the stuffy Willis Worthington. But Logan was quickly losing his patience with the man. Willis had referred to the previous evening's meal as a "God-awful concoction that would curdle a dog's stomach." When they had dined at Buffalo Station, Willis had stabbed at his biscuits and declared it was humanly impossible to swallow food that looked and tasted like rocks.

The thought of this crotchety old buzzard making his fortune off the seemingly personable young Samuel irritated Logan. Samuel was being used, and Logan was willing to bet Samuel was only being allowed a minimal percentage of the profits. The moment Samuel met his match and buckled in defeat, Willis would cast him aside to promote a new champion. Samuel would be practically penniless. Logan had seen it happen time and time again. The oversized farm boy was being taken for the ride of his life while he matched his meaty fists against every arrogant bully in California.

"Do you enjoy boxing?" Piper questioned, interrupting Logan's cynical thoughts and eliciting another adoring smile from Samuel.

Honestly, Piper mused as she returned the young man's grin, I can't imagine any man allowing himself to become a human punching bag. But then she couldn't explain why Logan risked his life with a gun either. She cringed at the thought of his muscular body riddled with bullet holes. Even though she resented how Logan had backed her into a corner, she didn't want to see him shot down in cold blood. Neither boxing nor gunfighting seemed healthy occupations for these two imposing men. Logan could wind up dead before his time, and Samuel could easily be knocked senseless and live out his life like a vegetable.

Only Jedediah Smith, the jolly merchant from Springfield, Missouri, seemed to have entered a safe occupation. The other men weren't making use of the good sense God graciously gave them. To Piper's way of thinking they were all a bit self-destructive. One would have sworn the brains of the entire male population had been frozen at the age of fourteen. They seemed to be constantly striving to prove their manhood and their domination over women.

When Samuel shrugged his broad shoulders, Piper tucked away her disdainful thoughts and focused on the young man beside her. "It's a living," Samuel responded in a soft voice that didn't seem to fit his gigantic physique. "Willis says we'll make piles of money fighting boxing matches in the gold fields."

After listening to Samuel drawl out several more comments about what Willis thought, Logan rolled his eyes and glanced out the window. Sure as hell, Samuel was allowing Willis to do all his thinking for him. Samuel ought to schedule a boxing match with his trainer and knock the scrawny old bird to his knees. He would be doing himself and the rest of the world a great favor.

"How long have you been married?" Jedediah questioned when the conversation hit a lull.

"Three days . . . a week . . ." Piper and Logan simultaneously contradicted each other.

Glancing sheepishly at the plump old man whose cheeks shone like polished apples, Piper murmured, "My husband is correct. I suppose it has been but three days. But it seems as if

144

we have been cooped up in this coach for at least a week since our wedding."

"This hasn't been an ideal honeymoon," Logan interjected, smiling in wicked amusement. He fully intended to embarrass this ornery minx. She deserved it after she had concocted her little charade. "We have been granted very little privacy and I can think of nothing I would enjoy more. . . ."

All three men cast him knowing smiles, causing Piper's face to turn a deep shade of pink. Discreetly she ground the heel of her shoe in the toe of Logan's moccasin. How he managed to suppress the yelp of pain was beyond her. She had stabbed him a good one!

"I found myself a charming young lady," Jedediah declared as he crossed his thick arms over his even thicker chest. "I was a man of many vices before Kathryn came into my life." He sighed theatrically and chewed on the tip of his unlit corncob pipe. "For months Kathryn pleaded with me to stop smoking this offensive pipe. Now I only nibble at it without stuffing it full of tobacco. Then Kathryn decided I was drinking to excess." His tawny eyes twinkled as he smiled at Piper. "That relentless woman convinced me to sip wine only once a week, if at all, and to avoid whiskey. Then she concentrated her efforts on my frivolous habit of gambling on the horses and draining my pockets at card games. If not for that perseverant woman I wouldn't be the man I am today."

"Did you marry her?" Samuel questioned curiously.

"Oh my, no," Jedediah snickered, his eyes twinkling with amusement. "By the time she finished reforming me I was too good for her."

Logan chuckled quietly at the round little man. His sense of humor was a refreshing change from Willis's constant criticisms. But in the hours that followed, Logan began to wonder if Jedediah's loquaciousness wasn't also a vice. Once the ice had been broken, Jedediah talked incessantly, hopping from politics to economics and then onto a various sundry of topics. The man also snored loudly while he slept, keeping the other passengers awake. And when Jedediah woke he babbled nonstop while the coach rumbled from the timber and brush country onto the rolling plains of Indian territory.

145

Only when the coach halted before fording Clear Boggy Creek did Jedediah draw in the reins on his runaway tongue. The tenseness showed in his chubby face as the horses and coach eased into the swollen stream and precariously rocked like a canoe that was about to capsize.

Piper, who had taken a position beside the door after their last ten minute stop at Atoka, was craning her neck out the window to monitor their progress across the frothy creek. When the coach bumped against the bed of rocks, the cab bounced sideways, causing the door to which she was clinging for support to spring open.

With a startled squawk, Piper found herself swinging out on the open door. Frantically, she stuck out a foot in hopes of anchoring herself to the carriage, but all she accomplished was to paw the air. The second jolt, caused when the coach rammed into another jutting rock in the creek bed, yanked the door from Piper's grasp. In an instant, she was dumped in an unceremonious heap in midstream.

After swallowing half the water in the creek, Piper sputtered to catch her breath. Her flailing arms flapped about her as she struggled to untangle her feet from her saturated skirt. Blinking to see through the mop of wet hair that was plastered against her face, she watched Logan, as calmly as you please, step out to retrieve her.

Humiliated and embarrassed to no end, Piper glared at Logan as if the unfortunate incident was all his fault. "You could have caught hold of me while I was dangling from the door," she hissed furiously.

Nonchalantly, Logan scooped up the dripping bundle of beauty into his arms and forded the stream. "I could have," he agreed, his body shaking in silent laughter. "But you have twice mentioned that you would relish the opportunity of bathing. This might be as close as you come to a bath the next few days."

Piper had her heart set on spouting off a barrage of insulting remarks, but the feel of her body engulfed in Logan's powerful arms sent her thoughts skipping off in a most arousing direction. She could feel the steady thud of his heart against her breasts. The clinging fabric of her bodice dampened his shirt, leaving her with the tantalizing impression that there was little between her bare skin and his.

The sudden intensification of his gaze suggested that Logan was also stung by the same arousing thoughts that had blazed through her betraying body. And indeed he had been. Her wet clothes hugged her shapely form like a second skin, revealing every luscious curve and swell.

For a long, breathless moment, Piper's eyes locked with those disturbing pools of rippling silver. Her imagination ran wild and her heart somersaulted in her chest. Her unblinking gaze fell to the sensuous curve of his lips, lips that could take sweet possession of her mouth and instigate warm, sizzling emotions that bore into the core of her being. The feel of his masculine torso brushing familiarly against hers reminded Piper of the intimate moments they had shared. She recalled, with vivid clarity, the wild flight of her senses that afternoon in Fort Smith when his muscular body had settled familiarly against hers. She remembered the reckless abandon she had experienced, the gnawing ache that demanded fulfillment. . . .

Before she did something crazy—like kiss him in front of their captive audience—Piper glanced the other way. Willfully she gulped down the forbidden knot of desire that clogged her throat. It still baffled her that this man could so easily stir her emotions. One would have thought she had misplaced the good sense she had been born with! Whenever Logan's body made contact with hers, no matter how harmless the gesture might have been, she was left to drip all over him like heated syrup. She meant nothing to him and she knew it. Men like Logan only used women to appease their sexual appetites.

"Are you all right, ma'am?" Samuel inquired as he rushed toward her like a knight on his way to rescue a damsel in distress. "Here, let me carry you. You're white as a sheet."

Before she could accept or reject his chivalrous offer, Piper found herself uplifted into another pair of commanding arms and jostled toward the waiting coach. Logan didn't know what had overcome him when Piper was whisked from his side. He rather liked the oversized farm boy . . . or at least he had until Samuel took the liberty of folding his muscled arms around Piper and making off with her like a dog with a bone.

"She's my wife," Logan heard himself growl ferociously. "If I didn't think she was capable of standing on her own two feet I wouldn't have put her down!"

Samuel's head swiveled on his wide neck to stare at Logan's thunderous scowl. "I was only trying to help," he insisted.

"Put her down before you strain something," Willis chimed in. Since that possibility was laughable, considering Samuel's size and stature, Willis felt compelled to add, "Heaven knows you must be weak after surviving on skimpy meals that are hardly fit for human consumption."

Although Samuel obediently obeyed his trainer, his brown eyes were full of gentlemanly concern for the saturated beauty. "You took an awful spill, Mrs. Logan," he said as he cautiously set her down. "Begging your pardon, but I feared you might up and faint on us."

"The name is Piper," she corrected with a wet smile. "And I appreciate your concern. I am more embarrassed than injured after my unexpected bath." With as much dignity as she could muster, Piper shoved the renegade strands of hair away from her face and then readjusted her soggy gown. "As my husband pointed out, I have been waiting for the chance to bathe. That was not the method I would have chosen, but I suppose I have satisfied the need in a roundabout way. . . ."

To Piper's astonishment, Logan pushed his way in front of her like a shield. And even more abruptly, he clamped a hand on her waist and elbow and swung her into the coach. Suggesting the other passengers squeeze onto the seat across from them so they wouldn't become as wet as husband and wife, Logan parked himself beside Piper.

It was comical to see Willis wedged between Samuel's broad shoulders and Jedediah's rotund form. The small man looked extremely uncomfortable, and Logan relished the sight. Unfortunately, the ride to Boggy Depot was relatively short. Logan would have preferred that Willis spend agonizing hours crammed in his small space. Then he truly would have something to complain about.

When the coach rolled to a halt to change horses, Logan tugged Piper's soggy body into his arms and retrieved their luggage. A wry smile pursed his lips as he aimed Piper toward the small cubicle located in the back of the store.

Piper cast the grinning rake an apprehensive glance as he kicked the door shut with his heel and began peeling off his damp shirt. "I can wait outside while you change," she offered.

One thick brow slid to a mocking angle. "And have the other passengers wondering why a married couple wouldn't relish this moment of privacy? No, my lovely wife," he cooed in taunt. "We don't want our friends gossiping about us more than they already are."

Her eyes traveled over the broad expanse of his chest, following the dark furring of hair that dived into the band of his breeches. When Logan unfastened his trousers, Piper gasped at the possibility of seeing him strip naked before her eyes. Like a spinning top, she twirled around to stare at the shelves of supplies that lined the walls.

"You derive perverted pleasure in humiliating me, don't you?" she sputtered furiously.

Logan surveyed her back, as rigid as a fence post. Leisurely, he shucked his breeches and grabbed a dry pair from his satchel. "You have it coming, sweetheart," he teased mercilessly. "You're the one who declared we were married. I warned you this masquerade would backfire in your face." A low chuckle reverberated in his massive chest. "I think perhaps this is what is referred to as *paying the piper*, Piper."

She found no amusement in his pun. Indeed, she found it necessary to count to ten to control her seething temper. When she was sure Logan had had ample time to fasten himself into his breeches, Piper pivoted to glower at his smug smile. "If you had one shred of decency, you would have allowed me to remain outside until you were dressed."

Her attempt to insult him failed miserably. Logan buttoned his gaping shirt, grinning all the while. "I drained the last of my noble decency in Fort Smith. Now strip off that wet dress," he ordered her.

Piper's chin elevated to a proud angle. "I will not! Not until you leave and it's safe."

One thick brow lifted as his eyes slid over her heaving breasts. "Are you implying that I'm dangerous?" he queried, distracted by his visual explorations.

"Extremely," Piper declared, "and I will not change with you in here!"

Like a tiger stalking his prey, Logan approached her. His silver eyes locked with flashing green. "Did you perchance take time to survey this quaint community here at Boggy Depot?" he questioned. "Envision yourself wintering here. It may take me months to corral this band of outlaws who are antagonizing the stage." An utterly roguish grin carved deep lines in his craggy features. "Take 'em off, sweetheart, or prepare to spend the rest of the year here. . . ."

Piper's answering glare was meant to maim and mutilate. Logan spun on his heels and strode toward the door. "Fine, have it your way. I'll notify the conductor of your lie and he'll scratch your name off the passenger list without paying you a refund. . . ."

As he reached for the doorknob, Piper expelled an exasperated breath. "All right, dammit," she grumbled bitterly.

Logan pivoted to prop himself against the door. His astute gaze flooded over her clinging gown, eagerly waiting for her to remove it. Raising her chin in defiance, Piper reached behind her back to struggle with the lacings. Oh, how she would love to clench her fingers around his ornery neck and shake him until his teeth fell out!

It wasn't the first time Logan had seen Piper partially naked. But at the time, she had been so overcome with passion that her modesty had fallen by the wayside. Having Logan undress her and doing it herself while he stood there watching her like a hungry shark were two different matters entirely. As Piper tugged the gown to her waist, exposing the chemise that stuck to her as if it were stitched to her skin, her face turned every color of sunset. She suffered through Logan's hawkish stare with mortified indignation.

When she was wearing no more than her wet chemise and petticoats, her lashes fluttered up to meet his shimmering silver eyes. The laughter had evaporated and he was staring at her with an undecipherable expression. For a moment, Piper thought he looked a mite angry. Why? She couldn't imagine since she was the brunt of his joke. He knew full well what a

150

strain he was putting on her modesty. He was forcing her to strip naked in front of him, to unveil herself for no other reason than to humiliate her.

Piper was learning more about her character with each passing day. Logan had put her to one test after another. She knew he was waiting for her to burst into embarrassed sobs like the weak, emotional creature he assumed her to be. And if she did, he would use her vulnerability and cowardice against her. Logan preyed on people's weaknesses. He was constantly probing to seek them out. He was a master at breaking men down, infuriating them until they became impatient and careless. That was why he was the best there was in his profession. His reputation as a shootist was only part of what made him a living legend. But little by little, Piper was beginning to understand what made Logan tick. She could now analyze his motivations. Piper was learning to react in an unexpected manner that caught him off stride.

Deliberately, she pushed the strap of her chemise from her shoulder, allowing the garment to rest temptingly against her barely clad breasts. "I had imagined myself disrobing one day in front of my husband . . . the man I loved above all else," she added for dramatic effect. "I presumed my deep affection for him would smother all modesty, that I would welcome his eyes on me. I had hoped that he would cherish this gesture of my love for him, that he would understand that I was sacrificing not only my modesty but all else to him. I had wished this moment to lead to the precious baring of hearts and bodies and souls." Her lips quivered slightly as she forced a tremulous smile. "It was to have been a symbolic moment that I had eagerly awaited. I would have wanted to come to him, hoping to please him, wanting his visual caresses, his touch. But now I will have nothing to give him that no other man has—"

Logan turned abruptly and flung a few of the colorful expletives in his vocabulary in the direction of the door. Her well-aimed remarks stung his conscience. He had integrity, even if most folks didn't expect a man of his profession to possess any. He wasn't bloodthirsty, trigger-happy, and ruthless unless the situation left him no other alternative.

He had never taken a job until he had studied all the facts.

He considered himself an extension of pioneer justice, not a mercenary who would dispose of anyone if the price was right. And it was that same sense of honor that spun his body around even as his eyes hungered to devour every inch of Piper's exposed body. Jeezus, she was gorgeous, and he could have received an eyeful if Piper hadn't forced him to be so noble.

Although Logan was staring directly at the door, in his mind he could still see the wet fabric clinging to the luscious mounds and the taut peaks of her breasts. He could picture the tiny indention of her waist, one that he could easily encircle with his hands. He had calculated the measurement of her curvaceous hips beneath the petticoats that wrapped themselves around her petite form. In another instant, Piper would have unveiled her naked beauty to him, not willingly but she would have nonetheless, just to protect her charade. He could have ogled that which dreams were made of. He could have rediscovered her silky skin, the same exquisite skin he had dared to caress that day in Fort Smith.

The rustle of clothing behind him caused Logan to grumble under his breath. Piper would be standing naked now. He could be memorizing every shapely curve and swell. But he wasn't, dammit! Piper's carefully chosen comments had forced him to behave like a gentleman, even when he had no aspirations of being one. He had allowed her to disrobe without embarrassing her. Why? Damned if Logan knew. He had purposely backed this saucy sprite into a corner and now he had graciously allowed her to escape. She really didn't deserve the courtesy, he reminded himself sourly. She should be stewing in her own juice after she pretended to be his loving wife. He should be entitled to a few privileges, blast it! This should have been one of them.

When Logan felt Piper's arms slide around his waist from behind, he flinched as if he had been stabbed in the back. He could feel her cheek resting against his shoulder blade, her breasts mashing into his spine.

"Thank you for sparing me, Logan," she murmured, giving him a grateful hug. "I shall always be indebted to you. And somehow I will repay you for forcing you to play this masquerade. You truly are a decent man."

"Don't tell my enemies that," Logan scowled disgustedly.

"It is enough that I know it," she whispered.

As she slipped out the door with her wet clothes clutched in her hand, Logan inhaled a shuddering breath and then swore a blue streak. He had seen the gloating smile that curved her lips upward as she sailed away unscathed. Confound it, he had been *had!* Piper had outfoxed him with feminine finesse.

That quick-witted imp had maneuvered him with her well-aimed remarks. She had allowed him to think it was his idea to grant her a moment's privacy. But in truth she was the one who planted the notion in his head with her touching soliloquy.

Dealing with a woman like Piper was a new experience for Logan. Most people were afraid of him, afraid to make visual contact for fear he would drop them in their tracks for looking at him the wrong way. They were always cautious about what they said, afraid they might accidentally offend him. But Piper was the exception to those rules. She would just as soon offend him as not. And she was not beneath manipulating him if she thought she could get away with it (which she just had, damn her).

No one crossed Logan except other gunslingers who were eager to match their talents with a pistol against his. And then, of course, there was this blond-haired pixie. She challenged Logan in her own unique way. She turned those enormous green eyes on him and probed into the depths of his soul. He had spouted orders at her on several occasions and she permitted him to rant and rave. When he was quite finished, she proceeded to do as she damned well pleased, *because* of him or in *spite* of him.

Logan suddenly realized he had never been able to control Piper in ways that really mattered. She let him think he won all their arguments while she savored her silent victories. Despite his overpowering strength and legendary reputation, Piper ultimately got what she wanted—his assistance in her crusade to retrieve her missing inheritance.

His breath came out in a frustrated rush. Well, that vixen was right about one thing, he mused. She was damned well going to repay him one day. And when that time came he was going to be the one to decide on the type of compensation that would appease him. He let her off the hook this time, but next time he wouldn't be so lenient with her. And he wasn't going to let her manipulate him again either!

This last encounter, compounded with a dozen others, left him wanting that gorgeous goddess in the worst way. Each time Logan stared at her in the future he would remember how she looked standing there in her unmentionables. He would recall the way the damp fabric hugged her well-sculpted physique. And those arousing thoughts would remind him of that day in the meadow when he had come so close to satisfying this maddening craving to possess her.

Each confrontation between them was like tossing another log in the hearth of desire. The tension between them fairly crackled. One day he would become immune to her evasive techniques of tapping at his conscience. Nothing she could say would dissuade him from appeasing this gnawing hunger, from taking possession of that luscious body of hers.

The trouble was that he was far too aware of Piper Logan. . . . He scowled sourly. Piper *Malone,* he quickly amended as he stomped out of the storage room.

As Logan stalked through the store the proprietor smiled kindly at him. Yes, by God, he smiled instead of glancing the other way as he had a habit of doing. Again Logan heard the same comments.

"Congratulations, Mr. Logan. I didn't know you had gotten married. Your new wife is lovely."

His questionable reputation was no longer as newsworthy as the topic of his wedding to that breathtaking and highly resourceful young minx known as Piper . . . Malone . . . Logan. Mumbling a thank you, Logan pulled out a two-dollar bill and lit his cheroot from the globe of the lantern. He wasn't sure if he performed the gesture out of habit or in symbolic defiance—as if he were silently assuring himself that Piper held no influence over him.

Holding true to form, Piper snatched the bill from his fingertips and stamped out the fire. With a condescending glare, she tucked the singed bill in her purse and breezed out the door. When she had rounded up Abraham she eagerly accepted Samuel's assistance in boarding the waiting coach.

Logan growled as he watched Samuel fold his thick fingers around Piper's trim waist. He didn't know why it irritated him that the gallant farm boy was fussing over Piper, but it did. Logan wanted to strangle both of them.

As he crawled into his corner, Logan leaned close to Piper. It may have appeared that he was whispering sweet nothings in her ear, but he was actually breathing down her neck. "You needn't feel so smug, my dear wife," he cautioned her. "Don't think I don't know I've been *had*. The technique worked once but it will not work twice. And when the time comes, nothing is going to save you from me. When I take you, you will be the one who has been *had*. . . ."

Piper managed a smile for the benefit of the other passengers, but on the inside she was trembling. Logan's hushed tone held a quiet warning. Her evasive tactics had saved her this time, but it seemed she had done more to challenge him than to discourage him. One would think she would have learned her lesson by now. There was no such thing as winning against this silver-eyed demon. Ultimately, he would have his way with her, just to prove he could. And she could anticipate no gentleness from him. Piper feared he would resort to savagery just to frighten her, to ensure that she found no enjoyment in his powerful arms. That was to be her punishment for manipulating him once too often. If he didn't stop eyeing her as if he were the rat and she were the cheese, she was going to sic Abraham on him! Dammit, this waiting game was playing havoc with her emotions. She might as well lie down and let him take what he wanted. Logan would take possession one time or another. She couldn't fight him. She was only prolonging the inevitable.

Frustrated, Piper heaved a sigh. She was so tired of riding, so weary of battling this mental tug-of-war with Logan. He was accustomed to the hunt, accustomed to biding his time before he struck. He had been hunting down better men than she for years. Did she honestly think she had a prayer against such a man as this? Piper swore she should have had her head examined for placing herself within Logan's reach. She would never gain his respect or his affection. He wanted her body, just to say he had had it. He would be rough and forceful, proving his male domination. That was what motivated him when he insisted she would pay for her scheming.

That depressing thought nagged at her mind as she stared out the window, seeing nothing, hearing only the haunting voice that echoed in her ears. She might recover her inheritance from that swindling Grant Fredricks, but she would lose her innocence to a man who saw her as nothing but another of the many challenges he had faced in his lifetime. Logan would see to it that she regretted coming west. Indeed, it seemed his goal was to make her sorry she had ever been born!

Chapter 11

As the stage tumbled along the fifty-mile stretch of rough road between Boggy Depot and Colbert's Ferry, which provided the crossing of the Red River into Texas, exhaustion overcame Piper, but each time she tried to sleep she was rudely awakened by Jedediah's loud snoring, the conductor's bugle, or the grumbling thunder that echoed overhead. Groggily, Piper glanced out the window to study the looming gray clouds that blotted out the late afternoon sun. The hours she had gone without sleep wore on her disposition. She contemplated smashing the conductor's infuriating bugle and stuffing a gag in Jedediah's mouth to muffle his snoring. Jedediah was the only passenger who had managed to catch a nap; the rest of them were totally exhausted.

Even Abraham had become surly after endless hours of confinement in his basket. The one time he had escaped to inhale a breath of fresh air he had very nearly lost his head—literally. His route to freedom had landed him in Logan's lap. Abraham was quickly learning that that was not a good place to be. When his claws sank in Logan's crotch, the tomcat found himself yanked up by the neck and roughly thrust into his basket. And Logan held a grudge. Each time the coach skidded to a halt and Piper allowed Abraham to crawl from his basket, Logan purposely kicked the pesky cat out of his way.

When gigantic raindrops pelted the canvas cab, Piper heaved a weary but constricted sigh. There wasn't room to inhale deep breaths when she was squashed between Logan's

157

muscular body and Willis Worthington's bony one. The dampness in the air settled about her like a wet cape, causing her to shiver uncontrollably. The driving rain formed rivers on the low-lying flatland and turned the roads slicker than ice.

The coach stalled in the mud and then lurched forward as the team of horses found firm footing. Whenever they skidded on the slippery road, the coach careened sideways. Piper's neck had suffered so many instances of whiplash that she swore it had turned to rubber. Her throat had been stretched out like a giraffe's, and she was already having difficulty holding up her head from lack of sleep.

Aware of her discomfort, even if Piper hadn't voiced a complaint, Logan wrapped his arm around her, drawing her body against his. Gently he pressed her cheek to his chest. Piper didn't know why a man who had been so antagonistic was suddenly being nice to her, but she welcomed the chance to lean on him.

Like a kitten cuddling up to a cozy hearth, Piper expelled an exhausted sigh and closed her eyes. The scent of the man who held her protectively against him—the feel of his muscular strength beside her—lured her into dreams. It had been impossible to sleep more than a few minutes at a time for the past few days. But when she snuggled against Logan she was asleep in a matter of seconds. She had never considered this brawny giant the kind of man who would make a comfortable pillow, but when she fitted herself against him, she could think of nothing more luxurious than sleeping in his arms. He was like a toasty blanket she could cuddle into. Even a feather bed couldn't have provided such protective comfort.

Logan's gesture of compassion and courtesy brought a quiet sense of satisfaction—something he hadn't anticipated. The feel of Piper's soft body nestled against his worked like a sedative for him as well as for her. Her arm was flung across his lap and her head was tucked in the crook of his arm. Despite the pounding rain and lurching motion of the coach, Logan drifted off to sleep, cradling Piper against him as he would have a pillow. Never could he remember such blissful sleep. Usually he slept with one eye open and one ear tuned to the sound of danger. But this late afternoon nap was the exception to the rule. He didn't rouse when Jedediah broke into another chorus of snoring that kept Samuel and Willis from nodding off. Logan merely snuggled against the soft cushion of Piper's body, rested his chin against the top of her head, and slept like a baby.

The bugle that announced their arrival at Colbert's Ferry abruptly awakened Piper and Logan. When Piper realized her hand was resting on Logan's lap, she jerked it away as if she had been stung. A becoming blush stained her cheeks, and she peeked up at Logan through a veil of thick, curly lashes. He was smiling slyly at her. But then that was nothing unusual, Piper reminded herself as she pushed into an upright position. Every time he glanced at her it was as if he had read her thoughts and was amused by them. He resembled a cunning cat who had feasted on a canary. Even Abraham never looked quite as smug as Logan. Abraham should have, being of the feline persuasion.

"You're enjoying this, aren't you?" Piper grumbled softly.

A mock innocent grin claimed Logan's bronzed features. "What is it you think I'm enjoying . . . and at your expense, no doubt?"

"You delight in reading my thoughts and wreaking havoc on my emotions," she muttered resentfully. "I cannot even enjoy a nap without you trying to make something of it."

For the sake of argument, one that would have been overheard by the other passengers, Logan shrugged noncommittally. Seemingly distracted, he drew back the leather curtains to stare at the rain and darkness. The coach was making slow progress on roads that were thick with mud.

A wry smile quirked his full lips as he listened to Willis gripe about the chill of the rain, their turtlelike progress, and any other grievance that came to mind. What a sourpuss Willis was, Logan mused. The little pipsqueak was a public nuisance who made an intolerable situation impossible. Logan was about to suggest that Willis get out and walk to Colbert's Ferry, but he finally piped down and pulled his derby hat down on his forehead and dozed.

When the stage finally slid to a halt at the stage station,

Samuel climbed down to assist Piper from the cab. His outstretched arms fell to his sides the moment Logan poked his head outside and flung him a warning glare.

"I'm perfectly capable of caring for my wife," Logan told Samuel in no uncertain terms.

A boyish smile, one that twitched with a hint of guilt, captured his face as he slowly backed out of the way. "I'm sorry. But Piper is the prettiest woman I've ever seen," he confessed to Logan. "I like her. I like helping her every chance I get."

"You and the rest of the male population," Logan grunted irritably before he pivoted to lift Piper into his arms and make a mad dash through the rain.

When Piper was set to her feet she straightened her tangled green gown and willed her heart to slow its accelerated pace. It puzzled her that Logan's touch continued to provoke these illogical reactions within her, even when she was annoyed with him. How could she deal with Logan if the most harmless physical contact caused mental imbalance? She couldn't think straight when he was so close. And with a man as devastating as Logan, it was most important that a woman keep her wits about her.

Concentrating on her ultimate purpose, Piper removed Abraham from his basket and aimed herself toward the stage agent. Without ado, she inquired about Grant Fredricks, just as she did at every stop. The agent recalled the man she described, the one who clung to his satchel as if it were glued to his fingers. Piper knew exactly why Grant was clinging to his carpetbag. He was toting her inheritance, and he would never permit it out of his sight. The lout . . .

The conductor's announcement brought Piper around with a start. "We're going to have to spend the night here," he informed the weary passengers. "The poor road conditions slowed us down all afternoon. It will be difficult enough to ford the river when it's swollen with rain, but it would be even more dangerous to attempt the crossing at night." An apologetic smile pursed his lips. "We are sorry about the delay, but Mr. Butterfield's chief concern is for your safety. He would prefer us to fall behind schedule than to endanger your lives."

Spend the night? Piper gulped apprehensively. Logan had already made it clear what he expected from her when they were allowed privacy. "Wifely duties," he had referred to them. Piper inhaled a steadying breath and fought down the blush of embarrassment provoked by the conductor's wink, one directed at Logan, who was leisurely lounging against the wall, monitoring her reaction.

Piper promptly glanced the other way, refusing to acknowledge Logan's gloating grin. There had been a time when she had nearly surrendered to the physical attraction between them. But there was conflict between them now. Piper knew she was the time Logan was killing before he assumed his job for Butterfield. She didn't mean anything to him. She was just a warm body that would appease his lusts. Any woman would have served his purpose. Unfortunately she was the only woman around and she had made herself all too available by charading as his wife. Blast it, she should have considered the dangers of announcing she was Logan's wife. It was the gravest mistake of her life!

"Mr. Logan and his wife can use the bedroom. The rest of us can make pallets in here on the floor," the conductor suggested.

The stage agent wheeled around to stare at Logan. Usually he ignored the notorious gunslinger, but the news caught him off balance. "I didn't know you had gotten married," he interjected.

Logan swore if he was subjected to that monotonous remark one more time he was going to draw his pistol and blow the place to smithereens. Unless of course he was allowed to enjoy the more intimate privileges of his supposed wedlock . . . And by damned, tonight he would be fully compensated for pretending to be this gorgeous minx's husband. When he had satisfied himself with this elusive sprite he could portray his role as the groom without feeling quite so frustrated. It was time Piper paid her dues. And judging by the expression on her exquisite face she was already scheming to avoid sharing his bed.

Well, he wasn't going to back away this time. He wanted Piper and there was no reason why he shouldn't have her. She intrigued him because he had yet to destroy the aura of mystique surrounding her. She knew the hazards of this trip and the complications that could arise from her charade. Logan had told her to go back home where she belonged. She had been warned, and now she was going to face the consequences of her defiance.

She couldn't remain a virgin in this wild country anyway, Logan rationalized, not with her compelling beauty and charming personality. Men buzzed around her like flies trailing sugar. If she were to find herself in some lusty man's arms after they parted company, she might as well know what to expect from him. And who better to teach her the facts of life than her supposed husband? The thought caused Logan to grin devilishly.

In order to expend the nervous energy that boiled inside her, Piper eagerly offered to assist with the evening meal. She had never prepared slumgullion, but she listened carefully while the agent rattled off the ingredients. After tasting the bland concoction he had brewed on the stove, Piper rummaged through the cabinet to retrieve spices and then added her own special touch to the recipe. While the main dish stewed on the stove, Piper rolled out the biscuits and popped them in the oven.

Her efforts caused a look of surprise to register on Logan's face. He ambled over to peer over her shoulder while she put the finishing touches on the meal she had prepared for the passel of men who had plopped down at the table to share a bottle of whiskey.

"I didn't know you were so handy around the kitchen," he remarked.

Piper didn't dare look at Logan. He would detect her nervousness at a glance. If he hadn't already. "My parents managed a hotel and restaurant in Chicago," she informed him as she lifted the lid to stir the slumgullion. "My mother was an excellent cook who drew hundreds of hungry customers. I suppose some of her culinary talents must have rubbed off on me."

"You worked . . . in the kitchen?" Logan chirped in disbelief.

162

The astonishment in his voice provoked a fair amount of irritation. Just enough to curb her nervousness and ignite her temper. Raising a proud chin she wheeled about to glare up into his ruggedly handsome face. "I will have you know I have not spent my entire life embroidering on tablecloths and handkerchiefs," she bit off. "There are a few things I can do and do very well. My knowledge is not restricted to the books I labored over at boarding school. Honestly, the way you're behaving one would think you consider yourself the only individual in the world with any talent."

A naughty grin dangled from the corner of his sensuous mouth. Logan grabbed her wrist to sample the slumgullion that clung to her wooden spoon, one that she was brandishing in his face. After nodding approvingly, he rinsed the spoon in the basin of water and handed it back to her. "Later, when we're alone, you can show me what other talents you possess, *Mrs. Logan.*" He bent to breathe against the side of her neck, causing a skein of goose bumps to fly across her skin. "I hope you can make love as well as you cook. . . ."

Piper dropped her wooden spoon. Her face was instantly aflame. Flustered, she fumbled to retrieve the cooking utensil. When she tried to lift the lid on the boiling potatoes it also toppled from her shaky hand and crashed to the floor.

Grinning in wicked amusement, Logan squatted down to scoop up the lid. "Nervous, my lovely wife?" he taunted. "You needn't be. I'll teach you the finer techniques of lovemaking and then you can teach me how you prefer to be kissed and caressed. We'll see if you prefer to be loved gently or with hungry impatience. Our night together will provide plenty of opportunity to experiment with the various methods of lovemaking. . . ."

Nonplussed, her mouth opened and closed like the damper on a chimney. Logan didn't think her enchanting face could turn a deeper shade of red, but it did. For once she was too rattled to counter with one of those guilt-provoking comments that subtly forced him to behave like a gentleman. Well, he had been an honorable gentleman once too often where Piper was concerned. She wasn't going to prey on his conscience tonight! They were going to be as close as two people could get, and he was going to appease this monstrous craving that had tormented him since the day he stalked into Sheriff Potter's office to see this lovely angel staring at him with those innocent green eyes.

Once Logan satisfied this unreasonable need to possess her, he would let her alone. Once he had made wild, sweet love to her the fascination she held would ebb. It always had in the past. He had always gone through women like a man thumbing through a file cabinet. Soon she would become another of his conquests and he wouldn't care where Piper turned her charms after that. Hell, she could even draw muscle-bound Samuel Kirby beneath her spell and Logan wouldn't give a whit. The poor farm boy would leap at the chance to become Piper's knight in shining armor. . . .

Logan didn't know why that thought disturbed him, but it did. Disgruntled by the unexplained feeling of jealousy that suddenly overcame him, Logan retrieved a two-dollar bill and bent to light his cigarillo in his customary manner. Piper reacted as she always did when Logan burned money. She grabbed the flaming bill and drowned it in the basin of water.

"It's time you stopped smoking those disgusting things. It is an offensive habit and I don't approve of it," she ground out. Her eyes darted to the table of men who were downing whiskey as if they had been stranded on a desert without an ounce of liquid to quench their thirsts. "And I don't approve of drinking either."

Logan eyed his unlit cigar and then fixed his smoldering silver gaze on Piper's defiant expression. "Are you trying to portray Kathryn, the stoic female who turned Jedediah's life around? Well, it won't work, honey," he told her point-blank. "I can give up smoking and drinking and gambling for one night of pleasure in your arms. And don't think I'll consider myself too good for you after you have relieved me of my vices."

A sly smile tugged at his lips as he loomed over her. Piper was overwhelmed by the urge to wipe the mischievous expression all over his craggy features. The fact that he loomed so well infuriated her to no end. She detested being swallowed by his intimidating size and stature. He towered over her like a stone mountain, casting a long shadow. She would have given most anything for a step ladder so she could stand face-to-face and give him the evil eye.

"You know what I want from you, Piper," he told her quietly. His consuming gaze toured the luscious landscape of her body, courting her with intimate promises. The impact of raw masculine power caused her to flinch involuntarily. "I want you in my bed. I can't remember wanting a woman quite as much as I've wanted you since I first laid eyes on you." His forefinger traced her quivering lips. "And I don't recall being quite so patient with any other female."

If that was supposed to be a compliment Piper wasn't flattered. In fact, she was downright furious—not so much with Logan but with herself. The subject of conversation stirred sensations he had evoked from her each time he dared to touch her. Those probing silver eyes penetrated her flesh to unlock the forbidden emotions she had tucked into the secret place deep inside her. She didn't want to want him, not in the intimate ways he suggested. He probably changed women like most men changed shirts. Sex was second nature to him. She would be the one hurt by this one-night affair, not Logan. Never Logan. His kind always walked away untouched. He wanted only brief, shallow affairs. To him, women were playthings who satisfied his male needs. He would make love to her with his body but not with his heart. And once she had become another notch on his bed post, he would no longer consider her a challenge but rather another conquest.

Well, she couldn't walk in and out of affairs the way he could. If he didn't mean something to her (which of course he didn't) she couldn't live with herself if she surrendered to passion. And if he did mean something she couldn't live with that either! Blast it, he was trying to force her into a compromising situation, and Piper refused to compromise. She had to devise a way to reject his advances without irritating him. She had to let him think it was his idea not to touch her. Only then would she be safe from his threats. She knew she didn't have the strength to fight him physically. And if push came to shove, he would become rough and abusive and spiteful. Surely there had to be a way to discourage him without offending him. . . .

His hand curled beneath her chin as he watched the thoughts chase each other across her bewitching face. "You don't think I intend to force myself on you, do you, naive little imp?" he queried softly. "If I did, you would enjoy the ultimate victory." His eyes dipped to sketch her sensuous lips, his gaze so potent that Piper swore she had been soundly kissed. "You will come to me without a fight, just as you did that day in the meadow. It will be the same between us . . . only better. . . . The waiting and wondering will finally be over. . . ."

His monumental arrogance stoked the fires of her temper. "Hell would sooner drip icicles," she hissed furiously. "If you think I will behave like one of your eager whores you had better think again. . . ."

"How long does it take to prepare that garbage the stage line calls a meal?" Willis grumbled crabbily. "My boy Samuel needs his nourishment, even if it isn't appetizing."

Suddenly Piper was back to cursing all men everywhere. They were such infuriating creatures—always wanting something from a woman. Logan haughtily supposed she would melt beneath him just because he possessed dark, mysterious charm. And Willis presumed that meals prepared themselves and then flew from the stove to his plate. Well, they could all sit there and starve for all she cared! Damn them all.

Piper stamped toward the bedroom, intent on locking herself in, but Logan snagged her arm when she buzzed by, madder than a hornet. His eyes were no longer dancing with seduction or teasing amusement. They were as cold and unyielding as granite. The pressure of his lean fingers increased, assuring Piper that he could crush her bones if that was his want.

She peered up into his chiseled face, seeing the man who struck fear in his challengers and his victims. There was not an ounce of warmth or compassion in his stony expression. The man she had come to know, the one who aroused her in reckless moments, had evaporated from sight. Logan looked blatantly dangerous from the top of his raven head to the toes of his knee-high moccasins.

"Put the meal on the table," he ordered in a quiet but foreboding voice. "I'll deal with Willis in due time and in my own way. Throwing a tantrum won't faze him. Don't lower yourself to his disgusting level."

"But it's perfectly all right for me to lower myself to yours?" she scoffed bitterly. "You expect me to play your convenient harlot? Because I'm just a woman, do you also expect me to spread myself beneath the rest of these men when you have appeased your voracious male appetite?"

Confound her! Logan had employed his unnerving glare on dozens of men on countless occasions. It was his trademark—a glittering silver glare that pierced flesh. The results had always been the same. He had never been on the receiving end of any backtalk when his competition knew he meant business. But this city slicker, this mere wisp of a woman, pushed and pulled on his emotions, stretching his well-trained temper until it was on the verge of snapping. Jeezus, didn't she know what he could do to her if she thoroughly angered him? He could make mincemeat of her in a matter of seconds!

"Fix the blessed meal," he growled into her rebellious face. His blistering tone squelched all argument, and the bone-crushing grasp on her elbow increased until she grimaced in pain. "If you don't do what I tell you I'm going to humiliate you by slinging you over my shoulder and toting you to the bedroom to finish what has been looming between us . . . right here . . . right now. . . ."

He not only looked as if he meant to carry through with the threat but also as if he would derive wicked pleasure in flaunting his domination over her in front of the other men. Jerking her arm away, Piper glowered back at his threatening frown.

"Damn you to hell and back, Logan," she growled as she yanked up the hot pad and clutched the kettle. "I have had just about enough of your grandiloquence and your debauchery."

Logan wasn't quite certain what Piper had had enough of, and he wasn't about to ask her to rephrase her comment. *Her* temper had been stretched until it was on the verge of snapping, and it would take little provocation to send her into a fit at this point.

A quiet smile rippled across Logan's lips as he watched Piper begrudgingly play the waitress. After she filled the plates, she walked, stiff-backed, to the bedroom, and refused to eat with the men. With her pistol stuffed in her purse and Abraham trotting along behind her, she then breezed outside and stormed down the steps. Although the rain had ceased, a cold wind nipped at Piper as she stamped around the outbuildings, looking for a suitable place to explode in frustration. Logan wisely let her go out alone, knowing he would probably be shot down by his "wife" if he annoyed her further. She was that furious!

"What's the matter with your wife?" Willis questioned between bites.

Logan stared at the scrawny little man for a long moment. "She was trying to prepare a meal to tantalize your palate, since you have been complaining about the food you ingested at every stop." The sound of a pistol barking in the night caused all eyes to swing toward the door. "It sounds as if she decided to polish up on her marksmanship again." His eyes circled back to Willis, flinging him a meaningful glance. "Although Piper appears to be a delicate young lady, I must warn you that she's a feisty little thing. I don't suggest arousing her too often. Even though we look to be an obvious mismatch there are definite reasons why we are suited for each other. We both have barks as fierce as our bites. . . ." A wry smile touched his lips when Willis blanched. "Next time try to remember not to offend my wife, for I too might take offense. . . ."

"I . . . I . . . didn't mean to insult her," Willis stammered. "Actually, this slumgullion is quite good."

"Maybe I should go outside and apologize for Willis," Samuel, who had swallowed his meal like a python, eagerly suggested. "We wouldn't want her to think . . ."

Logan clamped his hand on Samuel's broad shoulder and stuffed him back in his chair before he could gain his feet. "Women, like men, need their own space. Piper will be back when she regains her temper. Let her alone."

Jedediah paused from wolfing down his meal to cast Logan a pensive glance. "You seem to know your wife quite well," he mused aloud. "I'm sure it must be difficult for her to be thrust into a world teeming with men. We should all be as sensitive to her needs as you are. I never would have guessed that a man of your profession possessed such insight into women or anything . . ."

His shiny cheeks flushed with color as he clamped down on his tongue. Jedediah's eyes dropped to his plate as he took up his fork. Silently he prayed he hadn't aggravated the notorious gunslinger with that careless remark. Lord, he had been conversing with Logan as if he were just an ordinary man. Nothing could have been further from the truth!

My God, I have indeed become sensitive to that green-eyed leprechaun's needs and responsive to her moods, Logan suddenly realized. He had taken the time to get to know her. He still didn't understand her, but he knew her. He was constantly aware of her presence. For almost two weeks he had been trying to analyze her, to calculate her actions. And still he hadn't figured her out. For an Easterner, she had readily adapted to the discomforts of stage traveling. She made the best of every situation. She couldn't ride or shoot as well as most men, but that was about all she couldn't do. In fact, she seemed to be made of sturdy stuff, considering she was a woman and a bluestocking to boot!

Silently eating the meal Piper had prepared, Logan bided his time, awaiting the return of his "wife." As the minutes crept by he began to wonder if one of the stable attendants had pestered her. Logan was tempted to check on her, but he forced himself to remain in his chair. In her present frame of mind she would make short shrift of any man who dared to take advantage of her. Surely no man would dare, knowing she was Logan's wife. His reputation would be her protection from harm. But what would be his protection when she returned to the station? She had left, mad as hell. It left Logan speculating if she had gone outside to practice with her pistol so she could blow him to kingdom come when they were locked in the privacy of their bedroom.

Mulling over that unsettling thought, Logan made a mental note to check the location of her weapon when they retired to bed. It was unnerving to imagine his epitaph: "Logan. Died

1859. Gunned down by his own wife."

While the other men were listening to Jedediah chatter like a magpie, spinning another of his far-fetched yarns, Piper was pacing behind the barn, walking off her frustration. Walking was the technique she had employed to ease her irritation after she found herself saddled with her infuriating stepfather. After pacing back and forth, Piper was usually able to regain control of her chaotic emotions. But nothing seemed to help when Logan was the source of her frustrations.

It annoyed her that she had allowed Logan and her own temper to get the best of her. The group of men probably had her pegged as a temperamental, contrary female. But dammit, she had been so exasperated she had been forced to beat a hasty retreat before she erupted like a spewing volcano.

Damn all men, Piper silently fumed, wiping away the angry tears. Why the good Lord thought to populate half the world with them was beyond her. She could have tolerated their existence better if the whole lot of them had been planted on another planet. They considered women to be their chattel, their dutiful slaves. Women were supposed to know their places and assume the roles men had selected for them. Men labored under the ill-conceived notion that a woman was naturally a fool who needed constant guidance. Even in school Piper had been dissuaded from pursuing a career in law or medicine because men would not accept women in those professions.

It seemed women could only rise to respected positions if they inherited them from their departed husbands, even if the wives were the guiding force behind their husbands' success. Confound it, that wasn't fair! And why should she tolerate being knocked down and stepped on by men? She was strong-willed and she had a mind of her own and she wasn't going to be pushed around!

Chomping on that positive thought, Piper tucked her Colt in her purse and veered around the mudholes that stood between her and the station door. She was going to march back inside with her dignity intact. And if one of those impossible men asked her to do the dishes she was going to throw a plate in his face!

170

To her astonishment, Piper entered the cabin to find the entire group of men clearing the table and washing dishes. Piper shook her head and sighed. Here was another shining example of the total lack of consistency exhibited by the male of the species. They thought they were above women's work and yet here they were drying pots and pans, even after they had parked themselves at the table the previous hour and expected her to wait on them hand and foot. Men! Who could understand them?

The sight of Logan's callused hands in dishwater brought a reluctant smile to Piper's lips. His massive, muscular body was out of place when he was standing over a tub of soapy water. In the future, when Logan tried to intimidate her, she must remember to conjure up this domestic scene. It would strengthen her courage.

As Piper strode across the dining area toward the bedroom she was showered with unexpected compliments about the meal she had prepared. She couldn't imagine Willis Worthington being nice to anyone, but he, of all people, was plying her with glowing accolades. With a gracious nod of thanks, Piper entered the bedroom to discard her purse and offer Abraham the attention she had neglected to give him while she was venting her frustration with her Colt. When she turned around she found Logan negligently propped against the doorjamb, studying her with a faint smile.

"Is your marksmanship improving?" he drawled in question.

Her chin tilted to a proud angle. "Indeed it is," she proclaimed airily. "I blasted both you and Willis right through the heart with every shot."

One thick brow elevated and his silver eyes sparkled with amusement. "Did you now? Perhaps I should hire you as my bodyguard since you are becoming so proficient with pistols."

"You couldn't pay me enough," she sniffed sarcastically.

Logan moved deliberately toward her. He took note of the residue of recently shed tears before his astute gaze ran the full length of her tantalizing physique. "Then what would you prefer in the way of compensation, dear lady?" he murmured quietly.

Piper could feel the warmth radiating from him as he walked toward her. She could hear his husky words vibrating through his broad chest, one that was only a hairbreadth from hers. She could smell the manly scent of him, one that had become a part of her after she had nestled down to sleep in his arms earlier that afternoon. When Logan was in the mood he could charm the wings off an angel. And he was in that particular mood now, she observed. Piper felt herself falling victim to his magnetism. At the moment she couldn't name one of his flaws, even though he was plagued with scores of them. Fighting her way through the sensual web he had woven around her, Piper struggled for composure.

"For starters, I would like your heart fried," she told him tartly.

"And for seconds?" He moved even closer, drowning her in his musky aroma, attempting to hold her skittish gaze.

It was difficult to untangle her eyes from those shimmering silver pools, but she managed the feat. "All I want is the answer to one question," she insisted, sidestepping before he touched her and she melted like a witless fool.

"What do you want to know?" he inquired. His unblinking gaze remained fixed on her lips as if they were the first pair he had ever seen, as if he were mesmerized by them.

Piper sidestepped again and sought to draw in a breath of air that wasn't thick with his arousing scent. "What did you do to those men out there? Threaten their lives if they didn't offer me compliments and attend to the domestic chores?"

He gave his raven head a negative shake. "I threatened no one, Piper. They are doing the dishes in hopes of returning to your good graces. Surely by now you have become aware of your devastating influence on men. Most of them are willing to go to great lengths to please you."

His nearness was playing havoc with her emotions. Piper warned herself not to fall prey to his gentler mood. He wanted something from her; men always did. "And what motivates you, Logan?" she wanted to know.

"I want you," he said simply and directly. "You're an enigma that I haven't been able to puzzle out."

"Do you make it a habit of trying to seduce women you don't

172

understand?" she asked flippantly, steeling herself against his dark charm and the the low caressing huskiness of his voice.

Deliberately, Logan's head moved toward hers. His sensuous lips were poised a few breathless inches away from hers. "Only you," he admitted quietly. "You were aptly named. You are like the Pied Piper who lures innocent children to follow wherever you lead."

Since his repertoire was so limited, she was surprised to learn Logan had heard the fairy tale. It was probably the only story he knew. Too bad it was the one with her name in it, she thought resentfully.

"You are hardly an innocent child being led astray," she smirked as she dodged his intended kiss.

As if he had tired with toying with his prey for the moment, Logan sauntered toward the door. "But I am bewitched, just the same," he murmured. "Even if you are too cynical and mistrusting to believe it."

When Logan left her to wrestle with his parting remark, Piper frowned pensively. Her? Cynical? He had it backward. Logan was the one who trusted no one. How stupid did he think she was anyway? He was trying to sweet-talk her into forgetting her irritation with him. He was trying to demolish her defenses. But she wasn't going to succumb to him, not tonight or any other night! She hadn't eluded scores of lusty men these past few years, only to fall prey to this silver-eyed demon. She had come dangerously close once, but never again. Logan didn't even like her all that much. She was no more than a diversion. He was not going to make love to her when he had only been tolerating her presence the past weeks. That would only be adding insult to injury.

Piper would be damned if she let herself fall in love or give herself to a man who could never return her affection. She would be every kind of fool if she let herself in for that kind of heartache and humiliation. She was practically penniless already, thanks to Grant Fredricks. All she had left was the money Logan had given her, minus the two hundred dollars she had paid for her stage ticket. She couldn't tolerate being flat broke and heartbroken all at the same time. Coping with one or the other depressing situation at a time would be difficult enough. Piper swore she would avoid both humili ating states. She was going to hunt down Grant, retrieve her money, and elude Logan.

Where there was a will there was a way, Piper told herself confidently. Determination and perseverance had to count for something, especially when that was all she had!

Chapter 12

When the group of men finally called an end to their card games and scurried about, preparing their pallets, Piper's apprehension increased. The time when she and Logan would retire to their bedroom was rapidly approaching. She was as jumpy as a grasshopper, and Logan sat in his chair, quietly monitoring her actions. Knowing that Logan knew what she was thinking unnerved Piper. When he gestured his raven head toward the bedroom door, Piper gulped down her thundering heart, one that had galloped in her throat.

On legs that threatened to fold up beneath her, Piper walked to the bedroom with as much enthusiasm as a criminal marching to the gallows. When Logan closed the door behind them, Piper licked her bone-dry lips and pivoted to face him.

"I haven't been totally honest with you," she blurted out as Logan peeled off his buckskin shirt, revealing the bronzed expanse of his chest. Dragging her eyes from his masculine torso, Piper concentrated on the well-disciplined mask of his face, one that was frozen in an impassive stare. "Although it's true that I am tracking down Grant Fredricks to regain my stolen inheritance, I failed to mention that we were actually husband and wife. That's why Grant was able to take possession of my money."

As always, Logan's controlled expression revealed nothing of his thoughts. But the news hit him like a physical blow. When he recovered from his shock and contemplated her explanation, he frowned suspiciously. Piper wasn't an accomplished liar. Her eyes kept darting hither and yon. She was afraid to meet his probing stare. Pensively, Logan sank down on the edge of the bed to unstrap his moccasins.

"Where's your wedding ring?" he questioned, pausing to glance at her rigid stance, noting she looked as if she expected to be attacked from all directions at once.

Piper's eyes dropped to the emerald and diamonds that sparkled on her left hand. Nervously, she twisted the jeweled band Logan had given her. "I . . . I . . . was forced to sell it to acquire enough money for my trip west. Grant took everything I had."

With his head bowed, Logan permitted himself a smile Piper couldn't detect. She was afraid of the inevitable intimacy between them and she was grasping for any excuse to avoid lovemaking.

Logan frowned disconcertedly. Did she think he would be rough and abusive with her, even when he knew damned good and well she was innocent of men? Had he frightened her that day in the meadow? She had surrendered to the passion that sizzled between them, but now she was fighting it tooth and nail. What sort of apprehension provoked her standoffishness? Surely she didn't think he was intent on hurting her . . . did she? He may have been skilled with pistols and ruthless when he faced murderers and thieves, but for God's sake, he wasn't an abusive heathen! Why the blazes was she staring at him as if he were?

Deciding to play along with her lie, Logan sighed defeatedly (or at least that's how it sounded to Piper). He let her think he had accepted the fact that she was another man's wife.

"Although Grant used me to get his hands on my trust fund, he is still my lawful husband and I . . . well . . . I still have tender feelings for the man, even though he has betrayed me." Piper drew encouragement from her white lie and from Logan's apparent acceptance of it. "If I were to sleep with you, I fear it wouldn't be your face I saw, but rather Grant's. I suppose, even from the beginning, I looked to you for consolation, trying to forget how much I had been hurt."

There. That should put the finishing touches on my story, Piper assured herself. Logan had too much pride to permit another man's image to follow him into bed. Piper mentally patted herself on the back for eluding an intimate encounter.

Slowly, Logan raised his dark head. His expression was as undecipherable as ever. "If that is the way of things, I have only one request," he murmured.

Her delicately arched brow rose curiously. "And that is . . . ?" she prodded him.

"If I am to be deprived of the wedding night we were to have in this mock marriage of ours, would you at least consent to giving me a massage?" Logan tried to work the kinks from his shoulders and then grimaced uncomfortably. "My muscles have been tied in knots after folding myself into that cramped coach for so many hours. I ache all over." And indeed he did, but not solely because of the intolerable riding conditions. However, Logan didn't bother to tell Piper that. After all, why should he? Piper hadn't been honest with him.

Her shoulders sagged in relief as Logan's powerful body uncoiled to sprawl on the bed. A muffled groan erupted from his lips as he arched and stretched to relieve the pressure. Piper decided to accommodate him since she had deprived him of his lusty pleasures. It was small consolation, she reckoned.

Gracefully, Piper eased onto the edge of the bed and placed her hands on the whipcord muscles that bulged above his shoulder blades. Meticulously she kneaded his hard flesh, amazed that her touch smoothed away the tension in his body. Logan "oohed" and "aahed" as she massaged the wide expanse of his back. She was enthralled by the feel of his masculine body beneath her fingertips. It was as if she held some strange power over this swarthy giant. Piper likened the odd sensations she experienced to taming this ferocious tiger. Although Logan was the epitome of strength, he succumbed to her gentle stroking and purred in contentment.

Piper had not been allowed the chance to appease her curiosity about Logan that day in the meadow. Now her sense of touch seemed eager to compensate. While her hands splayed over his back, her eyes toured his masculine terrain, learning him by sight and touch. His skin drastically contrasted hers. His flesh had been darkened by the sun while hers was pale from lack of exposure. Beneath that bronzed, rough-textured

177

flesh lay rippling muscle that could coil with amazing swiftness. But now he lay in repose, his massive body relaxed. Touching him, exploring him, was pleasure in itself. Piper felt an unexpected stirring in the core of her being.

"Now my legs," Logan murmured into his pillow, along with a wry smile. "They feel as stiff as a corpse."

Her gaze drifted down his buckskin-clad backside to focus on the long, muscular columns that were twice the size of her own. Tentatively, Piper squeezed the flesh of his thighs and blushed at the direction her thoughts had taken. Was Logan tanned all over? Were his powerful legs covered with dark hair, just like his arms and chest? And what did he look like on the flip side. . . .

Banish the sordid thought! Piper fiercely scolded herself. She had seen too much of this man already. It was none of her business how Logan would look in the altogether. She didn't want to know.

"Is something wrong?" Logan mumbled when her gentle hands suddenly jerked away from the back of his calves.

Something was wrong all right! She was fantasizing and it wasn't something she could discuss. Touching him had unleashed the forbidden memories of their passionate afternoon, memories she wanted to leave buried. But they rose from their shallow graves to torment her.

"No," she lied as she forced her hands to massage his muscular calves. "I was just giving my fingers a rest."

Before she completed her ministrations on both legs, Logan rolled to his back. "You should hire yourself out as a masseuse," he suggested. "Your gentle hands work wonders on bodies." His calculating gaze gauged the effect he was having on her. "Now my thighs." He indicated the taut muscles that were revealed by his form-fitting breeches.

Swallowing hard, Piper kneaded his upper thighs, but her fingers had suddenly become thumbs and her face was pulsating with color. When the back of her hand inadvertently brushed against the private parts of his anatomy, Piper gasped in embarrassment.

Logan grabbed her hands and set them on his belly. It was all he could do not to burst out laughing. Piper looked as if she had swallowed a pumpkin, and her face turned so white he wondered if she were about to faint. "You're as jittery as a gun-shy rabbit," he observed as he moved her quaking hands up the rough landscape of his chest. "I'm not going to attack you. All I want is for you to soothe away the tension so I can enjoy a decent night's sleep." A long sigh tripped from his lips. "I was expecting more, but since you confessed that you were married to Brant . . ."

"Grant," she corrected shakily.

"To Grant," he continued, "I will respect your obligation to your lawful husband. Although why you married a swindler and a cheat in the first place puzzles me. I pegged you for a far better judge of character."

"They say love is deaf, dumb, and blind. I suppose I exemplify that statement," Piper mumbled, distracted by the feel of his hair-matted chest beneath her inquiring hands.

Piper wasn't aware that her touch had transformed from a massage to a leisurely caress, but Logan was. Jeezus, it was becoming increasingly more difficult to control the arousal that bubbled inside him. In another minute he was going to be forced to lay the pillow over his loins so Piper wouldn't know how strongly she was affecting him!

Her wide green eyes dropped to his ruggedly handsome face. "Do you realize we have known each other for almost two weeks and I still don't know your first name," she blurted out unexpectedly.

His gaze tracked across her bewitching face. "Take your hair down," he requested just as unexpectedly. "Does it feel as soft and silky as it looks?"

As if hypnotized, Piper pulled the pins from her long hair and the silver-gold waterfall cascaded over her shoulders. Reverently, Logan reached up to tunnel his fingers through the thick, curly strands of sunbeams and moonbeams. His chest rose and fell in a contented sigh as he smoothed the renegade tangles across her shoulders. He had been too caught up in the heat of passion that day in Fort Smith and hadn't taken the time to study her lustrous hair. But it was worth the wait. The shiny tendrils felt like silk in his hands.

"My name is *Tsungani*," he whispered huskily. "Vince

179

Logan is the name I gave myself when I made my place in the white man's world."

Those piercing silver eyes held Piper entranced. She knew she should gather her feet beneath her and move away, but her body was paralyzed from the neck down. And when his straying hand glided down her arm to set her hand on his thudding heart, her own heart leapfrogged around her rib cage.

His right hand lifted to trace the delicate arch of her eyebrows and the tempting curve of her lips. His left hand tracked a tantalizing path across the slope of her shoulder to brush lightly against the taut peaks of her breast. Sensations crackled through her like a fire. Piper stared helplessly into those shimmering eyes, wondering why she had been stung by this insane urge to press her lips to his.

"I was almost beginning to believe we were married," Logan murmured as his caresses continued to explore and excite. "I was beginning to feel protective of you, as if I had acquired something very precious, something I wanted to share with no other man. It was a satisfying feeling." A quiet skirl of laughter rumbled in his chest. "Funny thing, isn't it? I had started thinking in terms of *us* instead of just *me*."

Oh, why did he have to say such things? Piper wondered when she felt herself melt into sentimental mush. Logan made her feel guilty for lying to him, for using him in her masquerade. She had been conniving and deceitful for the first time in her life and it wasn't setting well with her conscience. Her problems were her own, not Logan's. Not every man would have been so tolerant of her foolish ways.

Piper suddenly realized there was more to this powerful Goliath of a man than met the eye. Despite his notorious reputation, there was a great deal of good in Logan. He had allowed her to see between the cracks, to find the warmth that lay beneath that cold, unapproachable shell.

"You've taught me things about myself I didn't know," Logan murmured as his hand curled around the nape of her neck, bringing her face steadily toward his. "I think I might have even found myself in love with you, given time. You would be easy to love . . . to cherish. . . . We might have created something rare and special, if not for the man who stands between us. . . ."

The distance Piper had tried to keep between them shrank to breathless inches. Sweet flames burst inside her, channeling through her quivering body like a fiery river. The last sediments of self-restraint washed away with the flood of aroused sensations that poured over her. She was left to wonder what it would be like to be loved by this awesome man. Would his lovemaking be an extension of the protectiveness he claimed to feel for her? Would he savor her instead of punishing her for using him in her charade? Would she become a part of his strength when he took possession or would she feel like a conquered slave without an identity?

Piper was as curious as the next person, perhaps even more so. The questions whipped through her mind, seeking to find answers. Her apprehension bowed to her inquisitiveness and she initiated their kiss. Calling upon the skills Logan had taught her, and inventing a few of her own, Piper nipped at his full lips. Her tongue darted into his mouth to explore the contrasting softness, to steal his breath and then graciously return it before he gasped for air.

Her adventurous hand trekked across the bulging muscles of his chest, the lean wall of his belly. Even more boldly did she trail her fingertips along the band of his breeches, eager to learn all of his masculine body by touch.

Although Logan swore he was about to go up in flames, he allowed this curious leprechaun to go on caressing him in ways that threatened to destroy his self-control. Never had he permitted a woman such privileges. He had always instigated and controlled lovemaking in the past. He had taken what he wanted from women without giving of himself. But then, he reminded himself dazedly, he had never been inclined to seduce a virgin. The women in his past knew where passion led. They were familiar with a man. Piper, however, was a novice who was just beginning to realize the difference between a man and a woman. Her feminine curiosity made her daring, and for Logan that was dangerous.

A gasp burst from his lips when her wandering hand dived beneath his waistband. It was as if he were suddenly deprived of oxygen. He couldn't draw a breath to save his life. Her light caresses were doing impossible things to his body and his brain. Although he knew it would have been wiser to let her do her exploring elsewhere, he didn't remove her roving hands to less intimate places. And if Piper suddenly regained her senses and pulled away Logan swore he would explode with frustrated passion. Sweet mercy! he had never endured such exquisite torture. He wanted to crush her body into his, to yield to the primal needs that engulfed him. But if he yielded to those savage cravings he might hurt or frighten her, leaving emotional scars that would never heal—the kind his own mother had suffered.

Finally, Logan thought to distract himself. His restless hands drifted over the delicate buttons of her gown, watching intently as the garment fell away from her breasts. His eyes devoured her as he pushed the thin chemise from her alabaster skin. She was so perfectly formed, so soft and exquisite. Logan ached to touch her, to arouse her as thoroughly as she had aroused him. He wanted to appease this maddening craving that had been eating him alive for almost two weeks.

Fighting for hard-won composure, Logan removed the hindering garments that deprived him of seeing all her natural beauty. His silver eyes swept over her in total possession long before he set his hands upon her. It was like unwrapping a priceless package that he alone could enjoy. She was a gift of pure, rare beauty and he worshiped the sight and feel of her.

Piper didn't know what devil possessed her. She peered up at the mountain of masculinity who was poised beside her, surveying every magnificent inch of him. There was no blush of embarrassment on her cheeks this time when she watched him watch her. She moaned in quiet surrender as his fingertips slid over her shoulder to encircle each dusky peak of her breast. Piper wanted his hands and lips upon her flesh, just as she had that day in the meadow. But this time she wanted to explore his masculine torso until she knew him as well as she knew her own body.

All inhibition flitted away, to be replaced by a passionate craving that encouraged her to discover where these feelings ultimately led. It was wild and sweet and glorious to return each kiss and caress. One reckless sensation after another avalanched over her. Her senses took flight, coming to life like a butterfly spreading its wings to soar for the very first time.

Each place Logan touched became instant flame. He created insatiable needs. His skillful caresses caused Piper to arch helplessly upward, as if she couldn't get close enough to the blazing fire that consumed her. She was back to wanting him as she had in the meadow, and she feared she would die if she were deprived of his lovemaking.

A gasp of pleasure died beneath his ravishing kiss as his fingertips splayed across her abdomen. Her body melted in a wave of ecstasy as he teased and aroused her with intimate caresses, leaving her to ache in places she didn't know she had. His gentle fondling provoked an even wilder, more breathless need that spilled from every fiber of her being. And suddenly, it was as if Logan had sprouted an extra dozen set of hands. He touched her everywhere at once, totally arousing her, leaving her trembling with the want of him.

Piper was afraid she was going to faint, even though she hadn't been prone to such spells. But she wasn't sure she could survive this rapturous pleasure. Her breath came in short, ragged spurts and her body burned like fire. And then the most remarkable sensation overcame her. There weren't words to describe it. And in the wake of that ineffable feeling came convulsive tremors that provoked her to cry out in disbelief, a cry Logan skillfully muffled beneath his devouring kiss.

Piper swore she was dangling in time and space, searching for a cure to this wild, undefinable feeling of frustrated pleasure. As Logan's muscular body settled exactly over hers, she found the satisfaction she had sought. Even the initial pain didn't diminish the rapture that held her suspended. In a matter of seconds, the splendor seemed to intensify. He moved within her, slowly at first, and then in sweet, sensuous rhythm. His masculine body became a living, breathing part of her, and she reveled in the phenomenal sensations that converged upon her.

Piper's nails dug into the taut muscles of his back as he set the cadence of lovemaking. He took her higher and higher still. Tears of pleasure streamed down her cheeks as he possessed her body, heart, and soul. In wonderment, Piper felt another wave of rapture splashing over her. But this time a feeling of complete satisfaction accompanied it. Logan's body had blended into hers, bringing an incredible sense of contentment. It was as if they were two pieces of living puzzle that completed the mystical picture, one that had made no sense at all until they were one.

Logan had become the flame within her, the cause and the cure of the wild, maddening cravings that had assaulted her from every direction. Had she known what awaited her at the rainbow's end she wouldn't have been so apprehensive. For an endless instant that blew the stars around and inflamed the sun, Piper had transcended time to experience the epitome of emotion. Logan had taught her the meaning of pure, unique passion and she was dazzled by the streams of pleasure that pulsed through her as Logan shuddered and clutched her to him as if he never meant to let her go.

In the aftermath of love, Logan shook off the numbing ecstasy that had engulfed him. He raised his raven head to peer down into the enchanting face that was bathed in golden lantern light. Passion-drugged eyes blinked up at him. Lips that were still swollen from his ravishing kisses curved into a hint of a smile. A glorious mane of silver-blond hair spilled over the pillow. Spellbound, Logan lowered his head to help himself to another honeyed kiss. Lord, he felt as if this sweet angel had drained his strength. The feel of her satiny body was imprinted on his, just as the memory of this magical moment would be forever implanted in his brain.

When Logan broke the tender kiss, Piper recovered from her temporary lapse of sanity. Sweet merciful heavens, the things she had done! She knew the feel of Logan's powerful body as well as her own. She knew the exact location of each scar, knew where to find each sensitive point that aroused his passions. She had kissed him and caressed him, making intimate gestures that she had never thought herself capable of performing!

The thought caused Piper to turn a darker shade of red. Like an ostrich, she buried her head in the pillow. A gentle smile pursed Logan's lips as he eased down beside her. When Piper tried to worm away, he cupped her face and lifted it to his.

"Don't spoil the moment," he whispered, his voice husky with the aftereffects of passion. "What we shared was special, Piper . . . very special. You needn't be ashamed of your responses. They were natural and instinctive. We gave and received pleasure from each other's bodies. Is that a crime?"

Piper nodded mutely, but she was afraid to speak. She swore her voice would shatter like eggshells.

Logan leaned out to snuff the lantern, exposing the broad expanse of his back and hips to her admiring gaze. It still amazed Piper that she was so intrigued by the sight of this muscular giant. She wanted to feast her eyes on him, touch him, kiss him, over and over again.

Heaving a tired sigh, Piper peered at his rugged face through the shadows and moonlight. "Logan, I . . ."

His index finger grazed her lips, shushing her. "It's been a long week with little chance for sleep," he reminded her. "It may be another week before we're allowed the luxury of a bed. Sleep now, little dove. We said enough to each other without speaking at all."

As his muscled body nestled against hers, Piper swallowed her confession. She had intended to explain her lie, one provoked by apprehension. But Logan was in no mood to listen. The thought of cuddling into the protective circle of his arms lured her into dreams, ones that were scented with the taste and fragrance of the man who had unleashed her forbidden desires and then satisfied them one and all.

Like a trusting child, Piper relaxed beside Logan. Her head rested on his sturdy shoulder. Her bent knee was draped over his thighs and her arm was flung across his chest. It was a serene sleep, provoked by exhaustion and the side effects of splendid lovemaking. Piper didn't even remember when Abraham had hopped up beside her to take his place. And she should have heard him grumbling about being crowded out by Logan's oversized body. But instead, Piper slept contentedly until the drugging sedative of being loved finally wore off in the early hours before dawn.

Chapter 13

Unaccustomed to sleeping with a man, Piper roused to the feel of Logan shifting beside her. Drowsily, her mind drifted back to the magical moment that defined rhyme or reason. The purr of her tomcat gradually brought her awake and left her to reminisce. It had all begun so innocently, she mused as she glanced at Logan's shadowed form. He hadn't put up a fuss as she expected him to do when she insisted she was already married to Grant. In fact, he had accepted her confession more gracefully than she had anticipated.

A pensive frown clouded her brow. Come to think of it, Logan had taken the news a little too well. For a man who had been determined to have his way with her, to spite her for dragging him into her charade, he had been a mite *too* lenient and understanding. . . .

The more she thought about it, the more she wondered if she hadn't been too busy gloating to realize she had fallen prey to a scheme of Logan's making. He had requested that she offer him a harmless massage to ease his aches and pains. With his subtle coaxing he lured her into bed. . . .

Piper silently seethed. Logan had preyed on her naivete and her vulnerability for him. He knew her feminine curiosity would get the best of her when she was allowed to touch him, to investigate his masculine physique. With her lack of experience it took very little to transform a massage into an exploring caress. She had been towed into the whirlpool of tantalizing sensations, becoming a victim of a carefully

187

planned seduction that Logan let her think she had instigated! And all the time she had believed that nonsense about his feeling responsible for her, about caring for her in new ways. . . .

Her body became rigid with outrage. She had been feeling guilty about plying Logan with lies, but he had told a few of his own. Damn that low-down, good-for-nothing varmint! All he wanted was to steal her virginity, and he didn't care what methods he employed to lure her into bed. She should have known better than to try to pull a fast one on that seasoned rogue. She would never forgive herself for falling for his wily scheme, and she would never forgive him for using her own vulnerability and innocence as weapons against her.

But what hurt the most was learning that he had no scruples. She had told him she was already a married woman and still he set about to seduce her. She had been the defenseless fly who was snared into a cannibalistic spider's web. He didn't give a whit whether she was married. She had been convenient and Logan had been eager to satisfy his lusts. Damn that man. She thought she knew him, but she kept discovering she didn't know him at all!

In frustration, Piper pulled Logan's pillow from his head and hit him with it. Logan was jostled awake by soft but repeated blows to his skull. He did what he always did when he was rudely awakened—he reflexively reached for his pistol. But it wasn't the Colt he grabbed, it was the cat. Logan wasn't sure who hissed the loudest, Piper or Abraham. But suddenly both of them were growling and yowling and clawing at him.

Cursing, Logan knocked Abraham off the bed after he had bit and scratched to gain his freedom. "What the hell . . ." Logan muttered as he watched Piper rise on her knees. After she punched him in the midsection, Logan expelled the rest of his sentence. ". . . is going on?"

"You tricked me, damn you!" Piper fumed as she doubled her fist and rammed it into his belly, once again for good measure.

"And you lied to me," he countered as he grabbed her clenched fist. "That makes us even."

"How did you know?" she questioned in surprise.

188

"I've grown adept at reading people's faces." It wasn't a boast, only a simple statement of fact. "You don't lie worth a damn, honey. But I'm sure you'll get better with practice. Women make a profession of lying."

Piper sputtered in fury, but she couldn't formulate a suitably nasty reply before Logan hurled his accusation at her.

"What happened between us was your doing," he had the audacity to say. "As I recall, I was simply lying abed when you started massaging parts of my anatomy that I hadn't asked you to work your gentle magic on."

It was a good thing the room was dark so Logan couldn't see how his off-color remark stained her cheeks with mortification. How was she supposed to respond to that remark? It was true that he had schemed to lure her into bed, but she was the one who initiated their lovemaking. But he calculated my reaction to exploring his body, she thought defensively. He knew exactly what he was doing and what she would do when overcome by curiosity.

Presenting her back, Piper stared at Abraham who had curled up a safe distance away. "I should insist that you marry me after what you did," she pouted spitefully. "You have considered yourself unwillingly strapped with me the past two weeks. But it would be nothing compared to having me underfoot for the rest of your natural life."

His quiet chuckle vibrated the bed. "Ah, the woman scorned," he mocked lightly. "I expected as much from a sassy bluestocking. You would probably marry me just to make my life hell. How vindictive you are, Piper." He pressed her to her back, looming over her in that infuriating manner of his. "But you fail to realize that no one ties me down permanently if it isn't my wish to be hobbled."

She hated this intimidation, this frustrated feeling that she could never win against Logan. He was like an unstoppable force who remained unaltered by external influences. Tying herself to him would be like trying to tame a lion, knowing he could turn on her at any moment. There was no way to defeat him without enlisting the services of an entire cavalry.

Tears of exasperation scalded her eyes and trickled down her cheeks. Piper wanted to beat the tar out of him, but she knew she couldn't fully satisfy her vengeance before he retaliated. The thought made her cry all the harder.

Logan scowled disgustedly. "Spare me the crocodile tears, honey," he snapped unsympathetically. "I don't decompose at the sight of sobbing females. You used me to track your cussed inheritance. You should have considered the risks involved. If you weren't prepared to pay the price you should have gone home where you belonged. I gave you ample compensation for your missing trust fund, but your greed provoked you to defy my warnings."

Did he think the money he had given her in Fort Smith was equal to her lost fortune, compensation for her lost virginity? Not hardly! Piper would have told Logan exactly how much money they were discussing if she didn't think he would have tracked Grant down himself and burned up her inheritance—two dollars at a time when he lit his offensive cigars.

The most peculiar feeling of vengeance overwhelmed Piper. She wiped away the tears abruptly and tossed her head. Piper stared angrily into Logan's chiseled face. There was only one way to repay him for the frustration she was experiencing, one way to touch a man who prided himself in remaining unaffected by those around him. She was going to enjoy the ultimate victory over him. And when they parted company, her memory was going to haunt his days and torment his nights. She may not have been experienced in seducing a man, but she was inventive and she would find a way to leave a lasting impression on him. He had stolen her innocence, but she was going to make him a slave to his own lusty passions, to the memories they had created. If another woman wanted him, she could have him. But his amorette was going to find Logan to be half a man, a man haunted by Piper's memory.

Piper may have been a sophisticated bluestocking, but she was quickly learning to adjust to this man's world. And the first rule of survival was to give as good as she got. With sylphlike grace, she sat up in bed, intent on her purpose. The first rays of dawn splintered through the window, casting slanted shadows across her flawless face. The golden sunlight caressed her bare flesh, wrapping itself around her shapely curves like unseen hands. The light glittered in her long hair like diamonds and gold nuggets, casting a halo about her head.

Although she possessed the face of an angel there was a bit of the devil in the smile she bestowed on Logan. He didn't quite trust this minx, especially when she was wearing such a cryptic grin. Logan would have taken time to analyze her expression if he hadn't been bewitched by the provocative picture she presented in dawn's first light. Lord, she looked absolutely breathtaking and it was impossible to think. And when she set her hands upon him, Logan forgot his own name—both of them.

"You made me want you," she murmured as her moist lips skimmed each nipple and then drifted over his shoulder. "And now you're going to want me in the same wild, wondrous ways." Her hand limned his craggy features, smoothing away his wary frown. "There is a fine line between possessing and being possessed." Like a witch murmuring incantations around him, Piper confessed the pleasure she derived from touching him. "Arousing you arouses me. From your strength I draw strength. What is yours will soon become mine, and I will use my powers to turn your own fierce energy back upon yourself. . . ."

Logan swore she had indeed performed black magic. Each time she touched him, muscle and bone melted beneath her gentle caresses. She weaved intricate patterns on his chest and thighs, leaving him gasping to draw a breath.

"I will hear my name tumble from your lips," she promised him as her kisses fluttered over his cheeks and eyelids. "You will want me, but this time it will be I who takes possession of you—body and soul. Your heart will be mine to do with as I please. And you will love me because you will be helpless to resist. And when the loving is over you won't have the energy to fight my spell. You will be at my mercy. The fallen giant will beg for the return of his strength and sanity. . . ."

Suddenly Logan found himself believing in ghosts and goblins. This she-devil had been sent up from hell to make him pay penance for every crime he had committed, along with several he hadn't. Even when he knew he should fight the tormented pleasure, he felt like a 235-pound weakling. Her silky body surged upon his and then receded like waves caressing a seashore. His flesh was aflame with erotic sensations that burned all thought from his mind.

Piper had him moving like a puppet on command when she tasted and touched him in such imaginative ways. A shuddering groan escaped his lips when her nails raked his chest and her knee insinuated itself between his thighs. Logan had dreamed of wild reckless fantasies but he had never lived one. And sure enough, he felt as if he had been possessed by a demon spirit who had materialized in woman's flesh. This witch with enormous green eyes and silver blond hair was forcing him to endure the most incredible form of torture known to man.

Each time he reached out to touch her, she withdrew to perform more of her maddening magic on his quaking body. He was living and dying in the same moment, wanting her, aching for her. Her caresses skimmed his flesh, time and time again, lifting him from one plateau of pleasure onto another. Logan groaned in unholy torment as her lips tracked along the same evocative path her hands had taken. He was burning alive, engulfed in a holocaust of fiery sensations that matched nothing he had ever experienced. He felt out of control, as if he were a senseless creature who could only respond to this sourceress's whims. She was going to let him die in tormented pleasure. He was sure of it. She held him suspended, teasing and arousing him, using her body to caress him without allowing him to appease the monstrous craving that was eating him alive.

Her enchanting face appeared above him, beside him. Her name tumbled from his lips in a pained plea and his body arched to meet hers, only to have her pull away. The agony of being so close and yet so far away was sweet, maddening torture, and Logan groaned when she touched him familiarly and bestowed a kiss that must surely have been laced with poison. He was dying, bit by excruciating bit!

Piper foolishly thought she could remain unstirred by her seductive ploy to humble this powerful man who had taken advantage of her. But she was trapped in her own bewitching spell. It was no longer vengeance that motivated her but rather a need to reexperience the pleasure of lovemaking. Trembling, she moved toward him, wanting him in the wildest way. This time she set the cadence of passion, guiding slowly over him, her breasts teasing his laboring chest, her thighs moving suggestively against his.

Why she wanted to prove her power over him no longer mattered. She was swept up in the churning storm she had created. And suddenly, loving him was her only reason for being. He was every breath she took, the essence of her existence. Piper responded mindlessly to the riveting sensations that converged upon her. They moved as one, skyrocketing past the turbulent storm, soaring past the distant stars, flying into the sun.

Ecstasy rippled through her as Logan clutched her to him, stealing her breath in a savage kiss. The rough urgency of passion tossed them like waves of fire cresting on a wind-tossed sea. Undercurrents of rapture towed her downward. The world turned a darker shade of black as she drowned in the wild, intense sensations that consumed her. Piper could feel herself letting go, drawn into the swift-moving currents of emotion that pulled her deeper into the fathomless depths. And then, from the darkness, pure white light exploded to sear her flesh with living flames. Her body shuddered convulsively against his rock-hard flesh as passion poured forth like molten lava erupting from an undersea volcano.

It seemed forever before Piper could find the energy to move away and sit up on the edge of the bed. Finally she drew her feet beneath her and weaved unsteadily across the room to retrieve a fresh set of clothes. She didn't want Logan to know she had enjoyed the same fulfillment, that she had not been the victor of this intimate battle. The passion they shared had devastated her, and it was all she could do to cross the room without wilting in a boneless heap.

In silence, Logan watched Piper prepare for another tedious day of traveling. He was at a loss to explain the strange sensations that lingered in the aftermath of their wild, reckless lovemaking. He had thought an inexperienced woman couldn't satisfy a man so completely. But Piper had taught him things he had never known about passion, even when he arrogantly supposed he had experienced it all.

Logan wanted to forget the sight of Piper bending over him while he was on fire for her. But he wondered if that tormenting vision would ever fade from his mind. She had been like a wild creature—the hauntingly bewitching contrast to the gently bred sophisticate he had met in Fort Smith. But beneath that veneer of civilized beauty was a woman with a dozen kinds of passion aching for release. So quickly had she shed her inhibitions to become the skillful seductress! And even more quickly had she shut him from her thoughts and turned away when the loving was over. He had possessed her for a time, and she, in turn, had taken complete possession of him.

Logan wondered if he could ever truly tame this complicated vixen. It was as if there were three completely different personalities housed inside that curvaceous body—the woman she had been, the woman she was, and the woman she would become. Those perplexing facets of her personality continued to intrigue him. Piper had undergone many transformations since their first meeting. Her new experiences had caused her to blossom into a spirited adventuress which her education and strict upbringing had suppressed . . . until now.

One day, Piper Malone would be a force to be reckoned with, and Logan doubted that any man could handle her when she finally came into her own. She had become more independent and confident with each passing day. She was already strong-minded, but she was becoming more resourceful and, Jeezus, even more seductive! It was a good thing he was going to step off the stage in another week so he could put her out of his mind. If he let her get closer to him than she already was, he was going to do something crazy like never let her go! And that would be a disastrous mistake.

Now wouldn't that be the crowning glory, Logan mused as he struggled to his feet to fetch his clothes and hastily shave. Imagine him shackled to a female—an Eastern bluestocking to boot! Well, it wasn't going to happen, Logan assured himself fiercely. He wasn't meant to settle down. He had been born under a wandering star. If he knew what was good for him he would never let himself forget that!

No matter how wildly this nymph aroused him, their affair

was not meant to be more than a fleeting moment of pleasure. They were still as different as dawn and midnight. Logan vowed, then and there, that he would not become more involved with this temptress than he already was. He had to be logical and reasonable. He and Piper were like oil and water—a combination that would never mix, no matter how many times it was shaken or stirred. She was a novelty to him, a new challenge, that was all. What they had shared was passion for passion's sake, nothing more.

Witches indeed! Logan snorted sardonically. He was accustomed to treading across the devil's playground. He had been to hell and back so many times in his life that he would never succumb to the powers of this gorgeous, emerald-eyed sorceress. He had confronted demon spirits far more devastating than Piper Malone and had walked away unscathed. Now that he had possessed her and she, him, the spell had been broken. The mystique was gone. He would be anxious to seek out another female conquest, just as he always had. Piper held no magical power over him. He was immune to her charms.

Famous last words, came a quiet, chuckling voice from deep inside him. But Logan ignored the taunt. Being the stubborn, bullheaded man he was, he thought he could tuck the sweet memories in a forgotten corner and never disturb them. Ah, arrogance! How it blinded a man to his own worst enemy—himself!

Chapter 14

After a hearty breakfast that Piper had taken it upon herself to prepare, the stage was ferried across the Red River on a raft. All five passengers settled into their niches for the jaunt to Sherman, Texas. During the hours and days that followed Piper practiced what she preferred to call civilized warfare in her exasperating relationship with Logan. She had meant for him to be tormented by the moments of passion they had shared before leaving Colbert's Ferry. *She* most certainly had been, even though she projected the image of carefree gaiety. But deep down inside she was hurting. As much as she hated to admit it, she did care about Logan, and it hurt to know her affection was one-sided.

It stung Piper's pride to admit the night they had spent in each other's arms was just another of the many nights Logan had shared with a woman. For him, there was nothing special to endear him to her. He had gotten what he wanted from her. Compensation, he called it—compensation for the use of his name and his part in her charade. But after the harsh remarks he'd made when she had succumbed to tears, Piper promised herself she would never *ever* let her guard down like that before his very eyes again. She was going to become as tough and unfeeling as he was. He would stare at her and see his own cold, callous reflection, just see if he didn't!

If nothing else, this rugged journey had convinced Piper that she could survive most anything. With each passing day she nurtured her newfound confidence, fed her strengths, and overcame her weaknesses. She had proved her resourcefulness on several occasions and she was assured of her abilities. Her strengthened self-esteem boosted her feeling of independence. Although she found herself in a man's world, having had very little association with women since she left Fort Smith, Piper had made her own niche. She had learned it was disastrous to trust men, and she had adopted the policy of depending on no one but herself, expecting nothing from men. Even though the men treated her with kindness, admiration, and respect, Piper became an entity unto herself. She was determined never to give Logan the satisfaction of having her lean on him, to depend on him for anything.

When the stage paused for meals, Piper took command to ensure their food was nourishing and appetizing. At one station the hungry passengers were greeted with rancid bacon floating in its own foul-smelling grease, and sourdough biscuits that could have stood up and walked to the table. Piper promptly tossed the kettle out the door, refusing to let her tomcat near it, and started from scratch. Although the stage was delayed a few minutes, the driver and conductor had no complaints when they bit into a succulent meal that tantalized their taste buds.

Logan had become watchful but distant during their five-hundred-mile journey from Sherman, Texas, to El Paso. There was little human habitation except for roving bands of Comanches and Kiowas, company stations, and a few military outposts. The scenery provided nothing but dry, rolling plains broken by rugged escarpments, cedars, and cottonwoods that canopied the creek banks.

Although conversation between Logan and Piper was strained, Jedediah Smith and Willis Worthington attempted to top each other's tales by babbling nonstop. For the most part, Logan chose to stare out the window and dwell on his own pensive deliberations. When the stage halted, he silently monitored the exchange of horses at swing stations, attempting to make some sense of the robberies that plagued Butterfield's stage route. According to the information Logan had dragged from Cactus Jack, a ring of spies marked the stages that were to be robbed and then sent messages to the outlaws who haunted the desolate stretches of road. Logan had kept a watchful eye on the stage and its attendants who loitered around it during the transfer of one team of horses to the other. But he kept finding himself distracted by the shapely blonde who had come into her own the past week.

A metamorphosis had taken place in Piper's character and personality. With each milestone she passed, her self-confidence increased proportionately. She was no longer the blushing bluestocking he had met in Fort Smith. Piper had become self-sufficient, expecting nothing from him and giving nothing in return. She was cautious, distant, and unapproachable and yet courteously polite. Although Logan admired Piper's blossoming strength he felt as if it were her gain and his loss. No longer did she prop herself against him when she was exhausted. No longer did she linger, expecting him to assist her from the coach when they were allowed to stretch their legs. Never once did she grasp his hand when they trudged through the soft sand that covered the plains, giving the weary horses a much-needed rest.

Logan had maintained a respectable distance from Piper because her glances and her attitude warned him to tread carefully with her. But Samuel still hovered around her like an attendant serving his queen. Piper even rejected his chivalrousness. She had proved to Logan and every other man that she was as sturdy and perseverant as the next person, and she practiced with her pistol each night after she had hurriedly downed her meals.

When the stage rolled into Fort Belknap, Piper was swarmed by troops who hungrily feasted on her beauty . . . at least until they were informed she was Logan's wife. Upon hearing the news the love-starved soldiers retreated a respectable distance. History repeated itself again at Fort Chadbourne and Logan found himself wondering at this lingering feeling of possessiveness that stung him each time the soldiers ventured too close to Piper. She could have had her pick of the troops, and Logan had the irritating feeling there would have been more than a few soldiers who would have taken liberties with Piper if they thought Logan would let them get away with it.

Piper means nothing to me, nothing at all, Logan reminded

himself daily. His sole purpose was to ensure that Piper could stand on her own two feet and fend for herself in a world that was unlike the society she had left behind. And she had adapted amazingly well, Logan mused resentfully, a little too well. Piper no longer needed him, even though he was still nursing this constant throb of frustrated desire. The splendid night they shared loomed like a haunting dragon in the dungeon of his mind. He didn't want to go on wanting that adorable minx. But dammit, he did. Once he had satisfied his passion for her, he should have been able to put her out of his mind. He never had any trouble discarding the other women in his life. So why did this green-eyed witch continue to torment his thoughts? Because, confound it, he could still envision her hovering over him in the pastel colors of sunrise, feel her gentle hands transforming bone and muscle to liquid desire. He could taste her lips melting on his like summer rain, still feel her luscious body molding itself to his. She had created fires that blazed out of control, and he could still remember. . . .

"If you are expecting to find scorpions floating in your stew, you are wasting your time searching for them," Piper smirked as she watched Logan stare at the bowl she had placed before him. "I merely squashed the pesky varmints flat and kicked them out the door."

Logan shook his head to shatter the thoughts that preoccupied him. "I suppose you clubbed the poor defenseless creatures with the same vigor you smashed the tarantula that wandered into the station yesterday," he remarked as he took up his spoon to taste the stew.

Piper nodded affirmatively. Abraham had sniffed out the pests that walked in as if they owned the place. She had pounced on them without shrieking in alarm as she might have done before she had been indoctrinated into the inconveniences and hazards of the West. There had been a time not so long ago when a huge furry spider would have sent her scrambling onto a chair, awaiting a gentleman to dispose of it. But no more. Piper took it upon herself to rid the stage stations of the creatures. She simply snatched up an improvised weapon and pretended each annoying varmint was Logan. The technique proved to be amazingly effective.

"I only hope I can become as proficient with a pistol as I am with a broom," she commented as she eased into the chair Samuel had pulled out for her. "There are some pests that can't be squashed with a broom, due to their enormous size."

Logan ignored the subtle jibe. He studied Piper's expressionless face, suddenly feeling as if he were staring in a mirror. Piper had become too much like him the past week. She was no longer the emotional creature who cried when she was frustrated or shrieked at the sight of a rattlesnake slithering across the plains. Again he was stung by the deflated feeling that his apprentice no longer needed his instruction. Piper seemed determined to become his equal. And indeed in many ways she was.

Piper had fiercely resolved never to let Logan know her heart was still bruised and bleeding. She wanted to feel no remorse when they went their separate ways. Logan had used her the way he used every other woman. He had cleverly manipulated her into his bed, and she didn't want to remember the rapture of lying in his sinewy arms, the heady pleasure of his masterful caresses. . . .

Abruptly, Piper set her spoon aside and rose from the table before the tormenting memories of splendor had her simmering like her stew. That night at Colbert's Ferry didn't happen, Piper told herself as she retrieved her pistol and stomped outside to practice her marksmanship. She was never going to let that infuriating man that close again. He was never going to hurt her the way she was hurting now. By damned, she was going to get over that brawny giant if it was the last thing she ever did!

After reloading her pistol and replacing the cans she had set upon the fence rail, Piper spun back around to see Logan leisurely propped against the barn. A cigarillo protruded from his mouth at a jaunty angle and a wry smile dangled from his lips. From beneath the brim of his hat Piper watched his silver gaze wander over her at will.

"Are you still hitting me between the eyes with every shot?" he questioned curiously. Logan had no doubt she envisioned his face in every target.

Why she felt the need to impress him was beyond her. But

Piper walked off twenty paces in stiff, precise steps and wheeled about to send Abraham into hiding and all six cans flipping into the air.

Logan was impressed all right! Dumbstruck would have been nearer the mark. Jeezus, who would have thought this feisty bundle of sophistication could have become so skillful with a pistol in three weeks?

While she swiftly reloaded the Colt .45, Logan sauntered over to retrieve a can. "Sometimes your targets don't stand still so you can take steady aim," he taunted her. Cocking his arm, he hurled the can high in the air, expecting Piper to test her ability with a moving target.

The pistol barked and Logan jumped out of his skin when two bullets zinged against the pebbles beside his feet. In mute amazement, Logan stared at Piper's mischievous smile.

"And sometimes they do," she told him saucily before she pirouetted, called to her tomcat, and gracefully walked away.

Logan grinned in spite of himself. He supposed he had that coming. Instead of complimenting her expertise he had challenged her to test her skills in the method he dictated. But Piper had put him in his place with two well-aimed shots at his feet. No man would have dared to do what she had done to a gunslinger. But Piper wasn't a man, Logan reminded himself as he studied the hypnotic sway of her hips. Piper was all woman, every well-sculptured inch of her. And she wasn't about to bow to him just because of his legendary reputation. If Logan wanted her admiration and respect he had the feeling it wouldn't come because of his expertise as a freelance shootist. Piper wasn't impressed with his talents, his character, or his personality. Her reaction to him implied that she disliked him intensely. Hell, he thought with a snort. Her haughty behavior toward him didn't imply her hatred. It was *shouting* it!

The nagging frustration of that incident tormented Logan as he pulled himself into the coach and huddled into his designated corner. After listening to Willis boast about how he had learned the techniques of boxing from British promoters who had instructed him in the East, and how he had taught Samuel the Englishmen's finesse of boxing, Logan had had his fill. The scrawny little pipsqueak used Samuel as an extension of himself. Willis was a nobody who was looking for fame by attaching himself to someone who possessed the abilities Willis did not.

"If you are so well-educated in the techniques of boxing, why aren't you matching your fists against challengers instead of nudging Samuel into the ring?" Logan questioned with an intimidating smirk.

Willis jerked up his head and his chest swelled up like a toad's. "If you knew anything about the boxing profession, which apparently you don't, you would realize lightweights do not draw the crowds that follow heavyweight boxing. People want to see muscled giants pitting themselves against each other, even if they are virtually unskilled in the sport."

Logan's silver eyes bore into Willis's inflated chest. "And how much are you paying Samuel to match his strength against other heavyweights? Since boxers are short-lived, I should hope he receives a high percentage of the gate."

"Actually, I only get paid . . ." Samuel began, only to be interrupted by Willis's indignant snort.

"That is none of your business, Mr. Logan," he shot back. "We haven't asked you how much Butterfield is paying you to rid the route of road agents. In my opinion, you have yet to earn a penny since we have met with no trouble."

Logan glared at Willis, who found his courage in the fact that Samuel was sitting beside him like a devoted watchdog. Purposely, Logan ignored Willis and focused his attention on Samuel. "I'll pay you an honest day's wage to work at my ranch in the Gila River valley," he offered. "I'm willing to bet you will make far more money herding cattle and repairing corrals than Willis pays you to taste other men's beefy fists."

"Where is your ranch?" Samuel asked, his eyes ablaze with interest.

"Just north of Tucson. The job is yours if you want it," Logan declared.

"Samuel is not taking on ranch chores when he could become the heavyweight champion!" Willis blustered. "He doesn't want to settle for herding cattle when he could be the toast of San Francisco."

Logan's stony gaze swung back to Willis. "That decision

should rest with Samuel, not with you. You've been telling him what to do, what to eat, and where to sit since we boarded at Fort Smith." An ornery smile pursed his lips as he pulled his felt hat over his eyes and crossed his arms over his broad chest. "It seems to me that Samuel is certainly big enough and old enough to make his own decisions. I know I wouldn't want some skinny know-it-all trying to tell me when to jump and exactly how high."

Willis's face turned the color of raw liver and Piper bit back a grin. She shared Logan's sentiments, but she wasn't about to give him the satisfaction of admitting it aloud. She would rather die than confess she agreed with him on any topic!

"Perhaps we should all put a wager on a bout between you and my man Samuel," Willis baited Logan. "The two of you are relatively equal in size and stature. I'd bet a hundred dollars Samuel could beat you to a pulp."

Logan reached into his pocket and unfolded several bills. Uncoiling in a threatening manner that caused Willis to flinch in wary anticipation, Logan flung the older man a defiant grin and stuffed the money in Samuel's vest pocket. "Here's an advance of the first month's wages, friend. You will work six days and take Sunday off, plus two days a month when you feel the need to carouse." When Willis sputtered furiously, Logan nailed him to the leather seat with a pointed glare. "If you want to see a fistfight, Worthington, I'll be glad to accommodate you. *You* can show me the English techniques you've been boasting about."

"You're a hypocrite," Willis burst out without thinking. "You hire yourself out to anyone who can afford your exorbitant price and yet you protest my promoting Samuel's talents with his fists."

"You seem to forget I'm well paid for risking my life," Logan countered.

The low purr in his voice may have sounded relatively harmless to everyone else, but Piper had heard that rumble often enough to know Logan's temper was being tested. Her body tensed when she felt the muscles of Logan's legs grow taut as they brushed against hers. If Willis knew what was good for him he would clamp down on his runaway tongue.

"In my estimation, Samuel is taking all the risks and you are hoarding all the money." Logan's stormy gray eyes cast ominous shadows on Willis, who had the good sense to wilt in his seat. "My gun is the extension of a justice system that doesn't reach far enough into the lawless frontier. I use it to protect upstanding citizens who can't defend themselves against desperados and marauders. There's a difference," he noted sternly. "And if this stage is attacked by road agents, you'll probably be the first one to insist I risk my life to save your hide. But I'm seriously considering letting the brigands make a feast of you."

The tension was so thick it could have been stirred with a stick. No one uttered a word for the next five miles. Willis looked in every direction except at Logan. Piper squirmed uncomfortably in her seat and craned her neck to peer out the window, hoping to call attention to the scenery, anything. But the land was featureless except for an occasional cedar or prickly pear cactus. . . .

Her eyes caught on a bewildering sight as she peered across the sandy plains. "What on earth . . . ?"

Her startled comment roused the sullen group, who poked their heads from various windows to determine what had captured Piper's attention.

"Am I seeing what I think I'm seeing?" Jedediah chirped in disbelief.

Logan nodded positively as he sank back into his seat. "Camels," he confirmed. "The one-hump kind. The secretary of war decided 'Operation Camel' was just what the army needed in these vast, isolated stretches of the Southwest. He insists that camels will give the military greater mobility, that they can make longer reconnaissances and move greater numbers of troops and equipment across rugged country where mules and horses would flounder."

Amusement danced in Logan's eyes as Piper practically climbed atop him to gain a better vantage point. Actually, he wasn't discomforted to have her shapely derriere planted in his lap. He rather liked it. Leisurely he looped his arms around her to steady her and then peered around her shoulder to converse with Jedediah.

"The camels were imported from the Mediterranean and put ashore in Texas. The army stationed their new recruits at a post eighty miles north of San Antonio. They have been using their camel caravans for excursions from Texas to military posts in New Mexico Territory." Logan shrugged a broad shoulder. "I'm not sure how effective the camels have been but they have given the Comanches and Apaches quite a start.

"Rumor has it that the camels will travel up and down steep rocky precipices that mules refuse to descend. They will eat anything from greasewood bushes to prickly pears, and amazingly, they stay fat on their unlikely diet."

When Piper realized she was using the man she had planned on hating as her armchair, she wormed back into her niche. Her abrupt movement caused Abraham's basket to tilt sideways. Caterwauling, Abraham scrambled from his basket. A pained yelp erupted from Logan's lips as Abraham repeated his infuriating habit of sinking his sharp claws into Logan's lap. Reflexively, Logan knocked the clinging cat away before Abraham rendered him useless to all women. The tomcat yowled and clawed the air as he went flying across the coach.

An agonized yelp burst from Willis's lips when Abraham sank his claws in to secure himself. Logan hadn't aimed the pesky cat at the scrawny boxing promoter, but he was glad to see Abraham hanging off Willis's chest.

After Piper apologized, she tucked Abraham back in his basket and squirmed into her narrow space. She was still rattled about the fact that she had climbed onto Logan's lap. The gesture had been all too natural, as if she permitted herself privileges with Logan that she could take with no other man. Nothing could have been further from the truth, Piper reminded herself grumpily. She and that impossible man were barely on speaking terms. He had tired of her after he had his way with her. She meant not a tittle to him, or he to her. And that was the last time she was going to feel his muscled thighs meshing against her hips, feel his sinewy arms enfolding her like a seat belt.

In fact, Piper resolved not to touch Logan at all if it could be avoided. A brief touch or a careless glance always stirred emotions Piper wanted to keep dead and buried. She was not going to find herself falling in love with a man who kept track of the women he had seduced by notching his pistol. Indeed, she wasn't going to let herself fall in love with any man. She was learning to survive quite nicely without the male of the species. They were nothing but trouble.

Out of the corner of his eye, Logan assessed the emotions that clouded Piper's dazzling green eyes, ones that dominated her lovely face. She was withdrawing from him again, receding back into her protective shell. Damn her. For a moment he thought . . . Hell, Logan didn't know what he thought, except that having that gorgeous female so close and yet so far away was driving him crazy.

Nursing that frustrating thought, Logan closed his eyes and begged for sleep. Trying not to think about that sassy vixen was exhausting. He wasn't sure how much more torment he could endure. For a man who had mastered his emotions he was having one hell of a time sorting out his feelings for that bewitching nymph.

Camels, I'll think about camels, Logan decided. Surely there could be no association between those pitifully ugly creatures and that breathtaking beauty with hair like sunshine and moonbeams and eyes like polished emeralds. . . .

The burning sand lay like an endless carpet, bounded only by the horizon. Heat waves undulated across the vast wasteland. Parched vegetation struggled to rear its head before it suffocated in the swirling grains that swept over the rugged terrain. Logan could barely tolerate the penetrating heat that scorched him inside and out. The camel on which he sat whined in protest at the prospect of stirring another step. Desperately, he nudged the hoary creature, forcing it toward the crimson horizon.

From the crest of the dune, Logan peered through sunbaked eyes, viewing an oasis that lay ahead of him. It had to be a mirage, he reminded himself. He had somehow wound up in hell and his torment was seeing things that weren't really there. In the distance, amid a boundless sea of drifting sand, palm trees swayed in the breeze.

And water . . . sweet, precious, thirst-quenching water! It sparkled in the scorching sunlight, luring him closer. The glittering pool was surrounded by a soft carpet of emerald green grass. And there, lounging beside the oasis, was a shapely goddess garbed in a gossamer robe of white. Her lustrous hair spread about her bare shoulders like a cape spun from silver and gold thread. Eyes as clear and green as the rippling blades of grass silently beckoned him nearer.

Logan held his breath, knowing the mirage would vanish and the cruel trick his eyes were playing on him would become another kind of torment. He focused intently on the inviting scene and breathed a thankful sigh when the mirage didn't evaporate as he approached. Upon command, the camel knelt for its weary rider to dismount. Logan dragged his wobbly legs beneath him to stare at paradise and its resident angel.

Gracefully, the lovely vision arose to drift toward him like a butterfly skimming over the earth. Her radiant smile smoothed the wrinkles from Logan's tormented soul. Her wide green eyes lured him closer still. In a dreamlike trance, Logan watched the beguiling nymph tip the silver cup to her own lips, depriving him of a much-needed drink. But then she offered him the cool liquid in a kiss that caused him to groan in pleasure. He drank deeply, unable to get enough of the sweet taste of her. The feel of her soft silky flesh brushing ever so slightly against his blistered skin was like a healing balm.

Without a word, she withdrew from his eager arms. The shimmering fabric of her gown fell away to reveal alabaster skin that appeared as soft as satin. Held entranced by her spellbinding smile, Logan remained motionless while she removed his dusty garments. Tucking her small hand in his, she led him beside the sparkling pool, and together they dived into the water to glide like graceful swans.

Her carefree laughter tickled his senses. Her mystical touch dissolved the weariness that had plagued him for days on end. Bewitched, Logan returned her arousing touch, caress for caress. Her curvaceous body responded to his explorations, and his to hers. He was on fire again, and the cool water couldn't douse the flame that consumed him. Her soft whisper encouraged him to do what he wished with her. Her gentle hands roved over him, giving wondrous pleasure in return, draining his will, stripping him of his sanity.

Logan wasn't sure how or when they had come ashore, but they were there, cushioned on the grass, entangled in each other's arms. His hands and lips whispered across the rose-tipped peaks of her breasts as she held his head to her, pleading for more. She murmured her need for him, assuring him that he pleased her with his practiced touch. She begged him to remain with her always, to give up his wandering and live in this mystical oasis with her forever.

And as the sun hid its head behind the far horizon and the stars winked down from the black velvet sky, Logan came to her. Forever was the promise that drifted from his lips before he bent to take sweet possession of her tempting lips, her luscious body. And there, beside the silver-studded pool, he made wild, passionate love to the green-eyed enchantress who . . .

"Logan?" An embarrassed blush stained Piper's cheeks as the passengers across from her watched her supposed husband curl his arms around her like an octopus.

It had been bad enough that Logan had been employing her shoulder as his pillow while he slept. But this was the straw that broke the camel's back. (Odd that she should employ that adage, since Logan was fantasizing about camels and mermaids.) At first she had suspected Logan only pretended to sleep, that he had leaned against her just to annoy her. But the quiet moans that erupted from his lips indicated he was not only asleep but was also dreaming. Undecipherable syllables broke the silence as he hugged her resisting body to his and nestled his head against her breasts instead of her shoulder.

"Logan, wake up!" Piper gave him a sound shaking. "Honestly, I cannot imagine how you could fall into such a deep sleep in the middle of a choking dust storm!"

The siren's voice was the same one that filled his dreams, but she was no longer whispering her need for him. The abrupt whack to the side of his head brought him awake with a start. Lifting bloodshot eyes, Logan found himself staring at Piper's bosom, one that was heaving in indignation. His arms were clamped around her as if the world were about to come to an end, and he intended to go out with something soft and cuddly clutched to him like a security blanket.

As Logan pushed himself into an upright position, his gaze lanced off Piper's annoyed frown. An amused grin tripped across his lips. "Camels," he said with a chuckle. "I was dreaming about camels."

Piper was prepared to bet her right arm he was lying through his teeth. More likely he was fantasizing about tumbling some wench to satiate his voracious lusts. And that wench better not have been her! Camels indeed!

Logan pulled back the leather curtain to survey the swirling dust. The wind blew grains of sand against the coach like the impatient drumming of fingers. Without a word, Logan unlatched the door and slammed it shut behind him. After climbing atop the coach, Logan assisted the driver and conductor in sighting the road markers that had been planted for just such difficulties.

The whipping winds and riveting sand stung his eyes, but he was thankful for the distraction. After that arousing dream, he wasn't sure he could trust himself to sit casually beside the shapely siren who had seduced him at his oasis in paradise.

Jeezus! Wasn't it enough that the saucy sprite haunted his thoughts? Now when he fell asleep his subconscious would be left to fight the frustrating hallucinations that constantly hounded him. If Piper had known what he had dreamt she would have pulled her pistol and shot him through the heart. She had made it clear that she didn't want him touching her, and she would have preferred that he didn't fantasize about her either!

Chapter 15

For another twenty-four hours the stage rumbled toward Guadalupe Pass in the jutting mountains east of El Paso. The station house where they paused for their evening meal lay beside a creek. Piper announced that she preferred to forgo nourishment to enjoy a long-awaited bath. The dust from the previous day's storm clung to her like an extra layer of skin, and Piper couldn't tolerate another moment. As she walked off to the creek with a bar of soap in hand and Abraham following at her heels, she breathed a sigh of relief.

Piper desperately needed this time alone as much as she needed a bath. Having Logan's masculine body wedged beside hers day and night was wearing her nerves thin. He stained all her thoughts and colored her conversation. His was the first face she saw when she roused from a nap, the only face that drew her eyes like magnets.

Her private room in hell was wallpapered with that man's ruggedly handsome face. It had not been Piper's way to string her male admirers along like some of her fickle classmates did at boarding school. She had never flitted from one man to another, plying them with false hopes of affection. So why was she suffering the torment of being closeted in a coach with the one man who knew how to stir her slumbering passions? Obviously there had been some mistake. The good Lord had mixed her up with some wicked woman who truly deserved to suffer for her sins.

Sighing heavily, Piper sank down into the cool spring-fed

creek, allowing the water to soothe away her aches and pains and the grime. Never again would she take the luxury of bathing for granted. Although her improvised tub was a far cry from the perfumed baths to which she had grown accustomed, it was heavenly. Piper made a mental note to be more appreciative if she survived to return to civilization. Bathing in the wild West wasn't a necessity, she decided. It was indeed a luxury!

After submerging to cleanse her hair, Piper arched backwards to float across the rippling water. Oh, how she wished the stage would delay for the night. She would be content to spend the evening adrift in this stream, relishing every moment of privacy. . . .

"As I live and breathe! I've discovered a mermaid in a desert oasis. And a lovely sight she is!" Logan's husky voice rattled with laughter and Piper jerked to her feet as if she had been snakebit.

Tugging the wild strands of hair from her face, Piper glared flaming arrows at the man who was propped against a cottonwood tree, puffing on his cheroot.

"What do you want?" Piper hissed furiously, attempting to shield herself from his devouring gaze.

The amusement evaporated from his eyes. For a long, brittle moment Logan didn't speak. He merely stood there amid the lopsided halos of smoke, ravishing her luscious body, remembering. . . .

"I want what we had," he said simply and directly.

Piper stiffened like a ramrod. How dare he even suggest things could be the way they had been between them. Did he think he could utter his whims and she would grovel at his feet, satisfied with whatever scraps of affection he might toss at her? The Sahara would sooner be besieged by a blizzard!

"What we had was the mere joining of bodies. You wanted mine because there were no others around. You were hopelessly addicted to your lusts," she snapped testily. "And I was too inexperienced and too curious for my own good."

Her green eyes were throwing fiery sparks. Piper looked madder than a wet hen. Logan chuckled at the comparison. If he had been more sensitive and less hungry for affection

212

he might have realized his laughter only infuriated Piper more than she already was.

"There was nothing wrong with what we had," he had the gall to say.

"Nothing wrong with . . ." Piper was so frustrated she couldn't complete the sentence, and it took a moment to recompose herself. When she did, she let loose with both barrels. "Dumb animals mate when the mood stirs them!" she spewed like a geyser. "Never again am I going to reduce myself to the degrading level of less intelligent life forms. As far as I'm concerned you can go straight to hell and take the rest of your annoying gender with you!"

Logan couldn't help himself. He burst out laughing again. "Next I suppose you're going to tell me you are swearing off men to become a dried-up spinster."

"I most certainly am, but hardly dried-up!" she spat in offended dignity. Long ago, Piper had abandoned the strategy of reasoning with Logan. Maneuvering him no longer worked either. He had become wise to her ploys. Besides, it was more satisfying to spout her irritation than to bottle it up inside her. "For your information, Mr. High and Mighty Logan, women can survive nicely without men in their lives, at least in the ways to which you are referring. You implied that if I couldn't take the heat I should get off the fire. Well, I can take it better than you can."

Her breasts heaved with every angry breath she took, providing Logan with an eyeful of ivory flesh that sparkled with water droplets. "I have adapted to your world and I have made the best of even the most intolerable situations. And all this without your assistance, I might add. All I want is to locate Grant Fredricks and ensure the return of my trust fund. I'm prepared to crawl through snake-infested deserts and tromp over cactus barefooted if need be! I want nothing from you, not sex, not protection, not conversation. Nothing! Do you hear me, Logan?"

Who couldn't? The woman's voice had risen to such a shrill pitch she could have roused the dead.

"You enjoyed the night we spent together so don't try to deny it," Logan parried in a gruff voice. "You may hate me

213

now but you loved me then."

"Loved you?" she parroted in astonishment. "Of all the arrogant . . . Oh!" Piper stamped ashore, oblivious to the fact that Logan had half collapsed from the enticing picture she presented. "You are so full of conceit and self-love there isn't room for anyone else's affection in that thimble of a heart. "Love? Ha!" Piper glowered up at his towering height, wishing she had an axe so she could chop this muscular giant down to her size. "You wouldn't know love if it marched up and sat down on top of you. I have been a fool once or twice in my life. . . ." She paused and then corrected herself. "Three times in my life. But never . . . *never* . . . will I let myself fall in love with a trigger-happy gunslinger who burns money the way most people burn wood in a stove!"

When Piper realized she was standing there stark naked, raving like a madwoman, she snatched up her discarded gown and held it in front of her. Since her hands were occupied, Logan took the liberty of hooking his arms around her waist and lifting her off the ground.

Her furious protests drowned beneath a ravishing kiss that stripped the breath from her lungs. Anger transformed into passion like a torch dropped on a keg of blasting powder. Wild, uncontrollable sensations spilled through Piper as his kiss deepened to explore the moist recesses of her mouth. Her betraying body melted against him and the old familiar feelings consumed her. No matter how long and loudly she declared her hatred for this mountain of a man, he still had the power to stir forbidden desire and leave her wanting the intimacy they had once shared.

Logan set her to the ground so abruptly Piper feared her legs would collapse beneath her. She blinked up into his craggy features like a disturbed owl. Displaying a roguish grin, Logan cupped her chin in his hand to close her sagging jaw.

"Thanks, Piper, I needed that," he murmured, his voice like a velvety caress. "Even if I had to subject myself to your tirade of insults (most of which I couldn't respond to since I have no defense), I've longed for your kiss."

As he shrugged off his shirt and gunbelt to wade into the

creek, Piper willed her sluggish body to walk up the bank. She intended to be fully clothed and long gone before Logan walked ashore. She wanted to feel nothing for him, and she would have if he would let her alone to brew her simmering hatred for him.

Although Piper was determined to keep her distance from the silver-eyed devil, the world and everyone in it seemed to have conspired against her. Willis was so exhausted from lack of sleep that he insisted they fold down the seats to form a makeshift bed in the coach. When darkness settled over the sprawling hills of West Texas, Piper found herself bookended by the inner wall of the cab and Logan's masculine body. Behind him lay Willis, Samuel, and Jedediah. Abraham's basket was shoved in a corner so he couldn't lift the lid and prowl around the sleeping passengers.

When the coach lantern had been doused and the curtains drawn, the interior was as black as pitch. Now that Piper's sense of sight was unavailable to distract her, she was hounded by her overactive sense of smell and touch. Logan's musky fragrance infiltrated her nostrils and clung to her skin. Her quaking body was meshed to his powerful frame as they lay side by side, facing the wall. Out of necessity (or at least under the pretense of necessity) Logan laid a brawny arm over Piper's hip to allow the other male passengers room to sleep. But Piper was as jittery as a rabbit when Logan draped his arm over her.

Each place his body made contact with hers burned brands on her flesh. And when his roaming hand discreetly investigated the terrain of her hip, Piper flinched. It aggravated her that Logan was taking unfair advantage. If she put up a fuss, she would draw suspicion from the other passengers, who believed her to be married to this ornery rake. It was her lot to endure the tingling sensations caused by the soft whisper of kisses against her neck and the light, teasing caresses that started fires that were left to flicker in every fiber of her being.

Logan knew he should turn his back instead of tormenting himself like this. But dammit, he couldn't keep his hands off this lovely nymph. He couldn't appease his passion, not in this cramped coach. Yet the opportunity to kiss and caress Piper

215

without having her pull away from him was too tempting to resist. His hand, as if it possessed a will of its own, glided beneath the hiked hem of her silk skirt to caress her leg and then ventured upward to map the soft flesh of her thigh. He felt Piper's quiet gasp vibrating against his chest, felt her body tremble against his. No matter what obstacles lay between them, Piper was still aroused by his touch, just as he was aroused by touching her.

All of a sudden Logan didn't care that there were five bodies wedged together on the makeshift bed. There was one body that interested him and it sure as hell wasn't Willis's! Logan didn't care if everyone else knew he was kissing his wife. All he knew was that he yearned for the honeyed taste of her the same way a starving man craves a feast. If he didn't relieve just an ounce of this pent-up passion that swelled out of proportion he was going to burst like an overinflated balloon!

When Logan's lips rolled over hers, Piper reminded herself that she detested this bold rogue . . . for all of a tenth of a second. By then, her brain had malfunctioned and she was kissing him back, arching against him like a shameless harlot, wanting him in the worst possible way. It was crazy and utterly insane, and Piper instantly decided *she* was crazy and insane for allowing Logan to embrace her here and now!

After Logan mustered the will to break their ardent kiss, he snuggled against Piper and breathed a shuddering sigh. He hadn't eased his lusty needs as he had hoped. If anything he had fueled them. It wasn't the coach lantern that blazed on a long wick during that night. The dark fires that burned between him and this stubbornly independent vixen provided enough light to illuminate the night sky.

When the coyotes howled, Logan felt the urge to accompany them. They were yowling at the moon, but Logan felt like yelping in frustration. Jeezus! This was going to be the longest night of his life. He felt as if he had been strung out on a medieval torture rack without being permitted to scream in agony. It would have been hollow consolation to know Piper was suffering right along with him. They were both dangerously close to reducing themselves to a pile of smoldering ashes out of their intense awareness of each other. Lying together on the improvised bed was nothing short of sweet, tormenting hell for both of them.

After the weary travelers forded the Pecos River at Elm's crossing, the distance between the company stations lengthened. Twice, when the passengers caught sight of roaming Comanches and Apaches, Logan swung atop the coach to lend an extra gun hand, should they need one. But the stage rumbled along the road without mishap, and Piper was thankful for the extra space provided by Logan's absence. Each time he crawled atop the coach Piper's emotions were allowed the long-awaited opportunity to regroup.

Heaving a dispirited sigh, Piper drew back the leather curtains to peer at the scenery. The featureless land of West Texas had transformed into magnificent buttes and mesas. The road had become a series of steep, long climbs that twisted through the El Capitan Mountains. Behind the foothills, tall mountains scraped the cloudless sky.

The trumpeting of the conductor's bugle heralded their arrival at Guadalupe Pass, located one hundred miles east of El Paso. The Pinery, as the terminal station was called, was high in the mountains. On one side of the road, the hills flattened into a sprawling mesa. On the other side, the jagged mountains shadowed the depot. Below the mesa lay the stone corrals, stage station, and hotel to house the weary passengers. Seven hundred yards below the depot lay an inviting spring, the first one Piper had seen in forty miles. After more than two weeks of traveling they had finally reached the halfway point between St. Louis and San Francisco. It was here that the east and westbound coaches met and made connections with feeder lines.

Piper would have been thankful to be halfway between San Francisco and her missing trust fund if she hadn't known what was in store for her. Logan had informed her, while he was wearing that infuriating grin of his, that there would be at least a two-day layover at the Pinery before they caught their stage.

The delay allowed the exhausted travelers an opportunity to rest their aching muscles and stretch out in bed. But unfortunately, there would be a man in Piper's bed, a man she had difficulty holding at bay. She had hoped that, by now, she would have mustered a spiteful hatred for Logan. To her chagrin, that had yet to happen. If wishing could have made it so, Piper would have detested the ground that raven-haired devil walked on. But it just wasn't so. Piper was still vulnerable to his touch and to that penetrating silver gaze that bore into her to unlock the hidden secrets of her soul.

With her confidence sagging, Piper stepped unassisted from the coach, purposely ignoring Logan's outstretched hand. Holding her head high, she strode toward the depot to inquire about Grant Fredricks, just as she always did.

The stage agent nodded recognition when Piper described Grant, but the news he gave Piper caused her to sit down before she fell down. "As you know, Mrs. Logan," he told her politely, "the stage line has suffered difficulties with marauding Indians and road agents. Mr. Fredricks's coach was held up four days ago. The driver reported that Fredricks was beside himself when his carpetbag was stolen. He wouldn't disclose how much money and valuables he had lost, but he ranted and raved like a madman until the conductor shoved him back into the coach to continue their journey. According to reports, Grant Fredricks got off the stage at Tucson, intending to form a posse to hunt down the desperados who robbed him. He didn't look to be the type who could endure the trials of a manhunt, but he was determined to try."

Piper felt as if someone had punched her in the midsection. The money Grant had stolen from her had been stolen from him? Lord, she was practically penniless as it was! All she had was the cash Logan had given her, and that was only a drop in the bucket compared to what she had lost!

Logan frowned bemusedly as he watched the color ebb from Piper's strained features. Her hands trembled as she restlessly knotted her fist in the folds of her skirt. She was visibly upset by the news, but Logan couldn't fathom why she was as distraught as she appeared to be. Hell, it was only money, and he had generously compensated her before they left Fort Smith. Obviously the news had caught her off stride and her weariness intensified her frustration.

"Oh, by the way," the stage agent added as he glanced at the swarthy giant who was lounging against the wall. "Congratulations, Mr. Logan. I heard you got married." His smile faded as he sighed. "I hope you can find a way to put a stop to these robberies. Grant Fredricks wasn't the only one who suffered losses. The other passengers lost their traveling money, and the mail was scattered hither and yon. Some of it was never recovered. John Hinkley, the stage driver, took a bullet in the shoulder. He'll be laid up a few weeks."

Nodding grimly, Logan grasped Piper's limp arm and hoisted her to her feet. After he had ushered her to their modestly furnished room, Logan turned to take his leave.

"Where are you going?" Piper interrogated him.

"To have a look around," he mumbled cryptically.

Piper hurled her purse at the bed in hopes of relieving her frustration. It didn't help. Her recklessness startled Abraham who leaped straight up in the air to dodge the oncoming missile. Piper didn't bother apologizing to her tomcat. She was exasperated and depressed. She wanted to sit down and have a good cry, but she had resolved never to let Logan see her reduced to blubbering tears again.

"Look around at what?" she asked belatedly. "The cactus, the lizards, the centipedes? I should think you could practically call all of them by name since this is your stomping ground." Her voice conveyed the turmoil of anger and disappointment that simmered within her.

"Hell no," Logan growled at the back of her head. "I was hired to scout around and to prevent another holdup, if possible. I'm trying to do the job I was paid to do. I thought you would be eager to have me out from underfoot for a few hours. You've given me the cold shoulder so often the past week I've got icicles dripping off my chest."

Piper pivoted, too tired to analyze why she felt the need to insult Logan, to anger him. Perhaps she wanted to share the company that misery loves so well. She didn't really know. She only knew she felt like yelling and throwing things, starting with Logan. She wanted to strike out and hurt him the way she was hurting, for a variety of reasons.

"Fine, just trot off into the sunset," she snapped, green eyes blazing. "Maybe while you're out scouting you can stop at Santa Anna and locate a señorita who can appease your animal lusts. And while you're carousing, you can get rip-roaring drunk and burn all your cussed two-dollar bills by lighting those foul-smelling cigars of yours."

Huffily, Piper stamped over to retrieve her purse and threw a fistful of coins at him. "And take these with you," she insisted. "After you finish your drinking and smoking and whoring, plant yourself in a card game so you can gamble away what's left of my money for me. What do I need with a few hundred dollars after all I've lost?"

Her voice had become higher and wilder by the second. She was very nearly screaming in Logan's face, one that was frozen in a muddled frown. In a burst of temper, Piper wheeled around to locate something she could throw against the wall to ease her irritation. Her anguished gaze landed on the lantern and she pounced toward it. Before she could put the projectile to flight, Logan snatched the lantern from her fingertips and returned it to its normal resting place.

"How much money did you lose?" he wanted to know.

Piper refused to glance in his direction, afraid she would burst into sobs and subject herself to his ridicule. "It's none of your business," she hissed bitterly. "I tried to hire you to find Grant for me, but you didn't want the job, remember? You're here to solve Butterfield's problems." Piper laughed humorlessly. "As if one man could rid this stage route of marauding Indians and ruthless thieves. Butterfield should have hired a mercenary army. I don't know why he thinks you can track every desperado in the area without getting yourself killed. And when you do, the road agents will rob and raid at will. If the superhuman Logan can't quell the disturbance no other man will dare try without assistance."

Piper inhaled a steadying breath and fought for composure. "Go ahead, go play leapfrog through the bordellos of Santa Anna and gamble the night away. Go tromp through these rocky ravines in search of desperados and get yourself shot in the back. What do I care?" Her voice crackled and her eyes sparkled with unshed tears as she clutched the bedpost for support. "I won't even be able to give my supposed husband a proper burial. I won't even have enough cash for the return trip east."

Logan gritted his teeth to prevent bellowing at her. He knew Piper was upset, that she was only ranting to vent her exasperation. But he wanted answers and he wanted them now! "How much, Piper?" he demanded as he yanked her around to face him.

Tormented green eyes landed on his craggy face, but she refused to respond to his question.

Logan gave her a hard shake, snapping her head backward, spilling the waterfall of silver-gold curls.

"Damn your stubbornness, tell me how much!" Logan snarled impatiently.

The jolt of having the stuffing shaken out of her freed the words that were trapped in her throat. "Two hundred and fifty thousand dollars," she croaked.

Her confession cracked the mask of cool reserve he usually wore. "A quarter of a mil . . . ?" Frog-eyed, Logan stared down at her anguished expression. "Jeezus!"

Logan let her go so abruptly that she sprawled backward on the bed in a tangle of petticoats. In two long swift strides, Logan was at the door and gone. Then Piper fell apart. She hadn't wanted him to leave and yet she didn't want him to stay. Logan had been right. She should have returned home . . . or what there was left of it after her stepfather auctioned off the hotel, the house, and the furniture to pay his gambling debts. She had waded through hell for almost three weeks and all for naught. Her trust fund may as well have been on its way to China for all the good it would do her now. She would have to track the band of outlaws to their hideout and demand the return of her money. And worse, Logan would probably get himself killed and she would hold that over him forever! She would be destitute and without a home, and would be left mourning a man who had made her fall in love with him even when she didn't want to. . . .

Piper burst into sobs and punched her pillow. Yes, dammit, she was in love with him. Why she cared, heaven only knew. But she did. Logan was like no other man she had ever known. He insulted her and taunted her and forced her to stand on her own two feet. He was long on criticism and short on compliments. He had made her aware of her own feminine yearnings. He had made her love him when there wasn't one logical reason why she should. He desired her, but he didn't love her. He used her to appease his needs because sex was second nature to him.

Now that he had forced her to survive in his world and had stolen her virginity, she couldn't go back to civilization. She didn't belong there anymore. She was no longer a naive bluestocking, as Logan insisted on calling her, and yet she wasn't truly part of Logan's world either. He had transformed her into a misfit, just like he was—an outsider, a loner!

Piper cried all the harder at that thought. But she, unlike Logan, couldn't hire herself out as a gunslinger when she was desperate for money. Perhaps she should just retrieve her pistol and shoot herself. At least she had become competent enough with her Colt .45 to manage that!

A pair of laughing silver eyes materialized before her— taunting her, ridiculing her. Oh, Logan would love this, she mused bitterly. He would delight in seeing her wail like an abandoned child. He would expect it of her and he would mock her for being a helpless, sniveling female who folded her tent when things got a little rough. And wouldn't he have a field day with the knowledge that she had fallen in love with him? He would never let her live that down.

Resolutely, Piper rose to an upright position and wiped away the tears with the back of her hand. Well, she wasn't going to take the coward's way out. She would show that arrogant rogue, she vowed rebelliously. When he returned, *if* he returned, she was going to greet him with dry eyes. She would react to adversity the way men usually did. She was going to become just like them. That was what Logan really wanted anyway, she speculated resentfully. He wanted her to behave like a man, not a woman. Men drank to forget their woes while women cried their eyes out. Well, she would see how Logan liked her when she assumed his role. If she couldn't beat him, she might as well join him.

What Piper was determined to prove to the rest of the world was anybody's guess. She wasn't even sure herself. She was simply rebelling against her monetary losses and the frustration of realizing she had fallen in love with a man who could never return her affection.

After washing her tear-stained face, Piper headed toward the restaurant and then went to the tavern to purchase a bottle of whiskey. She was sure liquor was the answer, and by the time the evening ended, she wouldn't even remember the question. After a few drinks she wasn't going to feel a thing. She would be numb to the world and everyone in it. She wasn't going to recall what had upset her so. She would drink herself deaf, dumb, and blind—just the way men did from time to time.

Get a Free
Zebra
Historical
Romance

*a $3.95
value*

Affix
stamp
here

ZEBRA HOME SUBSCRIPTION SERVICES, INC.
P.O. BOX 5214
120 BRIGHTON ROAD
CLIFTON, NEW JERSEY 07015-5214

BOOK CERTIFICATE

FREE

ZEBRA HOME SUBSCRIPTION SERVICE, INC.

YES! Please start my subscription to Zebra Historical Romances and send me my free Zebra Novel along with my first month's Romances. I understand that I may preview these four new Zebra Historical Romances Free for 10 days. If I'm not satisfied with them I may return the four books within 10 days and owe nothing. Otherwise I will pay just $3.50 each; a total of $14.00 (a $15.80 value—I save $1.80). Then each month I will receive the 4 newest titles as soon as they come off the press for the same 10 day Free preview and low price. I may return any shipment and I may cancel this arrangement at any time. There is no minimum number of books to buy and there are no shipping, handling or postage charges. Regardless of what I do, the **FREE** book is mine to keep.

Name _____
             (Please Print)

Address _____ Apt. # _____

City _____ State _____ Zip _____

Telephone (____) _____

Signature _____
             (if under 18, parent or guardian must sign)

Terms and offer subject to change without notice.

MAIL IN THE COUPON BELOW TODAY

GET FREE GIFT

To get your Free **ZEBRA HISTORICAL ROMANCE** fill out the coupon below and send it in today. As soon as we receive the coupon, we'll send your first month's books to preview Free for 10 days along with your **FREE NOVEL**.

Finally Samuel appeared, his ruffled hair jutting out [of hi]s broad head in all directions. He blinked at Logan like a [dazed] owl. Without apologizing for waking Samuel in the [middl]e of the night, Logan fired the question pertaining to the [wher]eabouts of his missing "wife."

[Sa]muel raked his blunt fingers through his wild hair. "I [thou]ght she would have retired to bed by now," he mumbled [gro]ggily. "She dined with us and then she left. I haven't seen [he]r since."

Muttering under his breath, Logan stormed down the hall [an]d out the door. The abrupt sound of a pistol split the [m]idnight air. Logan glanced in the direction of the noise and [ai]med himself toward its source, which seemed to be [so]mewhere beside the spring.

Logan skidded to a halt and stared in utter disbelief. Piper, [wi]th pistol in hand, was preparing to let loose with another [sh]ot. Like a pouncing lion, Logan leaped toward her to jerk the [gun f]rom her fingertips before she roused the entire depot. His [st]ormy silver eyes glided down her breeches and shirt, ones [th]at fit her curvaceous figure like a glove. Her long hair lay in [re]ckless disarray, and she was sporting the silliest smile ever to [be] plastered on a feminine face. As she wobbled around to [w]ave back toward the bottle she was cooling in the spring, [Log]an rolled his eyes heavenward.

"Jeezus, you're drunk!" he snorted disgustedly.

[P]iper grasped the floating flask and uncorked it. Raising the [bott]le in silent toast, she flung Logan a careless smile. "And [you]'re still alive. I drink to your health."

[W]hen she tipped the bottle to her lips, Logan yanked it away [to gu]lp a drink. He truly thought he needed the whiskey worse [than] she did. Seeing Piper in this condition knocked him [side]ways. When she reached out to retrieve her bottle, Logan [pro]mptly tucked it behind his back. A disappointed frown [clou]ded her face momentarily, but then she shrugged off the [loss] of the bottle.

"[D]id you and the señoritas in Santa Anna enjoy a fiesta?" [she s]lurred out.

"[H]ell no," Logan barked, and then swallowed another drink [to lu]bricate his parched vocal cords. "I've been scouting

ACCEPT YOUR FREE GIFT
AND EXPERIENCE MORE OF
THE PASSION AND ADVENTURE
YOU LIKE IN A
HISTORICAL ROMANCE

Zebra Romances are the finest novels of their kind and are written with the adult woman in mind. All of our books are written by authors who really know how to weave tales of romantic adventure in the historical settings you love.

Because our readers tell us these books sell out very fast in the stores, Zebra has made arrangements for you to receive at home the four newest titles published each month. You'll never miss a title and home delivery is so convenient. With your first shipment we'll even send you a FREE Zebra Historical Romance as our gift just for trying our home subscription service. No obligation.

BIG SAVINGS
AND FREE HOME DELIVERY

Each month, the Zebra Home Subscription Service will send you the four newest titles as soon as they are published. (We ship these books to our subscribers even before we send them to the stores.) You may preview them *Free for 10 days.* If you like them as much as we think you will, you'll pay just *$3.50 each and save $1.80 each month* off the cover price. *AND you'll also get FREE HOME DELIVERY!* There is never a charge for shipping, handling or postage and there is no minimum you must buy. If you decide not to keep any shipment, simply return it within 10 days, no questions asked, and owe nothing.

—Zebra Historical Romances
Burn With The Fire Of History—

No Obligation!

a $3.95 value

FREE

ANOTHER ONE
WE'LL SEND YOU
READING THIS BOOK,
IF YOU ENJOYED

Make This Special Offer...
Zebra Historical Romances

Chapter 16

Exhausted, Logan trudged up the steps to his room. Afte
several hours of hard riding, he was more frustrated than h
had been when he left the Pinery. Learning the exact amoun
of money Grant Fredricks had stolen from Piper knocke
Logan for a loop. He had flung a few hundred dollars at Piper
Fort Smith, thinking he had more than compensated her fo
her losses. She could have scoffed at his foolish arrogance an
taught him a thing or two about the difference between havin
money and being wealthy. Logan had made a fortune and b
built a cattle empire beside the Gila River. But Piper ha
full-fledged heiress before her stepfather and Grant
and whatever he was preyed upon her. The money he h
couldn't begin to match what Piper had lost.

Why hadn't Piper put him in his place when she
chance? Logan frowned in contemplation. He certain
coming after the way he had taunted and intimidated

As he eased open the door, he stared tow
unoccupied bed in the moonlight and shadows. N
Where the hell could she be at this hour? Pivoting on
Logan strode down the hall to rap on Samuel's door
had become her devoted puppy. If anyone knew
become of her, Samuel would. And she had bet
closeted in the room with Samuel, Logan mus
certedly. If she was he was going to beat the tar ou
them!

After rapping on the portal, Logan waited a

around the countryside."

"What a pity." She sighed melodramatically. "I'm sure all the ladies will lament the night they weren't allowed to spend in your arms." A mischievous smile pursed her lips as she peeked up at him through long, tangled lashes. "If they had consulted me, I could have told them they hadn't missed much." It was a baldfaced lie, but it was far better than offering him a compliment.

"Since when did you care where I satisfied my sexual appetite so long as it wasn't with you?" he inquired sarcastically.

Piper plopped down cross-legged beside the spring. Leisurely, she tossed her wild mane of hair aside and retrieved the cigar she had been puffing on before she decided to practice her marksmanship. "I don't care," she mumbled before she inhaled the cheroot. "I don't care about one damned thing."

Logan shook his head in amazement. How could anyone so lovely look so pitifully ridiculous? Piper was both comical and pathetic.

With lithe grace, Logan sank down on his haunches to peer into her bloodshot eyes. The moonlight reflected off those glassy green pools and cast shadows on the elegant curve of her cheeks.

"Do you do this sort of thing very often?" he questioned, biting back a grin. Lord, she looked silly puffing on his cigar and lounging beside the spring like an intoxicated mermaid.

Piper tried to blow smoke rings the way Logan did, but her attempts couldn't match his skills. But then, everything she did fell short of the mark when she compared herself to Logan. "No, actually, this is my first time," she confessed sluggishly. A pensive frown knitted her brow as she stared at the bottle Logan had placed beside her. "I thought drinking would help me forget what I didn't want to remember." She expelled a defeated sigh and reclined in the grass to stare up at the stars. "I still remember, but at least it doesn't hurt quite so much now."

"It will hurt much worse in the morning," Logan prophesied. His silvery eyes mapped her well-sculptured physique, imagining how she would look lying beside the spring without her concealing garments. He rather suspected she would be the identical image of the goddess he had envisioned in his dream.

Her bubble of laughter vibrated through the air. "I cannot imagine how that could be. I've lost my fortune and the man . . ." Piper caught herself before she confessed her feelings for this impossible man. "I hate you, Logan," she said suddenly.

Logan loomed over her, seemingly unmoved by her abrupt remark. "I know," he murmured as his eyes limned her enchanting face. "I hate you too, Piper. I always have." Slowly, his raven head came toward hers. "And I'm going to go on hating you until I can get you out of my blood. . . ."

His lips rolled over hers with such exquisite tenderness that Piper melted into a puddle of liquid desire. When his masculine body half covered hers, Piper arched shamelessly against him. Eagerly she returned his exploring caresses, rediscovering each sensitive point on his rugged body.

He was warmth and rock-hard muscle, and Piper longed to mold herself to his masculine contours. It was as if he were that special part of her that had been missing, as if she couldn't be whole and alive until she had absorbed his awesome strength. Her caresses glided up and down his lean belly, removing the garments that prevented her from seeing what she adored. Her lips whispered over his sensuous mouth, leaving Logan to shudder in barely suppressed passion.

Groaning in frustrated torment, Logan wrestled with the buttons of her shirt, baring her exquisite breasts to his devouring gaze. His worshiping caresses slid over the slope of her shoulder to encircle each taut peak. Bending, he kissed each creamy mound before flicking his tongue against the dusky buds. Tasting her only intensified his craving. He wanted to explore all of her, to lose himself in her luscious body.

When Logan's hands flowed over her like the incoming tide, Piper moaned in sweet torment. He could be so gentle when it met his mood, so loving. And when she confronted this usually well-protected side of his complex personality, she was helpless to resist.

228

Logan knew where and how to touch, to completely arouse her passionate longings. He made her glad she was a woman and he made her vividly aware of how long her feminine yearnings had lain dormant and unfulfilled.

Her body helplessly responded to his intimate fondling. She was like a wild thing in his arms, writhing and arching beneath his masterful touch. It was as if she couldn't get enough of the pleasure he bestowed on her. And Logan made certain Piper was adrift in rapture. It pleased him to give her pleasure. Hearing his name on her lips aroused him. Although they were worlds apart they had found common ground when they made love. They were just a man and a woman who were drawn by a compelling attraction. Their conflicting differences and their contrasting similarities no longer mattered. They needed each other's touch and they reveled in the potion of sweet magic they brewed when they succumbed to their forbidden desires.

Logan reverently caressed her satiny skin. He became addicted to the taste of her. This enchanting nymph was soft and supple, and her body fit so perfectly against his, complementing the hard, hair-roughened terrain of his masculinity. Life had never been so precious, nor passion as exquisite, as it was when Piper melted in his arms. She was his foretaste of paradise, and he ached with the want of her.

Piper's heavily lidded eyes fluttered open to see Logan's massive body poised above hers. He was so maddeningly far away. He was staring down at her in that mysterious way of his that made her wonder what thought clouded his mind. But Piper didn't ask him to translate his thoughts into words. She only wanted to feel his powerful body molded intimately to hers, to hold him until the storm of passion had run its course.

Boldly she reached up to touch him, to guide his body to hers. She ached to appease the monstrous cravings he so easily instilled in her. "Logan, I want you," she whispered longingly. "I need you."

"Do you?" he murmured, holding her unblinking gaze. "How much, Piper? Tell me how much. . . ."

Why was he tormenting her so? Wasn't it enough that she had sacrificed her pride and self-respect to enjoy the ecstasy she had discovered in his arms? "Must I tell you?" Her body arched suggestively against his. "I would prefer to show you. . . ."

And when she did, Logan swore he was reliving his erotic dream. Her hands migrated across his flesh, stirring him in ways no other lover had been able to do. Passion had once been no more than the satisfaction of physical needs, but Piper had given it new meaning and had widened the dimension of desire. She had touched the secret place inside him that he had protected from the rest of the world. It was as if she had touched him spiritually and emotionally as well, as if she had carved her initials on his heart.

Logan was unaccustomed to this odd feeling that transcended physical pleasure, but he could do nothing to fight it. This walking contradiction, this lovely enigma of feminine beauty and undaunted spirit, had bewitched him. Her gentle touch wove a tapestry of unparalleled ecstasy around him. She had composed a sweet, mystical melody that strummed on his soul as it took flight to orbit around the distant stars.

Her kisses skimmed his skin, igniting fires that burned back atop each other. The imprint of her shapely body seared his skin and his mind, unchaining old memories and creating wondrous new ones. Her hands continued to stroke his back as he lowered himself to her. Her moist breath whispered against his shoulder as she surrendered her all to him. And then suddenly tender patience escaped him. Logan feared he would crush Piper when the wild, mindless sensations swamped and buffeted him.

Lord, would he ever get this bewitching sprite out of his blood? Each time they made love she satisfied him completely, and yet he could never quite get enough of her. What he felt for this enchanting goddess was a paradox that constantly puzzled Logan. There seemed to be no end to his need for her.

When Logan's powerful body took possession of hers, Piper felt as if she were floating on a puffy white cloud of ecstasy. She was no longer an entity unto herself but rather a living, breathing part of this magnificent man. They moved as one in perfect rhythm, satiating the hungry needs. He drove into her and she clung fiercely to him, matching his ardent response, whispering his name over and over until even speaking became impossible.

The world suddenly exploded in a kaleidoscope of vibrant colors, and Piper gasped as the budding sensations burst inside her, spreading ineffable pleasure that channeled through every part of her. For what seemed eternity she was held suspended in a world of sublime rapture. Glorious sensations toppled over her like a waterfall. It was a river without a beginning or end that fed on her emotions and her passions. It was a stream of living fire that burned away time. . . .

When Piper drifted back from her splendorous journey she found herself in a peculiar mood. There had been times when loving Logan had drained every ounce of her strength. But now she felt miraculously rejuvenated. As Logan rolled away, Piper eased into the cold spring to dip and dive like a playful mermaid.

How she found the energy to move was beyond Logan. His arms, legs, and chest felt as if they had anchors strapped to them. Reclining on the bank, he watched the impish beauty swim in the moonlight. Her perfectly formed body glistened with diamond droplets as she glided across the silvery pool. Logan would have been content to lie where he was, watching her, admiring her, but Piper wasn't satisfied with that. It seemed she was determined to prey on his entangled emotions. Like a siren walking from the sea, she arose and floated toward him, stretching out her hand to beckon him to her.

Logan chuckled at the implication and gave his raven head a negative shake. His resistance only made her more determined. It was shameless to want him again, but Piper was long past caring what was decent or proper. This could well be the last night she spent in his arms. When they parted company she wanted to carry this precious memory with her always. She loved hopelessly, futilely, but she would never forget this brawny giant who had taught her soul to sing.

"No?" One delicately arched brow lifted provocatively. "Have you forgotten the powers we witches possess?" she teased him as she moved deliberately toward him. "Perhaps I should refresh your memory, my handsome rogue. Let me show you how easy it is to transform *no* into *yes*. . . ."

The moonlight enhanced her beguiling features and

231

sparkled in her green eyes and Logan choked on his breath. As his gaze drifted over her curvaceous body, he felt the stirring of desire, desire he thought he had fully satisfied moments before. But suddenly it wasn't enough. Her suggestive smile and her provocative movements aroused and excited him. Logan swore this nymph was indeed a powerful witch who had captured him beneath her spell. He could momentarily appease his craving for her, but she had somehow become his obsession. The more he made love to her, the more he wanted her.

Logan had contemplated that thought earlier, and he knew it shouldn't have been that way because it was totally illogical. He had never been so mesmerized by another woman. But Piper wasn't just another woman, he reminded himself. She was ever-changing, constantly growing. With each new day she had become stronger, more willful. Her beauty had blossomed like a stunning rose.

Loving Piper was like making love to many women—the ones Piper had been as she passed one milestone after another. He had witnessed each stage of her development, marveling at her newfound strengths, her resourcefulness. And Logan had become a part of this magical transformation from inhibited caterpillar to soaring butterfly. He felt responsible, and yet in awe of the changes Piper had undergone. She had come a long way since their first meeting, but Logan had the premonition this was only another phase through which she would pass before she fully came into her own.

"I want you, Logan," Piper murmured as she eased down beside him.

"You've had me," he chortled hoarsely.

"I've had your magnificent body, it's true," she whispered before she bent to brush her cool lips across his full mouth. "Now I want your heart and soul as well. . . ."

Logan flinched when her adventurous hand wandered over his hip. "We really should return to our room for a decent night's sleep. I'm sure Abraham is worried about you."

"Since when did you concern yourself with Abraham?" she questioned, distracted by the feel of his hair-matted flesh beneath her exploring caress.

Logan removed her straying hand. "I've become attached to that tomcat," Logan mumbled, his voice not as steady as he had hoped. "We better go check on him."

"Go then," she suggested as she flagrantly disobeyed his silent order to keep her hands to herself.

Her caresses became bolder by the second. They roamed everywhere, following the evocative path of kisses that left his skin tingling. Go? While she was doing impossible things to his mind and body? Logan suddenly was devoid of common sense. This shapely sorceress had bent him to her will and he had become passion's pawn. He couldn't have moved away from her arousing touch if his life depended on it.

Logan groaned when her silken caresses traversed every inch of his flesh, turning his muscles to mush. Lord, why had he bothered trying to resist her? It was a waste of breath and energy. . . .

That was the last sane thought to cross Logan's mind. Piper's seductive touch melted his brain. His body roused to the feel of her supple flesh making suggestive contact with his. She had stoked the fires of desire into a raging blaze. Indescribable sensations uncoiled within him when she came to him, giving herself freely, eagerly.

Logan felt as if he were reaching out to grasp some distant emotion that lay just beyond his reach and his understanding. And as his body joined with hers, seeking ultimate depths of intimacy, he found what he had been searching for. There, amid the twinkling stars that sparkled across the boundless sky, were the perimeters of paradise. And suddenly he was there, soaring in this angel's arms, exploring the heights and depths of ecstasy. This lovely goddess had led him down unfamiliar corridors in that mystical castle in the air. Logan knew he would never forget this night as long as he lived. He had discovered the pure essence of pleasure. And when the loving was over and he returned to reality, Logan was sure he had left part of himself behind in that wonderful world of sensations.

When Piper would have been content to nestle in his arms and sleep the rest of the night away, Logan forced her to dress. Grumbling drowsily, she pulled on her outlandish attire. The combined effects of the liquor and lovemaking left her wobbling unsteadily on her feet. Sighing impatiently, Logan scooped her up in his arms and carried her to the inn.

After he laid her abed, he stared down at her, knotted on the sheets in a tight ball. A reluctant grin pursed his lips as he peeled off her clothes, doffed his own, and joined her in bed. If Piper recalled any of the outrageous stunts she had pulled, he would be surprised. She had amused him with her antics and aroused him with her passion. And Logan wasn't going to forget even one rapture-filled moment.

Casting aside his sentimental thoughts, Logan pushed Abraham to the floor and stretched out in bed. Yes, Piper had affected him in ways no other woman had. But that didn't change who he was, who she was. They had made a space in their lives for a time, but that time was quickly drawing to a close. Logan had obligations and Piper . . .

Damn, what was he going to do about this nymph? He hadn't had any idea how much money she had lost. But now that he knew, he had to find a way to . . . Logan sighed wearily. He was too tired to think. Tomorrow he would determine what was to be done about Piper. Tonight he could easily be swayed by these lingering feelings that she stirred with her fervent lovemaking. Tomorrow he would be able to see clearly, to think rationally without her sweet, enchanting memories clouding his mind.

Chapter 17

As the sun rose over the mountains, casting hazy shadows on the foothills and valleys below, Piper moaned miserably. Nausea churned in her stomach and she swore she was dying a slow, agonizing death. The effort required to lift her head sapped what little strength she had mustered. Piper promised herself, then and there, she would never consume any alcoholic beverage other than dinner wine as long as she lived . . . *if* she survived her first bout with whiskey. At the moment Piper wondered if dying wouldn't be a blessing. She felt horrible.

Deciding it best to open her heavily lidded eyes one at a time before she attempted to hoist herself into an upright position, Piper's weighted lashes fluttered up to greet the sun. An instant headache, caused by the piercing light, plowed through her skull and thudded against her brain. Between the blinding shafts of sunbeams, Piper spied Logan lounging backward in a chair. His arms were folded over the back of the chair and his chin rested on his forearms. The wry smile that hovered on his lips drew her wary frown. Why was he looking at her like that?

"How's your head?" he questioned softly. His astute gaze worked its way across the tangled mane of blond hair and the colorless lines of her face, one that was puckered in a pensive frown. "Are you feeling a bit under the weather, little dove?"

Although she was as sick as a dog, Piper tilted a proud chin. "We are all under the weather," she rasped. "It is not humanly possible to be above it."

"You don't look good," Logan observed.

"I feel even worse," Piper sighed, unable to maintain her dignity. Her stomach was pitching like a ship on an angry sea. "I think I'm going to die. . . ."

Logan picked up the toast and coffee he had brought for her. "No, you aren't," he contradicted in a confident tone. "You just look and feel as if you have been dead two days. After a reasonable amount of time passes, you'll be good as new." He lifted the coffee to her lips, urging her to drink. "In the meantime, we've got to revive you enough to put you on the stage. I checked with the stage agent. The coach is scheduled to leave in two hours."

"Two hours?" Piper moaned dolefully. "It will be at least that long before I can stand up!"

To prove her wrong, Logan hooked an arm around her while he balanced the coffee cup in the other hand. "You're up and you're going to stay that way," he told her, grinning at the frazzled beauty who was wrapped in nothing but a sheet. "I want you on that stage."

The world spun furiously about her and Piper clutched at Logan for support before her knees wilted beneath her. "If I am to be on the stage, where are you going to be?" she questioned weakly.

"I'll be on the westbound stage. You're going east," he said matter-of-factly.

His terse command was like an injection of adrenalin. Piper reared back as far as his encircling arm would allow and glowered at him through bloodshot eyes. It infuriated her that he had been so warm and passionate the previous night and so cold and unapproachable this morning. His attitude only testified to her belief that she meant nothing to him. He had used her again to satisfy his lusts, but when the loving was over, he wanted nothing to do with her. He was tired of her and he wanted her out from underfoot.

"I'm going to Tucson to find Grant," she said between gritted teeth. "When he has been jailed for embezzling my money, I'm going to hunt down the desperados and retrieve my trust fund!" Her loud voice caused her to grimace. Damn, she

236

was inflicting more agony on herself than she was already experiencing.

"I'll see what I can do about getting your money back. But you're going home." His tone brooked no argument, but he found himself in the middle of one just the same.

"I most certainly am not," she announced, but not as loudly as before. "No one can be trusted with that kind of money. My stepfather tried to swindle me out of it by conspiring with Grant, who was in charge of the trust at the bank. When I refused Grant's romantic attentions he gave up his hope of marrying my fortune. Then Grant set out to double-cross Hiram and swindle me out of my inheritance. How do I know you wouldn't confiscate the cash and keep it for yourself so you could burn it up two dollars at a time?"

Logan scowled under his breath. "Thanks a helluva lot," he snorted resentfully. "Last night you wanted my body and this morning you don't trust me enough to let me do the job you tried to hire me to do in the first place!"

"You needn't shout," Piper groaned. His candid remark brought a rise of color to her otherwise colorless face. She might have known he would ridicule her for her outrageous antics. "I don't know why you sound so indignant," she sniffed. "You have been using women for years and then shuffling them out of your way. Well, women are entitled to the same privileges, Logan. Just because you seduce a woman doesn't mean you intend to keep her forever. And just because I took pleasure in your body last night doesn't mean I trust you."

Dammit, sometimes she made him so furious he wanted to shake her until her teeth rattled. But he wasn't going to permit her to divert his attention, not this time. The issue was her trip home and her lack of faith in him. And for some reason, her mistrust rankled him to no end.

"By God, you're going east," Logan boomed.

"By God, I'm going west," Piper snapped back, despite her headache. "You are supposed to be my husband. It would look suspicious if I suddenly turned around and went back where I came from." Inhaling a deep breath, Piper struggled to control

237

her temper and then proceeded in a softer tone. "Can't you understand, Logan? I have nothing at home. Hiram auctioned off all we had left to pay his debts. He bled my mother dry. All that is left for me is the trust fund that Grant stole. Without it, I'll have to take a job in the first town I happen upon. I have everything to gain and nothing to lose by searching for my inheritance."

Logan had always considered himself strong willed to a fault. But there was something in the way this wild-haired vixen was staring up at him that stirred more sentiment than sense. He couldn't think of one good reason why she should accompany him west, and yet he couldn't conjure up one excuse to make her go east when she had her heart set on searching for her money. It was absurd, and she would probably get herself into trouble. Jeezus, before he knew it, he was quietly nodding compliance to her whim. Logan had the uneasy feeling he would regret his decision.

"All right," he muttered grouchily, "but I don't know what you think you can do. . . ."

His grumbling remark was muffled by Piper's grateful kiss. It dawned on Logan that, somewhere along the way, he had lost complete control of this saucy minx. But confound it, how was a man supposed to resist those enormous green eyes?

Well, maybe he could convince Piper to take up residence on his ranch while he attended his duties for Butterfield and searched for her missing trust fund. Surely she would agree to that since that was where the supposed Mrs. Logan belonged. At least Piper would be safe there. It was better than having her running around loose in Tucson. With her arresting good looks she would need a stick to fight off the throng of men who would be vying for her attention.

"If the eastbound coach leaves in two hours, when are we heading west?" Piper questioned, drawing Logan from his pensive deliberations.

"Not until tomorrow morning," he reported. "We have to await the feeder line from the south to pick up another mail pouch." A teasing smile pursed his lips as he watched Piper wilt back onto the bed. "There will be a fiesta held tonight to entertain the stage passengers and other travelers who purchase supplies here before migrating west. I'm sure you will be eager to celebrate, just as you did last night."

The mere thought of imbibing liquor turned Piper green around the gills. "I think I will decline the invitation," she murmured as she snuggled beneath the sheet.

Logan strolled over to check his appearance in the mirror and inadvertently trod upon Abraham's tail. The tomcat's pained yowl stabbed at Piper's head, causing her to groan miserably. Logan wasn't the least bit sorry he had caught Abraham's tail. It would teach that pesky cat to stay out of his way.

When the cat darted onto the bed and Piper had pulled her head from beneath the pillow, Logan flung her a rakish smile. "You don't mind if I attend the celebration without you, do you, Mrs. Logan?" he questioned as he slicked back his hair. "If you don't care to dance with me, perhaps I can find someone who will."

For a long moment, Piper stared at Logan's ruggedly handsome profile. Was he trying to make her jealous? Was this another way of feeding his male pride? Well, if he thought to make her the laughingstock by gallivanting with another female while they were supposed to be married, he was in for a surprise. She would attend the cussed celebration. Besides, it would be worth it to see if Logan could dance. It might well be the only opportunity she had to outdo him. Just once, she would like to be better than Logan at something!

"I've reconsidered and I've decided to accompany you," she announced. "Since we are supposed to be married, I suppose we should keep up appearances. And it has been too long since I've enjoyed a dance. It should prove a refreshing change from sitting in the coach."

Logan's silver eyes fastened on the smug smile that rippled across her lips. Obviously Piper thought she could dance circles around him. And maybe she could, but at least he had accomplished his ultimate purpose. She was not going to spend the entire day and night in bed. She had been confined to the coach for days on end. The celebration was their one opportunity for diversion before they began the next leg of their rugged journey.

Dropping into an exaggerated bow, Logan smiled back at the rumpled beauty. "I would be honored to have you on my arm this evening, my dear wife."

"As opposed to under your thumb where you usually try to keep me?" Piper purred pretentiously. "Indeed, what a refreshing change that will be."

Dammit, she was doing it again—trying to bait him into an argument. Somehow their roles had become reversed the past few weeks. Now she was the one flinging jibes at him. But Logan refused to rise to the taunt. What Piper needed was a few hours rest to cure her hangover and sweeten her disposition. Keeping that in mind, Logan refused to snatch up the gauntlet. He merely ambled toward the door.

"While you're catching a nap, I'll do a little investigating," he told her.

"Until later then, Prince Charming," Piper cooed sweetly. "Try not to get yourself scalped by a roving band of renegades."

Logan swiveled his head around. "Prince Charming?" he questioned bemusedly.

"He's the one Cinderella met at the . . ." Piper sighed heavily. "Never mind, Logan, you are too old for fairy tales."

The strangest smile Piper had ever seen on Logan's face suddenly claimed his bronzed features. "I am at that," he agreed. There was a hint of remorse in his voice that Piper was at a loss to explain. "Sleep well. . . ."

As the door silently swung shut behind him, Piper frowned puzzledly. She had the feeling there was an underlying meaning in his quiet remark, but she didn't have the foggiest notion what it was.

Logan's comment was aimed more at himself than at Piper. He had needed to remind himself that fairy tales didn't come true. He had a way of forgetting that when Piper distracted him. She made him want things he knew they could never have together. And he was no one's Prince Charming. Piper was probably the image of Cinderella. Logan couldn't say for certain, having never heard the story, but of one thing he was certain, a lovely heiress and a shiftless gunslinger didn't belong together. There could be no happy ending for them. When the time came, Piper would go her way and Logan would go his. That was the way it had to be, simply because it was for the best.

By midafternoon, Piper had rallied enough to bathe and dress and venture downstairs without looking as if she had just crawled off her deathbed. But it was unnerving to realize she felt lost without Logan by her side. Attempting to preoccupy herself, Piper toured the supply store that was heaping with goods for travelers in search of the gold that had recently been discovered at Pike's Peak.

Several times she caught herself searching for Logan's face in the milling crowd. As time went by, she began to wonder if disaster had befallen him. The last rays of sunshine had disappeared and still he hadn't returned from wherever he had been. When he finally did arrive at the inn, he had very little to say about what he had been doing.

When Logan trudged upstairs to soak in the tub behind the dressing screen, Piper hurriedly changed into the garments she had purchased for the fiesta and then informed him that she would meet him downstairs. Piper wasn't sure why she felt the need to surprise him with her appearance. But for some reason she longed to make a lasting impression on Logan. It was the first time they had attended anything remotely close to a social function, and she wanted Logan to be proud to stand at her side. In the years to come, when he thumbed through long-forgotten memories, she wanted him to remember her as she appeared this night. If she couldn't hold him forever, she wanted to be the quiet smile that touched his lips when he glanced back through the window of time to recall the "wife" he had once had.

After examining her appearance in the mirror, Piper was satisfied with the extra time she had spent with her coiffure. With a quiet goodbye, she slipped out the door, following the sound of the Spanish guitars, violins, and harmonicas that serenaded the night.

241

Piper had just arrived at the refreshment table when Samuel Kirby approached her. Samuel's facial expression was compliment in itself, and Piper was pleased to note the amount of attention he was bestowing on her. She only hoped Logan would sit up and take note. It was a silly romantic whim, but Piper wanted Logan to be as attentive to her as Prince Charming was of Cinderella. Since Logan hadn't heard the tale, she would prefer to live it than to explain it to him.

That foolish notion whirled in her head the entire time she was dancing in Samuel's arms. It even lingered while Jedediah took Samuel's place during one of the slower tunes. Piper came to her senses three dances later while she was being held in Willis's bony arms. Almost an hour had passed and still Logan hadn't shown his face. Piper was stung by the disappointed feeling that Logan wasn't coming at all. Either that or some other female had caught his eye and he hadn't bothered searching out his supposed wife.

Disgruntled though she was, Piper politely declined the request of the young man who asked her to dance, and then lingered at the refreshment table. While she stood watching the other dancers twirl about, Piper heard Logan's deep, resonant voice behind her.

When she turned around she very nearly dropped the glass she clutched in her hand. Logan had shed his buckskins and had fastened himself into a black waistcoat that complemented his broad shoulders and trim waist. The form-fitting black trousers called attention to the muscled columns of his legs, and his white shirt contrasted his tanned face. He looked . . . Piper paused to select the precise adjective to describe his appearance. Logan looked beautiful, that's how he looked! Garbed in his sophisticated attire, with his eyes glistening and his hair glittering blue-black in the torch light, he was truly a sight to behold. Apparently she wasn't the only one who thought so. Piper's gaze darted sideways to note that every woman in the area was ogling him with blatant appreciation. Not that she blamed them. When Logan fastened himself into the fancy trappings of a gentleman he inspired a woman's wildest fantasies. He suddenly had the appearance of wild nobility mingled with sophistication—the subtle, intriguing combination of rugged masculinity tempered with dignified refinement. Piper felt her knees weaken as she peered at his striking physique.

It suddenly struck Piper that the evening she had envisioned had happened in reverse. She had hoped to bewitch Logan, but it was the other way around. Each time she tired to take her eyes off him, they kept sliding back to devour every well-structured inch of him. She was gaping at him like a lovesick schoolgirl. This wasn't at all what she had in mind!

Piper would have enjoyed a small amount of consolation if she had known Logan was just as mesmerized as she was. But she was too busy drooling over him to notice that he was simultaneously studying her with his hawkish gaze. Piper had purchased an off-the-shoulder peasant blouse and colorful skirt for the festive occasion. It had been her subtle way of assuring Logan that she could adapt to her surroundings.

It seemed Piper had dressed to please him and he had dressed to please her. The thought made Logan chuckle softly as he took her hand and led her away from the refreshment table. But the moment he took Piper in his arms to sway in rhythm with the music, Logan forgot the obvious differences between them, and he resented the clothes that separated them. Dancing with this stunning beauty only served to remind him of more intimate moments.

He had been vaguely tired when he returned from an afternoon of hard riding. An incident earlier that evening had clouded his thoughts and soured his disposition. When he returned from scouting the area, a young gunslinger who itched to test his abilities had sought Logan out, purposely antagonizing him. Logan had tried to shrug off the younger man but it had been impossible to avoid trouble. Although Logan had walked away unscathed, his challenger had lost the use of his right arm for several months to come. Logan had made certain the arrogant youth had been put out of commission with a well-aimed shot to the elbow.

When Piper's supple body brushed provocatively against his, Logan put the unfortunate encounter with the trigger-happy gunslinger from his mind. The feel of her arm curled about his neck was intoxicating. The scent of jasmine fogged

243

his senses. Jeezus, how was he to concentrate on dancing when his body was interested in more tantalizing activities?

Piper tried to control the accelerated beat of her heart as she swayed with the music. But it was damned near impossible. The feel of his hand lying against her spine set off a series of chain reactions and shock waves. Standing this close to Logan had always disturbed her. Dancing with him was even worse! She hadn't expected Logan to be so light on his feet. But he danced the way he did everything else—skillfully and superbly.

The moment the musicians struck up a lively tune, Piper threw herself into the folk dance, concentrating on the unfamiliar steps performed by the Spanish maidens. Logan stood back with the rest of the men to watch the women, who twirled in perfect rhythm with the music. As if entranced, Logan's eyes singled out Piper. All his senses were tuned to her, mesmerized by her elegant beauty, watching her move with the most sylphlike grace imaginable. The smile that blossomed on her lips held Logan spellbound, and he swore he would never grow tired of gazing at her. She was poetry in motion, the sum composite of poise, refinement, and loveliness.

When the dance ended, Piper dashed back to his arms, giggling giddily. She reminded Logan of a fun-loving child who had not a care in the world. Her lighthearted mood was contagious, and Logan found himself smiling for no other reason except that Piper was. He had somehow become the extension of her impish grin, her reservoir of overflowing pleasure.

Piper had never been so at ease in his presence, except perhaps the previous night. Last night, Logan had attributed her reckless mood to the generous amount of whiskey she had consumed. But he had no explanation for the gay abandon she displayed this evening. Even though Logan couldn't pinpoint the reason for her carefree manner, he reveled in this fascinating facet of her personality, one she rarely exposed to him. She was so full of life and laughter that Logan felt exhilarated just being near her. He wanted to capture this precious moment, to freeze time so this night would last forever. She had him riding on a carousel, spinning with the lively music. His eyes never left her face as they danced the night away. He was totally entranced by the emerald-eyed leprechaun who had materialized before his very eyes, and for the first time, Logan allowed himself to speculate on what life would be like with this bewitching nymph at his side.

It was almost midnight when the festivities ended and Logan and Piper ambled toward the hotel. Piper envisioned the perfect ending to a perfect evening with her very own Prince Charming. But her dream shattered in a thousand pieces when the hotel clerk intercepted them at the foot of the steps. When the young man handed Logan the message, informing him that its sender indicated the matter was urgent, Piper couldn't disguise her disappointment.

After reading the note, Logan heaved a heavy sigh. "I have business to attend," he told Piper as he pivoted on his heels. "Don't wait up for me. I may be late."

Forcing the semblance of a smile Piper watched Logan stride out the door. Although she knew Logan's business was none of her own, Piper was stung by curiosity. Knowing how easily Logan could detect the fact that he was being followed, Piper pursued him at a cautious distance. The last thing she wanted was to be caught snooping and be forced to explain herself.

Logan strode away from the lights of the small community nestled in the El Capitan Mountains and wended his way along the steep slope to the mesa. Piper inched up the incline until she had gained a vantage point that allowed her to peer down at the two men on horseback who had been waiting for him. Squinting in the moonlight, Piper surveyed the forms and faces of Logan's companions. She had never seen either of the men before, and she was annoyed that she was unable to hear their words.

Who were these men? Piper wondered as she eased away from her lookout point. What did they want with Logan? Well, whatever was going on, she probably would never know for certain. Logan was the world's worst about refusing to explain himself or his actions. All Piper had accomplished was to pique her curiosity. If she didn't quicken her pace, Logan would be sidestepping down the slope to return to the hotel before she could tuck herself in bed.

Scurrying along at a fast clip, Piper propelled herself toward the hotel. Thankful she had reached her destination before Logan realized she had chased after him, Piper bounded up the steps and prepared for bed. At least there was no harm done, she consoled herself. She had learned nothing from her nocturnal prowling, but fortunately she hadn't been caught snooping!

It didn't take Logan long to put the late night rendezvous out of his mind. The moment he pointed himself in the direction of the hotel his thoughts immediately turned to the enchanting nymph who awaited him. Logan intended to make this evening a memory that would burn brands on Piper's mind. The unexpected interruption had only delayed his opportunity to live his fantasy. The moment he stepped into their room he was going to . . .

"I hope nothing is amiss," the hotel clerk remarked, dragging Logan from his arousing thoughts.

"Amiss?" Logan eyed him with consternation.

"I became concerned when Mrs. Logan followed after you and then returned alone," the innkeeper reported. "I heard about your trouble with the young gunslinger today and I wondered if someone else had called you out to challenge your talents with a gun. I was afraid your wife might try to intervene in hopes of preventing another showdown."

Logan was on a slow burn. Damn that minx! She could have gotten herself in a peck of trouble by striking out alone at night. Had she learned nothing after being attacked on the streets of Fort Smith?

Although Logan calmly assured the clerk there was no need for worry, there was nothing calm about his demeanor by the time he reached the top of the steps. Piper needed to be taught a lesson about minding her own business. What Logan was doing in the wee hours of morning was none of her concern. She could have complicated matters for him if his associates had discovered they had been followed.

The door bounced against the wall, sending a trickle of dust from the woodwork, causing Piper nearly to jump out of her skin. She had pretended to be dozing, but Logan's loud entrance would have awakened the dead, so there was no sense feigning sleep. Before she could murmur an innocent greeting, Logan snatched her out of bed and shook the stuffing out of her.

Abraham, who had been peacefully lounging beside her, bounded to safety when he caught Logan's scent. The tomcat had learned it was best not to cross that powerful giant. Abraham occasionally sank his claws in Logan's flesh when opportunity permitted him to enjoy his vengeance, but his revenge was always short-lived. Logan usually got even. Abraham had learned that the hard way. In this instance Piper was on her own. Abraham showed his true colors by slinking under the bed.

"If you ever pull another stunt like that I'll tie you to the bed post before leaving!" Logan growled into Piper's shocked face.

"What stunt?" Had she sounded innocent enough? She certainly hoped so. Logan looked like black thunder, and she had no desire to bring down his wrath while he was in his present mood. He looked as if he wanted to strangle her, among other things!

The fact that Piper looked angelic enough to sprout wings and a halo had Logan snarling under his breath. "You know damned well what I'm talking about," he scowled as he sent her sprawling backward in a most unladylike manner. "You followed me. The clerk was kind enough to inform me that you didn't skip off to bed as I expected you to do."

The snitch! Piper fumed. That hotel clerk had no right to poke his nose in places it didn't belong. Never mind that she had done the same thing when she went trotting off after Logan as if she were his shadow! "I didn't know you had spies checking on me each time I stirred a step," Piper snapped defensively. "I was only . . ."

"So you do admit you followed me," Logan muttered angrily. "Woman, if you don't learn your place . . . and quickly . . . you won't have a place on this planet for very long! If I would have wanted your company I would have asked for it. What I was doing was none of your concern, and if you jeopardize my work you can damned well expect to answer for it."

Piper was standing on shaky ground, and Logan's glacial gaze threatened to turn her blood to ice. Those unnerving eyes could make her pay for sins she hadn't even committed! After she recovered from the effects of his frosty stare, her face flushed with irritation. Piper detested it when Logan scolded her as if she were a senseless child. He constantly put her on defense and she always felt inclined to justify her actions.

"Can I help it if I was worried about you?" she sputtered. "I was afraid you were headed for some sort of trouble. I only wanted to be there if you needed me."

A burst of incredulous laughter exploded from his lips. "And what, pray tell, were you going to do if I met with disaster? Lash my opposition to death with your tongue?" he questioned scornfully. "Having you come to my defense is like sending a lamb to protect a lion!"

Phrased as such, her actions did sound a mite ridiculous. But confound it, she had been concerned about Logan's welfare.

Piper decided to change tactics since she had lost the debate. "I don't suppose you are going to tell me who those two men were and why they wanted to see you in the middle of the night rather than in broad daylight."

"No, I don't suppose I am." Logan's tone softened, the direct result of having Piper peek up at him with those enormous emerald eyes.

Logan wasn't sure Piper had learned her lesson well enough, but he was quickly losing interest in conversation. This evening was all he had left to share with her in privacy. They had enjoyed a sweet, companionable silence until he had spoiled it with his burst of temper. Knowing they would be wedged in the stagecoach with other passengers the following morning left Logan grasping for a few moments of pleasure before the endless hours of monotonous drudgery.

Tenderly, he reached beneath her chin and bent to brush his lips over hers. His life was full of battles, and Logan didn't wish to go another round with Piper. He only wanted to enjoy her, to recapture those mystical moments while they were dancing, while they were aware of no one but each other.

"Logan, I only . . ."

"I haven't forgiven you for your foolish prank," he interrupted her as his arms glided around her waist, drawing her full length against him. "But you can make me forget. . . ."

And suddenly all was forgotten except the honeyed taste of her kiss, the wondrous way his body responded when it came in close contact with her silky flesh. Logan didn't want to think past the moment. He wanted to revel in splendor and lose himself in this angel's arms.

When his roaming hands pushed the gown from her shoulders to explore her quivering skin Piper dissolved into a pool of liquid desire. She longed for this moment of rapture as much as Logan did. They were at odds so often, and there was never enough time to explore the sensual world of passion Logan had revealed to her.

The previous day Piper had sworn she had nothing left in the world, but when Logan held her so tenderly and made love to her as if she were special to him, she realized she needed nothing else. Piper let herself pretend he felt the same deep emotion for her that she harbored for him. She cherished each gentle caress, each soul-shattering kiss. The feel of his hands sweeping across her pliant flesh was the quintessence of pleasure, and she returned each touch, worshiping him as if he were a precious gift.

Although the words were there, waiting to be voiced, Piper swallowed her confession. She knew Logan wasn't offering forever, but she loved him enough to make the sacrifice of living only for this night. Her deep affection for him left her grasping for whatever small amount of fondness he might have felt for her. Later she would probably regret giving herself wholeheartedly to him. But for now it seemed so right, so natural.

There was something in the way Piper touched him that left Logan suspended in time and space. She was weaving sweet dreams around him. He felt as if he were gently rocking upon a ship that was floating through a haze of indescribable pleasure. It was as if he and Piper had written their own whimsical fairytale. It was warm and tantalizing, and he would have been content to drift forever in this soft white fog of ecstasy.

Logan tried to assure himself that knowing this night was all they had was what bewitched him and left him clinging to each heart-stopping sensation. He was trying to make more of this moment than was really there. But this beguiling angel felt so unbelievably good in his arms, and her caresses were embroidered with loving tenderness. It was like nothing he could ever remember experiencing. It was a glimpse of paradise.

Her inventive ways thrilled and delighted Logan. He found himself in the midst of something that transcended physical satisfaction. Ever so slowly, Piper had led him onto one plateau of passion after another. Her unhurried caresses lifted him so slowly that he hadn't realized he was there until he was soaring to another towering height. And before he knew it, he was dangling on a lofty pinnacle where there was not one breath of air. And still she assaulted him with arousing kisses and titillating caresses that left him suffering from a deprivation of air.

She touched him everywhere, discovering each sensitive point, boldly fondling, massaging. Logan swore he would perish long before Piper satisfied this gigantic need that had somehow crept up on him through the cloud of heady pleasure. He had been drifting so peacefully, relishing her tender caresses. And lo and behold, he was suddenly consumed by a tormenting ache that demanded immediate fulfillment.

As if she knew how greatly he needed her, Piper settled exactly above him. "Love me," she murmured softly. "Love me, Logan. . . ."

A groan, an almost inhuman groan, tumbled from his lips as he surrendered to the savage passions that had arisen from out of nowhere to consume him. They were as close as two people could get, and yet it wasn't enough to appease this maddening craving. He was like a desperate man, impatient, hungry, devouring. Piper had aroused him so skillfully and completely that he could not control the tide of savage passion that crested over him. He was possessed by the desperate need to fulfill his primal needs. And yet in the darkness that accompanies mindless desire, there was one angelic face shining like the distant moon. It could not have been passion for passion's sake when Piper's hauntingly lovely face beckoned him even while he was engulfed by such innate instincts. There was more to this moment of maddening desire, something that touched his heart and soul, as well as his male body.

Before Logan could contemplate the reason for his wild, reckless reaction to Piper's unique brand of lovemaking, a shudder rocked the very core of his being. It was as if internal combustion had taken place and he was being flung helter-skelter through time and space, scattering in a million pieces. Logan wasn't sure he had a mind left, and he knew his body had disintegrated. He was numb with rapture. Logan might have likened himself to Humpty Dumpty, had he been familiar with the story.

And so Logan lay abed, waiting for the fog of passion to rise and grant him strength and sanity. All Logan had wanted was to inscribe his initials on Piper's heart, but she left her mark on him instead. If he lived a century, Logan doubted he would forget this magical night.

When Logan drifted off to sleep, Piper eased down beside him, smiling contentedly to herself. For a few minutes she merely peered into his moonlit features soft in repose. Even if she couldn't enjoy forever with this man, she would be consoled in the fact that she held a certain inalienable power over him. She had pleased and satisfied him and Logan had made no attempt to disguise what he was feeling while they were navigating their way through the sea of windswept passion. Perhaps she would never earn his love, but she knew how to appease him. If only . . .

Piper tossed the wistful thought aside. Logan was Logan and he wasn't going to change. He had given himself up to his passion and his emotions this night. But come dawn, the gentle, affectionate man who had emerged from that hardened shell during the night would disappear. Yet, it was comforting to realize she had touched the gentle giant who loomed beneath that callous exterior. It was the best Piper could hope for when she had fallen in love with a man who was known to all the world as an invincible warrior. Most folks had labeled him ruthless and unfeeling because he had to be in order to accomplish the impossible feats they requested of him. But deep down inside, beneath those steely muscles and hard flesh beat the heart of a man who could yield to love, if only he would give himself half a chance.

Piper closed her eyes and snuggled against Logan's sinewy length, listening to the methodic beat of his heart. Oh, how she wished his heart belonged to her. She wouldn't need her lost inheritance. All the money in the world couldn't compensate for her need to be loved by this lion of a man. But Piper was growing accustomed to disappointment. She knew she couldn't keep Logan as her own. It would be like trying to hitch herself to a fleeting cloud or gather sunbeams in her hand. Logan was like the wind, constantly moving and ever-changing. He could be gentle and caressing at times, billowing and raging at other times. One day she would wake and he wouldn't be there to love, and she would be left to yearn for a night just like this magical night.

Stop being so hopelessly sentimental, Piper chastised herself as she begged for sleep to overcome her. She would only make herself miserable if she dwelt on things that could never be. Logan wanted to be no more than a smile and a moment, and she could expect no more from him. That was a fact of life and she would cope much better if she never allowed herself to forget that.

PART III

Disasters come not singly,
But as if they watched and waited,
Scanning one another's motions.
When the first descends, the others
Round their victim sick and wounded—
First a shadow, then a sorrow,
Till the air is dark with anguish.
                                    —Longfellow

Chapter 18

While the stage jostled over the rocky path on its way across its three-hundred-mile route in New Mexico Territory, Piper's head drooped against Logan's shoulder. Logan glanced down at the comely nymph who sagged in sleep. The fickle hand of fate had turned on him when he crossed paths with Piper. Logan had no complaints with life. He had no one but himself to fret over. And suddenly there was Piper—all naive innocence and stunning beauty. Now their lives were entangled in one another's because of her charade. He must have been crazy to allow her to drag him into this masquerade. He was in over his head and he couldn't walk away uninvolved.

Dammit, Piper had begun to matter more to him than she should have. If he hadn't cared, she couldn't have persuaded him to travel farther west when she should have sped off in the opposite direction. Hell's bells, he may as well have married this spirited sprite. He already felt responsible for her and she could certainly use the security his wealth provided if she never recovered her inheritance.

A woman like Piper could never love a man like me, Logan reminded himself sensibly. But she did need him, and maybe that was what Logan had been searching for all his life. Maybe he was trying to satisfy his need to be needed. Perhaps that was why he hired out his gun hand. In the beginning he thought it had only been for the money, that and the chance to rid the world of men like his father. But maybe, deep down inside, he wanted respectable citizens to depend on him so he would feel wanted—if only until he had resolved their problems. . . .

Logan shook his head to shatter his pensive thoughts. He had to keep a proper perspective where Piper was concerned. She would be like all the others, he reminded himself cynically. If he did manage to recover her money, she would walk away with a hasty thank you and without a backward glance. He would have served his purpose and she would be on her merry way. Well, it would be for the best, Logan convinced himself. They had no future together. What a mismatched couple they were—a sophisticated city slicker and a half-breed gunslinger.

Pensively, Logan stared out the window, unaware that he was cuddling Piper closer to him than necessary while she slept through Jedediah's snoring. The coach sped along at the accelerated speed of ten miles per hour as it weaved over and around the rocky cliffs parched by the blazing sun. The stage stations were spaced farther apart on this leg of the journey, providing perfect opportunity for Indian raids and holdups. But as of yet Logan had seen no sign of trouble. His astute gaze was glued to the flat-topped plateaus that lay at the base of the looming mountains. The brown mesas were covered with coarse grass, sage, and saguaros, and broken by occasional sand dunes. The lower slopes of the mountains were dotted with mesquite, piñon, and juniper. Higher up the jagged slopes, poplars and pines stretched toward the cloudless sky.

It was a barren land, Logan mused, inhabited only by Apaches and vagabonds. It was a rugged, untamed land where a man had to depend on instinct and resourcefulness to survive. Logan felt a part of this rough country. It was where he belonged and where Piper didn't fit in. And after hours of being confined to the coach with his thoughts, Logan was growing more perturbed with himself for allowing Piper to accompany him.

She really doesn't belong here, Logan thought as he squirmed uncomfortably in his seat. Nor did she belong with a man who was as restless as a tumbleweed. The more he thought about it, the blacker his mood became. He had permitted Piper to talk him into staying when he knew she should go. Dammit, there were gangs of ruthless outlaws haunting these buttes and secluded ravines. If they got their hands on Piper . . . Jeezus!

He must have been out of his mind to agree to this.

Although Piper had done nothing to provoke his irritation, she found herself the brunt of unjustified criticism when she awoke from her nap. It seemed Logan was holding her in contempt merely for being born and for crowding into space that he considered his own private property. Since they left the Pinery at the base of the El Capitan Mountains, Logan had become less receptive to conversation. He was bursting with bad temper and he sat in his corner like a proud, unapproachable Indian war chief.

Each time Willis opened his mouth to complain of the heat and cramped conditions, Logan pounced like a panther, growling one snide remark after another. When Piper tried to keep the peace, she found herself on the receiving end of Logan's annoyed glares and ridiculing taunts that sorely tested her temper. Piper had just about enough of Logan's foul disposition, and she intended to read him the riot act as soon as they were granted a moment of privacy at the upcoming station.

The sound of the conductor's bugle alerted her that the depot was nearby. Piper quickly formulated what she intended to say to Logan as soon as she had the chance to say it, but a muddled frown knitted Piper's brow when the coach jostled to a halt in front of the evacuated swing station. When she stepped down from the coach she stared at the abandoned building and empty corrals. There was no sign of life to greet them.

"I don't like the looks of this," the driver grumbled to Logan. His route took him only as far as the Pinery before he reversed direction. He could hardly believe this was the same bustling depot he had passed the previous day. "We were here yesterday and all was well." His suspicious gaze circled the abandoned station. "What do you make of it?"

Logan surveyed their quiet surroundings and then stepped inside to survey the disheveled supply room. "Indians," he said quietly. "It seems they took everything that wasn't nailed down." His somber gaze slid back to the driver. "Are you planning to give the horses a rest?"

The driver nodded his shaggy head. "Since we don't have

fresh horses, we'll have to rest the ones we've got or they'll drop in their tracks. We're heading into rugged country, you know. The climb to Apache Pass will exhaust them."

Piper impatiently waited for Logan to finish his conversation with the driver before she approached him. When Logan ambled away from the other men to peer off into the distance, Piper squared her shoulders and stamped toward him.

"I would like a word with you," she demanded. "I think you have been purposely baiting Willis."

Sparing her an intimidating smile, Logan glanced down at Piper, who reminded him of a wilted rose. The excessive heat and the grueling journey were showing their effects. Her frazzled appearance testified to the fact that she didn't belong in this wild, desolate country.

"Since when have you decided to come to Willis's defense?" he sniffed sarcastically. "Or is it that you simply prefer to take sides with anyone who disagrees with me?"

Her lips compressed in irritation. "Just what is it, exactly, that is bothering you, Logan?" she wanted to know. "I think you are annoyed with me and you're venting your aggravation on everyone else."

"That is exactly what I'm doing," Logan growled as he pivoted to stare into the distance. "You shouldn't be here. We're headed for trouble and I never should have let you talk me into bringing you farther west."

Piper peered at his broad back and her heart twisted in her chest. Logan seemed so distant, so unreceptive. It was as if there were two very different men bottled inside his masculine body. She had come to love the gentle giant who touched her so tenderly. But she had difficulty dealing with this stone mountain of a man who loomed beside her now.

Heaving a frustrated sigh, Piper attempted to battle her way through his stubborn defenses. "It was my decision to come west. You warned me of the risks involved and I chose to come anyway."

"This sudden streak of independence you've acquired could get you killed," he grumbled crossly.

"I'm here because I want to be, because I think I'm falling in love with you. . . ." Of all the things she had intended to say to him, that wasn't even on the list! But the words were out before Piper could bite them back. For the life of her, she couldn't imagine what possessed her to make that confession. Her timing was terrible and Logan was blatantly unreceptive.

Logan winced as if she had stabbed him in the back. Her careless confession only served to annoy him further. Doing an about-face, he glared down into her flushed face and enormous green eyes. "Love?" he scoffed cynically. "Lady, you don't know what love is, and I'm not sure I do either."

Jeezus, why did she have to go and say something like that? Was she trying to soften him so he would bow to her like a devoted servant? Well, it wasn't going to work. Empty confessions didn't faze him. Two days ago she had batted her big green eyes at him and begged him to let her come west. Now she was trying to wrap him around her little finger. She probably made that reckless confession to anything in breeches when she was determined to maneuver a man into doing her bidding! And if she thought he was going to be nice to that whining, complaining Willis Worthington just to appease her, she thought wrong!

Piper flinched when Logan's stormy gray eyes fastened on her. The way he was behaving one would have thought she had insulted him instead of paying him the greatest compliment a woman could offer a man! But what hurt the most was realizing Logan didn't want or need her love, and that worse, he couldn't return it. She had known that all along. Hadn't she lectured herself on that subject on numerous occasions? What a fool she was to think baring her heart to Logan would make a difference. What an imbecile she was to offer him any type of confession. She may as well have given aid and comfort to her enemy. It made just as much sense!

Spinning about with more speed than dignity, Piper intended to stomp back to the coach to compose herself. Before she could take one step, Logan's hand snaked out to snare her arm. His hollow laughter hit her like a slap in the face.

"What are you planning now, sweetheart? Are you going to stomp off in a huff because I didn't buckle beneath your glowing confession of love? Did you really think I would?" His sharp tone cut like a dagger, leaving her heart to bleed. "Your strategy may have worked on all your other male admirers, but it won't work with me." His features hardened like granite. "You're just like all the rest of the so-called respectable citizens I've dealt with. You tolerate me while you need my help, voicing compliments to assure my allegiance. But you went a little farther than most with your charade of pretending we were husband and wife. You gave me your body in exchange for my protection and assistance. . . ."

Piper couldn't stop herself. Her hand cracked against his bronzed cheek, leaving a bright red welt. When Logan struck her back, Piper glared at him through a furious red haze. "Contemptible cur!" she spat at him. "Never in my life have I told any other man I loved him. Never!" Tears misted her eyes, but anger and bruised pride restrained them from streaming down her cheeks. "I thought you were different. I cared about you, despite your faults. But you are far too cynical to recognize love unless it hits you right between the eyes. And if you think all I wanted was your protection you're a bigger fool than I am, Logan!"

Piper sucked in a ragged breath before she burst into tears right in front of his eyes. She was going to get through this with as much dignity as possible. "If that was all I wanted from you, I wouldn't have practiced with my pistol. I wanted you to see me as your equal, not some silly city slicker who couldn't fight her way out of a feed sack. Honestly, I don't know why I wanted to impress you, hoping to prove myself worthy of a man like you. Now you have made me realize it was a ridiculous fascination. I'm not going to waste another minute loving you, indeed, I'm never going to love any man. You and your entire species are despicable!"

In a burst of fury, Piper darted toward the stage before she was reduced to blubbering tears. Logan stood paralyzed, watching her hasty flight. He didn't know what to make of her tirade. A man had to be cautious when dealing with a woman like Piper. Her unrivaled beauty and lively spirit often kept him from thinking logically. It would have been easy to go slinking after her, apologizing all over the place. But he knew from past experience that Piper was the mistress of subtle tactics. She was trying to maneuver him again, and dammit, he wasn't about to fall into that trap. The only effective way to deal with that blond-haired hellion was to build walls between them and keep them there. Even if she did feel something for him (which of course she didn't) it wasn't the kind of affection that would last. Logan had been around enough to know!

The sight of Samuel scurrying off in Piper's direction had Logan growling under his breath. It only served to remind him how quickly he could be replaced. The big ox could provide protection for that sassy nymph. Let Samuel think the newly married couple had a lovers' spat. If Samuel wanted to comfort her, he was welcome to her. Logan had important matters on his mind and Piper had already distracted him more than she should have.

Love? Logan stamped back toward the coach, grumbling under his breath. Piper didn't love him. She wanted him to think that so she could lead him around by the nose. But by God, no woman was going to make him her faithful servant. Why, Piper would even have him being sociable to that sniveling Willis Worthington. And there was no reason to tolerate Willis. He didn't deserve one iota of courtesy.

The look that was chiseled on Logan's stony face dissuaded Willis from voicing another of his complaints. He was set to spout off in irritation over the fact that Logan had argued with his wife and that Samuel was fussing over her. Things had been running smoothly until Logan started putting ideas in Samuel's head. Now the complacent farm boy thought he should exert himself. Hell, he had even announced he was considering Logan's offer of becoming a ranch hand. That annoyed Willis to no end.

Impatiently, Willis waited for Samuel to come lumbering back with Piper in tow. Seeing Samuel cooing and fluttering about her played havoc with his disposition. It was all Willis could do to keep his mouth shut, especially when Samuel sat Piper back in the coach and folded himself beside her. If he had possessed an ounce of compassion, Willis might have felt sorry for the distraught young lady, but it was beyond him why such an attractive young lady would marry that unruly gunslinger in the first place. Piper should have known better. In Willis's estimation, she was getting exactly what she deserved for trying to tame a man with Logan's notorious reputation.

While the stage rumbled on its way, Logan sat across from Piper, who refused to acknowledge his presence. She stared at the clenched fists that were knotted around Abraham's basket. Logan's carefully controlled demeanor revealed nothing of his thoughts or emotions. He knew this was another of her melodramatic acts. Piper wanted him to feel guilty for talking cruelly to her. That was her reason for ignoring him. But Logan wasn't going to succumb to her clever strategy. He wasn't going to feel a thing—not guilt, not compassion, nothing. And he certainly wasn't going to fall in love with that green-eyed witch. That was the last thing he needed right now, or ever, he quickly amended.

If Piper got hold of her money she would be long gone. If she felt anything at all it was desperation. Her trust fund was what motivated her, and Logan knew that as well as he knew his own name. Hell, he ought to. After all, he had given himself his name. And he had given himself everything he ever had in this life. No one had ever done him any favors. He was a loner, a free spirit. There was no place in his life for a woman, especially one like Piper, who had the uncanny knack of turning him inside out! He had gotten along just fine before he met her and he would get along without her when she finally went trotting home where she belonged. Love indeed! Jeezus, how stupid did she think he was anyway?

As the coach rumbled over the rocky hills and harsh valleys of New Mexico Territory, Piper peered somberly out the window. She felt herself being transported over the sandy gullies and thorny slopes that clogged the countryside. The driver had warned them that the deep arroyos made perfect cover for waiting outlaws and Apaches. But Piper didn't fear for her life, not when her heart had already shriveled in her chest. Even the sight of the ruggedly spectacular mountains capped with blue-violet shadows didn't faze her. She felt as emotionless as the tall pines and furs that jutted from the distant mountains.

Logan's cynical rejection left her to wonder what she had

seen in him in the first place. Obviously, she had wanted to see something in him that wasn't really there. Abraham never had liked Logan. Animals were better judges of character than humans, and Piper should have followed the tomcat's instincts.

Logan didn't even possess a heart, she mused bitterly. She had foolishly believed there had been one, encased in granite though it was. But there was nothing inside that rock that hung in his chest except more rock! She should have known that, but she had been an optimistic fool. Logan's reputation should have provided her with all the evidence she needed. He was just a man, she reminded herself cynically. That, too, should have warned her to be wary of trying to befriend him, to love him. . . .

The sound of pistol shots screaming through the air jolted Piper from her deliberations. Her wide-eyed gaze flew back to the window, searching the rocky cliffs. From out of nowhere four masked men appeared on horseback to pursue the stage.

"Well, do something, for heaven's sake!" Willis screeched at Logan. "This is what you were hired to defend against. Why are you just sitting there?"

Logan's scathing glare picked Willis apart. The scrawny little man had held true to Logan's prediction. Willis rarely gave Logan the time of day, but he had been the first to demand Logan's protection when trouble arose. "Maybe I don't want to get myself killed defending someone like you," Logan snorted disdainfully.

"You should at least consider your poor wife!" Willis squawked frantically. "If those men get hold of her . . ." His jaw fell off its hinges when he saw Piper dig into her purse to retrieve her pistol.

As the coach bounced over the rough road at an accelerated speed, Logan clamped his hand on the door to brace himself. His silver gaze landed on Piper's determined features. "If I die, I want one last kiss to sustain me through the eternity I'll undoubtedly be spending in hell."

Before she could accept or reject his request, Logan leaned forward to take her soft lips beneath his. It was an impatient, ravishing kiss that fit the man she had come to love . . . hate.

Blast it, she didn't know how she felt anymore. While she was gasping to draw a breath, he flung open the door to crawl atop the stage.

"Logan, no!" Piper shrieked as she tried to pull him back inside to safety.

Suddenly, bodies were toppling everywhere. The coach swerved and bumped along the road, throwing passengers hither and yon. Abraham's caterwauling mingled with the bark of pistol shots exploding around them. Willis's loud shriek drowned out every other sound as Abraham scaled his chest frantically, drawing blood along the way. But Piper had too many difficulties of her own to consider Willis's plight. In the next instant she found herself mashed to the floor beneath Samuel's gigantic body.

Samuel stirred like an overturned beetle, attempting to upright himself as the coach careened around the bend. When he finally untangled himself and climbed onto the seat, he hoisted Piper's wrinkled body up beside him. Craning her neck, Piper peered out the window to see Logan's leg dangling off the top of the cab. How he had managed to climb atop the coach while the rest of them were being bounced around like uncoiling springs was beyond her. But he was there, perched behind the driver and conductor like a human shield, firing at the highwaymen who were galloping after them.

Frantically, Piper retrieved her pistol from the floor and took aim. Her shot winged one of the outlaws in the arm, but he never broke stride. Another volley of bullets echoed through the canyon, their sound mingling with Piper's bloodcurdling screams. Before she could take aim a second time, she saw Logan tumble from the top of the cab and roll in the dirt. As he sprawled facedown, the riders shot at him, even while they jumped their horses over his lifeless body.

Piper swore she was living a nightmare. Over and over again she saw Logan fall to his death, heard the fatal shots. And over and over again she screamed his name at the top of her lungs. Although Samuel was cradling her in his protective arms, Piper felt nothing but aching emptiness. Tears that had been so carefully held in check that afternoon burst free like flood waters. She swore she would never stop seeing that tormenting sight as long as she lived. Logan was dead. . . . She had watched him die. The horrible thought made her cry all the harder.

Two of the highwaymen leaped onto the stage to slow the laboring horses. Piper closed her eyes and quietly uttered all the curses in her limited vocabulary of profanity. She didn't care what the desperados did to her. Nothing mattered now. After Logan rejected her she had spitefully hoped the Lord would call down His wrath on one of His most obvious sinners. But she hadn't meant for Logan to be wiped from the face of the earth! It had only been her anger and wounded pride speaking. Oh, how she wished she could retract the terrible things she had thought about Logan after he rejected her.

"Step out here so we can keep an eye on you," one of the desperados demanded tersely.

With hands held high, the passengers climbed from the coach. The hombre who was clutching his wounded arm cast his dark eyes on the apprehensive group. "Which one of you fired the bullet with my name on it?" he snorted contemptuously.

"She did." Willis pointed an accusing finger at Piper in hopes of sparing his own neck.

The small, wiry-looking bandito chuckled in disbelief as he glanced from his wounded compadre to the shapely young woman. "You were shot by a woman? That's a first!" His eyes swung around the group of passengers, and then he scoffed beneath the kerchief that covered his face. "You let a female protect you? It doesn't say much for your courage." His gaze fastened on Piper as he dropped into an exaggerated bow. "My compliments, miss. I wouldn't have expected such bravery from a woman."

"*Mrs.* Logan," the driver corrected bitterly.

"Mrs. Logan?" the bandito gasped in astonishment. His bug-eyed gaze flitted back to the lifeless body that lay somewhere in the distance. As if he were suddenly knocked to his senses, the bandito focused on the passengers and waved his pistol at them. "If you just stand there quietly, you won't wind up like Logan." Arrogant laughter tripped from his lips. "Butterfield was a fool to think one man could stop us." His eyes swung to the driver and conductor. "You tell Butterfield he wasted his time sending the best man he could find. We'll kill any other private detective he sics on us too!''

To everyone's amazement, the outlaws rifled through the mail bags as if they were searching for something in particular. They found what they were looking for and, boasting about how quickly they had disposed of the legendary gunman, mounted their horses and galloped away.

''We have to return for my husband's body,'' Piper insisted brokenly.

The driver gaped at her as if she had rose bushes growing from her ears. ''I'm real sorry about Logan,'' he said with genuine sincerity. ''But we can't go back with those bandits running around loose. They let us off easy this time because they got the man they wanted. But if we go back, we'll be inviting trouble.''

''Logan deserves a decent burial,'' Piper wailed in frustration.

The driver looked to Samuel, hoping he would deposit the distraught young woman in the coach, but Willis made the crucial mistake of opening his big mouth. ''Begging your pardon, Mrs. Logan, but you knew it would come to this sooner or later. A man who lives by the gun dies by the . . .''

Piper went for his throat with claws bared. If not for Samuel she would have scratched Willis worse than Abraham already had. The man had not one ounce of compassion or concern for anyone but himself. Logan had tried to defend all of them and Willis had expressed not a smidgen of gratitude, even when Logan sacrificed his life to save the other passengers. Damn that Willis. Logan was right about him. He deserved no consideration.

Holding Piper at bay, Samuel stared at Willis with contempt. ''She just lost her husband, for pity sake,'' he growled. His boyish face puckered in a frown. ''I think Logan deserves better than to be left on this desolate road. The rest of you can continue with your journey while we go back to bury him. . . .''

''Have you gone mad?'' Willis squawked in outrage. ''We are going to San Francisco and we aren't stopping in this godforsaken country where even a lizard can't make a living!''

Samuel tilted a determined chin. "I've decided to take Logan's offer. Mrs. Logan needs someone to tend the ranch and to see to her husband's last rites."

"You can't be serious," Willis croaked.

Samuel nodded his reddish brown head in affirmation. "Logan was right. I can think for myself and it's high time I did. When the stage arrives at the next station you can send someone back to fetch us."

Grumbling, the conductor climbed back onto the coach. He was responsible for the passengers and he wasn't so sure he should leave some of them behind. But neither did he wish to argue with the muscular giant who held Piper protectively against him. Samuel wasn't budging from his stand and neither was Logan's wife.

When the coach bounced down the road, leaving a cloud of dust behind it, Piper inhaled a steadying breath. She wasn't sure she wanted to see Logan's broken body sprawled in the dirt, but she was compelled to go back. She had loved him, and no matter what anyone else thought of him, she grieved for him. Even if Logan hadn't loved her, it didn't stop her from caring for him.

Resolutely, Piper trudged down the winding path with Abraham's basket clutched in her hand. Her mind was numb and her body moved mechanically. Logan was gone . . . gone. A shudder rocked her soul and a burning ache simmered in the pit of her stomach. What was she going to do now? Her money had been stolen a second time. The man she loved was dead. . . .

A trail of tears scalded her cheeks and then evaporated in the blistering heat. How much more torment was she expected to endure? she wondered dispiritedly. She was being tested, just like Job had been. Lord, it was hard not to crumble to the ground and sob like a lost soul. She had lost everything—the man she loved, her inheritance. She had nothing left. She wanted to lie down and die with Logan, to follow after him, even if their ultimate destination was hell.

It seemed trouble traveled in triplets. The moment Piper and Samuel started down the steep slope, the jingle of bridles and the creak of leather split the air. Dazed, Piper found herself staring at the same four men who had murdered Logan. A hoarse chuckle erupted from one of the banditos as he trotted alongside Piper, plucking her and her basket off the ground.

"You couldn't leave it alone, could you, honey?" he snickered as he dragged her into the saddle in front of him. When Piper tensed as if she intended to leap to freedom, the hombre jabbed his Colt in her ribs.

The incident provoked Samuel to snort like an enraged rhinoceros. He charged at the bandit and Piper feared he would wrestle both horse and rider to the ground. Samuel looked that furious! But before he could save Piper from disaster, one of the other highwaymen rammed Samuel broadside with his steed. The butt of his rifle clanked against Samuel's skull, causing him to stagger momentarily.

"Christ! What does it take to bring Goliath down?" one of the desperados chirped in disbelief.

"Hell, hit him again," the small, wiry bandit commanded.

In desperation, Samuel plowed into the horse upon which Piper sat, upending Abraham's basket and sending him tumbling to the ground. While the tomcat shot off like a rocket, the other three outlaws swarmed over Samuel like angry hornets defending their nest. The repeated blows caused Samuel's knees to fold beneath him and he toppled to the ground like a giant redwood.

It took all three men to hoist Samuel's limp body over the back of a horse, which protested its heavy burden by stepping sideways. Grumbling and cursing, the highwaymen weaved down the rocky ravine with their captives in tow.

Piper made no more attempts to escape, not with a pistol burrowed between her ribs. Besides, what was the use? she asked herself. Where could she go to escape these riders while she was afoot? It would be impossible to navigate through the ravines and arroyos. They all looked the same to the inexperienced eye.

Logan's words came back to haunt her. He had constantly criticized her naivete, her lack of practical experience. Piper's only consolation was that she might locate her trust fund, one that these men obviously had in their possession. Not that it would do her any good, mind you. She might see her inheritance again but she doubted she would live to spend it. From the look of things, Logan was the lucky one. She, on the other hand, was about to endure a dozen kinds of hell before she died. And poor Abraham. How would he survive in the wilds? He was a lap cat who had been pampered and spoiled. He didn't know the first thing about enduring in the desert!

While the small party wound its way down from the slopes of Apache Pass, a lone rider watched their progress from the precipice above them. A wry smile pursed his lips as he tugged his hat from his head and slapped away the dust. Things had gone according to plan, he mused as he followed his men from a distance. Well, all except the part about taking the two hostages. That shapely female and her guard dragon weren't supposed to have come searching for Logan's mangled body. But having the stunning blonde underfoot might not be so bad after all, he decided. Now that Logan was dead he was free to do as he pleased.

Chomping on that thought, the rider eased his steed between the jagged rocks as the sun sank behind the mountains, bathing the world in shadows of muted blue and gray. The wail of a cat caught his attention. The abandoned tomcat appeared from beneath a scraggly mesquite bush, and for a few moments man and cat studied each other before the rider continued on his way, leaving Abraham to fend for himself.

Chapter 19

By the time the procession reached its destination, darkness had long ago settled over the desolate hills and arroyos. Piper was exhausted from the grueling trek across rugged terrain and from the emotional turmoil of losing Logan. When her captors set her on her feet she didn't care what happened to her. She was hot, frustrated, and downright angry, and she demanded answers.

"I demand to know what you intend to do with Samuel and me!" she blurted out.

Samuel said nothing. He had roused to find himself bound and gagged and hanging upside down on the back of a horse.

"My, isn't she the sassy one," the small, wiry outlaw chortled as he removed the kerchief from his face.

The other banditos also tugged off their masks and Piper's eyes widened when she recognized two of the men as the scoundrels she had seen conversing with Logan that night on the mesa near the Pinery. They had purposely set Logan up for his last fall, her tortured mind screamed. These men knew Logan was on that stage and it had been their true intent to dispose of him! Oh, how Piper wished she could get her hands on her pistol. She would blow all of these murdering varmints to smithereens.

While Piper's mind was twirling with mutinous thoughts, the smaller thief grabbed her arm and shepherded her into the shack. "It seems Logan found himself quite a prize," he snickered to his companions. "Too bad he won't be around to enjoy her."

The remark provoked several horselaughs, but Piper didn't find the comment the least bit amusing.

"Yeah, who would've thought Logan could've latched onto something this pretty." Laughing brown eyes fell onto Piper's sunburned face. "What did he do, honey? Threaten to shoot you down if you didn't marry him?"

All that prevented Piper from pouncing on the man she had wounded during the holdup was the taut arm that was clamped on her elbow. Damn men everywhere, she muttered under her breath. They were mocking a dead man. Was nothing sacred in this lawless country?

"You didn't answer my question," Piper hissed as she was propelled into the bedroom.

Although she resisted, she was promptly tied in a chair and left alone while the bandits hustled Samuel into an adjoining room and secured him in like manner. The sound of the voices in the front room of the shack drew Piper's attention, but she couldn't decipher their words. Idly, she wondered where her money had been stashed. Contemplating that thought, she surveyed the crudely furnished quarters. If these desperados had hidden their loot in this dingy room, she couldn't imagine where it might be. There were no closets, only a lumpy bed, the chair she was tied to, and a dusty nightstand.

A deflated sigh tumbled from her parched lips. Piper stared unblinkingly at the door. If someone didn't come along, and quickly, to appease her curiosity about her future (or lack of it), she was going to screech the walls down. Piper counted to ten and then screamed bloody murder. She didn't stop screaming until she heard the creak of the door latch. Those ogres weren't going to stash her in this musty room without informing her of their plans! she told herself fiercely.

A shaft of golden lantern light sprayed across the dark room, silhouetting the intruder's bulky form. The man who had planned the holdup and the untimely demise of Vince Logan stood arrogantly before her. Piper's eyes bulged in astonishment when she recognized the ringleader. Sweet mercy! She couldn't believe what she was seeing. This was the mastermind of the desperados? My God, she never would have guessed it, never in a million years!

The shocking sight knocked the wind out of her. Over and over, Piper told herself she wasn't going to faint. The last few weeks she had spent in this lawless land had increased her strength and her self-control. She was no longer a naive sophisticate who wilted at the first sign of trouble. She was stronger now, much sturdier, and the room was spinning furiously about her.

Piper strained to glare at the shadowed face that wore a mocking grin, but the swirling darkness came at her from all directions. Her heart thudded in her chest like a stampeding stallion, and her tormented brain grappled with the haunting revelation of what she had discovered. Try as she might, Piper couldn't overcome her shock. She fainted dead away, even after she had promised herself she wouldn't. The only thing that prevented her from collapsing on the floor was the restraining rope that held her steadfast in her chair. The haunting face pursued her into the whirling abyss, torturing her mind with unanswered questions.

Grant Fredricks strode into the mercantile store on the main street of Tucson. He had been beside himself since the satchel heaping with money had been stolen from him the previous week. Upon arriving in Tucson, Grant had made a beeline for the sheriff's office. The sheriff had been little help to him, despite Grant's constant demands that he form a posse.

Finally, Sheriff Epperson suggested Grant seek out Burgess Channing. Grant was told Burgess supplied the Butterfield stage line with beef and other necessities required at the stations in New Mexico Territory. Since Burgess was familiar with the area and was an influential citizen he might be willing to help Grant recover his catastrophic losses. Why Burgess Channing would be more help than a sheriff was beyond Grant, or at least it had been until he learned Burgess practically owned the entire town. He supposed Burgess possessed the kind of power needed to get things done. But Grant didn't care what Burgess Channing did, as long as he would help form a posse of men who could track down the missing money. Grant was prepared to offer a reward or sell his soul—anything to retrieve the stolen cash.

After rapping on the office door and being invited inside, Grant introduced himself. Nervously he adjusted his wire-rimmed glasses and stared at Burgess. Grant was a whiz at figures but diplomacy wasn't one of his strong points. He did not interact well with people and was more content to count stacks of money than to converse at any type of social function. It did not ease his apprehension to learn Burgess Channing was not the kind of man who invited conversation. Indeed, Burgess's physical appearance shouted that he was the stern, unapproachable type. Burgess's mouth naturally turned down at the corners, and his hooked nose and beady eyes gave him a foreboding look. He was a stout man, a somber man. If Burgess had dared to smile, Grant found himself wondering, would his leathery face crack?

Flinging aside his musings, Grant cut to the heart of the matter. "Sheriff Epperson has been absolutely no help," he grumbled sourly. "He finally suggested I come see you. I want you to help me locate my money, which was stolen during a stage robbery." Grant inhaled a deep breath and plunged on, not the least bit encouraged by Burgess's poker-faced expression. "I was told you have connections with the stage line and that you have formed posses of concerned citizens who wish to stamp out these pesky thieves who are giving the stage company fits."

Burgess eased back in his chair to regard Grant. The man looked so frail and defenseless it was a wonder he hadn't blown away in a dust storm. His glasses were as thick as ice cubes and they drooped on the bridge of his blunt nose. Burgess couldn't think of one reason why he should help this Eastern dandy. He couldn't imagine why Sheriff Epperson had sent him over, unless it was to shuffle him out of the way. Burgess certainly had better things to do than play nursemaid to this bungling fop.

"You aren't the first passenger to lose his cash," Burgess grunted in his gravelly voice. "I've sent out dozens of posses in search of these desperados. As of yet, we haven't located their hideouts or confiscated a cent of missing money. Although we

274

suspect several of the drifters who wander in and out of town to be involved, we can't pin anything on them." He looked down his parrotlike nose at the scrawny Easterner. "You should consider yourself lucky that you escaped in one piece. Some folks wind up shot all to hell."

Grant came unglued. He had been patronized by every Western know-it-all he had confronted since the robbery. His temper, sorely put upon already, snapped. "Perhaps you aren't concerned about these thieving pests in your territory, but I want something done about them! It's no wonder this part of the country is so sparsely populated. There aren't enough upstanding citizens to shake a stick at, and the place is overrun by rapists, murderers, and thieves."

It was just like Grant to offend anyone within shouting distance. He didn't have enough tact to fill a thimble. He was the classic example of a man who protested thieving and skulduggery and then set about to cheat everyone he could.

"We are discussing a large amount of money here, Mr. Channing," he went on to say in that shrill, whining voice that could make the hair on the back of a man's neck stand straight up. "I was on my way to California to establish a bank in the gold fields. I have no intention of sitting back on my heels while those thieving renegades squander my hard-earned money."

If Piper could have heard his baldfaced lie she would have cut out Grant's tongue. But she was stashed in an out-of-the-way hideout, struggling to revive herself from a dead faint, one caused by receiving the shock of a lifetime.

Burgess's winged brows flattened over his dark eyes. He disliked the frail Easterner on sight and would have ordered him out of the office if Grant hadn't piqued his curiosity. "How much money are we discussing, Mr. Fredricks?"

"Well, it's nothing to sneeze at!" Grant declared hotly. "A man does not open a bank with pocket change."

"How much?" Burgess snorted gruffly. "If you want my assistance, you are going to have to be specific. I'm not sending out a search party of some of my own hired men for one or two thousand dollars and risk having them killed."

Grant gnashed his teeth. "The amount we are discussing is

far more than that," he said evasively.

Burgess wasn't known for his rosy disposition or saintly patience. He expected everyone else to possess a good deal of forbearance when dealing with him, but Burgess was not long on patience. When his associates beat around the bush it infuriated him. "Stop hedging and answer me," he snapped brusquely. "Either tell me the exact amount or get the hell out of my office. I have no desire to play guessing games with an Eastern dandy!"

Grant scowled under his breath. "We are discussing a quarter of a million dollars," he begrudgingly confessed.

Burgess's beady eyes opened wider than they had in his lifetime. "A quarter of a million?" he croaked. "Are you mad? You shouldn't have been carrying that kind of money on a stage line that has been plagued with robberies! For Chrissake man, you were asking for trouble!"

Grant didn't know why Burgess should be upset. It wasn't his money that was floating around some outlaw hideout. A little sympathy and concern was what Grant had counted on from Burgess. What he didn't need, on top of all his other frustrations, was a lecture from this sour-faced patriarch who controlled Tucson.

Biting back his irritation, Grant stared into Burgess's blanched face. "Are you willing to help me, Mr. Channing? I will, of course, offer a reward for the return of the funds."

Burgess wilted back in his chair and laced his stubby fingers together. For a long moment he stared deliberately at the undersized young man. Finally he nodded his consent. "I'll see what I can do. But you must have patience. Our methods will require a great deal of trial and error. I'll have to pose a few questions around town to determine if we can come up with some encouraging leads. If we can track a few of these drifters to their hideouts in the mountains, perhaps we can recover your money . . . for a worthwhile percentage."

After Burgess suggested that Grant return to his hotel room to wait, he stared at the closed door. Two hundred and fifty thousand dollars? If he had known there was that kind of money floating around he would have been combing the mesas and arroyos to find it. And I will find it, Burgess promised himself with a confident smile. Grant Fredricks was a fool for carrying such an enormous amount of cash with him, and Burgess was going to have his fair share of it.

Harley Newcomb fiddled with the kerchief that hung around his neck and stared at the lovely but unconscious woman who was draped in her chair. A tangled mane spilled over her shoulders and her bewitching face was the same pale color as her hair. Piper wasn't as well adapted to the West as Jenny Payton was, but this shapely goddess had apparently caught Logan's interest or she wouldn't be in New Mexico Territory.

Dragging his eyes off the fetching beauty, Harley focused his attention on the not-so-dead Logan, who had propped himself against the door to puff on his cheroot. "It seems to me you could have been more delicate about telling the lady you were still alive," he grumbled to his friend. "You just don't barge in on a person who presumes you to be dead and scare the living daylights out of her!"

"No?" Logan's thick brows elevated to a mock innocent angle as Harley stamped around the room to relieve his nervous energy. The man never could stand still for more than a minute. It was Harley's habit to pace about like a high-stepping rooster, and it was always easy to tell when he was irritated. He tossed his head and strutted. "If I hadn't barged in, Piper would have screamed and carried on and we couldn't hear each other talk. Now we can discuss our plans without yelling over this yowling minx."

"I still contend that was a cruel way to treat your wife," Harley muttered.

"And I told you she really isn't my wife!" Logan growled back at his outspoken friend.

"Well, she may as well be," Harley sniffed distastefully. "I suspect everyone between here and Fort Smith thinks you're married."

"No," Logan corrected. "Everyone presumes I'm dead, just as we planned. Those desperados who are harassing Butterfield's stage think the coaches will be easy prey once again. Now we can monitor their activities and discover who is behind this network of robberies. Cactus Jack was kind enough to report that the outlaws with whom he worked have also been selling rifles to the Apaches in exchange for raids on the stage stations."

Harley paused from his pacing to peer over at Logan. "Why would they want to do that?"

Logan's broad shoulders lifted in a shrug. "Damned if I know. But it appears this is more than just a gang of thieves looting and stealing. If they destroy Butterfield's business they'll lose their livelihood. They can't very well rob a stage if there is no longer one serving this part of the country. And there won't be one for very long if we don't corral those thieves."

Harley spun about to glare disdainfully as soon as he realized Logan was trying to divert his attention away from the issue. "Don't think you can steer me off track. I want to know why you sent us back to retrieve Piper and her oversized bodyguard if you didn't really want to find yourself strapped with a wife."

"You know my reasons," Logan snorted. "She was coming back to retrieve my body. I couldn't very well leave Piper and Samuel out there, wandering around in search of a body I'm still using. Since you and the men used blank shots she wouldn't have found a mark on me, even if I had lain in the dirt, pretending death."

Harley let out his breath in an exasperated rush. "And now that you have her here, what do you intend to do with her?"

"How the hell do I know?" Logan exploded.

"Well, if you ask me, you ought to go ahead and marry her."

"I didn't ask your opinion," Logan muttered before turning to stare at Piper's ashen face.

"You should," Harley grunted. "What if she winds up carrying your child?" When Logan bit down on the end of his cigar, Harley wagged a thin finger in his face. "And don't bother denying the possibility might exist. I wasn't born yesterday, you know. And a saint you ain't!" he added with a volcanic snort. "If the two of you have been posing as man and wife, you wouldn't have been gentleman enough to bypass the privileges of matrimony. I'd bet a king's ransom she was pure and innocent until she met you." His simmering blue eyes

278

nailed Logan to the wall. "You don't take advantage of a gently bred lady like this one without doing right by her, Logan."

"Stop annoying me," Logan muttered disdainfully.

"I think you should marry her," Harley repeated with firm conviction. "You need a wife and you couldn't do better than this pretty little thing. Hell, you'd be lucky to have her. . . ."

When Piper stirred slightly, Harley scampered toward the door, but not without flinging Logan a meaningful glare. "I'll start supper while you straighten out this mess."

Logan peered down at Piper's curvaceous form. Dammit, he hadn't wanted to hear Harley's lecture on propriety and he didn't want to think about what he was going to do with this troublesome sprite.

Squatting down on his haunches, Logan tunneled his fingers through the renegade strands of silver-gold hair. His mind was in a quandary. He had decided to let Piper go on thinking he was dead, even if he had only been shot with blank bullets. But she had taken it upon herself to come searching for his mangled body. He had no choice but to send his men to capture her and Samuel.

And as much as Logan had wanted to abandon that pesky cat he had found in the mesquite bush, he couldn't. Muttering all the while, Logan had turned his horse around and gone back to fetch Abraham, even if the damned cat had scratched him twice during their ride to the shack. Now he was strapped with a defenseless tomcat and a woman who hadn't had the good sense to remain on the stage instead of setting out on foot to read the last rites over her departed husband.

He should have known Piper would thwart his plans. She had been tangling up his life since the day he met her. Perhaps he should instruct Harley to deposit Piper and Samuel at the ranch for safekeeping. Hell, she could even take possession of the ranch and the entire herd of livestock if she wanted it. He could take up residence elsewhere—anything to get this female out of his life before she drove him crazy!

Lost in pensive thought, Logan untied the restraining rope and scooped Piper's limp body into his arms. When he laid her on the bed, her head rolled from side to side, fighting the haze of darkness that enshrouded her.

She's going to be mad as hell when she rouses, Logan predicted. He was a man of few words and he wasn't very good at explaining himself because he had never bothered to try. Now he needed to be eloquent, and he doubted he could select the right phrases to soothe Piper's frustration at learning he wasn't quite as dead as she thought he was.

The faintest hint of a smile rippled across Logan's lips as he stared at Piper. It was hard to believe this was the same woman he had met in Fort Smith. Her outward appearance hadn't changed all that much. She was still as gorgeous as ever with the blush of sunshine on her elegant features. But Piper had transformed drastically these past weeks. She had discovered herself, tested her weaknesses, and fortified her strengths. Her pride and self-confidence had increased daily. She was no longer a flighty, sentimental female. She was strong and stubborn and full of fire—and he would probably be singed when she awoke. Now that she had come into her own, she wasn't going to appreciate suffering the shock of her life without Logan offering her a reasonable explanation. He only hoped he could make her understand his need to go underground before she wrestled his pistol away from him and blew him to smithereens. He was going to have to do some fast talking!

Piper's eyes fluttered open to view the same haunting face that had sent her into a faint. But this time her shock incited her fury. Piper was seeing Logan through a mutinous red haze.

"You scoundrel!" she screeched as she whacked him on the chest. "What a rotten trick! You let me grieve for you, cry over you! Honestly, I think you derive wicked pleasure in scaring people half to death!"

"Did you prefer me dead?" Logan chuckled into her animated features. "Maybe I'm just a ghost. When you wake from this nightmare, I might not be here at all. . . ."

"Oh, that I could be so lucky!" Piper spewed furiously.

Before Logan could pin her to the bed, Piper vaulted up in a single bound and shot toward the door. Logan was so startled by her reaction that it took him a moment to give chase. By the time he reached the front door she was long gone and four amused faces were grinning at him.

"My, you certainly handled that well," Harley snorted sarcastically. "What did you do, scare poor Goldilocks half to death again?"

"Goldilocks?" Logan glowered at Harley. He needed to fetch a book of fairytales and catch up on his lost years of reading, since everyone kept referring to Goldilocks, Red Riding Hood, and Cinderella. Jeezus, he didn't have the faintest notion what they meant!

Since Logan was fumbling with his thoughts, Harley took the opportunity to fling another jibe. "I can't believe you let that female talk to you the way she did."

"You shouldn't have been eavesdropping. She's too damned stubborn to listen to my explanation," Logan defended huffily.

"Being an authority on stubbornness, I would have thought you could have found a way," Harley smirked. "You never had much trouble dealing with other stubborn people before now. Admit it, the lady has gotten under your skin."

The challenge had Logan burning on a hot blue flame. With a wordless snarl, he barreled out the door. Squinting, he surveyed the crisscrossed shadows to locate the fleeing nymph. When he finally caught sight of Piper he charged like a mad bull. But Piper's fury made her swift of foot, and it was a long breathless moment before Logan could chase her down.

Snatching her off the ground, Logan gave her a quick shake. "Will you listen while I try to explain?" he grumbled. "I'll not chase you all over the damned country trying to make myself understood."

"I understand perfectly," Piper hissed. Wiggling and squirming to no avail, Piper finally resorted to biting his hand.

Logan released her more quickly than she anticipated. She didn't have time to gain her balance before she fell in an unceremonious heap. And before she could tear off again, Logan was looming over her. Oh, how she hated it when he loomed. He did it so well, damn him!

"Don't try to ply me with lies," Piper spat at him. "I know what you are doing. You are the ringleader of this gang of thieves. You've been robbing Butterfield blind. And then to top off your wily scheme, you let Butterfield employ you so

281

you could further drain his funds." Bitter laughter burst from her curled lips. "Poor John Butterfield paid good money to the very man who has been looting his stage line. Now you plan to play dead so you can go on with your raiding without being suspected of wrongdoing. You are the one who stole my money," she harshly accused him. "No wonder you didn't want to help me recover it. And no wonder you burn your money so freely. You're a damned rotten, miserable, good-for-nothing thief, just like those other four men in the shack! And I hate you!"

A cruel smile thinned his lips. His eyes burned down on her like boiling silver. "My, my, the fickle sophisticate," he cooed caustically. "Why, it was only this afternoon that you swore your undying love. How quickly the worm turns."

Piper slapped him with the vigor of a lumberjack swinging his ax. Logan retaliated by shoving her back to the ground with enough force to knock the breath out of her. "The next time you strike me, she-cat, I'll do more than hit you back. Do you hear me? Dammit, I'm not your human punching bag!"

His booming voice ricocheted off the rock precipices to come at her in a repetitive curse.

"You don't love me. You never did," he scowled down into her whitewashed face. "If you did, that goddamn fortune of yours wouldn't matter. Nor would you care how I made my living. You would have wanted me first and the money second." The coldest smile ever to lie on a masculine face hovered on his lips. Logan yanked her up by the hair of her head to breathe fire onto her cheeks. As he crouched over her, his face only inches from hers, Logan laughed sardonically. "Bluestockings can't survive without their little nest eggs, can they, princess? You already proved you would do and say anything to get your precious money back, even pretend to be my wife and vow a love you don't feel and never could."

He pushed her down again roughly, pinning her hands and legs beneath him like a mighty panther stifling his squirming prey. "Now that you've met the real Vince Logan, what do you think of him, sweetheart?" he sneered at her.

Piper wanted to kick and bite and scream—and also to cry

282

out her eyes. Logan made her positively furious. She couldn't see or think straight when he was manhandling her. "I despise you," she jeered back at his ridiculing smile. "You're a bastard, a cruel, selfish bastard and I wish I had never met you!"

Logan didn't know why he was behaving so ruthlessly. He didn't know what he wanted from Piper. He didn't know why he was taking his frustration out on her. But as always when dealing with this complex creature, he was swamped by a dozen conflicting emotions. For once he wanted to be in total command. But he never felt as if he had supreme control over this spirited nymph. Since the beginning she had turned him wrong side out and upside down.

The feel of her ripe body writhing beneath his stirred another emotion. Desire funneled through him, igniting memories that constantly tormented him. But Logan refused to buckle to his lusty passions, not when he knew Piper would ultimately draw the tenderness from him and become the victor in this battle of wills.

Grumbling under his breath, Logan bounded to his feet, yanking Piper up with him. Without another word, he marched her back to the shack—past the four men who were ogling her with obvious interest. Once he had secured her door, Logan went back outside to compose himself.

Although Harley knew Logan wanted the time and space to think after his shouting match with Piper, he refused to give the surly gunslinger a moment's peace. Like a ram, Harley bowed his neck and headed toward the stoop where Logan was standing in stony silence.

"Well, did you propose to her?" Harley questioned point-blank.

Scowling, Logan glanced down at the wiry man he had come to call his friend (although, at the moment, Logan didn't like anyone, least of all himself). "No," he answered gruffly. "Piper detests me and she thinks I double-crossed Butterfield. She also presumes I'm the leader of this outlaw gang that has been attacking the stage line."

Harley's blue eyes popped from their sockets. "Why would

she think that?" he chirped.

"Because Piper leaped to that conclusion and I didn't tell her otherwise," Logan muttered grouchily.

"Why the hell not?" Harley wanted to know.

Logan exploded like a keg of blasting powder. "Because she wants to believe the worst about me, just like everybody else," he growled. "I've never in my life defended myself to anyone and I'm not about to start now. I don't give a damn what she thinks!"

Harley regarded Logan's rigid stance and the black scowl. He had never seen Logan in such a snit over a woman. Usually females flitted in and out of his life without making much of an impression on him. Harley knew Logan was fond of Jenny Payton, but even she didn't preoccupy him the way this blond-haired hellion did. He could see why Logan was intrigued with Piper. She had it all—the delicate features, the flawless complexion, curves in all the right places, and spunk. Harley had caught himself staring at the green-eyed enchantress a dozen times during their trek to the shack.

Logan expelled a harsh breath and stared into the distance. "I need some time alone," he announced. "I want to scout around. According to Cactus Jack, the desperados have several roadhouses in these parts. I plan to locate them so we'll know how many men we'll be dealing with when we move in on them."

"But what about . . ." Harley's voice evaporated as Logan strode off the porch to become one of the shadows. Logan took nothing with him but his weapons, but Harley quickly reminded himself that Logan always traveled light. He knew how to live off the land, even on land where a coyote would have a difficult time surviving.

Harley's eyes swung back to the cabin and he breathed a determined breath. If Logan wasn't going to tell Piper the truth, Harley would see to the matter. There was no reason for her to labor under the erroneous theory that she was being held hostage by brigands. With single-minded purpose, Harley drew himself up and propelled himself toward Piper's room. It was time he discovered what was going on between Piper and Logan. There had to be a good reason why Logan was in such a tailspin. Never in his life had Logan had difficulty making decisions. But he was having one helluva time deciding what was to be done now. Harley wasn't going to allow Piper to hate Logan for all the wrong reasons, and Logan wasn't going to hide behind misconceptions. If he really didn't want Piper around then he should put her someplace safe. And if he did want her around, he should have told her so.

Chapter 20

Piper jerked to attention the instant she heard footsteps approaching. Her glower transformed into a frown when Harley entered her room. There was no telling what Logan had decided to do with her. Perhaps he planned to give her to his band of cutthroats. But Piper wasn't going to be used by any man, ever again. If any of these scoundrels tried to touch her they would have a fight on their hands!

To Harley's utter disbelief, Piper bounded out of her chair and then hurled it at him. He ducked away, only to find the pillow and nightstand sailing across the room toward him.

"For God's sake, Piper," Harley snorted. The veins of his face pulsated with vexation as he glared at her. "I didn't come in here to hurt you. I only want to talk to you."

Piper's snapping green eyes riveted on Harley's thin but muscular frame. Her chin tilted to a defiant angle. "Then say what you came to say and get out!" she hissed. "I want no association with Logan's band of thieves."

Harley righted the chair and gestured for Piper to plant herself in it. "That's exactly what I want to discuss. I don't know what burr Logan has under his saddle blanket, but he left you with the wrong impression."

Piper blinked bewilderedly. This desperado didn't sound like an illiterate bumpkin. Curious, she sank into the chair and stared at Harley.

"Logan and I have been friends for a long time. The other three men who joined me in that mock stage robbery are deputy marshals who have worked for Logan in the past. The men greatly respect his abilities. When Logan requests their assistance they drop everything and come running." Harley eased down on the edge of the bed to survey Piper's dubious frown. "Before Logan ventured to Fort Smith he organized this entire scheme. While you were at the Pinery we rode down to meet with him, decided on the location of the robbery, and rounded up a couple of stage agents who have been working as spies.

"Logan wants everyone to think he's dead so he can keep an eye on the thieves' activities without drawing their suspicion. The only way to catch the ringleader of the gang is for him to think he can come and go without the risk of being recognized," Harley explained.

"Do you mean Logan staged his death and didn't bother to tell me?" Piper asked in annoyance.

Harley smiled sympathetically. "Logan probably thought it was the only practical way to handle the situation. It wouldn't have been very convincing if all the passengers and stage agents knew it was a hoax. And as his wife, you might not have been so bereaved if you knew we had staged the murder."

Piper supposed he was right, but it hurt to know Logan didn't trust her enough to tell her the truth about anything. And after all the hateful things she had said to him in her burst of temper . . . Piper groaned miserably. Her behavior hadn't helped the situation. But then, neither had Logan's, she consoled herself. Logan allowed her to throw her tantrum and still he refused to tell her the truth. Damn, that man was absolutely impossible. He didn't like her and he didn't want her to like him either.

Harley watched conflicting emotions chase each other across Piper's bewitching face. "I'm sorry you got mixed up in this. I don't know why Logan has been acting like the very devil. . . ."

A pensive frown knitted Harley's brow. Come to think of it, he had a pretty good idea why Logan was behaving like an ill-tempered bear. A wry smile pursed his lips as he rose to offer Piper his arm. "You've been cooped up in here long enough. Let me introduce you to the other marshals who are helping us. And then I'll see what I can do about getting you back to civilization. This is no place for a proper lady. My only request is that you and Samuel keep Logan's secret. We don't want anyone to know he's alive just yet."

Piper liked Harley Newcomb instantly. He was courteous and sensible and he seemed to sense that she wanted to be as far away from Logan as possible. Piper cast all thoughts of Logan aside and pasted on a pleasant smile. It was odd how misleading first impressions could be, she soon realized. The men she had presumed to be ruthless ruffians, in part because of the masks they wore to disguise their identity, were very likable men after all. Jacob Carter, Anthony Danhill, and Gorman Rader treated her with nothing but kindness and respect.

Anthony readily forgave her for plugging him with a bullet during the holdup, and he graciously returned Abraham to her when she entered the room. Piper was surprised Logan had taken the time to retrieve Abraham, especially since he had no use for cats. For a split second she considered forgiving him, but then her heart hardened once again. She did hate Logan because of the way he had treated her. He could do nothing to redeem himself, even by saving Abraham from certain death in the wilderness. He was still a scoundrel, damn him.

When Piper gently reminded her group of admirers that Samuel was still bound and gagged, Jacob Carter tugged his dagger from his boot and handed it to her. "Why don't you fetch Samuel and explain what's going on while we put our meal on the table," he suggested with a grin. "I'd just as soon not tangle with that big gorilla until he knows we mean him no harm."

Nodding agreeably, Piper stepped into the adjoining room. The moment she removed Samuel's gag, his fierce frown melted into a relieved smile. "Are you all right? Lord, I was afraid those men were going to . . ."

"I'm fine," Piper hastily interrupted as she cut the ropes. "The men who brought us here are actually U.S. marshals. We have nothing to fear from them."

Samuel's jaw dropped off its hinges.

Her expression sobered. "I must have your word that you will disclose none of what I am about to tell you," she insisted.

"The robbery was staged to allow everyone else to think Logan had met his death. Logan hopes the desperados will become careless now that they think no one is attempting to hunt them down."

Samuel's boyish face lit up like a candelabrum. "Truly? You've seen your husband?"

Piper grimaced at his reference, but quickly composed herself. "Logan is alive and well and you and I will be on our way as soon as we have eaten. Logan and his men will remain here to keep a watchful eye on the desperados and incoming stages."

After introducing Samuel to the marshals, Piper saw to the final preparation of the meal. Her eyes involuntarily darted toward the door at regular intervals. But Logan never appeared. Piper wasn't certain if she was disappointed or relieved by his absence. Perhaps it was best if they parted without saying goodbye. At least Logan would have no opportunity to torment her again. She could walk out of his life, just as he hoped, and he would never have to fret over her. That was what he wanted, what she wanted.

With their appetites sated, Piper, Samuel, and Harley retrieved their mounts. Piper was thankful she had learned to ride. If this had been her first encounter with a horse in rocky terrain she doubted she could have kept her seat. Harley was considerate enough to travel at a slow pace, weaving his way through the winding passes with only the moonlight to guide him.

Although they remained in the saddle until well after midnight, Piper voiced no complaints. She was perfectly satisfied to put mountains and deserts between herself and Logan. She needed the time to convince herself she didn't want to lay eyes on Logan again. If he wanted to think the money was all that mattered to her, that was fine with her. And the money did matter, she realized. She had nothing else to motivate her while her broken heart mended. She was not about to wallow in self-pity, pining for a man who didn't want her affection and who could never return it. Logan didn't want her with him, so that was that. She couldn't change a man who had a chip on his shoulder the size of the Rock of Gibraltar.

To hell with Logan, Piper lectured herself sternly. She would retrieve her money somehow. And when she had her inheritance in hand maybe she would burn it up two dollars at a time, just to prove to that infuriating devil that money wasn't everything to her.

Piper slumped in the saddle. What purpose would it serve to squander her inheritance? Logan wouldn't be around to watch her do it. He didn't care enough about her to concern himself with her or her stolen money. She was deluding herself to think he would spare her a single thought. Why, he had probably ordered Harley to tote her away, and Harley was courteous enough not to tell her so. No doubt it was Logan's idea all along. He couldn't get her out from underfoot fast enough to suit him.

Silently brooding, Piper peered at the moonlit desert that sprawled before them. Screech owls serenaded them as they weaved down the craggy slopes and through the forest of towering saguaro cacti that rose forty feet into the star-studded sky.

The longer they rode, the more embittered Piper became. I do hate Logan, she assured herself ten miles later. She hadn't gotten over loving him just yet, but she did detest him. Logan was a cold, insensitive womanizer. He nourished his male pride by conquering women and bringing outlaws to justice. Well, she hoped he resolved Butterfield's problems and stuffed another feather in his cap. And one day, when he was all alone and old and gray, he would wish there was someone to love him. But Piper wasn't going to be around to provide companionship in his declining years. He could sit there and polish his pistol and count the dusty notches in his bed post all by himself. . . .

Startled, Piper blinked like the owls that were perched in the saguaros. And just where would she be while Logan was mildewing in his old age? She would be sitting alone in her rocking chair. Since she had resolved not to fall in love again there would be no one around to watch her grow old gracefully. She and Logan would be drifting in similar ships on the same lonely sea.

What a depressing thought! Logan had been such a drastic

influence on her that she would turn out to be just like him. Heaven forbid! He had teased and taunted her until she had learned to stand on her own two feet. He had taught her to depend on herself and to trust no one. Piper supposed she should thank Logan for broadening her horizons. But dammit, why couldn't he have come to love her, just a little? She might thank him for developing the depths of her character, but she would never thank him for breaking her heart. He needn't have bothered with that facet of her education. Piper already had a low opinion of men before Logan came along. He had done nothing to change that opinion.

When they paused to sleep, Harley drew Piper aside. "I'm really sorry about your problems with Logan. He is a good man and . . ."

"I would greatly appreciate it if you would never mention his name again," Piper snapped more harshly than she intended.

She had responded a little too quickly, in Harley's estimation. If she didn't care about Logan she would have shrugged him off. But the comely blonde was as testy as Logan. It was a good sign, Harley mused, grinning to himself. He had always contended there was a fine line between love and hate when it came to romance. Unless he missed his guess (and Harley was sure he hadn't), Piper and Logan struck sparks in each other. And where there were sparks there was fire.

"Not too many people understand the man you don't wish to discuss," Harley declared as he handed Piper the canteen. "They all use him to solve their problems. They give him money for his efforts but are all too busy gossiping about his reputation to look inside him. Actually, he is sensitive about being needed."

Harley removed his hat and raked his fingers through his hair. "I've told him a hundred times not to bother with those so-called respectable citizens, to find a woman who needs him for the man he is, not what he can do for her. But I guess a man with Logan's background and his bitter past feels he needs to make a difference, even if he can never truly be accepted by the Indians or the whites. Logan just wanders back and forth between two different civilizations, searching for something

292

he's never going to find, searching for someone who will love him the way he is without trying to change him."

"If you think Logan is so special, perhaps you ought to marry him," Piper suggested, peeking up at Harley through her curly lashes. Harley was trying to soften her toward Logan and she knew it. Well, she wasn't giving an inch! Piper had bared her heart to that calloused scoundrel and he had ridiculed her. She may have been a fool, but she certainly wasn't an idiot who was unable to profit from her mistakes. And she was not going to allow herself to fall in love with Logan all over again. Once had been one time too many!

Her saucy remark caused Harley to snicker. "I've done my part by befriending Logan."

"And I've done my part," Piper insisted as she sank down on her pallet for a short rest. "I tolerated him for over three weeks. And honestly, it felt like a lifetime."

As Piper sprawled out on the ground, Harley bit back a grin. Although Logan and Piper came from two vastly different worlds they were a great deal alike. They were both stubborn to the core and they possessed enough pride to build rock fortresses around themselves. They were meant for each other, Harley decided. The problem was, they were both too pigheaded to figure that out.

After they awoke from their naps, Harley led the way through the maze of saguaros to Tucson. If his calculations proved correct, these two contrary individuals were going to discover they were more miserable apart than they were when they were together. Time and distance would have to solve their problem because they were too damned stubborn to listen to reason. But Harley had the sneaking suspicion Logan was going to be more aggravated to find that Piper was gone than he was when she was at the shack. Harley couldn't wait to see the look on Logan's face when he returned to find Piper had been transported to Tucson. That should shake him up plenty, Harley speculated with wicked glee.

Exhausted from their long journey, Piper quickly located a hotel. Although Samuel had protested leaving her alone, Piper had insisted that he continue on to the ranch to assume his duties as Logan requested. She even convinced him to take Abraham with him and keep a watchful eye on him until Piper could resume the task. Piper didn't say Logan would be coming to fetch her in Tucson, but she left that impression to pacify Samuel.

To Piper's relief, she found the stage driver had been considerate enough to leave her luggage in Tucson. Willis, however, had kept Samuel's belongings with him, perhaps as incentive for the farm boy to follow him to California. But Samuel had shrugged off the loss and purchased a few extra sets of clothes before he ventured out to Logan's ranch with Abraham in tow.

After catching up on lost sleep, Piper returned to the depot to interrogate the agents about Grant Fredricks. She had learned that Grant had taken up residence at one of the hotels. Piper wasn't sure what she hoped to gain by confronting Grant now that he didn't have possession of her money. But she felt the fierce need to satisfy her vengeance.

Piper located the hotel where Grant had rented a room, but was annoyed that he didn't answer the knock on his door. Wearing a frustrated frown, Piper stepped back into the street, glancing in all directions at once. Tucson wasn't a large community. It consisted of a few adobe houses and several business establishments, and it didn't take Piper long to locate Grant.

When Piper spied Grant's thin frame her eyes narrowed resentfully. She lifted the front of her blue satin skirt and followed him. To her bemusement, Grant veered into the mercantile shop. After he marched into the office at the back of the store, Piper discreetly wandered about in the pretense of browsing while she eavesdropped on the conversation.

Apprehension filled Grant's expression as he parked himself in the chair across from Burgess Channing. "Have you had any luck?" Grant asked anxiously.

Burgess expelled a long-suffering sigh. Grant had approached him every morning except the two days Burgess was out of town, hounding him with the same question. Burgess had just about enough of the scrawny Easterner.

"I have found a few leads," he declared in his characteristically gruff tone, "but this sort of thing takes time, Mr. Fredricks."

"I'm running out of time," Grant blustered. "I have taken a job sweeping at one of those disgusting saloons to pay my room and board until the search begins. I don't wish to make a career of menial labor!"

Burgess's brows formed a single line over his deep-set eyes. "I'm a busy man with a business to run," he snorted. "I can't devote myself entirely to your problem. You took a ridiculous risk in the first place. Your capital would have been insured if you had consulted Wells Fargo and had the money shipped to California."

Grant bit back the terse comment that dangled on the tip of his tongue. Burgess was right, but Grant had been in a rush to leave Chicago. He had taken his chances, hoping his stage wouldn't be one of those assaulted by road agents.

Before Burgess could lecture him further on his idiotic blunder, Piper burst into the room, causing the door to slam against the wall, sending Burgess's portrait crashing to the floor. With eyes wide with astonishment, Grant swiveled in his chair to see Piper Malone holding a pistol that was trained on his chest.

"Piper? What on earth are you doing here?" Grant croaked like a waterlogged bullfrog.

"Following you and my money," she hissed furiously.

Burgess stared bewilderedly at the hot sparks that flew from Piper's eyes and then glanced at the pistol she held. "Young lady, put that gun down before someone gets hurt," he demanded sharply.

Piper was not to be put off. She had envisioned this moment for the past month. Indeed, she had lived for it. "Hurting someone is the very point of my being here," she snapped without unfastening her gaze from Grant's peaked face. "My name is Piper Malone and this scoundrel stole my trust fund in Chicago and then took the first train out of town. If you help him recover the money he stole from me and take a percentage

295

for your efforts you will be an accessory to the crime." Piper inhaled a furious breath, her breasts heaving. "I want Grant Fredricks hanged from the tallest saguaro in the territory!"

"It isn't exactly your money," Grant stammered as his face turned from bleak white to profuse red. "And stop pointing that thing at me. You don't know how to use it and it might explode!"

"You know damned well it's my money," she spouted at him. "And if you don't keep quiet, I'll blow you to kingdom come . . . just as I have been planning to do since I began this cross-country chase."

"You claim Mr. Fredricks stole the money from you to begin with?" Burgess questioned with a muddled frown.

"Yes!" Piper declared adamantly. "If you have consented to help Grant, I will pay you more than he offered for recovering the missing funds."

Burgess sighed heavily. "As I have been telling Mr. Fredricks, it is often difficult to track down the losses suffered by passengers on the Butterfield stage. We have been having these problems for months now. This wild country is a haven for thieves. There are too many natural hideouts for outlaws who have no wish to be found. Even the man Butterfield sent to alleviate the problem is reported dead as a result of another holdup. And the Apaches don't appreciate seeing white men wandering around on their land. They murder and scalp those who cross their sacred hunting grounds. And these wily outlaws don't wear name tags, you know," he added with a sarcastic snort. "Searching the mountains and deserts is like hunting a needle in a haystack."

Piper glared at the man across the desk. "I did not come this far to give up," she bit off. "If you won't help me, I'll find someone who will or I will begin the search myself."

"That's preposterous," Burgess scoffed. "All you will succeed in doing is getting yourself killed!"

"You needn't worry your conscience," Piper declared, tilting a proud chin. "I have decided to recover my fortune or die trying."

"It isn't your fortune," Grant sniffed and then snapped his mouth shut when Piper cocked the trigger.

"It certainly isn't yours, Grant," she growled at him. "You had no right to walk off with my money in tow. . . ."

"What's going on here?" Sheriff Epperson demanded as he entered the office. "Your clerk came rushing to me, claiming there was a squabble going on in here." His eyes bulged when he spied the Colt that was trained on Grant. "Lady, what the hell do you think you're doing?"

"Seeing justice served," Piper exclaimed self-righteously.

"Unless you've been sent west to relieve me of my duties, I would appreciate it if you would let me handle the matter."

Piper breathed an exasperated sigh and grudgingly stuffed her pistol in her purse. "Very well then, Sheriff, I want this man arrested for stealing my trust fund. If you can see your way clear to have him lynched this afternoon I would greatly appreciate it."

"Hanged?" Grant squawked like a plucked rooster. "I have a right to that money!"

"The hell you do," Piper shot back. With claws bared, she went for Grant's skinny throat. To her dismay, the sheriff hooked his arm around her waist to hold her at bay.

"Mr. Fredricks, I suggest you go back to your room if you value your hide," Burgess insisted. "This young lady seems eager to extract a few pounds of your flesh."

Like a mouse scampering to safety, Grant scuttled out of the office. Jerking herself free, Piper glowered first at Burgess and then at Sheriff Epperson. "Is this your kind of justice? Do you allow criminals to run this town? Grant should be behind bars and I will not stop until he is! And I also want you to form a posse to search for my missing money. If there is law and order west of the Mississippi, I should like to see some proof of it!"

Piper flung her nose in the air and breezed out of the room like a misdirected cyclone. Both men stared at each other in astonishment.

"Pretty though she is, I think Miss Piper Malone is going to be a peck of trouble," Burgess stated with great conviction.

Epperson nodded in agreement and then pivoted on his heels. When Burgess was alone he folded his hands on his desk. A meditative frown puckered his harsh features. He wasn't sure who to believe, Grant or Piper. And it would take weeks to send a letter to Chicago and check on the matter. But one thing was for certain. That quarter of a million dollars had become a curse. Greed was a funny thing, and someone always wound up dead when more than one person was in pursuit of the same fortune. It didn't matter if there was plenty to go around. No one was generous enough to want to share it. There was always a heap of trouble when people got wind of available money.

Squinting in the midday sunlight, Logan reined his steed through the crooked mountain passes that led to the cabin. For more than three days he had slithered around like a snake, keeping watch over the two out-of-the-way shacks he had located. What he had seen the past few days had provoked more questions that demanded answers. But the theory that there was a network of several outlaw bands under the command of one leader had become increasingly plausible. Logan's observations led him to believe there was more than just random stage robberies going on in New Mexico Territory.

From atop a ridge, Logan had monitored the activities of both roadhouses as if he were watching two bustling ant dens. After a time he began to see a pattern that led him to his conclusion that a mastermind was in charge of the activities. He had witnessed the transfer of whiskey and rifles from whites to a band of renegade Mescalero Apaches. At the second roadhouse he had observed the confiscation of supplies and livestock from three unfortunate miners, who were left with nothing but the shirts on their backs. That very morning he had watched a band of thieves ride off in the direction of the stage station that had been abandoned the previous week.

Besides the steady stream of traffic moving south and east, there were also couriers trailing westward who met with a man that Logan hadn't expected to be involved in the theft ring. Considering the pack train that had returned to one hideout, Logan had a pretty good idea what was going on. But he was still confused by the connection to the stage robberies. The *when* and *how* no longer had him stumped. It was the *why* that befuddled him. . . .

His thoughts shifted quickly when he spied the shack that

was nestled beside the mesa on the rocky cliffs. Piper . . . the green-eyed witch . . . Logan had tried to force her from his mind from the moment he left the shack more than three days earlier, but it was as if she had taken up permanent residence in his brain. Trying not to think about her was exhausting and futile. Her smile was always in the sun. The sparkle in those enormous green eyes winked down at him from distant stars. The mystical combination of her silver-gold hair was in the colors of dawn and midnight. And the endless aching of frustrated desire gnawed at him night and day.

Damn, what did it take to exorcise Piper's bewitching spirit? Her absence from his life hadn't eased his craving. Preoccupation hadn't fazed his obsession. She still loomed in his thoughts like a tormenting apparition.

Logan wasn't sure how he would react when he saw Piper again. He suspected his men would be drooling over her by now, each one of them the picture of manly devotion. No doubt, Piper would delight in maneuvering them with her beguiling smiles and soft, alluring voice. Hell, she would have them fetching and heeling like obedient puppies!

Pulling in the reins on his wandering thoughts, Logan effortlessly swung from the saddle and stared at the shack. Three days' growth of beard and the dark circles that clung to his eyes testified to his lack of sleep and his constant vigil over the outlaws' hideouts. His foreboding appearance disguised the churning emotions inside him. He looked like black thunder, but on the inside Logan felt like a mass of conflicting emotion held together by a single thread. Grimly Logan stepped onto the porch and strode inside. His silver eyes lanced off the four men at the table and then swung toward Piper's bedroom door.

Without a word, Logan ambled over to pour himself a drink of courage from the bottle of whiskey the marshals were sharing. "How is she?" he asked after a minute.

"She's fine," Harley volunteered with a nonchalant grin.

"She's better than fine," Anthony Danhill chuckled as he eased back in his chair to rest a boot heel on the edge of the table. "She's gorgeous. I only wish I had been on the stage when she selected her pretended husband."

Logan glared at Anthony and then fixed his stabbing stare on

Harley, who had obviously blabbed the story to anyone who cared to listen.

"It's a damned shame you let that one get away, Logan," Jacob Carter declared.

"Get away?" Logan parroted in a dubious tone.

"Yeah, by now Piper probably has another string of eligible bachelors and a few married men trailing after her," Gorman Rader interjected with a melodramatic sigh. "I could have been one of them."

"What the hell is that supposed to mean?" Logan growled in question.

"Harley took her and Goliath to Tucson the night you left," Anthony informed him between sips of whiskey. "The way you were stomping around, Harley figured you didn't want Piper underfoot, so he toted her off."

Logan exploded. "You what?" His bellowing voice reverberated around the walls like a discharging cannon.

Harley flinched as the sound penetrated his eardrums. After chugging a drink of whiskey, he nodded. "I thought I was doing you a favor. You left me to tell her the truth and I assumed you also wanted me to get her out of the shack so you wouldn't have to face her when you came back. Now you can do the job you're being paid to do."

"You assumed?" Logan mimicked with a volcanic snort.

"What do you care?" Harley snapped back, the veins of his face popping in irritation. "Piper is safe and sound in Tucson. There is no need for you to fret over her anymore."

"That woman is never safe and sound when she's running around loose," he hooted. "She thinks that just because I taught her to use a pistol she can take on the devil himself if he dares to cross her. Piper knows just enough self-defense to get herself in worse trouble by trying to fight it out instead of turning tail and running." His broad chest heaved as he expelled an angry breath. "Jeezus, Harley, that was a damned fool thing to do!" Logan stamped around the room like a caged bull, muttering under his breath at irregular intervals.

"I nearly drove a good horse in the ground getting back here before you did. And this is the thanks I get for removing your unwanted baggage?" Harley crowded like an offender rooster.

"If you wouldn't marry the girl it wasn't right that you kept her, Logan . . . Logan? Where the hell are you going now?"

Logan had turned to storm out the door, snatching up a handful of pemmican on his way out. "To Tucson," he grumbled sourly. "And while I'm gone, the four of you are going to round up the dozen desperados I've been watching for the last three days."

Jacob blinked like a startled owl. "How the hell are we supposed to do that?" he asked. "We don't even know where their roadhouses are."

"You're seasoned lawmen. You'll sniff them out, just like I did," Logan threw over his shoulder.

"You could at least give us directions, for Chrissake," Gorman scowled as he stomped to the door to watch Logan's hasty flight.

"The roadhouses are only fifteen miles apart, nestled between the cliffs. You can be lying in wait and surprise the thieves when they return from their most recent raid. Bring them here and interrogate them. When we compare notes, we'll see if you come up with the same conclusions I did."

Logan slung his saddle over Sam's back and reached beneath the stallion's belly to fasten the girth. "If my suspicions are correct . . ."

"What suspicions?" Anthony interrupted impatiently.

"Blast it, Logan, you can't go parading into Tucson," Harley interjected before Logan could answer Anthony's question. "You're supposed to be dead, remember? And you aren't exactly an unfamiliar face in this part of the country. Someone might recognize you and spring our trap!"

Logan flung Harley a withering glance as he hopped into the saddle. "I'll be as inconspicuous as a ghost and you better pay attention to your business. Piper has a quarter of a million dollars stashed somewhere in these hills, stolen by some of the men you're going to arrest. I'm sure she would appreciate it if you found her money for her."

"A quarter of a million!" All four men squawked in unison.

Logan's blistering gaze landed squarely on Harley. "And in case you thought otherwise, my friend, the lady's foremost concern is her precious inheritance," he growled irritably. "So don't get any crazy ideas that we mean anything to each other." Logan eased his steed beside Harley who still stood with his mouth gaping. Leaning down, Logan offered his friend the map he had sketched of the two hideouts. "This will make your job a little easier. And next time, don't do me any favors that are going to cost me a two-days' ride."

"You don't have to go after her," Harley reminded him as he tucked the map in his pocket. "I gave you an out. If you drag Piper back here, you better marry her first. I'm not letting you use her. For God's sake, Logan!"

Logan scowled. "I wish the hell you would stop minding everybody's business and tend to your own."

"If your business wasn't in such bad shape, I wouldn't have to bother with it," Harley snorted defensively. "If you don't want to keep Piper permanently, then leave well enough alone!"

"Jeezus! Don't you ever quit?" Logan groaned as he gouged Sam and thundered off as if the devil himself were at his heels.

An ornery smile spread across Harley's face as he stuffed a bit into his steed's mouth. "Take a good look, men," he insisted with a chuckle. "A man in love rides a mad horse."

"Do you think Logan will marry that pretty little thing?" Jacob mused aloud.

"Nope," Anthony declared with great conviction. "Logan knows no other way of life and he's too stubborn to change at this late date."

"A ten-dollar goldpiece says you're wrong," Gorman challenged as he stuffed a booted foot in the stirrup. "That pretty lady could change the mind of a ninety-year-old woman-hater."

"Twenty dollars says Logan will sprout roots and settle down," Harley ventured optimistically. "When those two get over hating each other we'll probably all be godfathers to their raft of children."

Jacob and Anthony took their bets against Harley and Gorman and then had a good laugh while they looked over Logan's map. The foursome debated how Logan would react if he ever did become a father, and another flourish of betting took place. Finally they settled down to the serious business at hand. Logan had made their job easier by jotting down his suggestions for catching the brigands off guard. The marshals still had a battle on their hands, but with Logan's instructions and directions the thieves found unexpected visitors in their shacks when they returned. But even though the four marshals ransacked both shacks they failed to locate Piper's missing fortune. But then, Logan hadn't expected them to. If his predictions proved accurate, that quarter of a million dollars would sprout wings and fly off into several sets of hands before it returned to its rightful owner . . . *if* it returned to its rightful owner.

Piper's nest egg was only God knew where. But the matter of the money wasn't Logan's major priority. He had to retrieve Piper before she got herself into trouble. And she would, he prophesied. With her newfound sense of independence she would probably do something crazy like strike out on her own to find her missing trust fund. Logan hoped that stubborn minx had more sense than to flirt with disaster, but he refused to give her much credit for that. Knowing Piper as he did (and he had come to know her quite well), Logan warned himself not to be surprised at anything she did. The woman had become totally unpredictable!

never in a million years!

Chapter 21

Even though Piper had hounded Sheriff Epperson and Burgess Channing for two days, she had obtained no results. Epperson was still hemming and hawing, dreaming up a dozen excuses why he couldn't gather a posse and ride off in search of her fortune. He claimed he was a busy man with local squabbles with which to contend. But each time Piper burst into his office, Epperson was lounging in his chair, reading a newspaper or napping under it. In her estimation, Epperson should have arrested himself for loitering!

Burgess Channing still clung to his excuse that he was quietly gathering information in a way that would draw very little suspicion. The only positive action he had taken was to make two passes at Piper when she ventured to his office. She had promptly informed the homely merchant that his attentions were unwelcome and that he would be paid in cash if he assisted her in locating her inheritance.

To make matters worse, Grant continued to proclaim the stolen money was his, not Piper's. They had clashed twice since their first confrontation in Burgess's office—once at a local restaurant where they chanced to meet and once right in the middle of Tucson's main street.

When Grant decided they should split the funds in half, Piper came unglued. Before she could clamp her fingers around Grant's neck and shake some sense into him, Burgess Channing arrived upon the scene to pull them apart.

Burgess informed both of them that he had heard rumors

about a band of outlaws who had intercepted a great deal of money in a raid. Refusing to share their ill-gotten gains, the thieves had separated from their cohorts and had holed up near Superstition Mountain. According to the local gossip, one of the thieves had returned to town to gather supplies and to celebrate. The harlot with whom he had spent the evening had been privy to the information that tripped from his whiskey-loosened tongue.

Encouraged by the news, Piper insisted that she would strike out alone to begin her search. When Grant declared he didn't trust Piper to split the money, Burgess offered to accompany both of them. Grant wasn't thrilled with the idea of draping himself over the back of a horse for a grueling ride, but he was even less enthusiastic about leaving the matter to Piper. Neither was he eager to trek northwest when Burgess mentioned they would be traveling through Apache country. Grant had heard the terrifying stories about renegade Apaches attacking ranches in the area and he had no desire to be separated from his scalp while he was still in need of it.

The discussion ended when Piper called Grant a swindling coward. Burgess had ordered Piper to return to her hotel room and suggested Grant do likewise. Tempers were flaring once again, and Piper looked as if she meant to do the skinny dandy bodily harm.

Still fuming over the frustration that had mounted the past few days, Piper flounced down on her bed and performed her nightly ritual of cursing all men in general and Logan and Grant in particular. Although she had thrust herself into her crusade of locating her missing inheritance, her attempt to forget the silver-eyed devil who haunted her thoughts hadn't proved to be completely effective. Her body tingled when Logan's darkly handsome image came uninvited to her dreams. She could be in perfect control of her thoughts and then, without warning, dancing gray eyes and a lopsided smile intruded into her thoughts, unchaining a riptide of emotions.

Sighing heavily, Piper eased beneath the sheet and stared at the fleeting shadows on the ceiling. A light breeze fluttered through the window of her two-story hotel room. A carpet of moonbeams shone on the bare floor. Lively piano music wafted its way up to her from one of the many saloons, but the sound couldn't drown out the tormenting voice that echoed through Piper's thoughts.

She could see Logan looming over her as he had the night she left the shack in the mountains. Moonlight had glistened in Logan's raven hair as he bent close to breathe his harsh words. His cruel, intimidating smile cut like a double-edged dagger, leaving her heart to bleed. And in that moment, while Logan was chewing her up one side and down the other, Piper had despised him and all he represented.

It baffled her that she remembered that painful moment and that yet her foolish heart clung to the memory of his long, lithe body brushing against hers. She truly hated Logan for making her so vulnerable, for hurting her in ways that no other man had been able to do. Although Logan had left no marks on her with his rough handling, he had left wounds on her heart— wounds that would take an eternity to heal.

"Forget him," Piper lectured herself as she punched her pillow, wishing she could take out her frustration on its true source. Logan didn't want her, so that was that. He had left, allowing her to believe the worst about him because it suited his purpose. He had never really given her a chance because he still considered her a defenseless sophisticate who was out of her element. Logan never had one smidgen of respect for her, simply because she was a woman. Some folks may have considered half-breeds second-class citizens but, in Logan's opinion, women were as second class as any human could get.

Well, dammit, she couldn't help what she was! She had been born and bred a female. Logan resented the fact that she had been raised in the lap of luxury while he was forced to carve his own niche in the world. Was that her fault? Of course not! But she couldn't convince *him* of that. Logan was so set in his ways that it would take an act of God to change him. Logan behaved as if he were the only one on the planet who had problems. He was so busy being defensive that he never took the time to really know anyone else. That stubborn blockhead never once realized that he wasn't the only one to whom fate had dealt a punishing blow.

Don't spare that devil another thought, Piper advised

herself as she squirmed to find a comfortable position on her hard bed. Logan was out of sight and he should have been out of mind. He didn't like her. He only used her body for his pleasure, then he grew tired of her. Logan was glad she was gone. He wanted it that way. And if she never saw him again for the rest of her natural life that would be all too soon!

After delivering this lecture to herself Piper drifted off to sleep. She needed to rest before she set out across the rugged terrain to locate the band of outlaws who had stolen her money. It was her money, not Grant's. He was not getting his hands on even a penny of her inheritance!

With the silence of a stalking tiger, Logan curled one leg over the window ledge and then crawled into Piper's room. Hardly daring to breathe, Logan stared at the petite form of the woman who lay abed. The moonlight sifted across Piper's delicate features, soft in repose. Even in sleep her lips curved into a natural smile. Her long thick lashes lay against her cheeks and a wild spray of silver blond hair stretched like a shiny river across her pillow. The drooping sheet exposed the gossamer fabric of her negligee and the creamy swells that lay beneath it. Her bare arms glowed like ivory in the light, presenting a tantalizing picture of serenity.

Logan sighed appreciatively. If only she were this calm when she was awake, he mused whimsically. But for the past month this saucy nymph had changed with each passing day. She had grown and blossomed into an unpredictable spitfire. There was no peace to be found unless Piper was asleep. Only then could Logan admire her classical beauty. And for a long, quiet moment he did just that.

Too late he realized what a mistake it was to stand and ogle this lovely goddess. Within an instant the old familiar feelings flooded through him. He ached to reach out and caress what his eyes beheld. Although he and Piper had parted on an unfriendly note, nothing could ease the desire that gnawed at him when he recalled the pleasure they had shared in intimate moments. They had created precious memories. The passion they had enjoyed had dissolved their differences and their conflicts. During those splendor-filled nights they had been just a man and woman sharing a single identity, charting a course through a mystical ocean of stars. . . .

It had been Logan's intention to sneak into Piper's room, snatch her up, and tote her to his ranch. But suddenly he was stung by the fierce compulsion to join her in bed, to relive those rapturous memories. If they delayed a few hours it wouldn't hurt, would it? Besides, he could use some rest. He hadn't slept on a bed in almost a week. He had been living like a rattlesnake, curling up beside a rock while he kept a constant vigilance over the outlaws. Logan decided he deserved to pamper himself a bit. And a bath! What he wouldn't give to sink into a warm tub instead of the cold spring he had employed before venturing into town . . . !

To Logan's surprise, he found that his footsteps had already taken him to the end of the bed. He stood there, longing to ease the maddening craving this vision of loveliness aroused in him. Ah, the mind was a dangerous thing, Logan realized with a shudder. He had yet to touch this bewitching siren, and already he felt as if he had. The poignant memories triggered a flood of exciting sensations. He could almost feel her alabaster skin beneath his inquiring fingertips. He could almost taste her lips, lips that melted like rose petals beneath his kisses.

Logan didn't consciously recall removing his garments, but he must have. Either that or the heat of anticipated passion had melted them into a puddle at his feet. His whipcord muscles bunched and relaxed as he leaned forward to crouch above the sleeping beauty.

His silent movement caused Piper to stir slightly and a quiet moan tripped from her lips. Piper experienced the most arousing dream imaginable. In her sleep, she felt gentle hands skimming over her flesh. Warm drafts of breath whispered over her skin, evoking tantalizing tingles. Her body involuntarily arched toward the tender caresses while her mind stumbled through the dark corridors of drowsiness. She was floating on a cloud, tantalized by invisible hands—patient hands—that mapped the soft contours of her body, bringing each sensitive point to life.

Piper didn't want to wake. The delicious dream would fade

309

all too quickly and it would never again coincide with reality. Her subconscious was playing tricks on her, but she didn't care. She adored the forbidden sensations. They reminded her of the man who had taught her the meaning of passion, even if he had deprived her of love. And for this space in her fantasy, Logan was hers and hers alone. The sweet memories were hers to cherish, and in her magical dreams she could recapture those precious moments of lovemaking.

Over and over again, unseen hands migrated across her flesh, worshiping her, cherishing her. Velvety sensations unfolded like the petals of a delicate flower opening to greet the warmth of sunshine. Piper could feel moist lips hovering softly upon hers like a bee gathering nectar. The fragrance of the whole outdoors invaded her senses and the taste of addicting brandy melted on her mouth. While sensuous lips skimmed over hers, skillful hands descended across her abdomen to sketch lazy circles on her inner thigh. The ache of desire rose steadily, leaving Piper to burn. Gentle fingertips probed to satisfy and further arouse, making her want more than these teasing caresses and tempting kisses.

A soft moan tumbled from her lips as her thudding heart tapped at her consciousness. The feel of hair-roughened flesh gliding over her body caused her tangled lashes to flutter up. She gave a startled gasp as the moonlight and shadows revealed Logan's chiseled features and dark beard.

"Don't say anything, sweet witch," Logan whispered as he bent to take her lips. "I need you. . . . If you deny me, Piper, I swear I'll die of wanting you. . . ."

Piper knew she should be screeching in offended dignity, and for a moment she did raise a feeble protest, but she was the first to admit she really wasn't trying very hard to resist him. The forbidden pleasure was too tempting, and Logan was in one of his gentler moods. It didn't matter how he had found her or why he was here, only that he was here with her. If Logan thought he would die of wanting, Piper swore she would suffer the worst tortures of hell if he didn't ease the monstrous craving he had aroused in her with his practiced touch.

Adoringly, Piper reached up to trace the week's growth of dark beard and rearranged the tousled hair that was as shiny as a raven's wing. There was a ruggedly handsome quality in his commanding features. There was no refinement in his bronzed face, only the lines of vast experience and questionable breeding. But to Piper, it was the grandest face God had ever created.

Yes, she loved in vain and without rhyme or reason. Yet Piper couldn't help herself. She couldn't have denied this awesome man, not when it meant denying herself the rapture she knew awaited her when she melted in his sinewy arms. They may have been all wrong for each other, she may have been every kind of fool for drawing him closer when she should have pushed him away, but it seemed so right when he held her tenderly. Although she had tried to fight the attraction, loving Logan had become as natural as breathing. Without him, she was half, not whole. He had become a part of her that time and distance couldn't erase.

"Piper . . ." Logan groaned in torment when her hand glided down the tendons of his neck to settle on his hip.

"Logan?" A sleepy smile tugged at her lips. "It is you, isn't it?" Her soft, teasing chortle tickled his senses. "I can forgive myself for submitting to a ghost, but not to a perfect stranger."

Her playful remark provoked Logan to chuckle as he laid a bent leg over her thighs. "Dead men spread no rumors, little nymph. And if this be heaven, I don't begrudge my untimely demise."

Piper eased to her side to watch the flight of her adventurous hands over his muscled flesh. It felt so good to touch him again, to explore the hard wall of his chest, the lean columns of his legs. She would have been content to continue her investigations for several more moments to ensure that this wasn't another tormenting dream, but Logan wanted much more than her hands wandering to and fro on his skin. He wanted to feel her soft body beneath his, to hold her to him, to lose himself in an eternity of splendor.

Impatiently, his arm stole around her waist, pulling her full length against him. The throbbing peaks of her breasts pressed against his laboring chest, her hips fitting themselves eagerly to his. But still it wasn't enough to pacify his savage passions. He wanted to possess her, to love her as he had at Colbert's

Ferry and again at the Pinery. Surely this time he would finally appease this insane obsession. The third time was supposed to be the charm that broke black-magic spells, wasn't it? After tonight, her memory would no longer haunt him. He would be free of this sorceress with eyes of emerald green and hair the color of the sun and moon.

But when Piper gave herself up to him with the same ardent impatience, Logan wasn't sure even *three times three* would be enough. Gentleness faded into oblivion and the world spun furiously about him. Her hands and lips moved across his flesh in hungry possession, arousing him, taunting him, unleashing his fervent desires. Suddenly he had become the prisoner of his own primal needs. He longed to crush Piper to him, as if holding tightly to her would satisfy these monstrous cravings.

His heart hammered so furiously against his ribs that Logan swore it meant to beat him to death before he eased his wild need for her. His breath came in ragged spurts as they kissed with reckless urgency. His hands were roving, drawing her to him, longing to share the sweet intimacy of unrivaled passion. Never had he felt so hopelessly out of control. He wanted this lovely sprite as a starving man craves a feast after fasting for weeks on end. His body shuddered like an earthquake, and Logan wondered if he would ever be the same again. It was as if she were absorbing his strength, taking command of his mind and his body. He needed her desperately if he were to survive, and yet he wondered if he could endure this holocaust of sensations that were burning him alive.

The moment his body settled over hers his restless soul escaped the confines of its fiery prison to soar in motionless flight. Pleasure streamed through him as they moved as one. Logan could feel the sweet crescendo of rapture building inside him as he drove mindlessly into Piper's pliant body. It was like riding on a whirling carousel. With each dazzling revolution the ecstasy swelled out of proportion. He was moving in all directions at once, holding on for dear life, experiencing a myriad of incredible sensations.

And from the distance, soft, compelling music filled the breathless silence. It was Piper's song—the enchanting melody that lured souls toward an unknown destination.

Logan could feel himself letting go to answer the mystical calling. Passion bubbled like a geyser, spilling forth, flooding his mind, his body, his heart. He was stung by the same strange feeling that had tormented him once before when they made wild, sweet love. Again his limbs felt as if they were scattering hither and yon.

How he could hold onto Piper while he was lying in a dozen dismembered pieces, heaven only knew! Briefly, Logan wondered if he were holding her with his heart, since it seemed to be the only part of his anatomy that hadn't been flung to kingdom come. It was the oddest phenomenon. When he had experienced this crazed feeling at the Pinery, he had chalked it up to his wild imagination, but now he was beginning to wonder if he had discovered a new realm of passion, one he could only experience when he was in Piper's arms. He had certainly never been stung by these peculiar sensations when he was with any other woman. That baffled Logan.

As the spell of ecstasy faded into a mist, Piper breathed a contented sigh. Loving Logan called forth every conceivable emotion. It was a madness of sorts, she supposed. Piper could never seem to get enough of him. Even now, when one would have thought one would have been satisfied, Piper craved more of this sweet, hypnotic magic.

Gracefully, she raised herself on an elbow, causing her waist-length hair to tumble over Logan's face. Grinning mischievously, she drew the silky mane from his eyes and graced him with a kiss. Impulsively, her hand wandered over the broad expanse of his chest to flick each nipple. Her slow caresses scanned his ribs and belly, memorizing the feel of his hair-matted flesh beneath her hands.

"Not now," Logan breathed wearily. "I'm dead tired."

"Is that so unusual for a dead man?" she teased as she continued to explore his muscled flesh. "This body is but the cast-off garment of the soul. I should think an apparition would be capable of doing most anything when the spirit moves him."

"Woman, I swear you would test the endurance of two good men," Logan mocked gently as he pushed her to her back.

An adoring smile pursed Piper's lips when she stared into his strikingly attractive face. "But I would be perfectly satisfied with one unique man. The sheriff in Fort Smith assured me that none came better than you." Her straying hand rekindled passion Logan swore had completely burned itself out. "I think even you underestimate yourself at times, Logan. Rumor has it that you can perform the impossible."

Logan caught his breath as he peered down into her moonlit features. The confident smile she bestowed on him made him feel as if he could move mountains. Piper was looking at him as if he were something special. At that moment, Logan let himself believe she honestly believed in him, trusted him, cared about him. He may have been deluding himself, but he didn't care. He only knew he wanted her again for whatever the reason and he wasn't going to sit himself down and analyze why. He was simply going to love Piper again, to appease the need she constantly aroused in him.

Later, when he could think straight, he would remind himself that he wasn't quite as important to her as she would have him believe. It was enough that she wanted him to make wild sweet love to her again, because suddenly he wanted it too.

Reverently, he lowered his head to taste her honeyed lips. His body roused instantly when she arched upward to caress him with her silky flesh. Desire seared through him like wildfire, and Logan knew he would lose control all over again. This time he didn't care if he did. There was no such thing as sanity when this bewitching enchantress was weaving magical spells of pleasure around him. . . .

The abrupt rap at the door caused Logan to growl in frustration. "Who the hell is that?" he muttered in Piper's ear.

"I haven't the faintest idea," she murmured, her voice conveying her own exasperation.

"Another of your devoted admirers, no doubt," Logan grumbled sourly.

Piper flung him a disdainful glance. "I don't entertain men in my room, except you, and why you're here is a question that will probably haunt me until the end of my days."

The second rap sent Logan scurrying to fetch his discarded clothes. Piper frantically wormed into her gown. When she spun around, Logan was nowhere to be seen. The man was indeed a disembodied spirit, she decided. He could appear from nowhere and vanish into nothing! How could he do that?

"Who is it?" Piper demanded crossly. "It's the middle of the night!"

"Miss Malone, I would like a word with you. Open this door," Sheriff Epperson ordered.

Piper's brow knitted into a curious frown. What the devil did Epperson want? The man had probably taken so many naps during the day that he found himself prowling all night. And wasn't it just her luck that he had come crawling to her door?

Snatching up her robe, Piper shrugged on the garment on her way to the door. Cautiously, she opened the portal just enough to recognize the stout, middle-aged man who hadn't earned a day's wage to support the shiny badge that was pinned to his chest.

"May I come in?" Epperson requested impatiently.

Reluctantly, Piper stood aside. "Whatever it is you want can surely wait until morning."

"I'm afraid it can't, Miss Malone," the sheriff contradicted. "I found Grant Fredricks shot to death in the alley behind the saloon where he has been working at night."

"What?" Piper gasped incredulously. "Who would do such a thing?"

An accusing frown claimed Epperson's leathery features. "You're the only one I can think of, right off hand," he snorted disrespectfully. "Mr. Fredricks hasn't been in town long enough to offend much of anyone else. But you've threatened his life on several occasions."

Piper's chin jutted out. "That is a ridiculous assumption. I may have had a conflict of interest with Grant, but I certainly didn't kill him!"

"Didn't you?" His eyes narrowed suspiciously on her. "You threatened him often enough. You were holding him at gunpoint in Burgess Channing's office. And I saw Burgess pull the two of you apart this afternoon on the street."

"I don't know how you could possibly see anything that goes on in Tucson since you have your nose stuck in the newspaper most of the time," she shot back. "The story would have to be in print before you ever learned of it!"

Epperson's chest swelled as if he would pop the buttons off his shirt. "I do my duty, Miss Malone," he scowled indignantly, "and part of my job is hauling murderers to jail, even if the murderer is a woman!"

"Jail?" Piper parroted in astonishment. "You can't be serious."

Unfortunately, Epperson was as serious as he could be. He emphasized that fact by grabbing Piper's arm and ushering her toward the door. But Piper set her feet, refusing to stir another step.

"At least allow me to dress," she insisted hotly. "I have no desire to parade around town in my nightgown. Honestly, I don't know why you are doing this in the first place. I have been in my room since dark."

"Can you prove that?" Sheriff Epperson challenged.

Piper bit her lip. She could prove it if the man she had been entertaining weren't a ghost. If she divulged the truth she would damage Logan's attempt to corral the whole lot of desperados who plagued the area.

"Did you bother to interrogate the hotel clerk?" she inquired. "He can surely attest that I haven't set foot in the lobby this evening."

"The hotel has a back staircase for the servants," Epperson reminded her tartly. "You could have sneaked out without the clerk seeing you."

Heaving an exasperated sigh, Piper gestured toward the hall, silently demanding that Epperson remove himself from her room while she dressed. When the door was locked behind her, Piper wheeled around to see Logan rising from his hiding place beneath the bed. He was staring quizzically at her. Piper didn't know for certain what he was thinking, but she could hazard a guess.

"I didn't kill Grant," she felt compelled to say. "I wanted to a few times, but I didn't."

"I know." His silver eyes swept over her comely figure in masculine appreciation. "I was here with you when you didn't." A slight frown plowed his brow. "Why isn't the man in jail? He should have been arrested for theft."

"He wasn't because . . ." Piper clamped her mouth shut and

316

wiggled into her gown. "He just wasn't . . ." she finished cryptically.

Trepidation claimed Logan's features as he watched Piper sweep her hair up into a sloppy bun atop her head. She wasn't telling him everything. He could sense it. "Who is he, Piper?" he queried quietly. "And why didn't you tell Epperson I've been with you most of the night? It could have been the alibi you needed."

"Dead men can't testify in court," Piper reminded him in a hushed tone. "No one in town knows I'm supposedly your wife either. I told the stage agent that I had come to collect Mrs. Logan's luggage because she was too distressed to see to the task herself. Confessing to Epperson will only bring more questions, none of which will make your job easier."

Drawing herself up, Piper heaved a heavy sigh. "You may as well make use of the bed since I won't be needing it. You look as if you have missed a few nights' sleep."

When Piper turned toward the window, Logan grabbed her arm. "What are you doing?" he asked, puzzled.

"What I am *not* doing is going to jail," she told him with determination. "I'm going out the same way you came in."

"And if you do, Epperson will think you're guilty for sure," he grumbled, tossed a hasty glance toward the door.

An angry blush stained Piper's cheeks as she wormed her arm free. "You'd love to see me locked in jail, wouldn't you?"

"At least I'd know where to find you. It beats the hell out of having to creep past a dozen windows to locate you the way I did tonight," Logan replied with an ornery grin.

Piper stared down her nose at him. "If I land in jail, I doubt Epperson will approve of your sneaking into my cell to seduce me the way you did tonight," she bit off.

The loud rap on the door brought quick death to their conversation. "Hurry up or I'm coming in after you," Epperson threatened.

Resigning herself to the fact that she was to spend only God knew how long behind bars, Piper stamped toward the door. When Logan had crawled back into his hiding place, Piper mustered her courage and stepped into the hall to join Epperson. It galled her to be arrested for a murder she didn't commit. But what was infinitely worse was being hauled to jail by an irresponsible sheriff like Epperson. The man was never around when he was needed, and he refused to succumb to her pleas to file charges against Grant. If he had, Grant would be in jail instead of dead.

Disgustedly, Piper plopped down on the dilapidated cot in her dingy cell. "If there is a lawyer hereabouts, I should like to speak with him immediately," she proclaimed.

"I'll find you one in the morning," Epperson told her stiffly.

"I intend to be out of here by morning!" Piper spumed.

"Not unless someone breaks you out of jail," he countered with a smirk. "But don't get your hopes up, Miss Malone. You may be here awhile. Murder is a serious offense."

"So is false accusation!" Piper shot back. "One doesn't drag a person off to jail and ask questions later. You just decided I was the probable suspect and you . . ."

The door slammed shut behind Epperson and Piper uttered several colorful curses. She could envision him planted in his chair, doing what he did best—nothing! Damn that man. He planned to convict her without concrete evidence. If she ever got out of this rat hole she would begin her crusade to have that lazy lout fired from his duties. Tucson was wasting its money by paying that lazy scoundrel to sit on his—

"Piper," Logan's voice jostled her from her spiteful musings.

Muttering at the entire incident, Piper stomped over to glare at Logan between the bars of her window. "What!" she grumbled crankily.

Logan couldn't help himself. He grinned. Piper looked so ridiculous behind bars. To place a veritable angel in jail was sacrilege, even if she did behave like the very devil at times.

"I need to know why you had no case against Grant," Logan demanded after he wiped the amusement from his face.

Piper counted to ten twice to keep from screaming in frustration. Logan was enjoying this unexpected twist of fate, but she didn't think it was a damned bit funny. "What do you care? You're fancy free and I'm off your hands. I got myself into this tangled mess and I can get out without your help."

Her stubbornness stoked the fires of Logan's temper.

"Dammit, who was Grant and what connection did you really have with him?"

Piper chewed indecisively on her bottom lip.

"Without my help you may not walk out of this dungeon until you're old and gray," Logan growled impatiently.

"He was my stepbrother, if you must know," Piper mumbled bitterly. "Hiram Fredricks is the man my mother married." Tears threatened to cloud her eyes once the shock of being locked in jail wore off. It suddenly hit her that Grant had died a violent death. She had been vengeful, but she really hadn't wanted to see him lose his life. Grant had lived in her home for the past five years since her mother's second marriage, and he had always been underfoot when she was allowed to return home from boarding school. Although she had no use for Grant, the thought of his death stabbed at the pit of her stomach. "Grant claimed he was entitled to half my inheritance because my mother married his father. But it was my trust fund, established by my natural father. Grant had no right to it, whether the law states he was to gain partial possession at the event of my mother's death or not!"

"Jeezus!" Logan groaned. "Why didn't you tell me the truth in the first place?"

"I told you the truth," she defended tersely. When Logan gave her the evil eye, Piper glanced away. "I just neglected to mention a few insignificant facts."

"A few insignificant fa . . ." Logan broke into several unprintable expletives. "No wonder Epperson suspects you of murder. If you threatened your stepbrother, you have the most to gain from his death."

"Well, you weren't totally honest with me either," Piper parried. "You let me believe you were the ringleader of the gang that is harassing the stage. You could have told me the truth, but you left that to Harley."

This conversation was going nowhere so Logan terminated it. Each time he scolded Piper she reacted by jumping down his throat. Switching tactics, Logan expelled a sigh and stared straight into her misty green eyes. "Since neither of us is a saint, let's forget all the other accusations and concentrate on the matter at hand. Just tell me exactly what has been going on since you arrived in Tucson. And if you can think of any enemies Grant might have made, for whatever flimsy reason, please tell me. I don't have a helluva lot to go on."

Attempting to compose herself, Piper formulated her thoughts. She presented Logan with a brief but precise account of all that had transpired since she spied Grant on the street of Tucson. Logan listened diligently, nodding at irregular intervals, but he kept silent until Piper had finished her explanation.

In Logan's estimation, Piper and Grant had compounded their problem. But he didn't bother to tell Piper that. She had enough trouble of her own without him scolding her for mishandling the situation.

"I'll see what I can do," Logan murmured as he stepped away from the window. "And no matter who comes to your defense, you must agree with whatever is said. But I will see to it that someone comes to provide you with an alibi. With any luck at all, you will be out of here by morning."

When Logan disappeared from sight, Piper collapsed on her cot and grumbled to herself. She didn't have a clue what Logan was planning. How was he to find someone to offer her an alibi when he was supposed to be dead? And poor Grant. Who had committed the murder and allowed the blame to fall on her?

Piper's shoulders slumped dejectedly. Her future looked bleak . . . if she even had a future. That dispiriting thought set her to wondering if any other women had been hanged for murder in New Mexico Territory or if she was to be the first. Piper had several aspirations in life, but becoming the first woman in the territory's history to hang for a murder she didn't commit wasn't one of them!

Chapter 22

Since Logan was supposed to be a ghost, he resorted to slipping into a second window during the night. It happened to be the bedroom window belonging to Jenny Payton, who lived with her father on a ranch west of Tucson. As quietly as a church mouse, Logan eased into the dark room and approached the bed. Logan had always considered Jenny to be a very desirable woman. He might have been stirred to passion if he hadn't had that troublesome green-eyed witch on his mind.

Damnation, why couldn't Piper have told him she was pursuing her stepbrother? The man would have a reasonable case in a court of law, whether Piper thought so or not. It all depended on what had been stated in her father's will . . . if he had one . . . and whether Piper's mother was named the first benefactor of the money. Now that Grant was dead, Piper seemed to be the only one with motive. Blast it, since Logan had taught that feisty female to handle a gun and stand on her own two feet she had gone off half-cocked! Now she knew just enough to be dangerous, especially to herself.

Casting his wandering thoughts aside, Logan clamped his hand over Jenny's mouth and sank down beside her. "Jen, it's me, Logan," he whispered softly.

Her wide blue eyes blinked in astonishment. When Logan was sure she had recognized him, he removed his hand from her mouth. He found himself the recipient of a hug that nearly squeezed the stuffing out of him.

"I heard you were dead," she murmured as she rained kisses

on his bearded jaw and sought out his sensuous mouth. Logan removed her arms before the encounter became too passionate.

"I'm supposed to be dead. That's what I want everyone to think. I would appreciate it if you kept my secret," he insisted firmly.

Again Logan found himself on the receiving end of a tempting hug. Jenny had never denied him what he wanted when he happened through town. And there were times when she was even more aggressive than Logan in instigating romantic tête-à-têtes. His reputation intrigued her as much as the man himself. He excited her and she never refused him when he ventured to her room from only God knew where. If Jenny had her way, Logan would never have left her at all.

Prying the affectionate female loose, Logan gave her an abrupt shake. "Will you listen a minute, Jen? A friend of mine is in jail and I need you to provide a believable alibi."

Jenny peered up at Logan like an acolyte adoring a saint. She had always been there when Logan needed her for whatever reason. Jenny had hoped her devotion would endear him to her. The other men in her life were only pastimes—substitutes for the handsome, silver-eyed rogue she wanted and had never been able to capture. Put quite simply, Jenny worshiped the ground Logan walked on. He was more man than she had ever known, and there had been plenty of them. It was just that she had her heart set on Logan.

"What do you want me to do?" she asked as she lovingly sketched his chiseled features. "You know you have but to ask, Logan."

Logan ignored the suggestive gleam in her blue eyes, the tantalizing way her sheer gown drooped over her full breasts. Lord, Jenny made it difficult to concentrate on the business at hand. She was so warm, so willing, so available. She always had been. But even this lovely elf was a dim shadow in comparison to that curvaceous blonde rotting in Epperson's jail.

Confound it, if Logan had any sense he would leave that minx where she was until he had completed his obligations to Butterfield. Piper would be locked away and Jenny would provide him with the kind of pleasure a man needed from a woman. Besides, Jenny understood him as well as any woman did, except maybe for Piper who understood him better than he would have preferred. When Jenny said she loved him, he knew she meant it, even if she allowed other men in her life while he was roaming around like a tumbleweed. At least Jen was open and honest and affectionate.

Come to think of it, there wasn't one good reason why Logan shouldn't stick to his own kind instead of becoming distracted by Piper. Jenny had grown up in the West. She could ride and rope and take care of herself. If Logan ever considered marriage he would have considered Jenny first because she could fit into his life far better than Piper ever could. They had been lovers for three years and they rarely argued. But there were several reasons why Logan hadn't tied the matrimonial knot. He wasn't—

Logan gave himself a mental slap. As much as he would have liked to walk away from Piper, his conscience wouldn't let him leave her in jail longer than necessary. Yes, she was trouble. Yes, she was out of her element. And yes, Jenny was more his type. But Piper was his one and only brush with refinement and sophistication. Logan couldn't quite let go of her, even when he knew he should.

"I want you to go to Sheriff Epperson's office first thing in the morning. He has locked up a woman named Piper Malone for a murder she didn't commit. Tell Epperson—"

"How do you know she didn't?" Jenny interrupted suspiciously.

"Because Piper was with me when the crime was committed," he told her candidly. Logan gnashed his teeth when Jenny's eyes narrowed. He had a feeling he and Jenny were about to have their first disagreement. Sure enough, he was right.

The idea of Piper nipped at Jenny's female pride. She would have done anything Logan asked of her except to protect one of his paramours. And she wasn't foolish enough to think there weren't other women in Logan's life. Women couldn't resist his devilish ways. He was wild and reckless and challenging. They might pretend to take offense at his reputation, but most envisioned themselves in his brawny arms, surrendering to his savage brand of passion. Jenny had never enjoyed many luxuries in life and for once she would like to be envied. Laying claim to a man like Logan could satisfy that craving, and she didn't like the thought of Piper whoever-she-was stealing the man Jenny coveted for herself.

"You're asking a lot, Logan," Jenny pouted. "You know I'd follow you to the end of the earth, but I'm not about to do favors for my rivals. Find someone else to assist her."

"I'll pay you for your time and trouble," Logan offered. "All you have to do is name your price."

A wry smile pursed Jenny's lips as her straying hand slid over his shoulder to toy with the shaggy raven hair that lay at the nape of his neck. "My price is marriage," she insisted.

Logan flinched as if he were sitting on a centipede. "I thought you and I had an understanding," he grumbled.

"And I thought you knew why I never accept marriage proposals from other men," she murmured provocatively. "The only man I've ever wanted is you."

Sweet mercy, things weren't going as he had anticipated. Heaving a sigh, Logan weighed his options, of which there were only a few. "All right, we'll talk about marriage," he said after a moment.

"When?" Her eyes brightened in eager anticipation.

"As soon as I finish the job I was sent here to do. And part of it includes freeing Piper from jail."

Jenny frowned bemusedly. "Are you working for this woman who is stuck in Epperson's cell?"

"In a way, yes," Logan hedged.

Reasonably assured that she hadn't lost Logan forever, Jenny nodded her consent. When she did, Logan promptly unfolded his scheme for releasing Piper. Although Jenny had intended for Logan to spend the remainder of the night in her arms, Logan insisted that he had several other errands to run during the cloak of darkness.

Jeezus! Logan grumbled as he headed toward Tucson. How had he gotten in such a tangled mess? He was presumed dead. He had a supposed widow locked in jail and Jenny was making plans for their upcoming wedding. There was still the matter of rounding up the desperados and their ringleader.

Logan expelled a frustrated breath. If he was smart he would turn his back on his professional obligations and his personal entanglements and ride off into the sunrise, never to be seen or heard from in Tucson again!

This is all Piper's fault, Logan thought disgustedly. She had thrown a wrench in the mechanical workings of his life. He would have had only himself to worry about if she hadn't complicated his scheme. Now one problem was linked to another, and that saucy blonde was the focal point of his troubles. Piper was a walking disaster searching for a place to happen. He had known that the moment he laid eyes on her, but had he followed his instincts? Hell no, he had been tripped up by his needs. And since he had crossed paths with Piper in Fort Smith, Logan had been wandering through a maze of conflicting emotions, none of which could master the others. Was there any way around that woman?

Mulling over those spiteful thoughts, Logan thundered off into the darkness. For the life of him he didn't know why he was wearing himself out trying to save Piper's lovely neck. She would inevitably stick her throat into another noose. That flighty nymph's middle name was trouble! Not only did she attract it, but she also attracted people who attracted trouble. And that was even worse!

The murmur of voices roused Piper from a fitful sleep. The rattle of the lock on the door that separated the foul-smelling cells from the outer office swung open to reveal Sheriff Epperson and a shapely brunette garbed in trim-fitting breeches and a skin-tight shirt. A pair of bright blue eyes flooded over Piper, registering surprise before they darkened in envy and displeasure. Jenny Payton quickly masked her irritation behind a greeting smile.

"Piper, for heaven sake! How did you wind up in here?" she questioned with a theatrical frown. "When I left your room last night you were preparing for bed."

"I tried to tell Sheriff Epperson I hadn't left the hotel all evening," Piper commented, flashing the stoutly built man a condescending glare. Fleetingly, her gaze scanned the comely brunette, wondering what connection she had with Logan. As if I don't know, Piper thought sourly.

"If you spent the evening visiting with Jenny, why didn't you tell me?" Epperson asked suspiciously.

Piper tilted a proud chin. "Because I didn't want you disturbing Jenny in the middle of the night the way you disturbed me," she retaliated. "It's bad enough that Jenny had to traipse over here to come to my defense. And if you would have thought the matter through, you would have realized I didn't take after Grant with a gun. That was the most ridiculous . . ."

"All right!" Epperson growled as he unlocked the cell. "You are free to go. God, it will be a relief not to have to listen to another of your lectures."

As the two women stepped onto the street, Piper peered curiously at Jenny. "What did you tell Epperson we were doing until all hours of the night?"

"I informed him that we had met the previous day and had taken an instant liking to each other. We spent the evening chatting about the latest fashions and the vast differences between people from the East and the West."

Jenny's pointed glance and subtle remark carried an underlying meaning. Piper knew exactly what the insinuation suggested. Jenny considered herself better suited for Logan than Piper ever could be.

"You are supposed to come with me now," Jenny murmured as she moved toward her wagon. "Logan is waiting for us."

Piper had just pulled herself onto the wooden seat when Jenny popped the reins over the horses, sending them lunging forward. With a startled squawk, Piper clamped her hand on the seat to prevent being flung backward. Restraining her temper, Piper swallowed the tart remark that was poised on the tip of her tongue. Jenny had spared her the agony of spending time in jail. For that Piper was thankful, even if Jenny seemed intent on disliking her at first sight.

"I think we should come to an understanding here and now," Jenny declared, flinging the comely blonde a sidelong glance. "The only reason I saved your neck was because Logan asked me to."

"I appreciate that," Piper said with genuine sincerity. "I

326

intend to pay you for your trouble."

Jenny turned to peer directly at Piper. "All the thanks I need is your promise to keep your distance from Logan while the two of you are working together. I love Logan and we are going to be married as soon as he finishes whatever job he is committed to."

The news hit Piper like a blow to the midsection. She didn't know why she cared that Logan and Jenny were to be wed. She knew Logan didn't love her. After all, he had soundly rejected her confession. But it still hurt to meet the woman who truly fascinated a man like Logan. Piper wasn't surprised by her rival's appearance. Jenny seemed Logan's type—if indeed that rascal had a type. The attractive brunette seemed a part of this country she called home. No doubt the two of them had a great deal in common. Even Piper was sensible enough to know she was Logan's mismatch and Jenny was his match.

For the next few minutes, Piper forced herself to imagine Jenny and Logan together. To her chagrin, she could easily envision them riding off into their own sunset astride black stallions. Jenny could probably ride like the wind and fire a pistol at full gallop.

Piper's newfound confidence drooped when she compared herself to Jenny. In a way, Piper was glad she had met Logan's fiancée. It would prevent her from harboring any foolish notions that there could ever be anything lasting between her and Logan. He had taken advantage of her because she was convenient, but Jenny was the woman Logan wanted beside him now that he had decided to settle down.

A burning ache singed Piper's heart when she spied Logan's muscular physique propped against the stone and timber corral. The mere sight of him caused invisible tentacles to wrap themselves around her wounded heart, crushing it.

Piper watched Jenny beam with pleasure when she too noticed Logan. The moment Jenny reined the horses to a halt, she bounded from the wagon and flew to Logan like a homing pigeon returning to roost.

With her heart shriveled in her chest, Piper sat rigidly on the seat, enduring the romantic encounter, finding herself dangling on the third side of the eternal triangle. Jenny showered Logan with eager kisses. He didn't seem to mind having Jenny slobber all over him. If Jenny pressed herself any closer to Logan she would melt all over him! The brunette had stamped her claim on Logan and he seemed to relish the attention he was receiving.

"Any trouble?" Logan asked. He darted Piper a discreet glance. She was staring off into space, her elegant features masked behind a carefully blank stare. That annoyed Logan. She didn't seem to be the slightest bit jealous. Come now, Logan, he chided himself. You really hadn't expected Piper to be envious. You are only her tool, the pawn she plays to get what she wants most—her inheritance.

Jenny gave her head a shake. "Epperson swallowed the story—hook, line, and sinker," she declared, grinning mischievously. "Lucky for you, I have a respectable reputation in Tucson." Her index finger traced his sensuous lips. "And very soon, you'll make a respectable woman out of me, after three long years. . . ."

As fate would have it, Piper glanced in the chummy couple's direction at that particular moment. The sticky sweet scene very nearly gave her a toothache!

"You run along home now, Jen," Logan commanded in a soft tone that he rarely used with Piper. (And that stung Piper like a wasp.) "I'll be in touch soon."

"I hope so . . ." Jenny murmured suggestively.

While Logan assisted Jenny onto the seat, Piper climbed down on the opposite side. Forcing the semblance of a smile, Piper focused on the bubbly brunette.

"I'm indebted to you, Jenny," Piper told her gratefully.

"Just stay clear of . . . Epperson's jail," Jenny finished with a meaningful glance.

It wasn't the sheriff Jenny was warning Piper to avoid. It was Logan, and Piper knew it. "I'll do that," she announced with a short laugh.

Reluctantly, Jenny bade Logan goodbye and sped away, leaving a cloud of dust behind her. The silence that settled over Piper and Logan could have been sliced with a knife.

"She's very pretty," Piper congratulated him, fighting for hard-won composure.

Logan gauged her reaction for a long, pensive moment. "Yes, she is." Clearing his throat, he changed the topic of conversation. "I've decided it's best if I take you to my ranch. Samuel can keep an eye on you until I've dealt with the man I'm looking for."

Piper's chin jutted out in defiance. Logan was crazy if he thought she would consent to that! Now that she knew of his wedding plans, she wasn't going to accept any favors from him, and she certainly wouldn't be caught dead at his ranch, even if Abraham was there. Jenny didn't want her near Logan, and Piper knew she would feel the same way if she were his fiancée.

All Piper had left was her quest to recover her stolen fortune. She was not about to sit and twiddle her thumbs while Logan went about his business. He didn't give a hoot about her lost fortune. He didn't give a hoot about her period!

"I made arrangements with Burgess Channing." Piper rapped out the words in staccato. "He has agreed to help me locate the thieves who took my money. I'm going nowhere until my inheritance has been found."

Silver eyes glistened with barely restrained irritation. "You are going nowhere with Channing or anyone else," he growled in a tone that anticipated no argument. He wasted his breath.

"You have no right to tell me what to do! If you want to browbeat a woman, save it for your fiancée. She loves to jump each time you snap your fingers," Piper retaliated bitterly.

A dry smile pursed Logan's lips. "So that's what put a bee in your bonnet," he speculated. "You can't stand the fact that there's a woman on this planet who actually respects me, faults and all."

Her dainty chin tilted at an exaggerated angle. "No, it most certainly is not," she answered almost at once. "You have my blessing. I hope the two of you will be very happy. I couldn't care less if you marry Jenny. All I want is my money so I can be on my way!"

"That's what I thought," Logan scowled sourly.

"You don't think, you presume. When the good Lord dished out your brains with a spoon, the devil bumped his arm and you wound up a half-teaspoon short," Piper sniped. She didn't know why she was spouting her irritation at Logan. She had intended to accept the news of his marriage gracefully. But it hurt like hell to know she was still carrying a torch for a man who obviously had eyes for someone else. Dammit all!

"And if your brain was put in a buzzard, the poor bird would fly backward," Logan bit off. "You can't have a lick of sense if you are considering trotting off with Burgess Channing on a wild goose chase!"

For a moment they glared at each other. Finally Piper turned a cold shoulder to him and stamped toward the horse Logan had brought for her. "If I ever retrieve my inheritance, I'll purchase an appropriate wedding gift for you and Jenny—a brass bed. I'm sure you will be spending more time on your back than on your feet."

In two long strides, Logan closed the distance between them and jerked Piper around so quickly her head spun like a top. "I'm not half the rogue you think I am," he muttered grouchily.

"Aren't you?" Piper sniffed in a caustic tone. "You couldn't prove it by me. You've used my body as a stopgap for the fiancée you had waiting in the wings."

"What the hell's a stopgap?" Logan muttered in question.

"Go look it up in a dictionary," Piper snapped at him. "I'm tired of translating for you."

"What difference does it make to you if I'm the rogue and rake you think I am?" Logan scowled into her flushed face. "You used me as your pretended husband to buy yourself a ticket west."

"It would have made . . ." Piper clamped her teeth together so quickly she nearly bit her tongue in two, ". . . absolutely no difference," she lied to save face. "Jenny is welcome to you. You are a domineering, intimidating bully, and a heartless, no-account womanizer."

Logan looked as if he wanted to strike her. To her surprise, he didn't yield to the temptation. When she flounced toward her mount, Logan merely cursed.

"Are you really going on this treasure hunt?" When Piper nodded, Logan cursed again. "Lady, you are a fool. If your money is truly stashed in some secluded shack you don't have a snowball's chance in hell against those ruffians who have

330

taken possession of it. You're going to get yourself killed!"

"That's not your problem," Piper reminded him as she grabbed the reins. "I'm not your responsibility and I haven't asked for your help."

"If you're smart you would," Logan smirked arrogantly.

Piper wanted to kick this infuriating man. He made her so angry she couldn't see straight, and her body was trembling with barely restrained fury. With her fist clenched in the reins, Piper swung into the saddle. When Piper glared down at Logan he was grinning in smug satisfaction, knowing he had gotten under her skin with his cocky remark. With her back as stiff as a flagpole, Piper spewed several curses. The words tumbled from her tongue in disjointed phrases.

Her inability to swear fluently provoked Logan to laughter, and that made Piper all the madder.

"You can go to the devil, Logan." Her accompanying glower was as hot as the hinges on hell's door.

"You're getting better," Logan complimented, undaunted.

"Heaven forbid that I should become as proficient at cursing as you are," she gritted out.

Piper was so furious that she forgot she hadn't mastered riding. Gouging the steed, she shot off like a cannonball. The buckskin mare was built for speed and she stretched into her swiftest gait. When the steed swerved to prevent stepping in a hole, Piper fell from her mount. With a squawk, Piper hit the ground, but dignity brought her immediately to her feet. While Logan's shoulders shook in silent amusement, Piper stamped after the mare and pulled herself back into the saddle. Employing more caution this time, Piper trotted back toward Tucson, wishing she were well-versed in profanity. If she had been she would have burned off Logan's ears with a sizzling string of curses!

As Piper disappeared in the distance, Logan's laughter died into silence. For several minutes he stood deep in thought. And then suddenly he growled in exasperation. It galled him that this blond-haired virago could arouse such a multitude of conflicting emotions within him. One moment he wanted to grab her and kiss away her defiant frown. The next instant he wanted to shake the stuffing out of her for being so stubborn and contrary. And in the *next* second he was chuckling at her antics. Jeezus! That little firebrand had his emotions rolling up and down like a damned yo-yo!

Why didn't that green-eyed hellion affect him the same way Jenny did? He never felt out of control with Jen. She was predictable—feisty but predictable. Piper, on the other hand, set a new precedent with each dawning day. There was no way in hell to predict the actions and reactions of a woman who was developing greater depths of character with each new experience she encountered. A man couldn't second-guess Piper. A month earlier she had burst into tears when she was angry. Three weeks ago Piper tried to outfox him when she was irritated with him. For two weeks she had stood up to him with courageous defiance, refusing to listen to reason, rejecting his sensible suggestions just because she didn't want a man trying to tell her what to do. Hell, tomorrow Piper would probably . . .

Logan expelled a harsh breath. Only God knew what tomorrow would hold. Within twenty-four hours that saucy spitfire could become another Joan of Arc!

I ought to wash my hands of that troublesome misfit, Logan lectured himself, even as he swung into the saddle to follow Piper at an inconspicuous distance. He wanted to let her go. Truly he did. He wanted to put her out of his mind completely. But he couldn't. The thought of that daring beauty ending her life in some dusty, out-of-the-way shack nagged at him. Piper needed him, even if she was too proud and stubborn to admit it.

By the time Piper marched into Burgess Channing's office, she had regained control of her chaotic emotions. Since the moment she trotted away from Logan she had resolved to consider him a page from her past. She had to bury the whimsical notion of loving that brawny giant. He belonged to another woman, one who was a far better match than Piper could ever be.

If I can fall in love with Logan, I can also fall out of love with him, Piper reasoned sensibly. She would concentrate her efforts on recovering her money. And when she did, she would catch the first stagecoach out of town.

"Well, Mr. Channing?" Piper drew herself up in front of the sour-faced merchant. "You promised to lead me to the shack where the thieves are holed out."

Burgess regarded Piper with a dark frown. "This will be no Sunday picnic, you know. I have no guarantee that my information is correct or that you will find your missing funds. We are merely following rumors. The region where the roadhouse is supposed to be is near Apache stomping ground."

"You have already made that clear," Piper said impatiently. "And you also gave me your word you would assist me. I intend to hold you to that promise."

Burgess pushed himself out of his chair. "Very well then, give me a couple of hours to gather supplies. But bear in mind I expect two thousand dollars compensation if we are fortunate enough to find your funds."

"You'll get your money," Piper muttered resentfully. "I'll meet you in front of your store as soon as I have ensured that my stepbrother receives a proper burial." Burgess's narrowed glance brought Piper's chin to an indignant angle. "And no, I was not responsible for his death. Grant and I had our differences, but I did not resort to drastic measures to dispose of him."

With that, Piper performed a precise about-face and marched from the office. When she returned exactly two hours later, dressed appropriately for her ride, Burgess was waiting outside. In silence, they reined their mounts east, following the sketchy third-hand directions Burgess reported he had received from one of the local harlots.

Piper ignored the heat and dust. She was driven by a singleminded purpose—to prove she was capable of managing her own problems. She concentrated on her riding, being careful not to topple from her perch in the same humiliating manner as earlier that morning.

When they paused to give their mounts a rest, Piper sank down beside the spring that trickled between the boulders. After cleansing her sunburned face she surveyed the surrounding rocks, juniper trees, mesquite, and mesas. With a start, she focused on the slight movement that had caught her attention. In the distance, a shadowed form of a man leaned leisurely against a huge boulder. Logan?

"We're ready to ride," Burgess announced in his characteristically gruff tone.

Piper glanced back to the spot Logan had occupied, but he had vanished. A bemused frown etched her brow. Why was he trailing after her? Wasn't he supposed to be tracking down desperados? What was he planning to do? Take credit for flushing out the scoundrels who were holed up in this secluded shack?

Heaving a tired sigh, Piper stuffed her booted foot in the stirrup. She wasn't going to waste her time trying to analyze Logan. If he wanted to sneak around like the departed spirit most everyone supposed him to be, that was his business. Piper was through thinking about him, through wanting him. She wasn't going to cherish the memories they had made together. She was going to curse them and then push them out of her mind forever. The meaningless affair was over and done. It was as if it had never happened.

But I did ask for this heartache in a way, I suppose, Piper mused as they weaved around the mesquite and piñon trees that clung to the stony cliffs. She had pretended to be Logan's wife. What had she expected him to do, behave like a gentleman? He was a lusty philanderer and she had known that. She just hadn't wanted to believe it.

Her only consolation was that she hadn't turned out to be as idiotic as Jenny. If that woman thought she could tame a man like Logan she was a bigger fool than Piper was. Logan used all women. There wasn't a faithful bone in that magnificent body of his. He suffered from the disease known as roving eye, and even if Jenny managed to place a ring on Logan's finger, she couldn't prevent him from seeking pleasure whenever another woman caught his eye during his treks across the Southwest. Logan had been born under a wandering star that had brought him from the Cherokee village in North Carolina to Indian Territory and beyond. Jenny's love for him would never tie him down.

She had vowed not to spare that silver-eyed demon another

thought and here she was dwelling on him! Her disgruntled gaze swung to Burgess. If the man had one iota of personality, he could have distracted her in conversation during their journey, but Burgess couldn't have commanded anyone's attention if his life depended on it. In Piper's estimation, it was little wonder Burgess was forty-five and still single. Wealthy though he was, he didn't possess enough charm to fill a thimble. A woman would have to be blinded by dollar signs not to notice what a lousy catch Burgess would be. When his deep-set eyes swept over a woman she was more offended than flattered. Piper had made it clear that she was offering Burgess no more than monetary compensation for his time and trouble. Why he continued to stare at her as if he were expecting more was beyond her. There was no way in hell she would suffer his repulsive touch!

Although Burgess provided little companionship, Piper made a stab at conversation. "I have heard you are the major supplier for Butterfield's stage stations," she commented as she mopped the perspiration from her brow.

"Yes," Burgess replied without changing expression.

Determinedly, Piper tried again. "Where do you purchase your supplies to equip the stations?"

"Santa Fe mostly."

Piper's shoulders slumped. She might as well have attempted to carry on a conversation with the rock precipices that towered above them. And so it went for the remainder of the day. Piper was forced to wrestle with her pent-up emotions. Their journey progressed with only one near catastrophe. A band of Mescalero Apaches appeared on the mesa below them. Piper and Burgess plastered themselves against the jagged boulders to prevent being spotted. The sight of the savages had an unnerving effect on Piper, but she mustered her courage. She had come this far and she wasn't turning back just because they happened upon Indians.

When the twosome made camp for the night, Piper collapsed on her bedroll, eager to sleep. And sleep came quickly for her. But somewhere in the night, she swore she felt warm lips hovering over hers, felt the gentle touch of a caress. She opened her eyes, expecting to find Burgess hovering over her, but Burgess was sleeping like a baby. She wondered if she wouldn't have preferred to fend Burgess off with a stick instead of confronting the handsome rogue who loomed over her now.

Logan gestured for her to follow him, and Piper rose from her pallet and tiptoed in the direction he had disappeared. As she rounded a boulder, only a stone's throw away from camp, a sinewy arm snaked out to entrap her.

"What are you doing here?" Piper hissed as she squirmed for freedom. Logan's touch, no matter how harmless it might have seemed, still had the power to stir unwanted sensations. Piper hated her lingering vulnerability. It served to remind her that her heart was still ruling her head where this devilish rake was concerned.

"I'm following a fool," Logan taunted, his warm breath dancing across the back of her neck.

"I'll be sure to tell Burgess what you said about him," Piper sniffed in the same sarcastic tone.

Logan turned her in his arms. Cupping her rebellious chin, he brought it down a notch. "I've met a lot of men who were bent on self-destruction," he murmured as he searched the shadows that claimed her flawless features, "but I've never known a woman who openly invited trouble the way you do."

"And I've never met a man who can annoy me as quickly and thoroughly as you can," she grumbled, removing his wandering hand.

"That goes double for me," Logan insisted, but his voice carried no bite. It rumbled with disturbed desire—something he had never been able to control when he dared to venture too close to this bewitching nymph.

Piper knew he meant to kiss her. Even the shadows couldn't disguise the passionate glitter in his silver eyes. But she wasn't going to enjoy it! She was going to stand there like a pillar of stone, feeling nothing, wanting nothing from him. Lord, let it be over, Piper thought in anguish. Let these compelling feelings die.

As his lips slanted across hers in the lightest breath of a touch Piper's will broke down. There was no nagging voice to scold her. Her body no longer had a mind attached to it, and primal need assumed control of her flesh. Surrendering to his

336

skillful touch had become as involuntary as the batting of an eyelash. It was wrong to long for the touch of a man who belonged to another woman. But Piper couldn't even recall her own name, much less Jenny's at that moment.

Logan's hands glided up her hips to map her ribs and then swirled across the throbbing tips of her breasts. Piper ached for more of this sensual pleasure that swirled through her. When his kiss deepened and his caresses became intimately disturbing, Piper yielded to the magical sensations Logan so easily evoked from her. Reflexively, her arms wound around his neck as if they belonged there. Her pliant body molded itself to his hard, muscular contours, and she lost herself in his passionate kiss.

Suddenly there was no past, no present, no future. There was only this sweet, glorious dream that defied the measures of time. Logan drowned in the taste of Piper's soft lips as she absorbed his strength, his thoughts. The feminine fragrance that was so much a part of her became a part of him. Even with his eyes closed, he could see those emerald pools rippling in the moonlight. They lured him nearer. Like a senseless puppet he moved upon command, aching to live a forbidden fantasy.

A groan of sweet torment bubbled in his throat when Piper's roaming hands dived beneath his buckskin shirt to make tantalizing contact with his hair-matted flesh. Bone and muscle melted beneath her inquiring touch, reducing his body to the consistency of grape jam. Her caresses provoked longings that mushroomed into maddening cravings. His heart thundered around his chest as her hands stroked and massaged, growing bolder by the second.

Mindless passion overwhelmed both of them. Although they had selected the most unlikely of places to begin what neither of them had the will to stop, Logan knew he wouldn't be content until Piper was his again—body, mind, and soul. He was seized by male instinct, hungry and impatient to appease a desire that knew no beginning, no end. The attraction was always there, lurking beneath the biting words and sharp glances, waiting to blossom and consume him.

As Logan drew Piper down beside him on their pallet of discarded clothes, he marveled at her exquisite beauty.

Moonlight danced in her silver blond hair and played across her ivory skin. Her pale body contrasted sharply with his bronzed flesh. Her shiny tendrils reflected the light that his raven hair absorbed. She was elegant satin and he was rough leather. They each represented what the other was not. They were like the light and dark side of the moon—each so different, and yet an integral part of the other.

A sigh of sublime satisfaction tumbled from his lips as his body fitted itself to hers. Only when they were one could Logan find peace. In this wild, mad world there was only one haven. Piper supplied far more than passion when she took him to her, when he became a part of that blazing fire. She was the soothing balm that smoothed the wrinkles from his soul. She was the taste of wine that quenched his thirst. And even while the winds of passion raged upon him, Logan was possessed by a sense of serenity that he had never known and was at a loss to explain.

Piper clung fiercely to Logan as she met his hard, driving thrusts. Jumbled thoughts whirled through her dazed mind. It was impossible to love and hate a man as thoroughly and completely as she did Logan, but when he clutched her in his powerful arms nothing was impossible. Wrong suddenly seemed right and necessary. He had become every breath she took as they sailed off on the most intimate journey through time and space.

And then, with wings widespread in motionless flight, Piper experienced the epitome of passion. Her body shuddered as a kaleidoscope of ecstatic sensations sprang to life. Her nails dug into Logan's back, holding him ever so tightly to her, as if the world were about to explode. And explode it did. Silver-white light erupted from the darkness, and the maddening ache became sweet, splendorous release. It was a unique emotion that transcended physical pleasure. It was pure love—a feeling that did not conform to conscience or logical thought. It defied reason, and Piper felt it channeling through every fiber of her being. Logan was the man of her dreams. It didn't matter that he was the keeper of many women's fantasies. For now, for this one precious moment, he was sharing her dream with her.

It was long, breathless minutes later that sanity and reality reemerged from the passionate fog that clouded Logan's mind. It was even longer before the side effects of their ardent lovemaking passed from his spent body. Logan resented the intrusion of sensibility. He would have preferred to spend the remainder of the night in this hazy cloud of pleasure. But he knew the angel in his arms would soon take shelter beneath her stubborn shell and they would be at cross-purposes again. Before the inevitable happened, Logan helped himself to one last kiss—a long, lingering kiss that conveyed what words could not express, especially since he wasn't sure what he wanted to say.

Piper felt so small lying beside Logan's long, sinewy frame, and yet she felt so protected, so secure. An odd sensation rippled through her soul when Logan kissed her with such rare tenderness. He had been gentle before, but he had never treated her quite like this.

"I'll be here in case you need me," he murmured as he gathered his clothes and stepped into them. He suddenly felt awkward, as if there were something he should have said or done. But damned if he knew what it was.

Reality came flying back. With more speed than dignity, Piper climbed into the breeches and shirt she had donned for this rugged journey on horseback. "You don't have to do this, Logan," she insisted quietly. "And you truly shouldn't have done *that* either."

An amused grin crinkled his craggy features. "I only kissed you. You did the rest," he teasingly accused her.

Piper's face turned scarlet and she could feel the explosion of color in her cheeks. "I didn't do anything."

"Neither did I," Logan declared with great conviction.

"Then it must not have happened," she announced.

Logan's broad shoulders shook in silent laughter as he stared down from his towering height at the proud beauty. "I love your logic, little minx," he murmured, flicking the tip of her upturned nose. "If you want to ignore an encounter you simply strike it out by mumbling your hocus-pocus. And poof. There is suddenly a gap in the chronicles of your life."

"It helps me cope," Piper muttered bitterly.

"With what?" Logan wanted to know. "With making love to

339

a man who isn't good enough for you?"

Piper felt her temper rise several degrees. "You're impossible!"

"And you're incorrigible," Logan proclaimed. "If anyone else tore off on as many tangents as you have the past month, they would have killed themselves at least twice."

"Those are ironic words, coming from a dead man," Piper sniffed sarcastically. Flinging her nose in the air, she stamped back toward camp. "Good night, phantom. Go haunt someone else!"

Logan watched Piper veer around the oversized boulder before he expelled the breath he had been holding. What was wrong with the two of them? One moment they were sharing sweet companionable silence. The next instant they were hurling swords and daggers at each other. Piper could draw him into an argument before he knew he was there. How could she do that? he wondered bemusedly. That was the one thing he could predict, and still he fell into the same trap, every blessed time! Each time they parted company Logan felt as if he slid off an emotional seesaw and landed flat on his back.

Jeezus! I must be a glutton for punishment, he decided. He had traipsed after this fiery sprite to protect her from harm and already he was the victim of a dozen battle scars, even when he had yet to double a fist or draw his Colt. Piper employed her own unique type of ammunition. It came in the form of invisible bullets that penetrated flesh and bone. And if she didn't find that cursed money of hers and quickly, Logan swore he would be shot all to hell!

Chapter 23

A feeling of dread drenched Piper's spirits when she spied the curl of black smoke that spiraled into the afternoon sky. According to Burgess, the shack that housed the desperados who were rumored to have taken possession of her inheritance was just over the next ridge.

When they reached a vantage point that enabled them to peer over the rocky landscape, they could see the rising flames that engulfed the cabin. War whoops echoed in the arid breeze like a song of doom. The band of renegades, armed with rifles, thundered down the mesa toward the forest of towering saguaro cacti that sprawled out to the west.

Piper grimaced when she noticed the bodies of five white men lying facedown in the dust. In silence, Burgess stared down at the burning shack. When the Apache raiding party disappeared in the distance, he reined his horse in the direction he had come.

"This looks like the end of your search," he told Piper in his monotone voice, a voice that was devoid of emotion, even after witnessing the results of a bloody massacre. "If those thieves had your money, the Apaches probably took it with them. Those renegades are always eager to purchase supplies, rifles, and ammunition."

Piper's mouth gaped as Burgess walked his horse down the steep slope. "Aren't you even going to inspect the shack or the bodies for the money?"

Burgess halted his steed and twisted in the saddle. "I know a lost cause when I see one," he snorted. "I'm going back to Tucson. If you know what's good for you, you'll come with me. The money is gone forever." His eyes took on a roguish twinkle and he smiled like a barracuda, much to Piper's disgust. "If it's money you want, I've got more than enough for both of us. All you have to do is cater to a few of my whims. . . ."

"I'd rather take up residence in a poorhouse!" Piper snapped. The nerve of that man! She had already made it clear she wanted nothing to do with Burgess.

An annoyed frown puckered Burgess's homely face. Gouging his steed, he approached Piper, very nearly yanking her off her horse. "You don't know a good deal when you hear one, woman," he growled as he tugged Piper onto his lap. His arms closed around her like a beaver trap. "After I sample your charms I'll see that you live in the lap of luxury, just like you've grown accustomed . . . Ouch!"

Piper bit into the arm that was clenched around her shoulder. When Burgess abruptly let go, Piper braced herself for the fall. Before she could make a dash to safety, Burgess had scrambled from his mount to give chase.

"You haughty little bitch!" he hissed as he reached out to grab a handful of her trailing blond hair. "I've played the gentleman long enough with you. I expect to be paid for my troubles."

At the risk of having her hair yanked out by the roots, Piper wheeled about to kick Burgess in the groin. The blow took him to his knees and drained the color from his face. While he was struggling to draw a breath, Piper grabbed the pistol she carried in the pouch that was strapped on the saddle horn.

"You'll be paid half of what I recovered of my inheritance," she hissed as she trained her Colt on Burgess. "Half of nothing is still nothing!"

Growling as much from wounded dignity as from the pain of having been kicked in the groin, Burgess staggered to his feet. He swung his arm in an attempt to knock the pistol from her hand, but Piper agilely backed away.

"Give me one more reason, Burgess," she challenged in the threatening tone she had heard Logan employ. It worked. Burgess watched her cock her pistol while she gave him the evil

342

eye. He decided raping this firebrand wasn't worth getting killed for. Piper looked as if she meant to blow him to kingdom come, and indeed she would have. She was that furious.

"Damned fool woman," Burgess grumbled as he hobbled back to his horse. "I hope you can find your own way back, because I'm not hanging around to ensure your safe return."

"It wouldn't be safe if you were within shouting distance," Piper scoffed at him.

While Burgess was making his way down the winding path, leaving Piper to her own devices, Logan was scowling from his lookout point above them. He had been tempted to come to Piper's rescue, but he had waited, hoping he wouldn't have to reveal himself to Burgess. He wasn't sure if he was annoyed or relieved that Piper had handled Burgess without outside help. It was growing increasingly apparent that Piper didn't need him as much as he thought she did, and that rankled his pride for some reason. Logan was amazed at how his heart had flip-flopped in his chest when he saw Burgess yank Piper from her saddle. He wasn't accustomed to being afraid for anyone. He wasn't accustomed to being afraid, period! But he had been concerned about Piper's safety and it had been several minutes before his overworked heart returned to its normal pace. Even now, when the worst was over and Burgess had ridden away, Logan felt a mite shaky. Him! The man with steel nerves and iron will! What the devil was wrong with him?

While Logan was grappling with this unfamiliar feeling of vulnerability Piper was growling in frustration. Damnation, what had she done to deserve this punishment? Why had she been subjected to this hell on earth? She had lost both her parents, had been manipulated by a greedy stepfather and stepbrother, had lost her virginity to a man who felt no affection whatsoever for her, and now, to top off a perfectly miserable year, her inheritance (one that had been stolen for the third time in less than three months) was probably strapped behind an Apache brave who was at this moment galloping across the desert. Damnation!

Piper felt like screaming in frustration. She had nothing left to lose. Logan was engaged to Jenny Payton, Abraham was settling into his new life with Samuel, and Piper couldn't go back to the life she had once enjoyed in Chicago. Her stepfather had sold her home out from under her and she was practically penniless. What else could go wrong . . . ?

"It's over, Piper," Logan's voice, quiet though it was, rumbled like thunder through her tormented thoughts.

Her misty green eyes flew to Logan, who sat like an invincible Indian warrior upon his muscular paint stallion. He looked like an impenetrable rock wall and she felt like a bowl of emotional mush. And that made Piper even more frustrated.

"No, it isn't over," she blurted out. "Those renegades probably toted off my money, and if they did, I intend to retrieve it."

Logan usually possessed perfect control of his facial expression. He only displayed emotion when it was his want. But Piper's outrageous declaration caused his eyes to bulge from their sockets and his jaw to open wide enough for a roadrunner to roost. "Lady, you are without a doubt the most stubborn fool on the face of the earth."

"At least I hold title to something," Piper snapped bitterly as she urged her buckskin mare toward the smoldering shack. "I've lost all else. I will not lose my inheritance."

Jeezus! She was really going to chase a band of renegade Apaches across the desert with limited supplies, without knowing where the hell she was or what she might encounter. Piper wasn't a daredevil, she was a full-fledged idiot who rushed in where angels feared to tread!

Cursing profusely, Logan nudged Sam in Piper's wake. If she's crazy, what does that make me? Logan asked himself sourly. Blast it, Harley and the other men were awaiting his return and he was delaying to pursue this muleheaded minx who couldn't recognize a lost cause when it slapped her in the face. If he had any sense he would turn around and leave this daring hellion to fry in her own grease.

When Piper climbed down to inspect the bodies of the banditos who had fallen beneath the rifles of marauding Apaches, Logan watched in aloof silence as the color seeped from her cheeks. He offered no assistance, no consolation, even when the grisly sight of mutilated bodies caused Piper to vomit. He simply sat on his steed, waiting for her to search for the missing money, waiting for her to realize there was no hope of recovering it. Looking white as a ghost, Piper wobbled back to her mount.

"We're going back to Tucson . . . now!" Logan growled in no uncertain terms.

White-faced, Piper focused her defiant stare on Logan's thunderous scowl. "You go back to Tucson and your fiancée. I'm following my stolen money all the way to hell if I have to!"

"If you are determined to get yourself killed, why not let me do it?" Logan sniped sarcastically. "I can ensure that it will be a quick and painless death instead of the slow torture you will experience at the hands of the Apaches."

"I can't afford your exorbitant prices now that my funds have dwindled to nothing," Piper sniffed caustically. "Besides, I have heard that Indians take white women hostage instead of torturing them to death. Life with the Apaches might not be so bad. Maybe I'll even get to live in my own wickiup if I behave myself."

"Dammit, Piper, I'm serious!" Logan roared.

"So am I," she said with stubborn conviction.

Logan rolled his eyes heavenward, requesting divine patience. He couldn't believe the way in which Piper thrust herself into danger. He couldn't tell this proud, obstinate spitfire anything! While Logan silently cursed her stubbornness, Piper turned her mount westward. Grumbling, Logan trailed behind her, repeatedly asking himself why he bothered. Before the day was out Piper would surely come to her senses, he assured himself. When she realized she was on the brink of disaster and that her crusade was over, she would consent to let him lead her back to Tucson.

But as always, Logan sold Piper short. Even though they endured blistering heat, she continued to trek west, following the tracks of the Apaches. At dusk she collapsed on her pallet with a pained groan. Piper swore she had worn blisters on the blisters that already plagued her backside. All 639 muscles screamed in complaint each time she moved. And when Logan ambled toward her with naked hunger in his eyes—a look Piper had come to recognize at a glance—she held up an aching arm to forestall him.

"The answer is no, so don't ask," she muttered, flinging him a go-away-and-leave-me-alone glare. "You are an engaged man and it's time we both remembered that."

What happened in the next instant occurred with such incredible speed that it blurred Piper's mind. To her disbelief, Logan whipped both Colts from their holsters. He had never flaunted his deadly swift proficiency with sidearms, but now she knew why Logan was considered the fastest shootist of his time. Logan moved with the lightning quickness of a crouched panther. He had armed himself before her brain had time to register his actions. The movement was so incredibly rapid and reflexive that it boggled the mind. And Piper thought she was becoming faster on the draw! Compared to Logan's astounding talents, she moved in slow motion!

Piper barely had time to marvel at his ability. She feared he intended to shoot her where she sat, just as he had suggested earlier that day. Did he really plan to kill her just because she rejected his amorous advances? That was ridiculous, but she was going to be just as dead!

The barking Colts shattered the silence and two bullets zinged past her shoulder. He wasn't such a sharpshooter after all, she thought smugly. He had missed her with both shots! She would never let him live it down. . . . Then the eerie rattle of the unseen snake caused Piper to twist around to seek out the source of the unnerving sound. In stupefied horror she watched the beheaded snake coil and uncoil beside her leg.

"Dammit, you don't bed down beside a rock without checking to see what varmint is lying under it!" Logan roared as he slammed his pistols into their holsters.

The thought of being bitten by a diamondback rattlesnake left Piper thunderstruck. Her mouth opened and closed like the flap on Abraham's reed basket, but no words came out. Her tongue was stuck on the roof of her mouth and her eyes were frozen in an astonished stare.

Logan knelt to grasp the snake and then shook it in Piper's face. "Supper," he grunted.

"Yours maybe," Piper croaked. "Not mine."

His stormy eyes billowed over her. "When one is on the desert, one makes use of what is to be had, which is mostly slim pickings," he declared. "We're fortunate. Rattlesnake is a delicacy."

"Not where I come from," Piper choked as she stared at the scaly reptile that had very nearly killed her.

Logan squatted down on his haunches to trace her peaked features with his forefinger. "That has always been the problem, hasn't it, Piper?" he murmured ruefully. "You're a refined debutante from an aristocratic society and I'm a renegade who grew up all by himself in the wild. We're still miles apart, even when we've been as close as two people can get. And that's what I want now. . . ."

It would have been so easy to fall prey to that deep, husky voice, to drown in the silvery depths of his eyes. But Piper knew she could never resist him if she didn't begin somewhere! She could no longer live with the false hope that he could return her love, that she could somehow make a difference in his life.

"No, Logan," she told him as she removed his lingering hand from her face. "Not tonight or any other night." Her voice wasn't as firm as she had hoped. It quivered with barely restrained emotion, but she struggled for composure. "My search isn't over, but what was between us is. Jenny is waiting for your return. I'll not let myself forget you intend to marry her, not again. I'm the first one to admit she is perfect for you. She is everything a man like you needs. I'm tired of being the time you're killing, Logan."

Muttering at the mention of Jenny's name, Logan unfolded himself and stalked over to build a fire and cook his supper. He wanted Piper. He ached for her up to his eyebrows—right or wrong. He knew she was sore from all the hours she'd spent in the saddle the past few days, but that didn't stop him from wanting her in the worst way.

Seeing that rattlesnake slithering out from its den hadn't helped matters, Logan grumbled to himself. Nothing had ever frightened him until he met this green-eyed witch. And suddenly it struck a peculiar feeling of fear when he considered the possibility of losing her. Knowing Piper was constantly out of her element triggered this overprotectiveness. The thought of her suffering a deadly snakebite was worse than enduring the bite himself. He wanted to hold her, to love her, to forget how close she had come to disaster.

Jeezus! Next time she would probably sit down on a Gila monster or a scorpion. And if they survived this wild goose chase across the desert he would undoubtedly be a nervous wreck. That thought provoked Logan to lecture Piper on watching where she stepped in the future. But the words died on his lips when he spun around to give her a piece of his mind. Her pretty features shone in the fading light. Her hair sprayed about her like streams of silver and gold. She was fast asleep and he was frustrated as hell!

Logan paced about, turning his rattlesnake steak over the fire and tending the horses, but nothing eased his exasperation. Even the cool of the evening that settled over the desert didn't ease the heat of desire that gnawed at him. One glance at Piper made him go hot all over. Remembering the passion they had shared left him burning with a fever only Piper could cure. Speculating on what Sheriff Epperson might have done to her while he had her locked in his jail had tormented him. Epperson was a lousy sheriff and certainly no saint when it came to women. And watching Piper ride with Burgess Channing for more than two days had him wondering if the man's true intentions were to get her alone so he could have his way with her. Men . . . they were always flocking around her. And trouble . . . Piper constantly embroiled herself in it, leaving Logan to stew over her welfare, to ache with a need that drove him to distraction.

A contemplative frown knitted his brow as a fleeting thought skipped across his mind. For several minutes Logan mulled over the events of the past few days. He had been so preoccupied with Piper that he had failed to put the facts together. After what he had seen from his perch above the two outlaw roadhouses, combined with the information he had collected from Piper, Logan began to see the single thread that tied the past events together. Sheriff Epperson's appearance in Piper's hotel room the night Grant Fredricks was murdered had Logan frowning again. And suddenly, from within the dark jungle of entangled thoughts the light of understanding dawned in his mind.

"Well, I'll be damned," Logan grunted. He had finally located the piece of the puzzle that had been floating around in his head for a week.

Leaning down, Logan lit his cheroot with a two-dollar bill. A wry smile pursed his lips as he stretched out his long legs and peered into the distance. Suddenly everything made perfect sense. The ringleader of the desperados was clever, Logan mused as he puffed on his cigar. The scoundrel had seen to it that no one suspected him of wrongdoing. There was always someone to take the blame. But very soon the mastermind who organized the band of desperados that terrorized Butterfield's stage line and frisked silver miners of their livestock and supplies would be behind bars.

Damn, why didn't I figure this out earlier? Logan scolded himself. His gaze strayed to the bewitching beauty who lay on her pallet. He was staring at the real reason he hadn't solved the mystery before now. Logan had been too distracted by Piper and her hopeless crusade to think the matter through. Of course, knowing the *hows* and *whys* and *whom* wasn't going to do him a helluva lot of good when he was wandering around the desert like a nomad. But if he ever dragged this stubborn misfit back to Tucson, he would see to it that the wily ringleader never plagued Butterfield again!

Chapter 24

Gusty winds whipped across the sand, pelting Piper's face until she roused from a sound sleep. The whistling breeze became a howl and then a roar. Sand and dust swirled around the towering saguaros and billowed into the sky, choking the stars. Within minutes, breathing became difficult. Piper blinked tears as the grains of sand stung her eyes.

Logan's grumbling was the only sound heard above the roaring wind. Within a moment she felt rather than saw him sidle close enough to cover both of them with his blanket. Despite the feelings that assaulted her when her body made contact with his hard contours, Piper cuddled into his protective arms. She felt safely anchored, even if the fierce gale threatened to uproot her. The aroma of the man who held her against him blocked out the smell of dust and doom. The steady thud of his heart against her breasts marked the seconds that ticked by while they huddled under their makeshift tent.

The storm raged through the night while Piper dozed and awakened a half dozen times to find herself plastered against Logan's sinewy length. Each breath she took was filled with his manly fragrance and the suffocating dust that had filtered inside their protective cocoon. How much longer was this dust storm going to last? she wondered as she coughed to clear her throat. She didn't dare poke her head from the blanket. It would have served no purpose. She couldn't see her hand in front of her face with the dust and the darkness. It was an unnerving feeling to be in the middle of a desert during a dust

351

storm. Piper felt so insignificant, so isolated.

While the hours dragged by Piper asked herself what she was doing in the West chasing a band of Apaches. Honestly, she should have her head examined for thinking she could take on a world that was as foreign to her as Australia! What had she intended to do? Attack the entire Apache tribe? She couldn't speak their language. She couldn't waltz up to them and calmly explain they had stolen her money by mistake. As if that would have made a tittle of difference to the Apaches, Piper mused dispiritedly.

She hadn't wanted to admit defeat, but the odds were heavily stacked against her. She was chasing rainbows, living on false hopes, determined to prove to Logan and herself that she was willful and perseverant. But all she had proven was that Logan was right and she was wrong. Determination didn't always bring about miracles. There weren't always silver linings in black clouds. Her futile search was over. The blowing dust had erased the Apaches' tracks and there would be no way to trail the renegades now. Her money was gone forever. . . .

Those depressing thoughts were accompanied by the grumble of thunder. Lord, what now? Piper sighed defeatedly. It wasn't enough that they were covered with a layer of dust. Now it seemed they were to be drenched with mud.

And sure enough, her grim prediction came true. The driving wind buffeted their blanket with rain. Jagged streaks of lightning darted through the overhanging clouds, illuminating the dark hours before dawn. Piper supposed this was Mother Nature's way of making amends after she had swept the dust from her desert carpet. Now she was completing her housecleaning by washing down the desert floor and watering her plants. It only served to remind Piper there was no justice in the world. Her nightmare might have been a blessing to the sun-baked desert, but it wasn't helping her situation. As always, I am the one to make the sacrifices, she thought in self-pity. Life went on while she was shuffled out of the way. This was just another of the many obstacles that cluttered her path, another burden for her to bear.

Logan stirred beside her and Piper forgot about the wind and the rain. She also forgot her vow to consider Logan no more than a companion. Depression had settled about her like a dense fog. She felt the need to be held and comforted, to forget all she had lost. Logan didn't love her but he wanted her. It was enough. It was all she had ever had. Her stubborn pride was not as important as it once was. Right now, Piper needed to be needed, if only in a physical sense. She wanted to escape to that glorious dimension of time that wasn't clouded by harsh reality and bitter defeat. This ruggedly handsome wizard could make her forget she was destitute and unloved. He could send her soaring beyond the stars and, for that time in space, she could pretend he truly cared about her.

After Piper turned to face Logan, her hand glided up his muscular chest. She couldn't see him, but she could feel his warmth beside her. It was better this way, she decided. If he mocked her with those silver eyes for changing her mind, she wouldn't have to view his intimidating grin. And being a man, Logan wouldn't refuse the physical pleasure she offered him. He would make love to her with his body, not his heart, just as he always did. And Piper would be satisfied with that because beggars weren't allowed to be choosy.

Logan's heart belonged to Jenny. It must, Piper mused as her light caresses mapped the beard that hugged his jaw. Why else would he propose to Jenny? She hadn't expected this rare breed of a man to ever settle down, but there was obviously one woman whose lure could make Logan want to try. Jenny had assured Piper that she and Logan had been lovers for more than three years. No doubt, Logan had always come back to Jenny, no matter how far he roamed. Piper envied Jenny's power over him. She was woman enough to satisfy him, to love him, even if he wandered from one shallow affair to another during his travels. Piper was just one of the many women Logan left behind to return to Jenny's open arms.

Piper refused to allow herself to dwell on that discouraging thought. She needed Logan, even if he only wanted her for the moment, even if she had never been more than his pastime. She had lived with her wounded pride before and she could endure it again. It was the price she paid for loving a man who would always remain just out of her reach.

"Love me, Logan," Piper murmured as she fitted herself to

his masculine length. Adoringly, her lips whispered over his, tempting him to take what she offered. She longed to lose herself in his skillful kiss, to feel the fire that chased away depressing thoughts. "I need you. . . ."

"Why? Because you have lost everything else?" he growled resentfully.

Piper hadn't expected his harsh reaction or his question. What did he care why she needed him? He had always wanted her body, never the problems or personality attached to it. Since when did men give a whit why a woman offered affection, so long as she satisfied a man's sexual appetites?

"Does it matter so much why?" she whispered as her hand followed the rugged terrain of his body.

"I don't appreciate being your consolation prize," he declared in offended dignity and then removed her wandering hand from his hip. "It must have finally soaked into that wooden head of yours that this wild goose chase is over, that you don't have a prayer of finding your precious inheritance." His derisive snort drowned out the incessant patter of rain. "You're feeling lost and defeated and I'm supposed to make you forget. Is that it?"

His biting remarks and the tone with which he spoke them inflamed Piper's temper. If Piper had taken the time to consider how ridiculous the situation, she might have laughed out loud. But she hadn't so she didn't. To her, there was nothing amusing about huddling under a wet blanket during the rain that followed a desert dust storm while she and Logan spouted insults at each other. If anyone had happened by, they would have concluded that both occupants of the improvised tent were raving lunatics.

"I've found myself the object of your lusts on several occasions," she reminded him tersely. "It didn't matter to you that I had never been with another man, that I haven't touched anyone else since the first time you made love to me! You went to Jenny the same night you sneaked into my hotel room in Tucson. I'm not so foolish to believe the two of you did nothing more than discuss my sojourn in jail!"

"Now who's presuming instead of thinking?" Logan glared at her, even though he could barely make out her face. But he didn't have to see her. Piper's image was implanted in his brain. He could envision her flashing green eyes, the exaggerated pout on her lips.

"Logan, just how stupid do you think I am?" Piper snapped at him. "Jenny made it clear to me that the two of you have been lovers. I have never known you to reject the chance to feel the lusty beast within you. Men's brains are situated below their belt buckles. They think with the private parts of their anatomy."

"Since when did you become such an authority on men?" Logan sniffed sarcastically.

"I don't claim to be an expert on the male population in general, only you in particular," she countered just as caustically.

"I'm surprised you took the time to attempt to figure me out," Logan smirked. "You've always been too selfish and self-centered to notice there were other creatures on this planet, all of them a notch or two below your lofty perch, I might add!"

That nasty rejoinder caused Piper to explode like a keg of blasting powder. The rumble of thunder overhead could have just as easily erupted from her. She was selfish? Ha! This cocky rascal had it exactly backward. "You are the one who is motivated by your own wants and needs," she sniped. "You feed your overinflated pride by waving your pistol at your competitors and glaring them down with looks that are potent enough to maim and kill. You order people around because you consider yourself right and everyone else dead wrong. You bully women around because of your superior strength—all that to remind yourself that you are better than the rest of us. If we want something done that we can't manage by ourselves, we call Logan—the immortal warrior who defies death and returns to avenge his foes. When you swagger down the street, the crowd parts like the Red Sea to let the Almighty Logan pass!"

Logan took a moment to contemplate her biblical analogy, trying to remember who had performed that particular miracle. But there wasn't time to deliberate for more than a second. Piper was raking him over the coals for something else before he could recall who opened the corridor on the ocean floor.

"You are proud of your self-reliance, your self-possession, your self-confidence. Honestly, sometimes I wonder if you possess any sentimental feelings at all for other people. To you, people are simply waves that crowd your shores. But they never really influence you. And each wave comes along to erase the ones that came before. The high and mighty Vince Logan stands alone, like a monument to be feared and revered." Piper inhaled a huffy breath and rattled on before Logan could interrupt her. "Well, I'm sorry, Logan. I don't think you're so damned special. All you have going for you is the fact that you are as big and strong as a gorilla. It's no wonder your clients are always glad when you finish a job and ride out of town. Who would want you to stay? You have the charm and personality of a rhinoceros!"

My, I really let him have it, Piper thought to herself. I might not have punctured a hole in his inflated pride, but I put a few noticeable dents in it. Let him stuff those criticisms in his cigar and smoke it!

"Are you quite finished?" Logan muttered sourly. "Because if you are, I'd like to say a few words in my own defense."

"Go right ahead," Piper smirked. "Defend yourself if you wish. But you'll never convince me that you aren't more self-centered than I am. In your opinion, you have never been wrong about anyone or anything in your life. I don't expect a bullheaded man like you to think so now. . . ."

"Look who's talking!" Logan grumbled. Dammit, sometimes she made him so furious he wanted to box her ears.

"Look who's interrupting," she pointed out.

Finally Logan expelled a frustrated breath. They were having another pointless argument, one of many. He insulted her, she became defensive and ridiculed every facet of his personality. Before they knew it they were yelling at each other under a wet blanket. . . .

The cease-fire in their verbal battle allowed Logan to hear the silence. Like a turtle emerging from his shell, Logan peered out of the quilt to note the rain had ended and the sun had broken through the clouds. A pale rainbow arched across a desert silhouetted with towering saguaros and organ-pipe cacti.

356

For a moment their argument was forgotten while they admired the beauty of the desert.

Rising onto all fours, Logan stared at the wet horses and damp saddles. With one lithe move he was on his feet, preparing their mounts for travel. Before he could attend Piper's buckskin mare she had laid the saddle blanket on the steed's back. Straining, she scooped up the saddle and set it in place. Logan knew she was watching his every move and copying his motions. When he reached under Sam's belly, Piper did likewise. When he pulled up the cinch, Piper followed suit. And when he bridled Sam, Piper wrestled with the buckles and reins.

Piper needed to feel a sense of accomplishment just now, Logan mused as he gathered their gear. Her spirit had been broken when she realized she was fighting a hopeless battle. She had offered her body to him earlier, only to forget her woes. But Logan refused to let her turn to him just because of her desperation.

She was right about one thing, he supposed. He had as much stubborn pride as she did. There were times when even his lust couldn't overshadow it. He wanted Piper to need him for himself, not because he could supply comfort, a moment's pleasure, a warm body. . . .

With a start, Logan realized he hadn't cared so much before, so long as he appeased his own desires. But it mattered with Piper. It mattered too damned much and it always had. It had always galled him to play second fiddle to her quest to recover her precious inheritance. He didn't appreciate being another stepping-stone on her treasure hunt. She needed him for all the wrong reasons, and he refused to be simply her champion, as he had been for the countless citizens who hired him to save the day. It just wasn't enough where Piper was concerned. He was tired of being her shepherd, her crutch to lean on when the going got rough. If she didn't want him for the man he was—the man beneath the hard exterior—then she couldn't have him at all!

Jeezus, what was he thinking? He sounded like some offended virgin who demanded a man's respect before she surrendered to his lusty whims.

A muddled frown knitted Piper's brow as she watched Logan close up like a clam. "What is the matter with you now?" she demanded to know.

"Nothing you would care to know about," he muttered crabbily. After he strapped his gear in place, he wheeled around to glare at the disheveled beauty. "Well, are we riding east or west? Are you ready to admit your crusade is over or are we going to traipse around for weeks without tracks to follow?"

Crestfallen, Piper's head dropped, as if the ground beneath her feet had suddenly drawn her attention. This was another of Logan's tactics in humiliation, she mused bitterly. He had heard her confess she loved him once and he had ridiculed her. Now he wanted her to admit she was an idiotic fool for trekking across the desert in pursuit of savages. While she was at it, she may as well declare she wasn't as good as he was at anything! Surely he would be satisfied once she had conceded all to him—her body, her pride, her spirit. That was what he had wanted from the beginning—to break her as he would a contrary colt. Once she admitted she couldn't compete with him in any arena maybe he would go away and leave her alone.

Mustering her courage, Piper raised her smudged face to stare him squarely in the eye. "All right, Logan, you win," she told him, striving for a firm tone that disguised her helpless frustration. "This trip was a will-o'-the-wisp. . . ."

"A will-o'-the-what?" Logan interjected. Damn, he hated it when she resorted to words whose meaning escaped him.

"A delusive goal I can never attain," she said, hurrying on before her voice cracked. "My money is gone forever and you were right. I was a fool to think I could recover my inheritance. You were also right when you told me I shouldn't come west. I don't fit in. I probably never will, even if I'm forced to seek a job doing whatever is available to support myself. I was driven by an obsession to retrieve my money. It was my motivation."

Her lips trembled as she inhaled a steadying breath. "But you were wrong about a few things," she clarified. "I wanted to search for my trust fund because I had nothing else. It was to be my consolation. When I said I loved you, I meant it. My motivation was not to sway you so you would help me retrieve my money. Chasing rainbows became my diversion when I realized I could never earn your affection."

Piper couldn't endure another moment of peering into those piercing silver eyes set in that expressionless face. She glanced away before she continued. "I do know what love is, at least the futile kind. It is caring for someone who doesn't respect or admire me for what I am, for what I am trying to become. It is a longing for someone I can't have because he belongs to someone else. What you saw in me was stubborn pride protecting a wounded heart. I had never loved a man before." Piper expelled a heavy-hearted sigh. "How was I supposed to know how to behave? When I am honest with you, you ridicule me. When I defy you, you intimidate me. To you, I'm just useless baggage, extra trouble when you already have an armload of it.

"But what I thought was love isn't really love at all," Piper said dejectedly. "For you see, if love isn't shared it doesn't really exist. It is only a one-sided emotion searching for its counterpart. It is like a path stretching into nowhere, joining nothing." Finally Piper found the nerve to glance back into his bronzed face. "Even if I can't have your love, I do love you . . . halfway. . . . *My* half."

"Do you truly? Are you so sure it isn't desperation, a need for security? Are you sure you aren't like a drowning swimmer who clutches at straws?"

There it was, that arrogant smile Logan wore so well. Piper itched to smear it all over his craggy features, but she knew better than to try. Logan would break her into a thousand pieces. He had warned her not to strike him again and he had proved that he offered no idle threats.

"Do you want my confession in writing?" she snapped, green eyes flashing. Damn him! She had bowed at his feet and still it wasn't enough. He was trying to tell her how she felt, just like he tried to tell her what to do. Well, blast it, she knew what she felt. It wasn't desperation, it was love, whether he wanted to believe it or not!

Piper's fingers curled into the front of his buckskin shirt, tearing away the lacings. With a sharp nail, she scratched *Be Happy* on his chest. "Now are you satisfied, or shall I also print it in the sand and carve it on a cactus? I love you enough to want you to be with the woman who can make you happy. I don't know what else I can say or do to prove I meant what I said!"

Without awaiting his reply, Piper stepped into the stirrup and took off like the wind. Much to her own amazement, her hours in the saddle had transformed her into a skillful equestrian, even when she hadn't realized it. That knowledge couldn't have come at a better time. Piper felt the need to gallop across the country, allowing her the opportunity to compose herself before Logan caught up with her to ridicule her again.

Logan monitored her reckless flight with a pensive frown. He had never expected such a confession from that defiant beauty. Nor had he expected her to concede he was the victor, even if it went without saying. He should have been strutting like a peacock, patting himself on the back. But her confession made him feel like a heel. He had broken her spirit and he hadn't meant to do that. He had only intended to make a point—that Piper needed to be with her own kind so she could resume the life she had known before being transplanted in the West. If she stayed he would never get over this possessiveness, this obsessive need to protect her from harm. Once Piper walked back into her world Logan could get on with his life.

What Piper thought she felt for him simply wasn't meant to be. She had mistaken desperation for love. Piper had lost everything. She had nowhere to turn and that was all there was to it. Logan didn't want to fall in love with that green-eyed leprechaun. What he felt for Jenny Payton was simple and easy to understand. They fit into each other's lives. She knew the limitations of his affection for her and she had accepted that.

But Piper Malone was another matter entirely. Her gentle breeding and background greatly contrasted with Logan's. And Piper wasn't the kind of woman who could be satisfied with his limited affection. With her it would have to be all or nothing. She wouldn't be content until he was hopelessly devoted to her, until she was every breath he took, until her memory stained every thought.

Loving a woman like Piper would be a lifelong occupation filled with nights of splendor and days of senseless arguments.

The only thing they agreed on was that they couldn't agree on anything! Jeezus, what kind of life would that be? They would grow old, loving and then fighting, and he would probably never learn to predict her moods because she would still be evolving while she adapted to his way of life. Every day would be another adventure, another challenge. . . .

Logan muttered at his meandering thoughts. He didn't have time to sit there thinking while Piper was galloping off at breakneck speed. She could tumble from her perch and wind up with a cactus stuck on that lovely derriere of hers. She might scare up a den of rattlesnakes and fall right smack dab in the middle of them. Dammit, that woman was disaster in motion.

Giving way to that thought, Logan gouged Sam in the flanks and pursued the reckless nymph whose blond hair was waving behind her like a flying carpet. When he caught up with her a half hour later, Piper had regained control of her fragile emotions. She stared straight ahead, refusing to acknowledge his presence.

"Piper, I . . ."

"Don't say anything," she insisted without glancing at him. "Just let it be. I don't want your ridicule or your pity . . . if you have any to give. I have accepted what I can't change. We are wrong for each other, but I was foolish enough to think my feelings for you could make everything right. Now I know they can't."

When she finally glanced at Logan, he swore he was staring at his own reflection. Her delicate features were frozen in a carefully blank stare. Sometimes she reminded him so much of himself it was frightening! In some ways, they had grown alike these past months, influencing each other when they hadn't even realized the changes they had undergone.

"Loving you would never be enough," Piper told him, priding herself in expressing her thoughts in a calm, controlled tone. "There has to be some give and take in a lasting relationship. I hope you'll remember that with Jenny. Although she loves you enough for the both of you, her feelings for you will wither and die if you don't give something of yourself to her." A mocking smile pursed her lips. "It is

361

fortunate for you that you and Jenny share a common ground. She thinks you're as special as you think you are."

"So now we're back to insults, are we?" Logan scowled. "I knew it was too good to last. For a woman who is supposedly in love, you don't seem to be taking it very well."

"I'm trying to be nice," Piper assured him.

"I'm sure you find it difficult after just a few short minutes," he taunted.

Piper compressed her lips, swallowing the nasty reply that ached to fly free. She hadn't meant to antagonize him, but her pride was still smarting, even while she was trying to be noble. Nothing could ease the hurt of one-sided love. Logan had never been pretentious with her, it was true. He admitted he wanted the pleasure she could offer. She was the one who had built dreams on false hopes.

My resentment is ill-founded, she reminded herself sensibly. There was no rule stating a man had to return a woman's love, especially not in the lawless West. Logan didn't love her. He never had and he never would, so that was that.

Lord, how many more times would she have to have this conversation with herself before she convinced her foolish heart? Ten times ten, Piper speculated glumly. She had gotten over hating Logan easily enough, but she wondered if she would ever really get over loving him.

Piper may have recovered from hating Logan, but Logan wasn't finished hating Piper yet. He still detested his weakness for her, his maddening preoccupation. Piper made him want things he knew he couldn't have. He would be doing himself a great favor when he married Jenny. She would spend every waking hour distracting him from his illogical attraction to Piper. He had agreed to discuss marriage when he finished his obligations. It should naturally follow that he marry Jenny. Their wedding date would signify the exact moment he forced Piper from his life, once and for all.

Oh hell, Logan thought with a frustrated sigh. It was best to let the future unfold and determine what it held before he started trying on gold bands. The ringleader of the desperados was still running loose. First things had to come first. And the moment he returned to Tucson he was going to complete the job he was paid to do. He had followed this Pied Piper long enough. He needed to send her back to familiar surroundings and forget they had ever crossed paths.

But deep down in his soul, Logan knew he would lose a part of himself when he bade Piper goodbye for the very last time. She was his touch with sophistication and gentle grace. She compensated for all he couldn't be. He would be doing them both a favor when he deposited her on the eastbound stage. And years from now, when she was married to a wealthy aristocrat who put her on a pedestal where she belonged, she would glance back through the window of time to remember the man who had sense enough to let her go. One day she would have children who were the image of her stunning beauty. . . .

Something snapped inside of Logan. It was all too easy to envision a blond-haired little girl who peered up at him with wide-eyed innocence, just as Piper had done eons ago in Fort Smith. When the naive little girl blossomed into a radiant smile, just like her mother, the sun would burn twice as brightly. . . .

Suddenly Logan was growling like an ill-tempered bear. The image that leapt to mind tormented him every mile of their journey. By the time Logan neared the outskirts of Tucson he was in just the right frame of mind for his conversation with Sheriff Epperson. In this particular mood, Logan could scare the living daylights out of Epperson, and that was exactly what that conniving bastard deserved after what he had done!

PART IV

Your character is what you have left
when you have lost everything you can lose.

Chapter 25

When Logan reined his stallion to a halt, Piper kept on riding, refusing to look back. She knew Logan wouldn't be accompanying her the last two miles since he was supposed to be dead. And since there was nothing left for them to say except goodbye, Piper didn't bother with a last farewell. It would have been too painful to stare into those spellbinding silver eyes for the very last time. The hours they had spent together the past two days had been agonizing enough. They had made attempts at idle conversation when they paused to rest, but it was stilted and forced at best.

Piper had watched in silent admiration each time Logan resourcefully provided them with food. He had made certain they survived off a land that seemed barren and unproductive. He knew which vegetation bore edible fruit and he found substitutes for water in cactus when their canteen ran dry. He had spied a scampering rabbit and took deadly aim from his perch on the saddle and they had feasted on juicy meat.

His remarkable abilities to survive when others might have perished served to remind Piper that she had much to learn about the West. She would have died without Logan. The man was never out of his element, except perhaps if he were thrust into an elegant ball in Eastern society. But with his self-assurance, Piper imagined he could even pass himself off as an aristocrat. Women would be intrigued by him. Females would eagerly accept him and he would have no trouble finding companionship if he desired it. Put quite simply, Logan would always stand out in a crowd. He was too dynamic to flounder, no matter where he was.

"That's it?" Logan snorted disdainfully. His narrowed eyes focused on Piper's rigid back as she trotted ahead of him. "No thank you for saving you from certain death? Not even a toneless goodbye?"

Piper heaved a weary sigh and reined her buckskin mare to a halt. She supposed she did owe him a word of thanks. But she couldn't bear to look at him. His image already haunted her and it would for the next century. Tormenting herself with one last visual picture would only make matters worse, so she didn't swivel in her saddle to glance at him.

"I do appreciate all you've done, Logan," she declared to the distance instead of his face. "If not for you, I wouldn't be alive."

Piper stilled the nervous flutter of her heart when she heard the clip-clop of Sam's hooves approaching her.

"Where will you go?" Logan questioned quietly

Her shoulder lifted in a noncommittal shrug. "It doesn't really matter. I'll travel until I deplete my funds and then I'll find a job as a teacher or a chef. I have the skills for both." Hollow laughter tripped from her lips, but still she didn't glance in Logan's direction. "I suppose I should be grateful for those two options. If not for my education I might be forced to resort to selling my body to men."

The thought caused Logan to scowl disgustedly. He could picture Piper poised before a classroom of children, filling their heads with the knowledge she had obtained from volumes of books he'd never had the chance to explore. He could envision her laboring over a hot stove as he had seen her do at the stage stations along the route. But the image of Piper in another man's arms, accepting his kisses and caresses, was so vivid it cut Logan like a knife. He was the man who had aroused her slumbering passions, the man who had taught her the skills of lovemaking.

That old familiar feeling of protective possession overwhelmed him. Logan reached into his pocket and fished out the roll of cash he always carried with him. "Here, take this," he insisted as he leaned over to fold the money into her clenched fist.

"I don't want your money," Piper informed him proudly. *I only want your love,* she silently added.

"But you're going to take it," he told her in a no-nonsense tone. When Piper glowered at him and opened her mouth to voice a protest, Logan snatched her from the saddle and deposited her on his lap. "For once, you aren't going to drag me into another argument. Just take the damned money. I don't want to wonder if you have enough funds to take you back where you belong."

The feel of his body meshed familiarly to hers sent Piper's heart somersaulting around in her chest. Warm sensations flowed through her like melted butter. She had never felt so safe and protected as she did in the circle of Logan's arms. And yet she had never felt so close to danger either. Loving Logan was an impossible paradox. He could protect her against all her vulnerabilities except one—her incurable weakness for him. As always when she was this close to him, Piper was her own worst enemy. She found herself wanting him, falling in love with him all over again.

"If I take your roll of two-dollar bills, how will you light your cigars?" Piper questioned, striving for a light, playful tone that would ease the mounting tension between them.

The stern frown that was stamped on his bearded face mellowed into a grin. Rarely had he seen this facet of Piper's personality. He usually badgered her, and she was usually too busy being defensive to bless him with those impish smiles. Suddenly, she reminded him of the way she had been during their sojourn at the Pinery. She had been gay and carefree and had totally bewitched him with her antics. He wondered if that was the real Piper Malone—the lighthearted beauty who had cast aside her protective shell and considered him to be her confidant and friend as well as her lover. Those two nights had been like a glimpse of paradise. Logan had hated to see them come to an end.

Piper was usually too preoccupied with argument or imminent disaster to reveal that radiant side of her personality. Yes, her carefree nature was still there, waiting to blossom under just the right conditions. It was a shame Logan wouldn't be around when the defensive shell finally fell away and this lovely monarch spread her velvety wings.

Logan made the critical mistake of peering into her emerald green eyes before uttering a rejoinder to her remark. The words evaporated as a compulsive need consumed him. Logan knew this feisty sprite would protest, so he didn't permit her time to do so. Swiftly, his mouth came down on hers, savoring the sweet taste of her. His arms contracted, crushing her ripe body against his muscular frame. He suddenly felt starved. Logan couldn't get enough of her. He was like a desperate child clutching at a long-awaited treat, fearing someone would rush in and snatch it away from him before he could gobble it up.

Piper didn't want to respond, but her body melted in his arms. She returned each hungry kiss, her lips slanting and twisting upon his, her tongue probing the moist recesses of his mouth, sharing a ragged breath. Her hands roamed impatiently —touching, kneading, clinging to his masculine strength.

When his wandering hand slid beneath her shirt to make contact with her flesh, Piper moaned in forbidden pleasure. She wanted his caresses, needed them, ached for them. Her body arched upward when his lips abandoned hers to suckle at each throbbing peak. Her shirt lay open, granting him free access to her silky skin. Piper trembled in barely controlled desire when his hands and lips practiced their sweet seduction on her flesh.

God, how was she going to get through the rest of her life without him? How was she going to forget these wondrous sensations? And why was she torturing herself like this? She couldn't fully satisfy her hunger for him, not here, not now. He was granting her another foretaste of heaven before he deprived her of this magical pleasure forever. Piper would leave him soon, and she would be left burning with an ache no other man could appease.

Sam stamped and snorted and shifted uneasily beneath them. The jingle of his bridle brought Logan back to his senses. Piper blushed profusely, wondering if anyone had ever attempted to make love on the back of a horse. And that was exactly what would have happened if Sam hadn't protested their amorous tête-à-tête.

With fumbling fingers, Piper fastened her gaping shirt. She glanced down to see that the money Logan had given her earlier had tumbled free when she clutched at him. But Piper didn't call the fact to Logan's attention. She hadn't wanted his money in the first place. Once she had gone he could gather his scattered bills and be on his way to Jenny.

"Piper, for what it's worth, I . . ." he began, only to be silenced when Piper pressed her index finger to his lips to shush him.

She shook her silver blond head, sending the waterfall of tangled curls rippling around her. Nothing Logan could say would change the way of things. Piper just wanted to be set to her steed so she could gallop away. Already she was wrestling with the mist of tears that threatened to scald her cheeks, and she refused to permit him to see her crying. Logan tolerated no weaknesses in others that he didn't possess himself, and Piper vowed never to give him more reason to mock her. Later she would find a suitable place to fall apart, now that it was all over except for the crying. But by damned, Logan would never again see her reduced to a puddle of salty tears!

When Piper twisted to retrieve her reins, her back stiff as a ramrod, Logan heaved a sigh and set her to her perch. Her standoffish manner assured him that the warm, responsive woman who lurked beneath her shell of defense had retreated behind her protective wall. The spell had been broken and there was nothing left to be said.

Without a backward glance, Piper thundered away with her long hair undulating behind her like a flag. Only when Piper disappeared from sight did Logan tear his eyes away from her to notice the scattered money. With one fluid motion he swung down to collect it. But each bill he touched became a burning memory of green eyes and golden hair. Logan counted and cherished each one before he folded it into a roll of gone-but-not-forgotten nights of splendor.

Growling in frustration, Logan stuffed his foot in the stirrup and reined Sam toward Jenny Payton's ranch, where he would remain until dark. In the shadows of the night he would venture to Sheriff Epperson's office. If Epperson could have foreseen the future he would have been digging a hole to crawl into instead of napping under his newspaper. His upcoming visit from a vengeful specter would prove to be one of the most terrifying moments of his life!

With both feet draped on the edge of the desk, Epperson lounged in his chair with a newspaper covering his face while he snoozed. He hadn't heard the quiet click of the latch that heralded the arrival of the nocturnal prowler.

After locking the door behind him, Logan crept across the room to loom over the snoozing sheriff. Slipping his dagger from his knee-high moccasins, Logan clutched Epperson (newspaper and all) and jerked him to his feet.

Epperson blinked like a disturbed owl when he felt the point of the dagger carving at his Adam's apple. His eyes froze in a wide-open stare when he recognized Logan's foreboding face behind the dark beard. "I thought you were dead," he croaked in astonishment.

"One of us may well be before the night is over," Logan said in such a deadly tone that Epperson's blood turned to ice.

"What do you want with me?" Epperson squeaked as Logan propelled him through the door that led to the empty cells.

"Answers," Logan growled ferociously.

Epperson panicked. He knew how brutal Logan could be. He had witnessed this gunfighter's tactics on several occasions and had seen the end results when Logan toted his victims back to jail—sometimes alive, sometimes not. But every outlaw Logan rounded up looked as if he had been to hell and back by the time Logan was finished with him.

Logan had no mercy or patience with Epperson. The instant Epperson tried to worm free, Logan pricked his stubby neck with the stiletto, drawing blood. Before Epperson could squawk in pain, Logan backhanded him across the mouth and slammed him against the bars. Epperson stiffened, staring frog-eyed at his assailant. He found himself strapped spread-eagled to the bars before he could inhale a breath. The dagger slashed the buttons from his shirt, leaving the garment dangling beside his ribs.

"I'll see you hang for this," Epperson hissed when he finally found his tongue.

A wintry smile glazed Logan's lips as he towered over Epperson. "You won't live long enough," he assured him spitefully.

When Epperson opened his swollen mouth to rattle off another worthless threat, Logan's doubled fist embedded itself in his victim's midsection.

"You've been drawing up fake bills of sale for the rest of your thieving friends and sending the men out to steal livestock and supplies from unsuspecting miners," Logan harshly accused.

"I don't know what you're talking about." Epperson grunted in an attempt to drag in a breath of air. The blow he received had bruised his insides and he could barely breathe without inflicting another stabbing pain on himself.

"You've been turning right around and selling the stolen stock and merchandise to Burgess Channing, who supplies equipment to Butterfield's stage stations," he growled menacingly.

"I did not!" Epperson hastily denied. "I never sent . . ."

Logan backhanded him so hard his head clanked against the bars. "You're going to tell me what I want to know," he spat venomously. To emphasize his demand, Logan cocked his arm. The crooked sheriff was more inclined to spill the truth and admit his guilt when Logan's meaty fist connected with his jaw.

"All right, it's true," he said raggedly. "I did write up those fake bills and warrants for the return of supplies that I claimed to be stolen property. It was easy money."

"You preyed on the miners who came to town to restock their necessities and when they returned empty-handed to complain to you, you pretended to search for their lost livestock and supplies, didn't you?"

Epperson nodded mutely.

"And every time some of your thieving friends held up a stage, you trotted out of town with the pretense of making a search. But you only ventured to their roadhouses to claim your share of the loot."

Logan elbowed Epperson in the midsection when he refused to answer the question. His vicious blow prompted the sheriff to nod his disheveled head.

"When you learned Piper Malone's money had been stolen, you knew exactly who had it," Logan scowled. "But you were awaiting your cut of the profits." Ruthless laughter exploded from his lips. "Now the money has been spirited away again and your thieving friends died in an Apache massacre. You have been providing rifles and supplies for the Indians so they could prey on Butterfield's stage stations. That was the Apaches' payment for guns, ammunition, and whiskey. They raided the stations as you demanded, didn't they?"

Epperson licked his bleeding lips and glared murderously at the avenging giant who loomed over him. "You're a son of a bitch, Logan," he spat out, and then regretted his loss of temper.

"You'll be cursing me worse when I'm finished with you," Logan prophesied.

Logan came uncoiled like a rattlesnake. Epperson only thought he had been hit by a beefy fist earlier. But he was quickly learning that Logan could deliver far more devastating blows when he was enraged. A fist of steel collided with Epperson's soft belly and a bent knee gouged him in the groin. Epperson would have crumbled to his knees if he hadn't been tied to the bars. Instead he hung there, sucking in spurts of air, his face powder white.

"The Apaches were only obeying your orders, weren't they?" Logan sneered as he grabbed Epperson by the hair of his head and forced his battered face upward. "Weren't they?" he repeated in a deadly growl.

"Yes," Epperson whispered sickly.

"Why are you trying to destroy Butterfield?" Logan demanded. "It can't be just for the loot you've stolen from passengers and the resale of supplies to the same man you confiscated them from."

"That was all it was," Epperson groaned. God, every bone and muscle in his body throbbed. He swore Logan had broken several ribs. They felt as if they were stabbing his innards every time he breathed.

"Then why have the Apaches ransacked the stage stations and burned a few of them to the ground when merely stealing the supplies to resell to Butterfield would have accomplished the same purpose?"

When the sheriff refused to answer, Logan, holding his victim by the hair, twisted his head upward, and laid the knife to his throat. "You're going to tell me, damn you," he snarled. "It might be the last thing you ever say. But you're going to tell me."

The sharp-edged knife drew another trickle of blood, but Epperson refused to answer that specific question. Instead, he offered the same information Logan had already dragged from Cactus Jack in Fort Smith.

"Dammit, I'm not the only one involved," Epperson chirped when the blade left another trail of blood across his throat. "Some of the stage agents marked the coaches with chalk to let us know they carried wealthy passengers like Grant Fredricks. The spies tie their kerchiefs in sailor's knots at the neck so we know which ones are working with us if we need to make contact. The miners we frisked and left penniless were given the chance to join up with us or starve. They served as replacements for men we lost."

The mention of Piper's stepbrother momentarily side-tracked Logan. "Who killed Fredricks?" he wanted to know.

Epperson clamped his lips tightly together, but the blow to his jaw loosened his teeth and the words came tumbling out. "I did, goddammit," he sputtered viciously.

With a malicious snarl, Logan jabbed Epperson in the tender midsection, evoking his howl of pain. "You let Piper take the blame so you could get rid of her as well," he snapped, giving Epperson another slap across the face. "She was to be tried and found guilty of murder so there would be no one around to lay claim to that quarter of a million dollars."

"Half-breed bastard," Epperson sneered spitefully.

Logan wasn't sure why he hit Epperson so hard that it knocked him unconscious. He wasn't through with the murdering thief, not by a long shot. Maybe it was to retaliate against being called a bastard. Logan couldn't help what he was. Perhaps it was to compensate for the humiliation Piper had been forced to endure when Epperson hauled her to jail. She had been Epperson's scapegoat, and he would have seen to it that she was convicted of a murder she didn't commit.

After cutting Epperson's limp body loose, Logan slung him over his shoulder and stalked out into the darkness. He had no qualms about leaving Tucson without a sheriff. Epperson was what the town needed protection *against*. The man had been fighting on the wrong side of the law since he had been elected to the office.

It was time he returned to the shack where Harley waited, Logan decided. Hopefully Harley and the other marshals had rounded up the brigands and had them all tied in knots. Logan would drag the rest of the answers from Epperson on the way to the cabin. Epperson would realize he didn't have an icicle's chance in hell if he didn't reveal the last piece of information Logan wanted. Epperson would learn that Logan would kill him or torture him until he wished he were dead. There would be no one to come to his assistance on the abandoned mesas. He could scream for hours and no one would hear him. But Epperson would sing like a bird, Logan promised himself. He wanted to know why Butterfield's stage line was the prime target of so many attacks, why the ringleader spent his time trying to bankrupt the company. And Epperson was going to tell him . . . sooner or later. . . .

A disgruntled frown knitted Piper's brow as she ambled from Tucson's stage depot. The eastbound coach wasn't due for a week. Piper had considered striking out toward Logan's ranch to retrieve Abraham, but she imagined her tomcat would prefer to remain in Samuel's care rather than endure another journey by stagecoach. Piper lamented the loss of her pet, but she had already lost all else. Leaving Abraham in New Mexico Territory was just another of the endless concessions she had been forced to make.

Piper had hoped to shake Tucson's dust from her feet as quickly as possible. But as always, fate had frowned on her, and she was stuck in Tucson for several more days. She was forced to remain in town even though she might risk seeing Logan again. Piper wasn't sure she could bear it, but as always, she was left with very few choices. She was hurting all over as it was.

The sight of Jenny Payton strutting out of the mercantile store spoiled what had already been a disappointing day. Although Piper turned toward the hotel, Jenny refused to let her walk gracefully away.

"I thought you might want to see the fabric I selected for my wedding gown," Jenny taunted as she hurried to catch up with Piper. Since Piper was the only one in town who knew Logan was alive and well and would soon be wed, Jenny had nowhere else to boast about her feat. All the other women in Tucson and the surrounding area would be envious when they heard the news, but until Logan came back to life Jenny could brag about her wedding to no one but Piper.

Piper's first impression of Jenny was that of a bubbly, personable young woman. It was becoming evident that Jenny possessed at least one annoying flaw. The shapely brunette tended to gloat, and she wanted to make doubly sure Piper knew Logan was her personal property.

Like a queen flaunting her jewels, Jenny tugged at the brown wrapping to reveal the expensive white silk she had purchased. With her dignity intact, Piper complimented Jenny's selection and wished her well in her marriage. But still it wasn't enough. Jenny seemed hell-bent on irritating Piper. Indeed, Piper swore the woman had come to town with her sewing kit, intent on poking needles and pins in Piper's pride.

"Logan came to see me again yesterday," Jenny announced haughtily.

Piper impatiently tapped her foot. She didn't wish to have this conversation. "How nice." Her tone wasn't exactly sarcastic, but neither was it brimming with sincerity. When she tried to walk away, Jenny hustled along beside her.

"Logan assured me he will have this case solved very soon." Her blue eyes flashed a spiteful glare. "We had a long, private discussion . . ." she purred, "the kind in which a man and woman never get around to doing much talking. . . ."

Piper flinched as if she had been stabbed in the back. She knew exactly what Jenny meant. Determinedly, she contained her annoyance and forced the semblance of a smile. "I'm sure Logan will get around to making wedding plans once he has solved Butterfield's problems."

"Of course he will," Jenny declared with an arrogant toss of her head. "He knows how much I love him, how long I've waited for him. He'll be ready to set our wedding date when he doesn't have so much on his mind."

Before Piper could comment Jenny looked down her nose at the comely blonde. "When are you leaving town?" she asked abruptly.

"I'll be taking the next stage," Piper informed her. "Unfortunately, it isn't due for almost a week."

As Piper turned to go, Jenny roughly grabbed her arm and spun her about. Her pleasantness evaporated. Suddenly she was like a hissing mother cat protecting her kittens. "I rather suspect you spread yourself beneath Logan like a common slut," she sneered. "Most women find him impossible to resist. And being a man, I'm sure he accepted your offerings of affection." Her eyes narrowed warningly. "But know this, Piper, I won't give Logan up to you or anyone else. His whoring days are over, and I will be most anxious to have his latest harlot out from underfoot."

Piper didn't know why she responded so sarcastically, but the words were out before she could bite them back. "I hope Logan doesn't mind marrying soiled merchandise," she smirked, her gaze scanning Jenny's shapely form with scornful mockery. "I have been in town just long enough to hear one of your paramours telling his friends about the night the two of you spent together. I believe his name was Will Gilmore. . . ."

Jenny's face turned the color of cooked liver. She reacted to the caustic remark by slapping Piper's cheek. Piper didn't know what demon possessed her to retaliate with a doubled fist, but she did. The well-aimed punch sent Jenny staggering back, covering her left eye.

"Bitch," Jenny hissed furiously. "I'm going to tell Sheriff Epperson about this. And then I'm going to confess that I made up that lie about being in your room the night you murdered whoever it was you murdered!"

Piper had already been to Epperson's office to inform him that her money was still missing, but he was nowhere to be found. "Go ahead," Piper suggested flippantly, "but you will probably spoil your reputation as an upstanding citizen, if you haven't already. I'm sure Epperson will be dismayed to learn you're not only a whore but also a liar." A taunting smile pursed her lips. "That should be the one reputation you wish to keep since you don't have an *upstanding* reputation with men. That is probably why Logan always returns to you—because he knows you'll give him what he wants. I only hope he can be satisfied with what he gets. And you needn't worry. I won't tell him what a spiteful, gloating female you are. He can find that out all by himself."

Jenny's lips curled in a snarl. With claws bared, she pounced on Piper, her package forgotten. But Piper had taken note of the fighting tactics Logan had employed on the drunken scoundrel who had attacked her in Fort Smith. She had practiced them on Burgess Channing and Jenny was next in line to see that Piper's bite was as bad as her bark.

Piper's foot shot out to hook her heel on Jenny's ankle. As Jenny toppled off balance, Piper's doubled fist smashed into the same eye that had been the recipient of the earlier blow. In an instant, Jenny was sprawled faceup in the dirt, her head cushioned on her discarded package.

A sense of self-satisfaction consumed Piper as she brushed off her hands, lifted her skirts, and stepped over Jenny's unconscious body. She expected to be hauled back to jail after Jenny tattled to Sheriff Epperson. But to her surprise, no one bothered her the rest of the day. Either Jenny had slunk home to lick her wounds or she hadn't located Tucson's lousy excuse for a sheriff.

Two days later, when Piper chanced to meet Jenny on the street, sporting a black eye, the huffy brunette took a wide berth around her. Jenny refused to glance in her direction, which suited Piper just fine. She was as anxious to leave town as Jenny was to see her go. But she was not about to tolerate any more of Jenny's spiteful ridicule. Apparently Jenny had learned her lesson. Piper may not have been intimidating in size or stature, but she wasn't afraid to fight and she packed a mighty whallop when she got her dander up!

Chapter 26

The gray shadows of darkness that stretched like long fingers across the eastern slopes of the mountains were just beginning to fade when Logan arrived at the shack. His trip had been fruitful even though he was weary. Epperson had indeed told Logan everything he wanted to know. In fact, once Epperson reached his threshold of pain he had squealed like a stuck pig, offering tidbits of information that Logan hadn't thought to ask.

When Logan nudged Epperson into the shack at gunpoint, all four marshals peered at him.

"Epperson is in on this too?" Harley chirped incredulously.

Logan escorted his prisoner to the bedroom where the other prisoners had been bound tighter than mummies. When he had tied Epperson in a dozen knots, Logan strode back to the table to guzzle a long-awaited drink of whiskey. As he reflexively reached into his pocket to retrieve a two-dollar bill to light his cigar, his hand stalled in midair.

A rueful smile pursed his lips as he rolled the crisp banknote across his fingertips. If Piper had been here she would have scolded him for being a spendthrift. But she wasn't, Logan promptly reminded himself, and then lit his cheroot in his customary manner.

Harley frowned at Logan's annoying habit, but he was too impatient to learn what was going on to chastise the brawny giant. "Well, are you going to tell the rest of us where you've been for a week or are we supposed to guess?"

Logan casually blew a few smoke rings in the air and then planted himself in a chair. "I've been tying up a few loose ends. Epperson is the man who delivered fake bills of sale and supplies to the thieves you have stashed in the back room," he reported. "The outlaws who attacked the stages were never hunted down or arrested because Epperson was receiving a cut of the profit. The thieves robbed unsuspecting miners with those fake bills of sale and then Epperson sold the goods he confiscated to Burgess Channing, who supplies Butterfield's stage stations. Naturally, Channing bought the goods at a reduced price so he could enjoy a greater margin of profit himself."

"Epperson has been selling Butterfield's stolen goods back to him? Well, I'll be damned," Gorman Rader snorted. "No wonder nothing much gets done in Tucson. Epperson was using his badge to turn a tidy profit and protect the ring of thieves."

Logan nodded affirmatively. "There is no sense taking our prisoners to Tucson for trial. The circuit judge won't be through the area for two more weeks. And to make matters worse, the sheriff is as guilty as the rest of his gang." He paused to down another sip of whiskey and then stretched his long legs out in front of him. "We'll take our captives to Fort Buchanan to stand trial, and the bounty on their heads will be your profit to split four ways."

"You should have a share," Anthony Danhill insisted. "It was your plan that made it easy for us to round up the outlaws when they returned from raids, carrying the stolen money and valuables they took for stage passengers."

One broad shoulder lifted in a reckless shrug. "You put your lives on the line to capture those men. The reward is yours."

"But . . ."

Danhill's protest died on his lips when Logan's steel gray eyes narrowed on him. "Just take the money and don't argue with me," he snorted gruffly. "You're being as contrary as Piper. I swear if I declared the sun rose in the east, that minx would claim the opposite!"

His sudden reference to Piper provoked all four men to grin. Logan scowled at each and every one of them.

"What's so damned funny?" he wanted to know.

"Nothin'," Jacob Carter mumbled as he unfolded himself from his chair. "Come on boys, we've got a lot of horses to saddle."

After the other marshals had filed out the door, Harley stared pensively at Logan's sour frown. "You didn't marry her," he guessed.

Logan jerked up his head. "I can't."

"You can't or you won't?" Harley pried.

"Both," Logan grunted before guzzling another drink. "When Epperson arrested Piper for murdering Grant Fredricks, I—"

"Arrested Piper for murder!?" Harley choked out, his eyes popping.

Logan nodded grimly. "The man who originally stole Piper's inheritance was her stepbrother. Epperson disposed of him and then accused Piper of killing Grant so no one would be around to claim the money."

"Epperson had her money all along?" Harley questioned curiously.

"Not exactly. The five thieves who robbed the stage Fredricks was on decided to keep the money for themselves. They lit out to the north to hole up in Superstition Mountain." When Harley tried to pose another question Logan waved him to silence. "That quarter of a million has been in so many hands it would take the rest of the day to explain. The point is, I had to promise Jenny I'd marry her if she would provide an alibi to free Piper from jail before Epperson had her convicted of murder."

"What!" Harley vaulted from his chair, upending it. "But what are you going to do about Piper?"

Logan stared incredulously at his companion. "What the hell's the matter with you? Four months ago you were insisting I marry Jenny and settle down. If that's what you wanted you don't look happy about my upcoming wedding," he smirked.

Harley uprighted his chair and then plopped into it. "I did say that four months ago," he acknowledged. "But that was before Piper showed up. You owe that girl something for dallying with her."

"What about Jenny?" Logan countered.

"You know what about Jenny," Harley snapped. "You knew before you started seeing her. But that's different. I'd bet my right arm that citified blonde was never with another man until she pretended to be your wife. You owe her for taking privileges." Harley wagged a lean finger in Logan's scowling face. "And don't try to tell me you didn't because I know you well enough to know you did. You were sharing the same room with her at the Pinery. The night Anthony and I rounded up the stage agents you suspected of working with the desperados I checked the guest register when I left the message for you. There were no female passengers listed at the hotel because Piper was sharing your room! You have a responsibility to her after what you did."

They had had a similar conversation once before and Logan detested having it again. His fist hit the table like a sledgehammer. "I owe her nothing," he growled. "She's given me more trouble than I could ever give her. Hell, she had me following her around like a damned guard dog to keep her from running headlong into disaster!"

"Did she ask for your assistance?" Harley inquired.

"Well no, but . . ."

"But you took it upon yourself to trail after her," Harley snorted. "I took her to Tucson and you went running after her. It seems to me that you can't quite let go of Piper. And if that's so, you have no business marrying Jenny Payton."

"It seems to me you should mind your own business!" Logan roared.

"You're in love with her, aren't you?" Harley chuckled. "Ol' hardhearted Logan finally found a female he couldn't handle, one he couldn't shrug off like he did all the rest."

Logan had lost his temper several days ago and he hadn't been able to find it since. Harley's nettling wasn't helping Logan's surly disposition one bit. "I am not in love with Piper!" he bellowed with great conviction.

Harley tapped the side of his head to stop the ringing in his ears. "You needn't yell."

"I won't yell if you'll quit badgering me," Logan shouted into Harley's grinning face.

"My, aren't we sensitive all of a sudden," Harley observed. "I mention Piper Malone and you go up in smoke. Mighty peculiar behavior for a man who claims he doesn't give a fig about her."

Logan bounded from his chair and was at the door in three long strides. "I've got more important things to do than listen to you," he muttered grouchily.

"Now where are you going?" Harley questioned.

"Back to Tucson to see Jenny."

"I'll purchase a new set of clothes for your wedding while I'm at the fort," Harley teased. "But it seems silly for you to get married to Jenny while you're in love with another woman. Even as understanding as Jenny has always been about your wandering ways, I don't think she's going to like having another female's image standing between the two of you on your wedding night."

"There is no other woman," Logan snapped crossly. "Piper is going back where she belongs with her precious damned money occupying the seat beside her."

Harley frowned in bemusement. "I thought you said you didn't find her money."

"I haven't yet, and if I can't recover it, I'll personally pay for her losses before I put her on the eastbound stage," Logan insisted.

"You're going to give her a quarter of a million dollars?" Harley croaked in astonishment. "You don't have that much money! You might have if you didn't burn it up two damned dollars at a time!"

"I'll have enough after I rob the stage headed for Fort Smith," Logan assured him.

Harley threw up his hands in exasperation as he followed Logan out the door. "What the sweet loving hell are you ranting about?"

"I'll explain later," Logan grumbled as he swung onto Sam's back. "This business with Butterfield isn't over yet."

Harley rolled his eyes skyward and muttered under his breath. Logan had never been one to explain what he was going to do until after he'd done it. He offered just enough information to play havoc with Harley's curiosity.

Logan was going to marry Jenny Payton after three years of avoiding a commitment and he was going to rob the stage he was sworn to protect? None of that made any sense. If Logan truly wanted to wed Jenny he would have done so long ago. Oh, Harley had suggested it a hundred times, but he knew Logan well enough to know that no amount of nagging would provoke him to do what he didn't really want to do. And this business about robbing a stage was crazy! They had most of the scoundrels rounded up and ready to be delivered to the jail at the fort. Why tamper with the stage now? It made no sense at all.

Grumbling to himself, Harley watched Logan trot his paint stallion down the winding path. What he had on his mind was anybody's guess. Harley couldn't begin to figure Logan out.

"Where the devil is Logan going in such a rush?" Anthony questioned.

"He said he was going to rob a stage and then marry Jenny Payton," Harley informed the other marshals. The men stared at him as if he had cactus growing out his ears. "Well, dammit, that's what the man said!"

Muttering, Harley and Anthony, who had wagered that Logan would wind up marrying the comely blonde, handed over their ten-dollar gold pieces to Gorman and Jacob. Harley let his money go with great reluctance. He had been certain Logan's conscience would get the best of him and that he would realize he had an obligation to Piper Malone. It was for sure Logan hadn't been himself since he returned from Fort Smith. Logan didn't seem to know what he wanted these days. That was strange behavior for a man who had once been as calculating and methodic as they came.

Logan had two women on a string and that was hard on a man's sanity. Jenny had always been a little too available and obvious in her intentions, and she had never confined her affections solely to Logan. Harley liked Jenny, but when he compared her to the saucy blonde, the brunette ran a distant second. Logan was frustrated by emotions he didn't want to experience, Harley mused as he helped saddle the string of horses. Logan was trying to be sensible but his heart kept getting in the way of his head. The conflicting feelings left him clinging to Piper even after he declared he was marrying Jenny. Logan had troubles all right, Harley thought to himself. He was meeting himself coming and going and he didn't *think* he should have what he *thought* he really wanted. Lord, it was no wonder Logan was confused. Harley was confusing himself just contemplating what Logan was *thinking!*

If Logan could have read Harley's mind, he might have realized how confused he had become. But Logan was too exasperated to think straight—had been since he breezed into Fort Smith to meet that enchanting green-eyed witch who was to pose as his wife. But when he returned to Jenny she would convince him that he had made the right decision. She would make him forget that haunting image of emerald eyes and silver blond hair. This is the best way for all concerned, Logan assured himself. Once he resigned himself to the obvious he could get on with the rest of his life and be satisfied with it.

Meditatively, Logan peered at the shaft of light that traced a golden path across the ground. Heaving a tired sigh, he dismounted. There had been a time when his footsteps took him to Jenny's room without a moment's delay. But the past three times he had come to see her he had dragged his feet. Tonight was going to be different, Logan promised himself. He would take Jenny in his arms and forget the woman he didn't want to remember.

The instant Logan slipped into the room, Jenny flew into his arms, but not before Logan noticed the black eye and cut lip she was sporting. "What the blazes happened to you?" Logan questioned, holding her at arm's length.

"That blond bitch did this," Jenny hissed, hoping to prey on Logan's sympathy. She wanted to turn him against Piper's bewitching powers, once and for all.

"Piper?" Logan fought back his astonished grin. He wouldn't have believed Piper would engage in a knock-down drag-out fight if he hadn't seen her make mincemeat of Burgess Channing. Jenny's black eye provided the evidence that Piper had done battle, not once but twice. "Why would she do a thing like that?"

Jenny presented her back to him, smiling wickedly to herself. "Because she is ungrateful and selfish and jealous. The sooner that woman is out of our lives the better. You should have heard the hateful things she said to me before she attacked me!"

"What did you do to her?" Logan wanted to know.

Jenny pivoted, her chin elevating to an indignant angle. "I didn't lay a hand on her," she lied.

Silver-gray eyes bored into her flashing blue ones. "You just passed Piper on the street and she punched you without provocation?" he smirked sarcastically. "Come now, Jen, I know Piper better than that. She doesn't act, she reacts. What did you do to set fuse to her temper?"

It galled Jenny to no end that Logan had come to that sassy bitch's defense. "I was only making idle conversation," she insisted as she sidled close to curl her arms around his neck. "But none of that matters now. You're here and we have wedding plans to discuss."

Her lips played softly against his, luring him to take what she was freely offering. Logan devoted himself to returning her tantalizing kiss. He closed his eyes and devoured the taste of her. His arms fastened about her, his fingers mapping her luscious curves and swells. But the feel of her ripe body meshed intimately to his wasn't quite right. Perfectly formed though she was, attentive and affectionate though she had always been, Jenny wasn't Piper. Her kisses and caresses left Logan wanting something that just wasn't there. Once upon a time Jen had been woman enough to satisfy him. She had come as close as any woman he had ever known . . . until Piper.

Logan squelched the betraying thought and hugged Jenny even closer. When she unfastened her blouse and granted him free access to her bare flesh Logan thought sure his body would eagerly respond as it once had. He thought wrong. There was no tingle of anticipation, no raging fire, only the nagging sensation that he had set his hands on the wrong woman.

Still struggling with his thoughts, Logan squeezed his eyes shut again and bent Jenny into his hard contours, but sparkling green eyes continued to torment him. It wasn't Jenny who was whispering to him. It was Piper's soft, alluring voice that echoed through his mind. He knew he couldn't have the blond-haired nymph, but he could no longer find consolation with Jenny. The spark simply wasn't there to ignite the flame of desire.

Dammit, it wasn't going to work, Logan finally admitted to himself. He couldn't make love to Jen when it was Piper he really wanted. He cared about Jenny, but he ached for that spell-casting witch. Blast her! She had spoiled what might have been a reasonably satisfying match for a man like him. If he spoke the vows he would be living a lie.

Jenny might be the best he could hope for in this rugged part of the country, but she would never have his love. And in Logan's estimation, there was no reason to marry if not for love. Women had always been convenient. There had always been one within shouting distance when he wanted one. And since Logan had money to burn there was no reason to marry just to acquire it. If not for love, what was the use of settling down? he asked himself as he set Jenny from him.

"It just won't work," Logan growled in frustration.

The look that etched his craggy features enraged Jenny. She had waited three years to entrap Logan. He had made her a promise and he would damned well keep it! Perhaps he didn't love her, but she could make him love her, given half a chance. She had bent over backward, always giving Logan his way, always catering to him when he came to her. She deserved marriage after the sacrifices she'd made for him. Why, she had even turned down two rendezvous with Will Gilmore, just in case Logan showed up!

"You promised!" Jenny reminded him with an angry hiss.

"I promised to discuss marriage," Logan corrected. "We are discussing it and it is my opinion that we should continue as we have the last three years—no strings attached."

Her eyes burned a hot blue flame. "It's because of Piper, isn't it?" she growled bitterly. "You've been sleeping with that prissy sophisticate and now you think you can do better than me! All of a sudden you have yourself thinking I'm not good enough for you, just because you've seduced little miss high society!"

"Shut up, Jen," Logan muttered threateningly.

"Why? Because I hit upon the truth and you don't want to hear it?" she sniffed sarcastically. "Well, you're a fool if you think that sassy Easterner would have a man like you. You're nothing but a novelty to her. Women like Piper toy with men like you. It gives them some perverted kind of thrill to be seduced by a rough-edged renegade. But in a month Piper will plead and cry and beg you to pull up stakes and take up residence in her society. She'll have you attending fancy parties where you wouldn't begin to fit in. You'll be as out of place in her world as she is in ours!"

Her spiteful, mocking tone caused Logan's brows to pucker in a scowl. "Shut your mouth before I'm tempted to blacken the other eye."

"Go ahead," she challenged him, "but it won't change anything. You can slink off to that haughty bitch, but she won't have you now. I told her you and I had been intimate each time you came here."

"That's a damned lie!" Logan growled into her smug smile.

"Piper thinks it's the truth and that's what matters," she assured him airily. "That's why she struck me. And if you think she'd have you now, you're in for a bitter disappointment."

Logan never wanted to hit a woman quite as badly as he wanted to hit Jenny now. She possessed many admirable qualities, or at least he thought she did. Suddenly Logan realized he only knew Jenny in the way he had known every other woman—except Piper. He and Jenny had shared a one-dimensional relationship that only involved falling into bed to appease their lusts.

Jenny had a jealous streak and she could be vicious when she didn't get what she ultimately wanted. When she was crossed she became cruel and vindictive. If she thought he didn't know there were other men in her life she was a bigger fool than he was! Will Gilmore, the neighboring rancher, had been paying her nocturnal visits for more than a year. Logan knew they were doing more than enjoying a friendly game of checkers. The sound coming from the bedroom window was not the click of checkers jumping across a game board!

When Logan wheeled around to leave through the window

in which he had come, Jenny grasped his arm. She was furious with herself for allowing her tongue to outdistance her brain.

"Logan, I'm sorry," she hastily apologized. "I shouldn't have said those awful things. I love you and I don't want to lose you. Stay . . . please. . . . I'll make you glad you did. And I won't force you to marry me if you don't want to. Things will be the way they've always been."

Shaking free of her grasp, Logan flung a long leg over the windowsill, but Jen threw herself in front of him, blocking his exit. Shamelessly, she shrugged off her blouse and wrapped her arms around him, clinging to him as if he were her lifeline. "Please, Logan. Just give me a chance. I can make you forget her. . . ."

Logan wasn't aroused by Jenny's desperate attempt to detain him; he was repulsed. He began to wonder if he really knew Jenny at all. It was becoming evident that she was willing to do anything to keep him with her. It also left him to wonder if Jenny had mistaken possession for love. She wanted him because of his reputation, because he had never coddled her or fussed over her. Will Gilmore had done exactly that and she had kept him on a leash, using him to satisfy her passionate nature when Logan wasn't around. Will Gilmore would probably have married Jenny long ago, but she had set her sights on a shiftless shootist because he was always out of reach.

In a way, Jenny and I are a great deal alike, Logan reckoned. *We both want what we can't have.* But that wasn't enough to hold them together for a lifetime. Disgusted with himself for coming to Jenny in the first place, Logan untangled her arms and slipped out the window, only to see Jen poke her head out to glare at him.

"Don't you ever come back here, Logan," she jeered contemptuously. "I'm going to marry Will Gilmore. And for your information, we were lovers while you left me alone for months at a time!"

Logan pivoted to display a wry smile that even the shadows couldn't conceal. "I know. I've been here a time or two when you and Will were nestled in bed. I never did think you were faithful, honey, only available."

His ridiculing remark caught Jenny flat-footed. Her mouth gaped in surprise. Logan knew? The thought made her even more furious. "Good riddance, half-breed," she hurled at him. "I hope you lust after that Eastern bitch for the rest of your life. Your penance for wronging me will be craving for a woman you can't have. You can go straight to hell—and take Piper Malone with you!"

If Logan had any regrets before, they were nonexistent now. He wasn't sure he liked the real Jenny Payton. Poor Will, he mused as he walked toward his stallion. The man was getting more than he bargained for. Logan had nothing, but it was better than what Will Gilmore was going to get!

With a scowl, Logan swung onto Sam's back. He had one more matter to attend to before he completed his job for Butterfield. And this particular matter involved Piper, whether she wanted to see him again or not. She deserved to ride beside him when he resolved this case. It would be Piper's consolation prize, of sorts. Piper was going to be Logan's accomplice when he robbed the stage. When they had completed this final task, Logan intended to deposit Piper in the coach and send her rumbling east to deliver the news to Butterfield.

Flinging his musings aside, Logan headed toward Piper's hotel. When this was over, he was going to treat himself to a week's sleep. He had spent so many hours in the saddle the past six days he was sure his backside resembled the shape of his horse. Although Logan was fond of Sam, he had no desire to look like him.

As Logan rode through the darkness, Jenny's words came back to torment him, just as she hoped they would. She had put into words the thoughts that had been buzzing around his head since the first time he laid eyes on Piper. The ill-fated attraction Logan and Piper shared was a curse, not a blessing. It was a temptation that could never become reality. They had made a space in their lives for passion, the likes of which Logan had never known, the likes of which Piper had never experienced until he had forced her to surrender to him. But the bitter truth was that their lives ran parallel to one another; they were always pulling in the opposite direction. What Logan felt for that shapely minx was a stumbling block that hampered his logic, but he had to be sensible and realistic, even if Piper had left a hole the size of New Mexico Territory in his heart. She needed to go back to the world to which she belonged.

It's over, Logan lectured himself sternly. His stormy affair with Piper had ended and his long-standing affair with Jenny was over and done. Logan had resolved himself to those truths by the time he reached Tucson. He had always been a loner who had no intention of settling into one place unless a bullet with his name on it or old age planted him in one spot.

By the time he completed his obligations and returned to his ranch there would be at least a dozen offers awaiting him in the mail. As always, he would select the job that appealed to him and then he would set off to become the long, expedient arm of law and order. Given time, he would praise himself for making the right decision about Piper. Occasionally, he would reopen the memories and recall the weeks and months when he had come as close to loving a woman as he could ever come. He would cherish those rare, radiant smiles of Piper's. He would remember the forbidden rapture they had shared, even if they never should have tampered with passion at all.

Rawhide and lace don't mix, Logan reminded himself. And one of these days, he was going to be glad he let go of this impossible dream. And that was all it had ever been—a fantasy, a sweet unrealistic fantasy that couldn't have a happy ending. But ah, what mystical splendor it had been while it lasted. . . .

Chapter 27

Logan slipped into Piper's room with the cool evening breeze that drifted through the open window. But no matter how quiet he had tried to be, his entry had aroused Piper. She hadn't enjoyed a decent night's sleep since her fight with Jenny. The fact that she had a stage to catch in a few hours also prevented her from sleeping soundly. Every few minutes she awakened with a start, afraid she had overslept.

It wasn't difficult for Piper to recognize the nocturnal prowler. One glance in his direction and Piper knew exactly who had been creeping around outside her window like a restless spirit. Her eyes reflected mixed emotion as she watched Logan tiptoe toward her bed. Part of her wanted to welcome him with open arms. Another part of her itched to snatch up the Colt that lay beneath her pillow and blow him to kingdom come. It was what Logan deserved for falling in love with that snippy brunette who obviously held the key to his heart (if indeed he had one)!

Piper hadn't wanted to see Logan again after what Jenny told her, but helplessly she savored the sight of him. She didn't want to feel this warm tingle running down her spine when he drew near, but she did. One would think she was a glutton for punishment. She knew Logan had been sleeping with Jenny, and still Piper ached for his touch. Now that was crazy!

"Tell me, Logan," Piper demanded as she rose on an elbow to point her Colt at his muscular chest. "Do you ever enter a room the normal way, even when you aren't pretending to be a ghost?"

Logan froze in his tracks. He hadn't expected to find Piper awake, nor had he anticipated being greeted with a pistol. But now that he thought about it, he wondered if he couldn't solve everyone's problems if he just let her shoot him.

"Why don't you pull the trigger and put me out of my misery," Logan suggested. "According to Cherokee legend, death comes as a long-awaited friend to ease all suffering and pain."

And Logan was in pain. The moment he laid eyes on this exquisite beauty he was stung by arousing sensations. His self-inspiring lectures hadn't helped a tittle. He was back to wanting this lovely goddess the way he always had, even when he swore up and down that it was over between them.

"If you came to retaliate for stuffing my fist in your fiancée's eye, you have my apology," Piper assured him. Unable to stare at him another moment for fear of being sidetracked by her wayward thoughts, Piper contemplated the shadows caused by the curtains fluttering in the breeze. "I shouldn't have lost my temper with Jenny. It was a most unladylike thing to do."

Like a moth drawn to a compelling flame, knowing damned well he would singe his wings, Logan moved deliberately toward Piper. As if he belonged there, he sank down beside her to brace his arms on either side of her well-sculptured hips. "I never suspected you could pack such a wallop," he teased softly. "If Willis Worthington gets wind of this, he'll probably come back to persuade you to test your skills in the boxing ring."

Piper refused to glance up at him. If she fell into those glistening silver pools she would drown. Thank goodness Logan had taunted her about her fracas. If nothing else, it supplied a topic for conversation that would distract her from his disturbing nearness.

"I said I was sorry," she grumbled bitterly. "If you want to exact a pound of my flesh, then be quick about doing it." Piper reached beneath her pillow for the other weapon she kept within arm's reach these days. She handed him the bowie knife she had purchased at Channing's store. "Here, cut off one or two of my fingers. That probably won't appease Jenny, since she prefers to go for the throat, but it will have to suffice unless she wants to see you toted off to jail for murder."

Logan took her pistol from her and swiftly laid the dagger to her neck, forcing her head to the pillow. "No matter what I choose to do to you, Sheriff Epperson won't be coming to apprehend me," he informed her. "He's on his way to Fort Buchanan with the rest of the desperados who have been preying on the stage line."

Piper might have demanded that Logan explain himself if she hadn't been so preoccupied by the feel of his powerful body sinking down beside hers. But it was impossible to think when her brain melted in the fire ignited by his touch. It had been an eternity since she had inhaled the musky scent of him. Her senses took flight when his masculine fragrance filled her nostrils. Her body burned each time his body brushed familiarly against hers.

The knife that had lain at her throat clanked to the floor as Logan yielded to overwhelming temptation. Despite his better judgment, he bent his head to press his lips to hers. This was what he had tried to forget when he clutched Jenny to him. This was the taste to which he had become so hopelessly addicted. The feel of Piper's luscious body beside his was the sensation that had been lacking when Jenny molded herself to him.

His hands tunneled through her silky blond hair, tilting her face upward so he could explore every inch of her soft mouth, so he could taste her fully, completely. His big body trembled with wanting as he savored and devoured her all in the same breathless moment.

The helplessness Logan experienced served to remind him that he would never be able to resist this sophisticated beauty unless they were miles apart. When she was in his arms, he didn't have the good sense God gave a duck. Piper had made him a slave to his passions, his foolish whims. When he dared to touch Piper he wanted her wildly.

It had been his intention to retrieve Piper and have her assist him in his last duty for Butterfield. But his body refused to rise from the bed until he had satisfied this maddening hunger. His hands seemed to have perfect recall, as if it had been minutes instead of endless days since he had caressed her satiny flesh.

Piper's soft moan of pleasure encouraged him to continue his explorations. Logan longed to rediscover every exquisite inch of her body. He wanted to cherish her, to love her for all the time he wouldn't be there to do so in the years to come. This was his touch with perfection, and he vowed to brand his memory on her mind, just as her precious memory would be emblazoned on his restless soul.

Piper tossed her head from side to side, adoring the feel of his skillful hands on her skin. And yet she detested herself for submitting to him. Logan was using her again, even while Jenny was waiting in the wings. That painful thought caused Piper to fight her way back through the haze of desire that threatened to cloud her thinking. Her hands caught hold of his, stilling their flight across her quivering flesh. She waited for Logan to raise his shaggy head and meet her anguished gaze.

"No, Logan." Her voice wobbled as she fought for self-control. "You have constantly told me to go back where I belong. Now you are the one who is out of place. Go back to Jenny."

"What was between Jenny and me is over," he told her in a voice that rattled with barely contained desire. "There will be no marriage. I only agreed to discuss a wedding in order to get her to provide you with an alibi. That was the price she demanded in compensation." His eyes glistened in the moonlight, burning down on Piper like starfire. "She lied to you, Piper. I haven't been with her since I met you. You were the woman I wanted. Jenny knew that and she antagonized you because of it."

Piper blinked like an owl. Logan hadn't exactly said he cared for her, but he had done a superb job of talking around it. Her heart swelled with hope for the first time in more than three months. She looked him squarely in the eye, holding his face in her hands, seeing the rugged lines that were shaded with shadows moonlight. But it wouldn't have mattered if she could see his face or not. Piper could have closed her eyes and sketched each beguiling feature which had long ago been committed to memory.

"You aren't trying to tell me you love me, are you?" she questioned softly.

Logan's heart flip-flopped in his chest as he peered down into her bewitching face. He couldn't remember saying he had loved anyone in all his life, though he must have loved his mother when he was a child. Logan had never expressed his emotions to anyone. There had been no reason to, nor was there now. What he felt didn't change anything. In fact, it only complicated matters.

"I am trying to say nothing of the kind," he grumbled. "Whether I do or not doesn't make a damned bit of difference."

"It does to me," Piper whispered to him. "If you love me, I have to know. It matters to me, even if it doesn't make a difference to you."

It would have taken a far better man than Logan to deny her request to state the truth. Logan didn't feel like an invincible warrior or a skilled gunman at the moment. He felt like a jar of peach marmalade.

"Jeezus, Piper! You're in my blood," he confessed, as if he resented the emotions and the admission. "I look at other women and I see you. I close my eyes and your memory colors every thought. I've spent months fretting over you, wanting you in the worst way. I know it's no good between us, but that doesn't stop me from aching for you up to my eyebrows."

"Then say the words, just once," Piper gently commanded him. "Say what you feel . . . even if it can't be forever. . . ."

His eyes searched her shadowed face. His index finger mapped her flawless features. Reverently, he bent to take possession of her inviting lips. "I do love you, Piper," he murmured with heartfelt sincerity. "God help me for saying so, but I've never loved anything so much in my life. If not for love I would never have known anything so precious . . . or frustrating. . . ."

Her radiant smile, one that Logan hadn't seen often enough to suit him, blossomed on her face and illuminated the room. "Honestly?" Surely her ears had deceived her. She had wanted to hear the words so badly she probably dreamed them up.

Logan chuckled softly and her hopeful expression provoked him to burst into a face-splitting grin. "Honestly," he confided. "Do you want it in writing?" His wandering hand drifted to the soft flesh above her heart. "I'd be happy to print it all over you. . . ."

Piper was satisfied to let him do just that. For the first time in their stormy affair there was not a hint of reluctance in their responses to each other. Piper surrendered in total abandon, returning each kiss and caress, worshiping his hair-roughened flesh. Loving Logan had never been quite so wild and wondrous. Now there was no riptide of emotions to torment her, only the rapturous bliss of loving this mountain of a man who honestly loved her, even if he wasn't offering forever. For now was enough. That was more than Piper had dared hope for.

As they rolled and tumbled on the bed, impatient for each other, Piper repeated her love in words and deeds. Logan answered just as fervently. The torture of loving Piper and refusing to acknowledge his affection was over. He had come to terms with his feelings for Piper. For once there was no reluctance when he yielded to the blazing flame of a passion that he had never been able to control when he was with her. The words *I love you* were embroidered in each caress, each devouring kiss. His hands and lips and body spelled out the precious words to her, printing the phrase on her silky flesh until he gave new meaning to the term *love letters*.

It was a wild coming together of bodies and hearts and souls. It was as new and splendorous as the first time they succumbed to passion, and yet love expanded the perimeters of ecstasy. Now there was no limit, no boundaries to confine his feelings for Piper.

But each time we make love is always like the first time, will always be like the first time, Logan reminded himself as he surrendered to the mystical sensations that swirled around him. Piper provided a special touch of magic that made each encounter unique. She was a kaleidoscope of ever-changing reactions and responses. Because she had blossomed with each passing day, the fire that burned between them never dimmed. It blazed higher with each hour of lovemaking, as if they were improving on what had been perfection.

Logan wondered if it would always be this way between them had they a lifetime to share. Somehow Logan knew it would be. Piper would never be the woman he had known the day before. She would continue to grow from within, broadening her horizons, meeting new challenges, gaining strength and momentum. And Logan adored each fascinating change that had come over her. Perhaps that was the reason he had chased her. Oh, he complained that she was destined for trouble. But the curiosity of wondering how she would react each time she confronted a new challenge intrigued him. He wanted to be there to watch her cope with each new experience, to ensure that she was free from harm. . . .

That was the last sane thought to skip across Logan's mind before passion completely consumed him. He could feel himself slipping away into that wondrous dimension of time he had come to know as paradise. This sweet, dynamic angel had spread her wings and sent him sailing in motionless flight. Rapturous sensations swelled over him until his body was riveted with sweet, maddening pleasure. Logan feared his encircling arms would crush Piper's delicate body, but he couldn't unclamp his fierce grasp on her. The intimacy of this precious moment sealed their bodies, forging their flesh into one living, breathing essence. Her alluring fragrance was now a part of him. The taste of her kiss lingered on his lips. The feel of her silky skin molded to his provided satisfaction that defined description.

Heaven was the unending circle of her arms. The immense pleasure he had found with Piper was worth the trials, the petty arguments, the constant ache of wanting. He had tortured himself for more than three months. He had paid his penance. Now he could enjoy this rare, unique brand of love he had discovered. And if not for this special kind of love, Logan would have walked through life without experiencing the most magnificent emotion of all. Piper had taught his soul to sing. She had given his rough-and-tumble life new meaning.

Logan and Piper had come full circle. No matter what tomorrow held, this night was the one Logan would cherish until the end of his days. When he sent Piper back where she belonged, he would carry this treasured memory in his heart.

He would think back and he would remember the time when he and Piper had stepped out of their own worlds to make a place of their own.

In the aftermath of passion, Piper felt as if she was a bubbly glass of champagne. The pleasure she had experienced, compounded by the sheer happiness of loving and being loved, overwhelmed her. She felt like dashing to the window and sharing her excitement with the world.

A muddled frown creased Logan's brow when Piper, giving way to impulse, tugged the sheet around her exquisite form and leapt off the bed like a mountain goat. Resembling a fleeing apparition enshrouded in white, she sailed toward the window.

"I love him and he honestly loves me!" she exclaimed to anyone who cared to listen.

A deep skirl of laughter rattled in Logan's chest as he watched and listened to Piper's outrageous antics. "You're crazy, lady," he chuckled, but his husky tone was far from condemning. "You must have gotten hold of some loco weed. Ugh!"

His breath came out in a pained grunt as Piper darted across the room to plop down on his belly. And then it came, that blinding smile that lit up the darkness. Logan melted in sentimental mush for the first time ever—soft, dripping mush—exactly like watered-down grits!

"I am crazy . . . about you," Piper clarified before planting an adoring kiss on his lips.

"The rest of the world might be a bit skeptical if they knew you claimed to be in love with a ghost," Logan pointed out as he nibbled at her soft lips.

"How long before you come back to life, Logan?" Piper murmured, distracted by his arousing kisses.

He had already come back to life! The feel of her pliant body caressing his set fire to a special brand of desire that would never burn itself out, even when Logan swore passion's blaze had consumed him and itself. "Very soon," he assured her as his wandering hands chartered the curvaceous terrain of her flesh.

Their playfulness vanished as desire again burst like a volcanic eruption. For a second time Piper felt herself being swept along in the fiery sensations of love. Knowing what they shared might not last forever made each moment rare and precious. His love was a long-awaited gift that might be stolen away from her at any moment. Piper wanted to revel in the splendor, savor and devour every soul-shattering sensation that channeled through her. She wanted to return every remarkable feeling, to intensify it, expand it. She wanted to love and cherish Logan for all the bleak tomorrows she would be forced to endure. She wanted to compensate for what she knew she couldn't enjoy ever again.

Piper longed to create a world of tomorrows in this brief but glorious moment. She gave herself to Logan, worshiping him with each breath she inhaled, relishing the feel of his masculine body upon hers. And yet, amidst the sublime pleasure of loving him so completely a hint of sadness shaded her heart, knowing the end would come too quickly. Their love was like a shooting star that sizzled across the midnight sky. For a time it blazed with fiery splendor before evaporating in the darkness. But Piper refused to dwell on the depressing thought of losing Logan. His love for her couldn't change what he was. He loved her, but not enough and not forever.

There was no changing Logan's ways. It was that wild, reckless nobility in him that had compelled her to him from the beginning. Piper knew he wanted her to go back to her world and leave him alone in his. He had harped on the subject for months. She wouldn't plead with him to let her stay, to ask him to make a permanent place for her in his life. She wouldn't follow after him, begging him to let their love live forever. If he wanted her with him, waiting for him each time he returned, he would have to come right out and say so. Piper wanted to remain with him even if she stuck out like a rose in a cactus patch. But if the love he felt for her wasn't strong and compelling enough to force the words from his lips, she couldn't make demands, not on a man like Logan. If he felt chained to her, bound by the love she felt for him, it still wouldn't be enough to hold him. It was the velvet chains of *his* love for *her* that would make all the difference, and Piper feared the invisible bond between them wasn't strong enough to compel Logan to consider her as a part of his future.

The jingle of harnesses and the rumble of a coach in the street below caused Piper to jerk her head up from its resting place on Logan's shoulder. Time had sped by and Piper had forgotten she was to catch the eastbound stage at four o'clock that morning.

When she tried to wiggle free, jump into her clothes, and sail out of the room, Logan hooked his arm around her waist. "I'll see that you catch your stage. Right after we rob it," he said calmly.

Piper stared at him as if he had lizards crawling out his ears. "Rob it?" she parroted in amazement. "We? You and me?"

Logan gave his ruffled head a shake and grinned cryptically. "You and me—the notorious Logan gang."

A dubious frown puckered her brow. "I thought you upheld the law instead of breaking it."

His muscular body rolled sideways, pinning her beneath him. "There are times when a man must break the law in order to enforce it," he insisted. "It is an extension of court justice. It saves time, and we don't have an abundance of it at the moment."

"I thought you considered my talents with a pistol barely passable," Piper pointed out.

Piper didn't like the sound of this, and as usual, Logan hadn't bothered to explain his ultimate purpose. Only Logan knew what he intended. Everyone else was left to make a stab in the dark in hope of second-guessing him. Why the devil was he being so mysterious?

"You don't have to shoot anybody, just look as though you might if they cross you," he informed her blandly.

"I don't know about this," Piper said warily. "It sounds to me as if you've forgotten which side of the law you are supposed to be on."

Gentle hands smoothed away her troubled frown. "Trust me, Piper," Logan urged. "For once don't judge me, just trust me. . . ."

How was she supposed to deny the request when he uttered it so softly, when he trailed his fingertips over her eyelids and lips, leaving them quivering in helpless response? "I love you, Logan, and it's for certain one of us is crazy. Now all I have to do is determine which one—you for inviting me to a stage robbery or me for accepting."

His brawny body shook with laughter. "You'll be glad you came along. It will be a tale you can relate to your grandchildren in years to come."

"If I live long enough to have grandchildren," she sniffed.

Logan rolled from bed and hoisted Piper up beside him. "Put on your breeches and try to look like a man." A wry smile pursed his lips a few moments later when he surveyed Piper's arresting figure. "For once I wish you didn't have so many shapely curves. We don't want parts of your anatomy protruding in places a man's doesn't."

Piper left her shirttail dangling, swept her hair in a bun, and pulled her hat low on her forehead. "Now will I pass for a man?" she inquired as she pirouetted in front of him for inspection.

Her question provoked Logan's laughter. "Not yet," he declared as his eyes raked her curvaceous form, missing not even one detail. "I brought along a jacket and oversized hat that might help camouflage your feminine assets."

One delicate brow shot up to an incredulous angle. "You planned this holdup, knowing I would agree to it, even before you asked me?"

"I did," he confirmed. "I had already decided you were coming along, even if I had to tie you to the saddle."

"Mighty sure of yourself, aren't you?" she smirked, her tone slightly accusing. "I love you, but don't think you can take me for granted."

She isn't going to drag me into an argument this time, Logan vowed. In measured strides he bridged the gap between them to tilt her face to his coaxing smile. "I want you with me every moment until we go our separate ways. We have two days left. I don't want to waste precious time debating my intentions. I just want to love you."

Piper felt her knees fold up like an accordion. Hearing his quiet words tore a gash in her heart. This was the beginning of the end, she reminded herself. Logan loved her, but he still intended to let her go. Even what they felt for each other was to be measured in time. Logan had calculated how long it would

405

take him to perform his duties for those who hired him and he had probably calculated (to the exact minute, mind you) when he would push her from his life and cease loving her. Dammit, he was already making plans to turn off his affection for her the moment he planted her on that eastbound stage!

Well, maybe he could switch his emotions on and off, but she couldn't. Piper would love him five hundred miles and ten years from now! She didn't fall in love with every man she met and then jot down a time schedule that would terminate her affection. It hurt her to think Logan could do so. It was a maddening thought, and Piper felt inclined to punch him soundly for even suggesting they had two days left to love each other.

The man was incredible. If he thought she would fit perfectly into his designated time slot he had better think again! If she had two days she would concentrate all her efforts into making them the most memorable forty-eight hours of his life. And he damned well better regret shoving her into that stagecoach and closing the door on the past. She didn't want to become a forgotten memory in the cluttered cavity of his mind! Blast it, what was it going to take to dissuade Logan from sending her away? Piper needed a miracle.

Piper contemplated her alternatives as they gathered her luggage and sneaked across the roof of the hotel. While they galloped east across the rough terrain she continued to ponder her dilemma. Piper decided to show Logan what their life would be like if she were allowed to spend the next century with him instead of the next two days. She was going to love him so thoroughly and completely that he couldn't imagine life without her. If he thought for one minute that she was going to give him up without doing all within her power to strengthen the feelings between them, he was the crazy one!

The rugged cross-country journey tested Piper's endurance, but she refused to permit weariness to overcome her. She never once complained about the long, grueling hours in the saddle as they picked their way along the shortcut to reach the site Logan had selected for the robbery.

Piper even let a few arguments pass for the sake of tranquility. She employed all she had learned from her experiences in the West to prove to Logan that she could fit into his world. Nor did she succumb to the nausea that had plagued her every morning for the past week. She knew the reason for her queasiness, but she was not about to tell Logan she was carrying his child. Piper promised herself she would not try to trap him, to make him feel an obligation to her. If not for love, she wouldn't want to stay with him. He had to love her without feeling trapped simply because he had fathered a child.

Logan will no longer be able to fall back on the excuse that I can't adapt to the code of the West, Piper promised herself. Maybe she couldn't match Logan's abilities and strengths, but she would be damned if she became more hindrance than help to him. If he wanted her to rob the confounded stage—for whatever reason—then she would do it, and he would have to admire her for her courage. Logan wasn't going to cast her off because she couldn't handle any situation he thrust her into! No sirree, he would have to dream up some other flimsy excuse to send her away.

In silent admiration, Logan watched Piper climb down from her steed to drink from the spring that bubbled up from the rocks. She had voiced not one discouraging word while they wound through the treacherous mountain passes to reach their destination. The time they had saved by cutting through mountains where the stage couldn't go would enable them to intercept the coach when it veered back to the north.

One would have thought Piper had been born in the saddle the way she was behaving, Logan mused. Her previous experiences had prepared her for this last test of endurance and she had met the challenge superbly. It left him to wonder if—

Logan squelched the whimsical thought. He had decided what was best for her and he was standing firm, even if he *had* begun to picture her at his ranch, settling into his way of life. This delicate beauty wasn't as far out of her element as she had once been, but he couldn't provide her with the luxuries she had come to know in the East, luxuries a woman like Piper deserved. He would feel obligated to import expensive furnishings that would match her elegant tastes. Arizona was still a raw country, most of the land resisted the influences of civilization. . . .

"Are we going to ride or do you intend to stand there dawdling for another quarter of an hour?" Piper inquired, dragging Logan from his pensive deliberations. She playfully patted his behind, urging him to his steed. "It's time to ride. We're wasting daylight."

An amused grin hovered on Logan's lips as he watched Piper settle herself in the saddle. Damn if she didn't beat anything he'd ever seen—from regal princess to sturdy tomboy in a matter of a few months. Why, she had even practiced riding all over her horse like the Comanches and Apaches. She had taken target practice each time they had the opportunity to ride at full gallop, shooting piñon trees and cacti as if they were desperados. Once, she had practically twisted his head off his shoulders as she breezed by to plant an unexpected kiss on his lips.

Piper had certainly come into her own these past few weeks. She was teeming with undaunted spirit and newfound confidence. These days, what she didn't think she could do (and the list had dwindled to a scant few) she didn't think needed to be done. She was living every minute to its fullest, even under the most adverse conditions.

She looked absolutely radiant! There was an unexplainable glow in her cheeks, a mystical sparkle in her eyes. Although Logan doubted it was truly love that made the difference, he was bewitched. If Logan hadn't been pressed for time he would have scooped Piper up, carried her off to a secluded spot, and made wild, sweet love to her instead of settling for those tormenting kisses that left him wanting more than a hasty embrace delivered from horseback!

But when this was all over Logan was going to treat himself to the pleasure of . . . Logan halted in midthought. There could be no more nights like the one they'd shared in her hotel room. When they stopped the stage, Piper would be placed inside it. There wouldn't be time for passionate goodbyes, not with the driver and conductor milling about. Knowing he would never be permitted to reexperience the rapture they'd shared soured Logan's mood. Suddenly, Piper's incessant cheerfulness irritated him. She had accepted the way of things better than he had, and he was the one who had declared this was the way things were going to be! Didn't she feel even any remorse about leaving him to return to her world? Was she planning to forget him the moment she took a seat on the stagecoach?

Logan growled under his breath. Whose crazy idea was this anyway? He should have told Piper why he was holding up the stage and he should have left her in Tucson to catch the next coach. All he had succeeded in doing was torturing himself by speculating on what life would be like if he kept Piper with him. Now it would be even more difficult to let her go than it had been before.

"Why are you looking as sour as curdled milk?" Piper queried when she noticed his unpleasant expression.

"Because I . . ." Logan caught himself before he translated his disturbing thoughts to tongue. "Because I have a rotten disposition," he mumbled lamely. "And I'll be glad when I can part company with Sam. We're beginning to look and smell too much alike!"

"Oh?" Piper bit back a grin. "The buckskin mare and I have developed quite a friendship. I'm going to miss her terribly. I've grown accustomed to her."

"I suppose you plan to take a job somewhere along the way, training horses," he smirked sarcastically.

"I might, now that I've got the hang of riding," she replied cheerfully. "And I'm beginning to prefer the wide open range. I don't think I will appreciate the city, where I'll be forced to share my space with a dozen other people."

Logan gaped at her. "You're serious," he realized and said it aloud.

"Perfectly serious," she declared with great conviction. "Who knows, Logan, you might be tracking across the Southwest one day and see me camped out on my own claim, raising horses." Her green eyes settled on his bearded face. "I'm not going back to Chicago. The city isn't big enough for my stepfather and me. I could barely tolerate having him under the same roof. Having him in the same town won't help matters all that much."

"If I decide to come looking for you, where do you suppose I might find you?" Logan asked and then frowned. He had never considered that possibility before. He shouldn't be contemplating it now, either. When this lovely bird spread her wings and migrated east, that was that. She would be out of sight and Logan would put her out of his mind. He had to if he intended to keep his sanity.

A mischievous grin alighted Piper's tanned features, giving them an enhanced glow. "You're the private detective, Logan. Legend has it that you can find anybody anywhere, even those who don't wish to be found. But to make the task easier, I will tell you this much. I might wind up somewhere in Texas."

"It's a big state," Logan snorted grouchily.

"But you have a nose like a bloodhound, eyes like an eagle, and a compass implanted in your head," she complimented him. "If anyone could find me, you could."

"People tend to mix fact with fiction," Logan grumbled. "I'm not an immortal god who knows all and sees all!"

"All this and modesty too," she exclaimed as she leaned out to bestow a fleeting kiss to his pouting lips. "I love you . . . even if you aren't an immortal god. But in my opinion, you are as close as anyone could ever get."

Logan's hand snaked out, intending to drag Piper from her saddle and onto his lap, but his hand dropped limply by his side when he realized they had reached their destination. They had last-minute preparations to make, and he was denied what he really wanted.

Gesturing for Piper to dismount, Logan strode over to brace his hands against the boulder that was perched on the rocky ledge. Together he and Piper set off a landslide of rock and dirt that tumbled onto the winding path below. The scattered debris would prevent the stage from rumbling east until a path had been cleared.

After picking their way down the steep cliff, Logan located two niches that would conceal them from sight. A stern frown clouded his brow as he peered down at the midget highwayman whose face was disguised behind a kerchief.

"Don't take any reckless chances," he warned solemnly.

"The idea is to get the drop on the stage agents, not to drill them full of holes like you did the trees and cacti we passed along the way."

Piper nodded and shifted nervously from one foot to the other. "You never did tell me what this robbery is supposed to accomplish," she reminded him.

Logan tipped back her oversized Stetson to press a kiss to her brow. "You'll find out soon enough, love. But with your help, we're going to tie up some loose ends for Butterfield."

Piper flung him a withering glance. "By robbing his stage? I don't see how . . ."

"Just follow my lead and obey my orders for once!" he instructed.

When Logan turned and walked away, Piper was stung by the realization that they had just ended their last private conversation, one that was being cut short by the sound of the approaching coach. She tugged the kerchief from her face and dashed after Logan. Leaning full length against him, she kissed him for a long, breathless moment. The kiss she delivered carried enough heat to wilt a saguaro cactus and fry a mesquite bush to a crisp. As she withdrew, her green eyes searched those shimmering pools of silver.

"I wish I had time to prove how much I love you," she whispered, her voice quivering with emotion.

Reverently, Logan's hand glided over her creamy cheek. "Enough to . . ." Logan compressed his lips. Dammit, he knew what was best for Piper. He had to bear that in mind and suppress his fanciful whims. The haunting words Jenny had spoken to him exploded in his head. She had predicted that Piper would tire of the inconveniences and lack of luxuries in the West and be gone in a month. It was difficult enough to let Piper go now. If he kept her with him for another month and then lost her it would be worse than tearing off a leg. "Piper, I . . ." Logan expelled a sigh and relinquished his attempt to speak.

Piper itched to reach down his throat and drag out the rest of the question he had very nearly posed so she could answer it. Damn this stubborn man. Why wouldn't he ask her to stay?

Mulling over a dozen tormenting thoughts, Logan stalked

toward his crevice between the rocks and squatted down on his haunches. Within a few minutes he would know whether Piper would even want to remain with him, whether she truly loved him as much as she claimed she did.

Logan had purposely refrained from explaining why he wanted to halt this particular stage. He wanted to view Piper's reaction when she learned the truth. Then he would know, at a glance, if what she felt for him was strong and lasting or if she truly had mistaken love for desperation, if she was simply grasping at security.

Of course, it wouldn't change anything, he reminded himself sensibly, but at least he would no longer be tormented by doubts—the same doubts that had lingered since he found himself so obsessed with this feisty beauty. In a few minutes Piper's life was going to change drastically. How she responded to the truth would provide Logan with important answers. For his own peace of mind he had to know if what she felt for him was truly love—the kind that couldn't be begged, borrowed, or sold if the price was right. . . .

Chapter 28

The sound of thundering hooves forced Logan to inch further into his corner. Determinedly, he focused on the cloud of dust that billowed above the winding path. As Logan had anticipated, the driver stomped on the brake when he rounded the corner to see the blockade of rock and dirt. The driver's abrupt attempt to halt the coach threw the conductor off balance, and he clung desperately to the belt that held him on his perch. Before either man had time to reach for his weapon, Logan charged from his hiding place with both Colts trained on the agents. Piper emerged behind the coach, her pistol pointed at the lone passenger who stared incredulously at the highwaymen.

"Step out, Channing," Logan ordered brusquely.

With his hands held high above his head, Burgess Channing clambered from the coach. A disgruntled scowl framed his harsh features, causing the corners of his mouth to turn down more than they normally did.

"You're not supposed to hold me up," Burgess grumbled quietly to Logan. He didn't know exactly who had committed this error since the bandit's kerchief and hat concealed his identity, but Burgess voiced the remark, just the same.

Piper was surprised to see Burgess Channing and even more astonished by his discreet comment to Logan. Just what the devil was going on here? she wondered.

"Get Mr. Channing's satchel," Logan ordered Piper, paying not the slightest bit of attention to Burgess's remark.

Burgess, heavy-footed though he was, scampered toward the coach.

"Take one more step and you won't live to stand trial for theft and murder." The click of the trigger emphasized Logan's threat. Burgess froze in his tracks. "The satchel . . ." he prompted Piper, who was glancing back and forth between Burgess and Logan.

Still bemused, Piper moved toward the coach, keeping a cautious eye on Burgess, who was suddenly as nervous as a caged cat. When she had retrieved the bag, Channing growled at the midget thief and then at the brawny giant.

Contempt swallowed Burgess's harsh features. "Who are you?" he demanded to know.

Logan tugged the kerchief from his face, exposing his devilish smile. It took Burgess a moment to recognize the man behind the dark beard and mustache. But when he did, his eyes bulged from their sockets.

"I thought you were dead!" the driver, conductor, and Burgess Channing croaked in unison.

"I got better," Logan smirked.

Burgess gazed frantically about him, searching for a means of escape, but Logan kept both pistols trained on him. When Logan ordered Piper to open the satchel for inspection, her startled gasp broke the brittle silence. The bag was heaped with money, and Logan carefully scrutinized Piper as she stared wide-eyed at the stacks of crisp bank notes.

"It's yours," Logan told Piper who was still gaping at the satchel in disbelief.

"But how can that be?" Piper chirped incredulously. "The Apaches stole it from the men who were massacred at the shack near Superstition Mountain."

Logan gave his head a contradicting shake. "What you saw were renegade Apaches, hired by Burgess Channing and paid with rifles, ammunition, and whiskey, to dispose of the desperados who had tried to double-cross him. Burgess is the ringleader of the outlaw gangs that have been terrorizing the stage line and preying on silver miners in the area. Sheriff Epperson was his right-hand man."

Piper's wide green eyes flew back to Burgess, who was

swearing under his breath after hearing the female voice. "But why would Burgess escort me to the shack if he was involved and already had possession of the money?"

"For the same reason he had Sheriff Epperson dispose of Grant Fredricks and attempt to have you convicted of his murder," Logan elaborated. "Burgess is the one who has been seeing to it that supplies and livestock were stolen from the stage stations. When Butterfield was forced to allocate money to replenish the stolen goods, Burgess sold them back to him. But Burgess didn't know about the stolen quarter of a million dollars until Grant went to him for assistance.

"When Burgess realized some of his men had kept the cash for themselves without informing him, he went to retrieve it. And then he sent the Apaches to kill the pack of thieves while the two of you were there to witness the massacre. It was Burgess's way of forcing you to relinquish your search for the missing money."

Logan's gaze was focused on Piper's shocked face, gauging her reaction to the information he was giving her. "But all the while your money was safely tucked in Burgess's safe. All those who knew about the cash were either dead or had been strongly discouraged from attempting to recover it." His steel gray eyes swung to Burgess, who was scowling furiously. "All except Sheriff Epperson, that is," he amended. "And Epperson was kind enough to fill in the missing pieces of the puzzle after I interrogated him."

"Where is he?" Burgess growled venomously.

"Epperson and the rest of your hoodlums are on their way to the fort to stand trial." He raked Burgess with scornful mockery. "I knew you were responsible for the robberies and the theft of Piper's money, but I couldn't figure out why you preyed so heavily on Butterfield until Epperson explained it to me and then confessed that you intended to travel to Fort Smith to make Butterfield an offer for his stage line."

"That bastard," Burgess snarled, his homely face twisting in a scowl.

"Don't misunderstand," Logan cautioned with a deadly smile. "It was pain that freed his tongue. I didn't let him alone until he told me why you were posing as a respectable business man while you ramrodded your band of thieves." Dry laughter tumbled from Logan's lips as he watched Burgess squirm in his clothes. "You thought you had come into a stroke of luck when you discovered there was a quarter of a million dollars floating around Superstition Mountain. You had been preying on Butterfield, hoping he would become discouraged and sell out to you. It was your belief that whoever owned the stage route to the West would be in perfect position to acquire vast wealth when the railroad finally joins with California. You were going to ensure the rail companies paid dearly for the right to follow the Butterfield Trail.

"After you laid your hands on Piper's money, it gave you the opportunity to approach Butterfield with a proposition to purchase his company without completely draining your ill-gotten funds." His intimidating smirk caused Burgess to jerk up his head and glare. "And of course, you had no fear of carrying so much money on a stage that has been plagued by outlaws because they all worked for you."

"How did you know I . . ." Burgess growled in frustration, only to be cut off by another round of goading laughter.

"I suspected you were involved because you have been replenishing Butterfield with livestock that he had been buying from me," Logan declared. "Suddenly, Butterfield was able to purchase stock from you for a lower price than I could sell it to him. You had been involved in setting up the stage stations and furnishing them with supplies ever since Butterfield won his contract to carry mail. You were on the inside, but it annoyed you that Butterfield was making money hand over fist and you were only making a decent living. Your greed provoked you to undermine his operation. You have been stealing Butterfield blind, coming and going, waiting the chance to buy him out and gain sole possession of the route that joins the East with the riches in California."

Piper, engrossed in Logan's explanation, made the crucial mistake of crossing in front of his line of fire to stand by his side. But Burgess was ready and waiting. The moment Piper passed directly between him and Logan, Burgess pounced.

A startled squawk burst from Piper's lips as her pistol was ripped from her fingertips. Burgess hooked his left arm around her neck and yanked her body against his as a shield. Her own pistol lay at her throat and Piper cursed her stupidity. Her critical mistake prevented Logan from firing at Burgess while she was held captive in his arms.

"Drop 'em, Logan," Burgess demanded gruffly.

Rage claimed Logan's chiseled features and he cursed himself for bringing Piper along with him. He had decided Piper should have the right to steal back the money that had been stolen three times. It was to have been her compensation for the trials and tribulations she had been forced to endure. Now she was held prisoner by a desperate man, and Logan would have to shoot through her to get to Burgess. Damn!

"Don't you dare drop your pistols," Piper screeched, as Logan looked as if he were about to lower his hands.

"You're a fool," Burgess hissed in her ear. "You'll wind up dead."

"But my consolation comes in knowing Logan will see to it that I will take you with me," Piper growled back at him.

Logan's body was taut. He wasn't certain what Piper's courageous performance was supposed to accomplish. But if she managed to distract Burgess for a split-second, that was all Logan needed. His aim was as good as his eyesight and he was eager to get the chance to fire at his target.

When Piper moved she set off a chain reaction. With no concern for her own safety, Piper elbowed Burgess in the midsection, causing him to bend at the waist. As he bowed slightly, she twisted to kick his shin. In a burst of fury, Piper jerked both arms upward, forcing the pistol away from her throat. Burgess was so surprised by her daring and her painful blows that he momentarily loosened his grasp on her. She ducked away before Burgess could recapture her. Frantic, Burgess glared into Logan's stormy gray eyes and grim frown. Burgess knew his only option was to put a quick bullet through the skillful shootist who stood directly in front of him.

Pistols barked like rabid dogs and the battle was over as swiftly as it had begun. When the gray clouds of smoke that exploded from the pistols had cleared away, Logan's features were frozen in a menacing glare. For several seconds he didn't move or even bat an eyelash. A few seconds later only the muscle in Logan's jaw twitched as he stood poised behind his smoking gun barrels. It was then and only then that Piper was allowed her first true glimpse of the legendary shootist. He had iron-clad control—like a well-oiled machine that defied death without the slightest hint of fear in those steel gray eyes. Only now did the full impact of Logan's dynamic personality hit her. Piper realized then and there that Logan had been generous in his dealings with her in the past. If she had seen him in action before she met him in Fort Smith she doubted she would have found the nerve to approach him. The look he gave Burgess Channing was enough to send a grizzly bear into early hibernation! There were times when Piper had purposely antagonized Logan, just to see if he would let her get away with it. She hadn't comprehended what privileges he had granted her until now.

Still standing before his challenger, Burgess stared at Logan with a mutinous sneer on his face. As he grimaced to cock the trigger of the pistol a second time, the color waned from Burgess's ruddy cheeks. With his last bit of strength, Burgess squeezed the trigger, but Logan's Colts barked again. Burgess flinched as two more shots penetrated his flesh.

"Damn you, half-breed bastard . . ." Burgess growled.

"The last two shots were for Piper and what you tried to do to her at Superstition Mountain," Logan sneered as he watched Burgess pitch forward to sprawl facedown in the dirt. His chest heaved as he expelled his last breath, and Logan felt no regret in seeing Burgess removed to a lower sphere.

In calm, smooth precision, Logan slid his Colts to their holsters, but relief didn't wash over his craggy features. They were masked behind a carefully controlled stare. Piper, however, was as transparent as glass. She was relieved and it showed in her lovely face as she scrambled to her feet and dashed to Logan.

To her amazement, she was grasped by the elbows instead of being cuddled in the protective circle of his arms. Logan shook her so hard her hat fell to the ground and her hair tumbled from its bun in wild disarray.

All the restrained emotion that Logan had kept bottled up for the past few minutes suddenly erupted. "Jeezus, woman!"

he scowled into Piper's peaked face. "You scared ten years off my life with that daring stunt! Dammit, you could have gotten yourself killed!"

His harsh, booming voice and his rough manhandling caused her temper to snap. "What do you care?" she hurled at him. "You wanted me out of your life anyway. One way is just as good as another. You are planning to deposit me on this cursed stage and wave goodbye."

Her brows puckered in an irritated frown. "And dammit yourself! You knew Burgess was leading me on a wild goose chase to that mountain cabin. You let me tear off across the desert on a will-o'-the-wisp, chasing after a tribe of Apaches, knowing full well they didn't have my money! You've been laughing behind my back the whole blessed time!"

"I didn't puzzle out what happened to your inheritance until we were on the desert," Logan maintained hotly. "I've been so damned busy watching you flirt with disaster that I didn't have the time to sit myself down and fit all the pieces together."

The driver and conductor smiled wryly at each other as they cleared a path around the fallen debris. They loaded the limp body of the ringleader of the desperados in the cab and climbed back on the stage. Logan and Piper were so busy shouting at each other that they failed to notice the stage agents were quietly going about their business.

"Well, you could have told me about your suspicions on our way back to Tucson," Piper bellowed in indignation. "But you purposely withheld that information and let me live through the torment of thinking my inheritance was gone forever. You even made me admit to you that I was tracking a lost cause!"

"I couldn't tell you where your money was," Logan countered just as loudly. "Knowing what a daredevil you are, you probably would have done something crazy like stamp into Burgess's office and hold him at gunpoint. If he suspected trouble and beat a hasty retreat it would have taken me weeks to round him up. I would still be rushing hither and yon, seeing to the arrangements of sending the outlaws to jail and preventing you from throwing yourself in harm's way all over again."

Logan thrust his growling face into Piper's. "And I don't

know what you're so damned fired up about anyway, woman. I made certain you got your money back. That's what you wanted since you migrated west. It wasn't love you claimed to feel for me. It was simple desperation. You only admitted you cared about me when you had nothing else left, when you thought your inheritance was gone forever. Now that you have your money back you're picking fights with me again!"

"I am not!" Piper argued.

"The hell you aren't," Logan snapped.

"I am merely pointing out that you are dead wrong," Piper assured him tartly.

"I'm dead right," Logan contradicted. "At first you clung to hope, praying you'd recover your fortune. And when you thought your crusade had ended in defeat you were content to settle for the second best thing around—an uncultured half-breed who had money to burn! I wasn't your sole concern. I was your consolation prize. And now that you have your goddamn money you don't need my love!"

"What love?" she scoffed into his thunderous scowl. "The forty-eight hours of love you intended to spare me before you shoved me on the stage and sent me packing?"

Piper was so furious she wanted to beat Logan to a pulp. His logic was twisted and his brain obviously consisted of wet noodles. He never listened; he always assumed what she was thinking. When she told him what was really on her mind and in her heart he reduced it to his own conclusions. Since they were not sharing the same brain it was impossible for him to know how she felt, but that didn't stop this domineering man from trying to analyze her thoughts!

With a wordless growl, Piper wheeled about and stamped over to retrieve the discarded satchel. Reaching inside, she clenched a wad of money in her fist and hurled it in Logan's frowning face. "You take this cussed money. I don't want it," she shouted for all she was worth. "I loved you long before I became desperate. The truth of the matter is I was determined in my search because I thought that was all I had, that you would never get around to loving me back. And when Jenny informed me that the two of you were going to be married, my quest for the stolen money was all I had left to motivate me. I knew I had lost you, that you loved Jenny, not me—not the misplaced bluestocking who couldn't fit into your world."

Piper inhaled a quick breath, her breasts heaving beneath her oversized jacket. "But you didn't want me to fit in. You constantly ridiculed me, discouraged me. I've heard you tell me to go back where I belong so many times I'm sick of it!

"You have decided what is best for me." Piper stabbed him in the chest with her index finger to emphasize her point, even though her sharp voice was punctuation in itself. "You kept the truth about my inheritance from me because it benefited your scheme to capture Burgess and his band of desperados. Well, what about what I want? You never once asked me what I wanted," Piper reminded him angrily. "You just keep telling me what you think I need. But the last thing I need is for a muleheaded man to tell me how to think and what to do!"

Logan stared incredulously at the fuming beauty. She looked like hell. Smudges of dirt and perspiration were smeared on her elegant cheeks. Her waist-length hair was in such a tangle it resembled a bird's nest. The man's garb she wore was powdered with dust.

Is this the same cultured, sophisticated Easterner I met in Fort Smith? he asked as his gaze ran the full length of Piper. She had once been an inexperienced city slicker, but not anymore. She was a full-fledged hellion who wouldn't back down from the devil himself if he made the foolish mistake of crossing her. There was a time when harsh words and burning insults reduced Piper to tears. But no longer. This feisty female had gained confidence in herself and her abilities. No one could tell her what to do now that she had acquired such self-assurance and daring.

Jeezus! I've created a monster, Logan realized. If he dared to scoop her up and set her on the stage she would be kicking and biting and screaming. . . .

Startled silver eyes swept the abandoned road. The conductor and driver had removed enough rock from the barricade to ease the coach around it and they had quietly gone their way during the shouting match. Logan had been so involved in bellowing accusations and insults that he had failed to notice the coach's departure. Hell, he would have to hold up the confounded stage a second time if he wanted to stuff this spitfire in it!

Taking advantage of the silence, Piper dragged in a deep breath and proceeded to tell Logan what she wanted since he wasn't considerate enough to ask. "What I want is to stay in New Mexico Territory and buy half interest in your ranch," she informed him. "I want to raise horses and supply Butterfield with sturdy livestock to draw his coaches. I want to live in sin with you, sharing your bed and your home without marrying you because I don't want to lay claim to half your fortune when you get yourself killed by some vicious murderer who would shoot you in the back if he gets the chance. I don't want to marry a gunslinger and live with the fear that you might not return from one of your crusades for justice. I don't want you to think I am interested in your money, so don't think I would marry you, even if you got down on bended knee and proposed!"

"Now wait just a damned minute," Logan blared in annoyance. "I'm not raising bastard children who don't carry my name. I've lived with that stigma all my life and my children are not going to endure the same humiliation." His chest swelled to gigantic proportions as he glowered down into her flushed face. "If we're going to live together I demand legal license to fight with you. We're going to do it right and proper or we will not do it at all!"

"Since when did you become so blasted noble and respectable?" she sniffed sarcastically. "I thought you didn't give a fig about propriety. You certainly condemned me for it on dozens of occasions. It didn't sting your conscience when you stole my virginity. I certainly can't see why it would bother you now."

"Because I love you, dammit!" Logan barked sharply. "And that makes all the difference."

Two perfectly arched brows jackknifed over her sparkling green eyes. "How much, Logan?" she wanted to know. "Enough to let me stay and share your life with you? Enough to consider my feelings instead of deciding what I need without asking me? Enough to share decisions that concern both of us instead of making up your mind and plowing ahead like a stubborn mule? Enough to take off your pistols and lead a normal life?"

Logan growled under his breath as he reached down to unfasten his trousers. She had him making all sorts of concessions. Why not give her his masculinity as well? Hell, she had practically taken everything else! "Don't you want to wear the pants in the family too?" he smirked caustically. "Here, take them if that will satisfy you, but for God's sake stop arguing with me!"

A hint of a smile tugged at the corner of Piper's mouth as she stared at Logan's drooping trousers. "I don't want your breeches, only one leg of them. But most important, I want the man in them," she specified.

"Well, don't expect me to ask to share your wardrobe just because I'm willing to give you a leg of my breeches," he snorted in offended dignity. "Jeezus, Piper, what am I to get out of this arrangement after all the demands you've made?"

"Me," she answered, batting her big green eyes at him.

"And what makes you such a bargain?" he scoffed sarcastically.

Undaunted, Piper reached up to soothe away the tension in the taut tendons of his jaw. "You love me and that makes me special," she murmured proudly. As of yet, Logan hadn't said she could stay and share his life, but neither had he ordered her to go, even when he admitted he loved her.

"Honestly, woman, you are impossible." Logan laughed at himself. Just listen to him! Now he had resorted to uttering Piper's favorite expression. She had become so much a part of him that he was beginning to sound just like her.

"Does that mean you'll sell me half your ranch and let me reside there with you?" she questioned in a softer tone.

It was staring into those enormous green eyes that dominated her face that finally did it. Logan was instantly reminded of the wide-eyed, innocent expression that tugged at the strings of his heart when he first met her. That vivid memory, compounded by the bewitching face that was staring up at him at this very moment, made up Logan's mind for him. He could easily picture an emerald-eyed little girl who was the lovely image of her mother—the mother of *his* children. . . .

For the first time in his life Logan let his guard down completely. He didn't care what was for the best anymore. He only knew he wanted Piper with him always. Reason couldn't counteract the love he felt for this feisty pixie. He wanted the chance to love her as he had loved no one else in his life. But he was not, *not*, he fiercely assured himself, not going to live with this gorgeous creature without giving her his name. Hell, she had everything else except his name. And once he had nothing left to give away he would have everything to gain. . . .

Logan frowned at his paradoxical thoughts. Was he making any sense at all? Of course he was. If giving in to this proud beauty meant he could keep her forever, then he would have all he ever wanted, all he had once doubted a man like him could ever possess. If not for love, what was there in life? Logan asked himself. He had already learned from experience that fame and fortune formed the stuff of empty dreams if there was no one to share them with. If not for love, he would be burning two-dollar bills all his life instead of laying gifts at Piper's feet—gifts to complement her rare beauty, gifts to express all the tender emotion he felt for her.

Beneath the fringe of thick black lashes, Logan peered down at the disheveled minx who had come to mean more to him than life itself. Deftly he drew his pistol and aimed it at her, causing her to stare at him in bewildered astonishment.

"So that's the way of things, is it?" Piper snapped in irritation. "If someone disagrees with you, you just whip out your Colt and blow them to kingdom come."

"Yes, that's the way of things," Logan assured her, biting back a sly smile. "You are going to agree to marry me or I'll use the same methods of persuasion on you that I used on Epperson."

Piper didn't dare ask how many kinds of torture his methods of persuasion entailed. She didn't want to know. But she wasn't backing down, no matter what Logan threatened to do to her. There would be no marriage unless Logan turned from a freelance gunman to a full-time rancher. She wasn't going to spend the weeks while he was away, wondering if she were soon to be a widow, nor did she want his fortune when she had one of her own.

"There isn't going to be a wedding," Piper told him courageously.

Logan's shoulders slumped. He had been able to stare down everyone except this daring nymph. She didn't believe he would shoot her. There had been times the past few months that he would have liked to, but he hadn't.

"All right," Logan conceded begrudgingly. "I won't hire myself out to anyone, if that's what you want. Now will you marry me?"

Piper removed the Colt from his hand and replaced it in its holster. Her arms wound around his shoulders to bring his lips down to her kiss. "Then in that case, I would very much like to be your wife." Her supple body moved provocatively against his, arousing needs that had lain dormant for more days than Logan cared to count. "And about those ten years I scared from your life . . ." she murmured softly. "I promise to love every one of them back on again. . . ."

"Now?" Logan chirped in surprise.

"Have you something better to do?" she inquired with a seductive smile.

"I can't think of a solitary thing," he breathed as he bent to taste her inviting lips once again. "Jeezus, woman, do you know how much I love you?"

"I honestly believe I do." The fact that Logan had consented to relinquish his dangerous way of life without putting up too much fuss was testimony in itself. "But I'm eager to see some proof of your devotion. . . ."

Logan located an open-ended cave formed by the boulders. A cool breeze wafted its way through the secluded tunnel. Distracted by the radiant smile that claimed Piper's enchanting features, Logan spread the pallet he had retrieved from his stallion.

In open admiration Piper studied the whipcord muscles that flexed and relaxed as Logan doffed his shirt. He had the body a Roman god would envy, she mused with feminine appreciation. He was bronzed and masculine and perfectly formed. His jet black hair, thick brows, and curly lashes complemented his appealing characteristics. Piper swore she would never tire of gazing at him. He was so tantalizing to the eye—all rippling

425

muscle and potential energy waiting to burst into action. What she felt for this rough-edged giant defied words and left her trembling with heartfelt emotion. She longed to convey what words couldn't express, to assure him that he meant more to her than all the riches life had to offer.

Removing one garment after another as she approached, Piper stood shamelessly before him. She adored the way those shimmering silver eyes roamed possessively over her. She wanted his eyes, the gentle stroke of his hands, the warm draft of his breath mingling with hers. Piper had never felt so whole and alive, so in love. It was a wild, heady sensation that caused her to arch toward him, to twine her fingers behind his neck and hold him close.

Logan's hands settled on her trim waist. A shudder riveted through him when the peaks of her breasts teased his hair-matted chest. In the past, Logan had held back that one small corner of his heart when he surrendered to the chaotic emotions Piper aroused in him. It had been a protective instinct within him. He had always thought in terms of a future without this bewitching nymph there beside him. Logan told himself there would still be life after Piper had gone home where she belonged. But now he had no defense left because the plain simple truth was he couldn't imagine life after Piper. She was here with him and she was going to stay. Logan was hopelessly devoted to ensuring her happiness, to protecting and cherishing her with every breath he took. They would share each precious tomorrow together and he would go on loving her through eternity.

As if he were handling fragile crystal, Logan lifted Piper from her feet. Her pliant body moved softly against his, dragging a tormented groan from his lips. Bending her into his hard contours, Logan took her with him to their pallet and stretched out beside her.

The world careened about them as his open mouth sought hers once again. Her body quivered in excitement as his bold caresses spread a path of living fire over every inch of her flesh. It was sweet, maddening torment, the kind that left Piper wondering if she could survive and yet not caring if she didn't. She was prepared to sacrifice her last breath for a dozen more kisses like the one Logan bestowed on her.

Like a dedicated sculptor, Logan kneaded and stroked her pliant body until she felt like clay in his skillful hands. And then, like a master craftsman, Logan brought her to life, leaving her writhing with the want of him.

Waves of fire rippled through Piper when Logan's kisses drifted over each throbbing bud. Her body went up in flame as his sensuous lips followed the titillating path of his hands. Longing uncoiled within her, intensifying her ardent need for him. Her overworked heart hammered inside her chest and her breath came in ragged gasps. He was doing the most incredible things to her body and she ached to the core of her being, ached to take him to her and love him for all the yesterdays they had been apart.

His name burst from her lips as his kisses and caresses descended across her quaking flesh. Her voice echoed through the shadowed cavern and then rolled back upon her as Logan continued his exquisite fondling. Piper swore he had sprouted an extra dozen set of hands. They were everywhere, stirring, massaging, arousing. She could feel his soft utterances upon her skin as his lips glided to and fro, worshiping her, enticing her until she arched toward him in wild abandon.

But each time she reached up to him, yearning to have all of him, Logan stilled her restless hands. "In time, sweet nymph," he promised huskily, "but for now, let me show you all the ways I love you. You have much more to learn about passion. . . ."

Piper thought Logan had taught her all there was to know about lovemaking. But she soon discovered how wrong she had been. The wild desire she had experienced in the past was a mere stepping stone that led into this dark, sensual world he now unveiled to her. Passion embroidered with love was not the "little death" the French called this wondrous pleasure. Piper swore it was the acquisition of infinity. There was not even one distant star she couldn't touch when she was soaring in Logan's arms. She could fly into the sun to be consumed by its holocaust of fire and yet the flames couldn't destroy her. She could reach out to grasp the pastel colors of the rainbow and hold them in the palm of her hand. She could glide through one corridor of ecstasy into another—seeing, feeling, touching each wondrous sensation.

Only one door in that magical castle in the air hadn't opened to her, could not open until she was one with Logan. She pleaded with him to satisfy her greatest whim, to love her with his body, mind, and heart.

Logan couldn't believe how wild her passions, how sweet the emotions that surged through him. Piper rasped his name as she welcomed him with open arms and took him into her, holding him as if she meant to go on holding him forever. Mindlessly he thrust into her, setting the frantic cadence of passion. His body was molten lava flowing upon hers, melting into her to become one living, breathing flame that illuminated the darkness.

The mere thought of the unrivaled intimacy they shared sent shivers chasing each other down Logan's spine. Never had loving Piper been so savage and yet so sweet. It contradicted itself each time one ineffable sensation avalanched upon the other. His ravenous need for her was so fierce and all-consuming that it truly frightened him, and yet his love for her was the essence of gentleness. The combination of enigmatic emotions that churned inside him baffled him. Piper had somehow managed to prey on all his feelings until they converged in a single purpose—loving her with every ounce of his being.

If not for this rare, unique love, Logan would never have known what life was all about. He realized now that in their petty arguments they had voiced the same affection, but in a different way. He had been expressing his love, even when he tried to send her away, when he scolded her for taking reckless chances. He hadn't said the exact words, but the feelings had always been there. He had loved her, even when he hadn't wanted to fall prey to these miraculous emotions.

From the beginning he and Piper had been fighting this magnetic attraction for each other. Beneath those harsh words they were conveying subtle messages, the same ones that passed between them now. They cared enough to become angry and jealous and concerned for each other. They cared so deeply that it took very little to set sparks flying between them—all sorts of sparks. They had tried to resist what their hearts and souls must have known from the beginning. For a time reason had restrained love, but the incredible attraction had always been there, boiling beneath the surface. And now the armor of stubborn pride and the shield of fear that protected them against being hurt had fallen away. Raw emotion spilled forth to engulf them. Love had always been there. Fighting the feelings didn't make them go away, it only intensified the needs until they grew and thrived like a lovely cactus flower blossoming in the desert.

That wondrous revelation converged on Logan just as passion diverged to channel through every fiber of his being. A shuddering groan escaped his lips when sublime rapture flooded over his body. For what seemed eternity, Logan was held suspended in flight, somewhere on the other side of a sparkling rainbow.

When his strength finally returned, Logan gathered his feet beneath him and strode, stark naked, to the entrance of the cave. Inhaling a deep breath, he expelled a declaration that raced along the stone precipices and echoed on the road below.

"I love her and she loves me!"

Logan swiveled his head around when he heard the soft giggle behind him. Piper's bewitching smile caused his legs to wobble beneath him. She looked breathtaking lying there, her face flushed with passion, her lips moist from his ravishing kisses, her hair cascading over her shoulders like a waterfall of sunshine and moonbeams. From beneath a veil of curly lashes dancing emerald eyes peeked up at him. She smiled a smile that gave her an inner radiance, and it made Logan go hot all over.

"When I said that you called me crazy," she reminded him in another soft whisper of laughter. She delighted in seeing the boy in this awesome man. Knowing of his past, she doubted Logan had been allowed to be a boy for very long. It was heartwarming to see him succumb to a silly antic.

The late afternoon sun silhouetted Logan's profile as he leaned negligently against the rock wall. "When you said that I thought we were both crazy for loving each other when I knew you would be better off without me . . ."

His quiet remark brought Piper gracefully to her feet.

Holding his silvery gaze she closed the distance between them. Adoringly she traced his craggy features, memorizing each distinct line and curve. "I would have been miserable without you," she assured him. "You color my every thought. You touch each and every emotion. Now that I have your love, the sun burns twice as bright. Because of you, life is full of promise, and if you ever stop loving me, if another woman comes along to pique your interest, I swear my heart will shrivel up and die."

Piper looped her arms over his shoulders and laid her cheek to his chest. "I don't think I could bear losing you now that I know how greatly you have enriched my life."

Logan rested his chin on her head and cradled her against him. He had never felt so loved, so needed. He supposed he would have gone through life trying to satisfy his need to be needed, but Piper had fulfilled that craving to overflowing. "Put your fears to rest, love," he murmured as he hugged her tenderly to him. "No one else has ever stirred me the way you do. I don't know if I'll ever overcome this fierce possession I feel for you. I know how other men's eyes follow you, and there were times when I felt like shooting a few of them for being so obvious in what they were thinking about you, for wanting you the same way I do."

Piper leaned back as far as his encircling arms would allow. "You were jealous?" She was surprised. Logan was adept at disguising his emotions. She never gave it a thought that he might care who stared at her and for what reason.

A bubble of laughter burst from his massive chest. "Hell yes, woman. I could have clobbered Samuel Kirby a time or two when he drooled over you. But, big as he is, I wondered if he would pound me into the ground. I couldn't let him do that while I was so damned busy trying to impress you!"

"I wonder how Samuel is managing at your ranch," Piper mused aloud. "By now he has probably given us both up for lost and Abraham has probably decided I will never come to retrieve him."

Logan sighed heavily. He would prefer to spend the evening in this secluded cave, but it was time he returned to his ranch on the Gila River. Harley and the other marshals would be there waiting for him. There was still the matter of several other unscrupulous stage agents who had yet to be apprehended. Epperson had named names and Logan had to see to it that Burgess Channing's spies, who marked the stages for robbery, were put behind bars.

Although Logan headed toward his ranch, he refused to keep the same relentless pace that had brought him east. Each time he came upon an inviting oasis or spring he paused to reassure Piper of his affection. But she didn't seem to mind the delays. And with each passing day Logan found himself growing deeper in love. And that did indeed seem to be the case. Either that or he was coming down with some rare disease that affected his physical and emotional constitution. Whatever it was, Piper's amorous attention cured his affliction . . . at least temporarily. But the condition continued to flare up each time Logan permitted himself to peer overly long at the shapely beauty who rode beside him.

Logan had one helluva time staying on Sam, and he conjured up a thousand excuses to dismount. It took him days to reach his ranch, but he arrived with a smile on his face and the taste of kisses sweeter than cherry wine on his lips.

PART V

One pair of hands to twine
Love's flowers fair and gay,
And form a wreath divine,
Which never can decay;
And this is all I ask,
One gentle form and fair—
Beneath whose smiles to bask,
And learn love's sweetness there.
                    —Mignon

Chapter 29

From the well-furnished parlor of Logan's hacienda, Harley Newcomb peered out the window at the tall figure of a man and the dwarf rider who approached the ranch. It was Logan all right, Harley assured himself. A man of Logan's size and stature was hard to miss, even at a distance.

"It's about time," Harley grumbled as he moved toward the front door.

The other three deputy marshals, who also awaited Logan's return, followed in Harley's wake. The foursome propped themselves against the supporting beams of the veranda that ran the breadth of the spacious home.

"Who's Logan got with him?" Gorman Rader questioned with a muddled frown.

"Damned if I know," Harley grunted. "Maybe he's dragged home more help." He squinted into the distance to survey the smaller rider. "But the boy doesn't look to be worth his weight, not like Samuel, who boxes the ears off Logan's prize bull each time the ornery scamp charges at him." His amused chuckle drifted in the breeze that caressed the river valley. "The boy Logan has with him must be a new house servant. He doesn't look big enough to wrangle cattle and horses."

While Harley and the other marshals were speculating on what duties the newcomer would attend, Piper peered at the sprawling hacienda from beneath the brim of her oversized Stetson. To hear Logan talk one would have thought he lived in a two-room shack surrounded by stone fences and corrals. But his home couldn't be referred to as a shack, not by any stretch of the imagination. The two-story adobe structure sat like a Spanish-style castle in the desert. Roof timbers extended through the walls and corners and a veranda, shaded by ivy, wrapped around the front and east sides of the house. Iron railings surrounded the balcony of the upper story, providing a perfect lookout to view the vast acres of the ranch.

Piper's surprise and pleasure died beneath the wave of nausea that splashed over her. It had been difficult to hide her queasiness from Logan the past few days, and exhaustion wasn't making it easier to deal with morning sickness that lingered long past noon. Although Piper was assured of Logan's love for her, she hadn't worked up the nerve to confide in him. She wasn't sure how he would accept the news that he would become a father. The adjustment of having her constantly underfoot and having to relinquish his wandering ways was enough for a man like Logan to handle. But the arrival of a child so soon might cause problems. Piper didn't want more trouble after enduring more than three months of it.

Logan reined Sam to a halt and peered down at the four men who had been enjoying his hospitality during his absence. They were all clean-shaven, starched, and pressed, while Logan looked like a bearded vagabond. Lord, what Logan wouldn't give for a bath, a shave, and a soft bed!

"Where the hell have you been so long?" Harley snorted, ignoring the young "lad" whose face was veiled by the shadow of the wide-brimmed hat. "We've been lounging around here for four days and the mail is piled so high it will take a week to answer the correspondences. We've gotten letters, pleading for your assistance in every state from Indian Territory to California."

"A simple hello would have been nice," Logan snorted as he swung from the saddle.

"And what about the wedding?" Gorman Rader wanted to know. "I've got other obligations, but I don't want to miss this monumental occasion."

"The clergyman will be here tomorrow," Logan informed his curious friends.

Harley's brow furrowed. "What about the bride-to-be? Why didn't you bring her with you?"

"I did," Logan replied, biting back a wry smile.

Four pair of wide eyes swung to Piper who, nauseous though she was, tipped back her hat to bless the men with a smile.

Harley sat down on the step before he fell down. "Piper?" he croaked in disbelief. "You're marrying Piper instead of . . ." He bit his tongue when he realized the young lady in men's clothes probably wouldn't appreciate hearing her rival's name blurted out the day before the wedding.

Befuddled, Logan watched all four men dig into their pockets. In a flurry, the ten-dollar gold pieces that had been exchanged after their last wager were tossed back to their original owners, along with an extra ten dollars of winnings. Logan swore he was watching the ritual of the betting exchange that preceded a horse race.

"What was that all about?" Logan queried curiously.

Harley shrugged slightly as he stuffed his newly acquired gold pieces in his pocket. "We had a wager, but those who thought they lost actually won. We were just settling up," he answered cryptically.

A dubious frown furrowed Logan's brow. "I don't suppose you want to explain what the bet was."

Jacob Carter shook his head and grinned. "You don't want to know so don't ask."

Logan had the feeling the wager had something to do with him and Piper, but Jacob was right, it was probably better that he didn't know what was going on.

When the money had been put away, all four men scuttled over to assist Piper from the saddle. After receiving a round of congratulations she was herded into the hacienda for food and drink. Logan couldn't squeeze a word in edgewise since his companions were chattering nonstop to Piper.

Thoughtfully, Logan assessed Piper from over the rim of his glass. For the past few days he had been plagued with the nagging feeling that something was amiss. Although Piper strove to be cheerful he had noticed the meditative frown that knitted her exquisite features when she thought he wasn't looking. Logan began to wonder if Piper was having second

437

doubts about remaining with him in Arizona.

Logan was confident that Piper loved him as much as she claimed she did, but he still detected a hint of remorse, even in her smiles. He was stung by the premonition that she was keeping something from him. Piper had very little appetite of late. Long ago, Logan had learned that Piper refused to eat when she was worried or upset. It was her nature to starve her frustrations rather than to feed them. He was willing to bet something was wrong. And if she dared to spirit away, leaving him standing at the altar, he would hold it over her for the rest of her life . . . !

His meandering thoughts dispersed when Piper rose from the table, murmuring an apology, and left to locate a spare bedroom so she could lie down. The moment she disappeared from sight, Harley focused his full attention on Logan.

"Shall we sift through the correspondence while Piper rests?" he questioned.

Logan gave his shaggy mane a shake and unfolded himself from the chair. "There's no need. You can send an apology, informing each client I can't take the job."

"Reject all of them?" Harley chirped. "But you haven't even heard what—"

"It doesn't matter," Logan interrupted. "I'm retiring my guns."

Harley and the other marshals nearly fell from their chairs. Logan was giving up his rambling ways, forfeiting his legendary reputation? Harley had been after Logan for years to settle down and run his ranch and now, all of a sudden . . . . Piper. A wry smile pursed Harley's lips as Logan moved swiftly toward the door. Who would have thought a woman could have made such a difference in Logan's life? Piper had turned him inside out to reveal the man who had been hiding beneath that hard, callous exterior.

"Well, if that don't beat all," Anthony chuckled. "It looks like I lost another bet."

Harley wanted to bound up the steps and squeeze the stuffing out of Piper. She had accomplished the feat Harley had battled for more than two years. But neither did Harley want to interrupt, since Logan was on his way to see his bride-to-be. Besides, Harley had to collect on another of his bets with Anthony and Jacob, who had wagered Logan would never change his wild ways. They paid for making an error in judgment—twice in the last two hours!

The door banged against the wall as Logan's massive frame filled the entrance to the room Piper had selected to catch a nap. "I want to know what's wrong," he demanded.

Piper rolled onto her back and forced a faint smile. "Nothing is wrong. It's been a long three months and I'm just a mite weary," she lied, but not convincingly enough to suit Logan. He wasn't fooled for a minute.

"Something is wrong and you are going to tell me what it is . . . now!" he growled in irritation. "If you've decided to back out of this marriage, tell me. I don't want to stuff myself into the fancy trappings of a gentleman and stand downstairs tomorrow, wondering if you're planning to sneak off."

"I wouldn't do that to you," Piper protested sharply.

"Oh-ho! Then you are considering calling off the marriage," he accused. His silver eyes narrowed to probe the depths of her soul. "Why?"

"What is bothering me has nothing to do with marriage," she hedged, and then grimaced when the food she had consumed hit like a rock on her queasy stomach.

The harsh frown evaporated from Logan's features. His expression bore evidence of his concern. In two long strides he crossed the room and eased down on the edge of the bed. The mattress sagged beneath his heavy weight and Piper's stomach pitched and rolled, provoking her to groan miserably.

"Dammit, what is wrong with you?" Logan questioned as his hand brushed across her brow. "It's the climate isn't it? You're not accustomed to the heat. Now you're thinking maybe you should go back where you belong."

Irritably, Piper shoved his hand aside. "I am thinking nothing of the kind! Will you stop trying to tell me what I'm thinking." Her lashes fluttered up to note the worry lines that crinkled his ruggedly handsome features. "What I am actually thinking is you are not going to be able to handle this on top of all else just now. . . ." Piper licked her bone-dry lips and gulped hard.

Logan growled in frustration. "Now you're trying to tell me what I'm thinking! Jeezus, woman, what is it I'm not going to be able to handle on top of what else? If you don't stop talking in riddles you'll drive me mad!"

It was obvious Logan wasn't going to leave her to her misery until she confided in him. And he was a master at dragging information from people, even if he had to resort to drastic measures. Piper formulated and discarded several tactful methods of broaching the subject but she was too tired and nauseous to be diplomatic.

"You have yet to adjust to the idea of marriage and already you are going to be forced to grow accustomed to the idea of being a father," she blurted out. There, she had said it. Now all that was left to do was watch Logan cope with the news.

Logan bounded off the bed as if he had been sitting on live coals and gaped bug-eyed at Piper. "Me?" he chirped like a sick cricket.

Piper was apprehensive and Logan wasn't helping matters. He looked as if he had swallowed a watermelon. "Of course, you," she muttered crankily. "Who else could it have been? I certainly didn't do this all by myself!"

"How . . . when . . . ?" was all Logan could get out.

Piper flung him a withering glance. "*When* is an easy question to answer," she sniffed. "It was our first night together at Colbert's Ferry. And honestly, Logan, you should be able to puzzle out *how* all by yourself!"

"A father . . ." Logan tested his new title. He didn't know beans about being a father, never having had one of his own. But he was going to love their child the way he had never been loved. A father? He liked the sound of it. The title gave him an extra added feeling of respectability.

Absently, Logan ambled toward the door, bumping into furniture along the way, still murmuring the word *father* and envisioning himself in his new role. Piper stared bewildered at him. He was behaving a mite strange, even for Logan.

"Logan? Are you all right?" Piper called after him. But Logan wasn't listening. His mind was filled with thoughts of cradles and wooden toys and all the other paraphernalia associated with babies.

Harley glanced up when he heard Logan's footsteps echoing through the hall. When Logan barged into the room his face was beaming like a lantern on a long wick. Harley couldn't remember seeing such pleasure on the face of a man who usually disguised his emotions behind a carefully guarded stare.

"You look like the cat who swallowed the canary," Gorman observed with a teasing smirk.

Logan peered at each of the four men as his chest swelled with pride. "I'm going to be a father!" he announced. "Can you imagine that?" Logan was bursting at the seams.

Logan wasn't certain what sort of reception he would encounter after his announcement, but he was puzzled by his companions' reaction. Another flurry of coins exchanged hands. Anthony and Jacob, who had wagered they would never become the godfathers of Logan's children because he wouldn't have any, handed over their coins to Harley and Gorman, who had speculated on that very possibility.

A muddled frown clouded Logan's brow. Instead of receiving congratulations he was forced to watch another betting exchange. When the coins had resettled in a different set of pockets, the marshals finally got around to voicing their surprise and delight. Before Logan could return upstairs to check on the mother of his unborn child, Samuel Kirby came lumbering through the front door with Abraham trailing one step behind him. The oversized tomcat sniffed the hall and then bounded up the stairs to locate his mistress.

"I just learned you had returned," Samuel said with a pleased smile. His eyes darted around the group of men who were whacking Logan on the back. "Where's Mrs. Logan?"

It was obvious Harley hadn't explained that Mrs. Logan wouldn't actually be Mrs. Logan until after tomorrow's ceremony. Mr. Logan, however, had no time for lengthy explanations, so he delegated the task to Harley and then leaped up the stairs two at a time to pamper Piper.

441

By the time Logan returned to the room Abraham had curled up beside Piper, who was soaking him and her pillow in a river of tears. The smile slid off Logan's lips as he strode toward the bed.

"Since when did you revert back to crying?" he grumbled. "I thought we had passed that phase long ago."

It suddenly dawned on Logan that Piper hadn't seemed all that pleased with the prospect of carrying his child. She hadn't wanted to tell him and he had practically forced it out of her. The thought hurt Logan as nothing else could.

"I can cry if I feel like it," Piper mumbled through her tears. "I knew if I told you you would go into shock. You couldn't face me until you had time to recover from the news. And now you have come trotting back to make amends, but it isn't going to work. I know you weren't the least bit pleased so you don't have to pretend."

"I wasn't recovering from shock," Logan snapped in offended dignity. "I was announcing my fatherhood to my friends. Isn't that what a proud father is supposed to do? Obviously you aren't excited about the possibility of motherhood or you would have told me the moment you realized your condition. It seems to me that I'm accepting the fact that I am to become a parent far better than you are." Logan glared at her tear-swollen eyes. "And will you stop crying before the confounded bed floats away!"

Piper blinked up at him. How could he possibly think she didn't want his child? That was ridiculous and she proceeded to tell him so. "I want to be the mother of your children," she insisted, muffling a sniff.

"And I want to be the father of your children. Jeezus, Piper, if you're happy and I'm happy, what the blazes are we arguing about?" Logan finally broke into a smile and eased down beside her.

Sick though she was, Piper flung her arms around his broad shoulders, drawing his face to hers. "As usual, we are arguing for nothing," she murmured against his bearded cheek. "Oh Logan, I don't want for anything more than your love and your baby. Our child will grow up knowing I love him as deeply as I love his father. I only wish I felt up to expressing my affection."

Logan cuddled her close and Abraham meowed in complaint when he narrowly escaped being crushed by Logan's brawny body. Of course, Logan had purposely squashed Abraham, just to get the pesky tomcat to leave. But Abraham had developed his own character after roughing it in the wilds. This time he sank his teeth into Logan's hand and spiked his claws in Logan's crotch, just for spite. With a yelp, Logan flung Abraham off the bed. Like an exploding cannonball, Abraham shot across the room and out the door to locate Samuel, who had befriended him in Piper's absence.

Glancing sideways to monitor the flight of Abraham, Logan smiled to himself. He was glad that nuisance was gone. He never had any use for Abraham or his annoying habit of digging his claws into his lap. When he refocused on Piper, all thoughts of Abraham evaporated. Lord, she was the loveliest creature he had ever laid eyes on. He had known a score of women in his life but Piper was his first and only lady. A deep sense of pride and satisfaction consumed him when he peered into those misty green eyes. Logan had what he wanted. Nothing was as precious as holding Piper.

"Sometimes just hearing you say you love me is enough," Logan whispered softly. "If you are fretting over the fact that I might grow restless in days to come when you grow round with my child, you worry for naught, my saucy nymph." His voice was husky with emotion, his silver eyes shimmering with love. "You are all I have ever wanted, all I will ever need to make my life complete. Watching our baby grow inside you will be a wondrous reminder that you are blossoming with the love I feel for you."

His gentle hand traced her elegant features, adoring the feel of her creamy skin beneath his fingertips. "I never knew what love and fear were until you came into my life, Piper. And now, loving you as I do, the only thing that frightens me is the thought of losing you. From the very beginning, I think I was purposely trying to make you strong enough and tough enough to survive in my world. I knew I could never conform to your

443

world and yet I couldn't let go of you, even when reason bade me to sever the bond between us. I want you here with me forever," he whispered tenderly. "Without you, I would become the half a man I was before you came along to fill my heart and my life to overflowing. You once said half a love was a road leading to nowhere. But this love we share is a pathway paved with gold, and I will cherish every step I take with you."

Piper was crying again, and for the life of her she didn't know why. Perhaps it was Logan's tender words or the gentle voice with which he conveyed them. Whatever the reason, she was spilling an ocean of tears. But Logan didn't complain this time, not even when she soaked his shirt. He just held her to him, waiting for the flood of emotion to ebb, offering the compassion he had never allowed himself to show her before now.

Carefully, Logan withdrew to wipe away the residue of tears. "Rest now," he murmured adoringly. "There will be time enough later for us to express what we feel for each other." A faint smile hovered on his lips as he brushed his fingertips through his heavy beard. "As for me, I believe I'll see how close I can get to a razor. I hope to be a new man by the time you wake."

Piper looked up at the mountain of a man who towered over her, love shining through the mist in her eyes. "I'm well satisfied with the old one," she assured him.

"Then you should be doubly pleased with the new one," he declared as he swaggered toward the door. "He's a respectable gentleman who adores his wife-to-be and he is bursting with pride, now that he is to become a father."

Perfectly content, Piper sighed and closed her eyes, hoping a long-awaited nap would ease her queasiness. And while she slept, she dreamed the most pleasant of dreams, one she promised herself would collide with reality once she was feeling her old self again.

Chapter 30

Logan leaned down to light his cheroot in the lantern and smiled quietly to himself. He had discarded his habit of burning two-dollar bills and had begun a fund for his child which consisted of the cash he would have burned up two dollars at a time if Piper hadn't broken him of setting flame to money. Logan looked and felt like a new man. He had no regrets at having sacrificed his wandering ways to assume control of his ranch. There was nowhere else he wanted to be as long as Piper was with him.

Lost in thought, Logan ambled onto the terrace outside his bedroom to gaze across a ranch dotted with cattle and horses. Piper had yet to awaken and Logan had tired of the celebrating that was going on downstairs. Several times the past hour he had been tempted to slip quietly into Piper's room to check on her, but he had restrained himself. She needed her rest and he didn't wish to disturb her. But damn, it was difficult to prowl around his room when he longed for Piper's company, even if he had to be content just to watch her sleep.

Aimlessly Logan strolled back into his room to plop on the bed. The creak of the door jarred Logan from his contemplative musings. Reflexively, he reached for the pistol that no longer sat on the nightstand. His eyes darted toward the door and he bit into the end of his cigarillo when a vision of pure loveliness drifted into his room.

Piper's face radiated renewed color, and her waist-length hair lay like a shimmering cape about her. The sheer, off-the-shoulder negligee caught in the lantern light, revealing her luscious curves and swells beneath it. Logan's heart flipped over in his chest when Piper peeked up at him through a fan of long lashes. Lord, she took his breath away! It was several seconds before he could inhale a draft of air.

Piper drank in the magnificent sight of the man who lounged on his bed. His hair glowed blue-black in the pale light. His clean-shaven face was alive with unmasked desire. The cream-colored linen shirt that lay open to the waist contrasted with his bronzed flesh, flesh that rippled with whipcord muscle and potential strength. His tight black breeches revealed the hard contours of his legs, and Piper blatantly admired the picture of masculinity that he represented.

"I'm feeling much better," she murmured as she walked over to retrieve his cigar from his fingertips and lay it aside.

His eyes roamed over her in total possession. "That's good," he said absently. "I wish I could say the same, but I ache all over."

A provocative smile tripped across her lips. Deftly she drew away his shirt and recklessly dropped it on the floor. "A thorough massage should cure your ailments," she diagnosed. "It seems to me you were suffering the same affliction that night at Colbert's Ferry. If my calculations prove correct, it was that night which got us in the condition we are in now. . . ."

"I may not have been educated in the finest schools in the East, but I don't think we are both sharing the same delicate condition," Logan teased as he drew Piper down beside him to caress her bare arms. "I don't think it is physically possible for you to have gotten me pregnant at Colbert's Ferry or anywhere else. And you're wrong if you think a massage is all I need to ease this maddening ache that plagues me."

"What a coincidence," Piper chortled as her lips whispered over his sensuous mouth. "I hadn't intended to stop at that. . . . I couldn't before, nor can I now. . . ."

And sure enough she didn't, not that Logan minded one bit. Piper had come to his room to give and share the love she felt for him, to erase any doubt that she wasn't exactly where she wanted to be—in the magic circle of his arms. This desert was

446

paradise when she was with the man who had come to mean all things to her.

I love you was embroidered in each soft kiss and caress that Piper bestowed on Logan. She had come to him, weaving wondrous dreams around him. And if not for love she couldn't have crocheted a single stitch on that flying carpet that transported them on their intimate journey through the stars. Logan swore Piper was sent from heaven. She was his angel, his guiding light, his breath of life. Admitting to love was the most difficult thing he had ever done, but loving Piper came so easily. He was eager to spend his days by her side, watching her smile up at him with adoration in her eyes while they watched their children toddle about under the concerned eyes of their four godfathers. And each night, when Piper got their children to bed, Logan intended to be there to hear the fairy tales he had missed during his childhood. But for now he was going to love the lady whose wide-eyed innocent gaze had tugged on the strings of his heart since the first moment he saw her.

Much later, when passion had run its wondrous course and dawn came creeping silently across the darkened sky, Logan eagerly dressed and ventured downstairs to oversee the preparations for his wedding. If not for Piper, Logan would have never known what true happiness was. It still amazed him that this mere wisp of a woman could have made so much difference in his life. Jeezus, he never believed it possible that he could be so hopelessly in love! But nothing was impossible when he was following this Pied Piper. She filled his days with pleasure and his nights with splendid passion.

Logan had made several concessions so he could fully enjoy his dreams and he encountered only one frustration—allowing Abraham free run of his hacienda. It galled him to see Abraham prance around as if he owned the place, but Logan tolerated the pesky tomcat's presence for Piper's sake. Logan knew he was gong to love Piper forever and ever, but he was never going to like that ornery cat!

HEART-THROBBING ROMANCES BY
KAY MCMAHON AND ROCHELLE WAYNE
FROM ZEBRA BOOKS!

DEFIANT SPITFIRE (2326, $3.95)
by Kay McMahon
The notorious privateer Dane Remington demanded Brittany
Lockwood's virtue as payment for rescuing her brother. But once
he tasted her honey-sweet lips, he knew he wanted her passionate
and willing rather than angry and vengeful. . . . Only then would
he free her from his bed!

THE PIRATE'S LADY (2114, $3.95)
by Kay McMahon
Shipwrecked on Chad LaShelle's outlaw island, lovely Jennifer
Gray knew what her fate would be at the hands of the arrogant
pirate. She fled through the jungle forest, terrified of the outlaw's
embrace—and even more terrified of her own primitive response
to his touch!

FRONTIER FLAME (1965-3, $3.95)
by Rochelle Wayne
Suzanne Donovan was searching for her brother, but once she
confronted towering Major Blade Landon, she wished she'd never
left her lavish Mississippi home. The lean, muscled officer made
her think only of the rapture his touch could bring, igniting the
fires of unquenchable passion!

SAVAGE CARESS (2137, $3.95)
by Rochelle Wayne
Beautiful Alisha Stevens had thanked the powerful Indian warrior Black Wolf for rescuing her as only a woman can. Now she
was furious to discover his deceit. He would return her to her
people only when he was ready—until then she was at his beck
and call, forced to submit to his SAVAGE CARESS.

UNTAMED HEART (2306-5, $3.95)
by Rochelle Wayne
Fort Laramie's handsome scout David Hunter seemed determined
to keep auburn-haired Julianne Ross from doing her job as a re-
porter. And when he trapped her in his powerful embrace, the
curvaceous young journalist found herself at a loss for the words
to tell him to stop the delicious torment of his touch!

*Available wherever paperbacks are sold, or order direct from the
Publisher. Send cover price plus 50¢ per copy for mailing and
handling to Zebra Books, Dept. 2809, 475 Park Avenue South,
New York, N.Y. 10016. Residents of New York, New Jersey and
Pennsylvania must include sales tax. DO NOT SEND CASH.*